PURE CANE

by

DAVID ABIS

Sweet Spot Publishing

Pure Cane

Sweet Spot Publishing

Paperback Edition

Copyright 2015 David Abis

All rights reserved.

Cover images courtesy of Hillwoman2, Sumroeng Chinnapan, dreamstime.com, & istock.

Cover by Joleene Naylor

ISBN 978-0-9907739-3-1
eBook ISBN 978-0-9907739-2-4

Chapter 1

Forgive me father for I have sinned. That's how confession always begins, followed by a frantic scramble for an offering, racking your brain for something to tell the priest. Nothing too juicy, of course. Just enough to get by. Enough to qualify as a confession. Like the time when we were little, and Boy Delgado buried that stray cat alive. Not that *I* had buried it. Just that I didn't tell. I should have told. Sometimes telling is a sin. But *not* telling can be worse. Damned if you do. Damned if you don't. Never mind he threatened to kill my whole family if I did. I never believed he would. It wasn't in him. Boy wasn't a bad person. Not even close. Some people are bad. Evil bad. Others, like Boy, just do bad things. I still think there's a difference.

You see, I have it all figured out now. That's where guilt comes in. It's all about guilt. The truly bad ones don't have a drop of it. Everyone else, I'm sure, carries a certain amount of guilt around with them. Some more than others. And while we're talking about guilt, what about sin? After all, there are sins and there are sins, right? I mean a 14-year-old girl stealing her best friend's crush is not the same as the lust felt by that same girl three years later at 17, right? And lust, of course, is not the same as murder. And what about the sins of a priest versus those in his trust? That's got to rank pretty high, doesn't it? I mean, a priest should know better, right?

Anyway, getting back to guilt, I guess the object is to get through life without carrying so much around that the load itself kills you, slowly, insidiously, like a cancer, until the weight drives you straight down through the soles of your shoes into the grave, and maybe even to hell. Oops. See, I've done it again. You'll have to excuse me. God, I can be so melodramatic.

At least that's what Wing always tells me. I know. I know. What kind of a name is Wing, you're asking? Well, I guess everyone in the Philippines has nicknames. Her real name is Mary Elena, but she's called Wing, short for Wing Ding, after a cartoon character. A lot of our nicknames sound similar. Sometimes I think we just like the sounds they make. I personally know two Bings, a Beng, a Ming Ging, a Ging Ging, and a Ginguy. Of course, the wealthy families always have a son nicknamed Boy, and a daughter nicknamed Girlie. This whole nickname thing seems to be distinctly Filipino, or Pinoy, as we say.

I was raised in Manila. A city girl. My real name is Mary Salonga. Of course, just about every girl in the Philippines is named Mary, after the Blessed Virgin Mary. So they call me Lisa. Don't ask.

Wing's my cousin from the farm. Well, maybe farm isn't the right word. But that's what we called it. Actually it was a huge sugarcane plantation, the biggest on the island. Wing's family, the Delgados, owned it. They also grew coconuts and raised some livestock. Oh, and prawns. The Japanese would buy every prawn the Delgados could produce. The Japs just love those things. But sugarcane was the main thing. That's what the farm was really all about.

Anyway, Wing was raised on the farm in Bais, pronounced Bah Ees, on the island of Negros, pronounced Negg Roes. That's just one of the Philippine Islands. There are only about 7,000 of them.

Wing wasn't just my cousin. We were the same age and she was my best friend. Everyone confuses relatives and friends in the Philippines anyway. I don't know if that's because we're such friendly people or because everyone is somehow related to one another. After all, I bet the whole population was begat from a single ménage à trois between two pretty Chinese girls and a Spanish priest. That's where we get the great tans, from the Spanish. And our boobs, too. We're like tan Chinese girls with boobs. I guess that's why the men can't resist us. But more about that later.

Wing spent winters with me in Manila, for school. And I spent summers with her on the farm, to get away from my mother. My mother was a pain in the ass. I'm sure, to her, *I* was the pain in the ass. But ever since my dad died, I guess she'd been trying to find a new husband, and I probably complicated matters. I don't know why. It's not like she ever had anything to do with me anyway. See, in the Philippines, kids are raised by yayas, our word for nannies. They're servants, but they're more than that. Since they're actually paid to be your mom, they don't carry around the resentment a lot of moms do. They're like moms without attitude. When I was little, mine used to happily jog along behind me while I biked around the neighborhood, in case I fell or needed anything. I know how it sounds. Spoiled rich kid. But everyone I knew had yayas. Labor is so cheap in the Philippines, it's cheaper to have a maid live at the back of your house to do your laundry than it is to buy a washing machine.

True, not everyone had maids and yayas. Most people didn't, I guess. I just never knew them. I mean, all the good neighborhoods were surrounded by high walls and had armed guards. I only saw the poor when our driver would take us on the highway from which you could see the lines of tin shacks on the other side of the barbed wire. I don't imagine they had yayas there.

Of course, if you didn't have a yaya, you probably didn't have shoes either. And if you did have a yaya, you probably had lots of shoes. People love shoes in the Philippines. And it seems like there are only two classes of people there. Those with lots of shoes, like Imelda Marcos, our former First Lady, and those with none.

That's probably where the communists came from, those with none, I mean. But what did a 14-year-old girl know about communists and revolution in the summer of 1983? I thought everyone was happy. All I knew about communists was what my relatives on the farm told me. Stay away from them. They're trouble.

And it was easy to tell who the communists were in the Philippines. They were the ones who never smiled when you looked at them.

I would learn a lot more about it later on. I'd learn about a lot of things. You just never see these things coming. Kind of like typhoons. That's what we call our hurricanes. We get a load of typhoons in the Philippines. Just when you think you have everything all figured out, they sneak up on you, out of nowhere, hit hard, shake everything up, and then move on. It's like walking through a car wash without a car. You get pretty beat up. But when you come out the other side, you sure are clean. Kind of like confession.

I think everything is in God's hands, and typhoons are God's trump cards. See, I knew I'd end up talking about God again. I guess you can take the Filipino girl out of the church, but you can't take the church out of the Filipino girl.

Anyway, hardly anyone wore shoes on the farm. I loved the farm. And as long as I could remember, I always wanted to live there, like the Delgados. I wanted to *be* a Delgado. I wanted to be one of the hacienderos as we called them, the plantation owners.

Life there was so different from life in Manila, the big city. Manila was black and white, tasteless, like a big ubé root, before adding the sugar, cream, and purple food coloring to make it into ice cream. Everything in Manila was so formal, so starched, that all the fun, all the flavor was dried out of everything. Maybe it was the ever-present heat and humidity reflected off the dirty gray pavement that was everywhere.

Going to the farm, on the other hand, was like the scene where Dorothy steps out of her house in the Land of Oz and suddenly everything's in color. Maybe it had something to do with the sugarcane. But everything about life on the farm was sweet. All of it. Even the water in Wing's pool, so sweet the fruit bats would swoop down at night for a sip of nectar, their tiny tongues hardly leaving a ripple in the glassy surface of the water.

Of course, the boys would go after them with slingshots. But the girls, mostly Wing and I, we'd scoop up the injured or orphaned bats to nurse them back to health. The boys were always so mean. At least to us 14-year-old girls they were. They would either tease us or ignore us. I don't know which was worse. It's different when you grow older though, when suddenly the boys are everywhere, like mosquitoes, as if they only had 24 hours to mate before they die.

But that's getting ahead of myself. Fourteen. That's how old I was that summer the first time Johnny mysteriously appeared on the farm like some kind of alien from another planet. Like someone dropping an ice cube down the back of your shirt. An unwanted jolt, yet in the oppressive summer heat, somehow refreshing.

I remember Wing and I were playing with Molly Moo Cow. That was our calf. Each summer, Papa, that's what everyone on the farm called Wing's father, would give us a baby cow to play with. We could have had any kind of animal from the farm, but the cows were so cute, we always asked for a cow. We got to feed them if we wanted to. Sometimes we even dressed them up.

Wing saw him first. I was busy trying to feed Molly her milk with a baby bottle, but she was giving me a hard time. I think she preferred her real mom.

"Who's that?" Wing asked, looking over my shoulder, beyond the vine-covered entrance gate of her cobblestone driveway, to where the farm offices and courtyard were.

"Who?" I said turning around, seeing only the sweaty cane workers getting ready to head out to the fields. I recognized Captain. He was Papa's foreman, the one who handled all the workers. I didn't know his real name. But everyone called him Captain. He was very nice, at least to us. I heard he was really strict with the workers though. He was in his forties, I guess. Not a big man, but strong and wiry from working all his life on the farm. I remember his hands felt like sandpaper. But he was always gentle with all the kids, and always smiling. He loved the farm as if he owned it, and took pride in his work. Papa trusted him to run the farm, and that meant he trusted him with his life.

"There. Behind Captain. The white one," said Wing, pointing with her lips. That's how Pinoys point, with a thrust of our puckered lips, as if throwing a kiss.

I noticed the music first. Electric guitars. I think it was "Sweet Home Alabama," by Lynyrd Skynyrd. Then I saw him. As Captain turned to bark some orders, Johnny was standing behind him with a boom box, tall and lanky. He was 17-years-old, I would learn later. He stood out from the crowd like when you see one of those white tigers at the zoo. No, not albino. He was nicely tan. Just not that leathery over-tanned look of the cane workers. I guessed he was Eurasian, or mestiso as we say in the Philippines, half Pinoy and half European, like a haciendero. Many of them are more Spanish than Asian. He wore a T-shirt with a confederate flag on it, a cowboy hat, and sunglasses.

"Turn off that noise!" Captain shouted. Johnny took his time turning the boom box off, his slow motion response barely affecting an insubordinate slouch. "And take off the hat and sunglasses. I want to see the fear in your eyes when I'm talking to you."

Now that was strange. I'd never seen Captain raise his voice at anyone but the workers, much less a foreigner. I was trying to make sense of the scene, that is until Johnny took off his hat and sunglasses with a defiant glare in Captain's direction. That's when things started to get kind of weird for me.

His hair was dark and straight, like the other workers, but it was longer, shoulder length. I'm sure Captain would have something to say about that. And even from a distance, I could make out the most beautiful set of blue eyes I'd ever seen. Standing out against his long dark hair, they were like two gleaming oceans, blinding you on a sunny day at the beach. I dropped Molly's bottle. Something happened to my knees and I had to grab Wing to keep from falling.

"What are you doing?" she asked pushing me away, annoyed that I almost knocked her over.

"Wow," was all I could mutter, still dazed.

Wing slowly turned to me with that look she always uses when she knows what I'm thinking, staring straight through me with narrowed eyes. "I saw him first," she said firmly, laying her claim, marking her territory. And she wasn't fooling around.

It wasn't like anything was really going to happen between them. After all, we were only 14. It was just another game of pretend for us. Like the posters of movie stars and rock idols we'd tacked on the walls of our bedrooms. We could dream. But we certainly wouldn't have known what to do with them if they'd actually entered the room. Back then, in the Philippines, Catholic school was for real. Sex was just a big blur. Like that time one of the nuns was forced to stop teaching and leave the school. We just thought she was getting fat. Well, before we knew it, she was married and the baby arrived a couple of weeks later. Seemed kind of soon to us. But we weren't allowed to talk about it.

Besides, complexion aside, he seemed to be one of the cane workers. And certainly nothing would ever happen between one of the workers and a Delgado, or a cousin of a Delgado for that matter. Yet something wasn't right. We knew there was more to this story.

"Where'd they get that one?" asked Wing, still eyeing the stranger, like a rancher at a cattle auction.

"He looks foreign to me," I said. "European maybe."

"Or Cano," suggested Wing, meaning Americano, from the States.

"He's hot. That's all I know."

Wing's look again. Then, "Well let's go find out who he is."

"You mean, go talk to him?" I asked, surprised by Wing's newfound boldness. My palms were starting to sweat.

"Are you crazy? No, I'm not going to talk to him. Let's go ask at Casablanca. I'm sure one of the maids will know."

We called Wing's house Casablanca, meaning White House in Spanish, partly because that's where Wing's family lived. Like in the States, it was our little way of considering Papa the president, commander in chief, and Wing a member of the first family. But it also just happened to be the only building for miles that had paint. And the paint, of course, was white.

We turned to head up to the house when we realized Molly was gone.

"Where's Molly?" I asked, grabbing Wing by the back of her shirt.

"Oh shit!" said Wing, staring at the milk bottle in her hand.

That's when we heard Captain's voice coming from the end of the driveway.

"Hey girls. You might want to get your pet out of Mama's flowers."

Mama was what everyone called Wing's mother. And she was worse than mine. If she found out that Molly trampled her flowers, there'd be hell to pay. And sure enough, there was Molly, near the entrance gate, making mulch of Mama's newly planted impatiens.

We raced past the workers, hoping to save what was left. But in our panic, I tripped on the cobblestone driveway. Wing would later say I fell on purpose. But no sooner had I hit the ground than I felt someone helping me up. I assumed it was Captain. But when I turned to thank him, I froze. It wasn't Captain. It was *him*. It was Johnny who'd come to my rescue. I could feel the heat coming from his lean six-foot frame, and I stood there like a deer in those deep blue headlights. I tried to form words, but they wouldn't come. Then, to make things worse, as if to cover for my failing voice, my knees decided to give way. Johnny caught me, preventing any further damage, at least the physical kind. Unfortunately, when I felt his strapping arms around me, strong but gentle, it was all over. There were bright flecks of light everywhere. Then darkness.

When I woke up, it was that look of Wing's again, staring down at me. I was in bed. Yaya was holding a cool wet cloth to my forehead. Yayas were usually called by their first names. But this wasn't just any yaya. At 72, she'd been with the Delgados since Papa was a baby. She'd raised him and then his children, including Wing and Boy. They didn't really need a yaya anymore, but she'd become a member of the family, earning a place of honor and respect for the rest of her life. Her job now was to oversee all the maids at Casablanca, of which there were five at the time.

But mostly her job was to do whatever the hell she wanted. Aware of her position in the family, Yaya didn't take orders from anyone, not even Papa, unless it suited her. Skinny as a rail, and wrinkled like a prune, she would preside over Casablanca, barking orders laced with profanity, that ever-present cigarette butt dangling from her lips. A hopeless chain smoker, she preferred chewing tobacco or a good cigar when she could get one.

"Ah, you've decided to come back to us," she said with a semi-toothless grin when I opened my eyes.

"Aye, thank God," muttered Hortensia, one of the maids, making the sign of the cross.

"God!?" snapped Yaya, blowing smoke. "What the hell's he got to do with this?"

"Yaya, please," implored Hortensia as she ran from the room with her hands over her ears at hearing the Lord's name used in vain.

Yaya and God didn't exactly get along. She'd stopped attending church long ago and would actually spit at the ground every time she saw the priest, spreading panic among the maids, who would all go running for cover, as if God had already launched a lighting bolt in Yaya's general direction, and they didn't want to get caught in the cross fire. It embarrassed Papa and especially Mama, who would always feel obliged to fall all over themselves apologizing to Father Rivera. But, as I said, Yaya did whatever the hell she wanted. And even Father Rivera seemed to accept the insult without a struggle, which was odd in itself for the usually strict priest.

We didn't really know the history behind Yaya's feud with the church, but it was certainly one of those mysteries we'd pursue every summer I spent on the farm, each year blackmailing one of the maids caught at some minor indiscretion into supplying another strand of classified intelligence, another speck of tsismus, our word for gossip. All we knew by that point was that it had something to do with Yaya's daughter and some forbidden affair resulting in her banishment from the farm. She was forced to work as some kind of hostess in Manila to support herself. Yaya never talked about it. Just as well. Looking back, at 14 years of age, I don't think we'd have understood it anyway.

"Yaya?" I began, testing the waters, "Who's the mestiso boy we saw with Captain and the cane workers?"

Yaya couldn't hide a small smile as she took a drag on her Marlboro and raised one eyebrow. "Cute. No?" Then with a full belly laugh, "Maybe you want to marry him?"

I looked over at Wing, embarrassed to admit I found him cute.

Being the owner's daughter, Wing was more bold than I. "He's gorgeous," she added.

Suddenly Yaya's smile was gone, as she whirled around to Wing. "Not for you!" She was practically shouting. "You stay away from him!" She was threatening Wing.

I would have cried from such an attack. But not Wing. Defiantly, she stood her ground with the servant. "Hey. What did *I* do?"

"He cannot be for you," continued Yaya, grinding out her spent cigarette in the palm of her own hand.

"That's not fair!" Wing wouldn't drop it. Like a spoiled child pouting because her sister got a larger slice of cake, "Why is he OK for Lisa and not for me?"

"Wing," I interrupted with a chuckle, "It's not like I'm going to marry him. After all, he's just a cane worker."

Big mistake. Now Yaya turned on ***me***. "Just a cane worker?" she began, rising from her chair. "You think he's not good enough for you?" spittle flying from her lips. "Is that what you think?"

I thought she was going to strike me. I didn't know what to say. Then came the obvious.

"Well, who is he?" I asked.

No sooner had I said the words than I wanted to take them back, recoiling at the possibility that 98-pound Yaya might take a swing at me. In the momentary silence filling the room, many more questions raced through my mind. Why did he have to come here anyway? This was supposed to be *my* summer vacation. Coming to the farm each summer was my pilgrimage, a sacred thing. Who was *he* to shake things up and ruin it?

I looked over to Wing as if I could transmit my thoughts to her through the air. What was this boy to Yaya? What made her so angry with us?

But when I turned back to Yaya for her reply, I couldn't believe my eyes. Tough as nails Yaya, Yaya the drill sergeant, was slumped over in her chair, crying.

Chapter 2

Wing and I had intended to open the investigation the very next day, to immediately start grilling the maids about this mysterious Johnny, and Yaya's connection to the whole thing. Unfortunately, all that would have to be put on hold, as it was Saturday, and on the first Saturday night of each month, a party was held for all the neighboring farm owners, the haci\u200benderos. The haciendero social represented just about the only social life there was in Bais, and this week it was at Casablanca. There were a million things to do in preparation.

Casablanca was no mansion. It wasn't a stately home you'd see in Europe, or one of those manors you'd find on an old southern plantation in the States. It was really just a farmhouse with white paint and bad plumbing. Of course, in Bais, plumbing alone, good or bad, made a house special. You see it was all relative. Floors and running water equaled castle. Mama would have torn the place down to put up a proper mansion, but Papa wouldn't have it. He always considered himself just a part of the community. No better. No worse. And the people of Bais appreciated that.

I loved to hang around the big kitchen where Marylou, the cook, was busy preparing all the local delicacies. Except for Lou, as we called her, I was probably the only one who knew all the secret unwritten recipes. I was privileged to know, for instance, that the ingredients for dinuguan called for four cups of internal organs, not necessarily species specific, and two cups of blood. I couldn't be absolutely certain, but I assumed the source of the blood was other than human.

The crown jewel of the feast, however, was always the lechon. That was a pig, slow-roasted all day on a spit. The honey-colored skin would get so nice and crispy that one time Mama broke a tooth chewing on a piece of rind. At the time, I got scared that Lou would be fired or maybe even beheaded or something, but when I looked her way out of concern, I saw, instead, a strange sense of self-satisfaction on her face. You see, apparently when someone breaks a tooth on the rind of a lechon, it is looked upon as one of the greatest compliments a chef could receive. What can I say? My people are crazy.

Besides the lechon, hundreds of lumpya, or Filipino egg rolls had to be cooked, and vats of pancit, our favorite pasta dish. There were bushels of mangos, and chico, the small brown fruit of the sapodilla tree.

Boy Delgado, Wing's older brother, spent the afternoon going through his record albums selecting music for the event, mostly American and British rock and roll of the 60's and 70's. If he were in a good mood, he'd allow Wing to choose a disco record, but just one. He didn't want to scare off his friends. The guests would bring some of their own music as well. There was always guaranteed to be at least one mellow slow dance record for late in the party, after all the boys had had enough rum to drink to get up the nerve to finally ask the girls to dance. That was the best part for Wing and me. No, we didn't slow dance yet. We danced the fast ones together. But the slow ones, that's when we'd stay off to the side, spying for any new romances blossoming among the older kids, gathering ammunition to blackmail them with at a later date.

The gardener was on his hands and knees all morning trimming Papa's putting green with a pair of scissors. After manicuring the fine Bermuda grass to perfection, he would use a can of green spray paint to touch up any brown spots. Papa was insanely meticulous about his putting green, especially when the other haci[n]deros were expected.

The day was so hectic, and it appeared as if Casablanca would never be ready, yet, as always, at six o'clock sharp, Papa and Mama were already out front welcoming the guests on their arrival. Papa looked so dashing in his barong, the traditional Filipino formal wear, a long white shirt weaved from pineapple fiber with intricate embroidery. A barong is worn instead of suit and tie in order to survive the oppressive heat and humidity. It also served to hide Papa's expanding belly, but did nothing for his already receded hairline.

Mama, perennially model-thin, wore a white evening gown and the crown jewels, or at least what appeared to be every piece of jewelry she could muster in order to impress her friends. For Mama, it was all about appearances, a contest between the wives, at least in Mama's mind. The other wives never knew they were competing.

Unlike the others, though, Mama was an outsider, raised in Hong Kong, and resented being brought to the farm, stranded so far from civilization. Given the choice, she'd have spent all her time in Manila. In fact, according to the maids, that's pretty much what she'd done after Boy was born. She figured she'd done her duty by bearing Papa a son, and her dreadful days on the farm were finally over. She'd earned an early parole. But two years later, she came back.

I used to ask what made her change her mind. I knew it wasn't the farm. If the farm were mine, I'd never leave. They'd have to kill me first. But Mama was different. She didn't get it. She was never awake to see the sun rise over the majestic purple mountains encircling the farm. She couldn't hear the sugarcane blowing in the breeze or smell the sweet ash of molasses in the air when the fields were burned after the harvest.

No, I knew it certainly wasn't the farm. Not for Mama. I kept hoping, instead, to hear of some romantic love story, that she and Papa couldn't bear being separated from one another. But no such tale was ever forthcoming. The maids all became very hush-mouthed whenever I pressed them on the subject, looking to one another for moral support in withholding vital intelligence from my interrogation. It always ended the same way, though. "You'll have to ask Yaya about that," they would say. I early on learned that would be fruitless. Yaya was one tough cookie that couldn't be cracked. She wouldn't even discuss it. Big taboo, apparently, which meant it was probably real juicy. I vowed one day to get to the bottom of it all, but for now, there was a party getting under way.

The other hacienderos dressed in similar fashion to Papa and Mama. The kids, however, went by a different dress code. We hadn't yet realized in the Philippines that designer jeans and polyester shirts, so popular in the 70's, were no longer cool back in the States. The girls' jeans were so tight, I'm sure they'd needed assistance from their maids or yayas to help pull them on. All sense of style on the farm was, by definition, badooey, our word in Manila for provincial, out of date, uncool. They just never knew it. And it would be considered bad form for those of us from Manila to point it out.

Speaking of badooey, Papa's golf partner, Ron Fanlo, always arrived first. Ron wasn't his real name. Just a Pinoy nickname again. It seemed too ordinary for one of our nicknames, but apparently it was an inside joke among the men. Like all the women, I never suspected that, as I would learn much later, he was called Ron because he looked just like Ron Jeremy, some chubby American porn star known for his ample body hair who, in fact, had his own nickname, The Hedgehog. As I said before, all these nicknames were ridiculous, but they were all terms of endearment, and Ron always managed to get a wink and a chuckle from the other guys when being greeted.

While Mama and Mrs. Fanlo, or Girlie as she was called, split off to catch up on tsismus concerning the other hacienderos before they had a chance to arrive, Papa and Ron were already handicapping for their next golf match, competing for who had the worse injury, Papa's back, or Ron's sore elbow.

"Aye, it's terrible getting old," Papa would begin.

"Old?" said Ron, rubbing his right elbow. "You're not old. You're just a pathetic golfer."

Papa would fake a punch to Mr. Fanlo's stomach, Mr. Fanlo would flinch at the feigned threat, and they'd both walk off laughing like kids. Papa didn't drink alcohol, but most of the other haciendaros did. So he was sure to have on hand a hardy supply of San Miguel beer and Tanduay rum, both produced in the Philippines.

After a few drinks were had, the men's conversation would drift predictably from golf to basketball and soccer, and then, inevitably, to The Case. They thought I didn't know what The Case was. They talked almost in code so as to hide the true meaning from me. But I figured it out. And I could tell from Papa's face that he knew I knew. He was the only one who knew how smart I really was. But he didn't rat on me. He let them talk.

The Case, as they referred to it, was a claim by one of the maids at one of the cane farms that one of the haciendaros had raped her. As the maid's father was seeking a big payoff to drop the charges, everyone assumed it was all a scheme made up just to extort money. There was no evidence. And the haciendaro refused to pay. But his reputation was tarnished.

Once everyone was brought up to speed on The Case, the conversation inevitably fell to work. Like observing the cook, listening in on the politics of farming was one of my favorite things. Wing wanted nothing to do with it. "Borrrring," she would moan, leaving me on my own with the men. And Boy would rather be with his buddies showing off for the girls. But for me, it was like being a member of an elite club. And the men even got used to me being there, like some kind of mascot. After the first time or so, they even stopped asking me to go fetch them drinks or food. Soon they had the maids do it instead, so that I wouldn't miss anything. Sometimes they even asked my opinion on matters. I didn't know at the time that they were just trying to be funny.

After comparing their production of sugarcane, like boys competing over who could pee the farthest, they'd move onto external forces beyond their control.

"Prices are down again," began Scooby Montero. "Since the government began setting the price of sugar, it's gone nowhere but down." There were nods of agreement all around.

"It's classic government mismanagement," stated Chica-ting Arroyo. "It's President Marcos and his cronies."

"It's more than mismanagement. It's corruption," countered Scooby. "Marcos never seems to have enough."

"Well, they have to take their share, don't they? Like the mafia," said Chica-ting. "To buy more shoes for our First Lady, Imelda. Right, Lisa?" he added, slapping me on the knee.

I looked proudly over at Hortensia who was busy fanning the flies away from the guests' food with a palm frond. She would nod back her approval that I was accepted among the men's inner circle.

"But they control everything," Scooby complained, taking another swig of his rum and coke, mostly rum with just enough coke for color.

Papa often couldn't get a word in among his boisterous companions, but when he did, I noticed mouths would stop and ears would open. I could tell they all had a great respect for Papa. Even Hortensia would ignore any annoying calls for help by the other servants when Papa spoke, so as not to miss anything profound.

"I wish they'd control these communists the way they control the price of sugar," he said.

Papa's serious tone was met with a solemn silence, finally broken by Scooby's joke. "You're right, José. They should supply us with mosquito repellant to take care of those annoying pests."

They all laughed at the comparison of communists to mosquitoes. All but Papa.

"You laugh now. But those bloodsucking mosquitoes of yours will not be scattered by Hortensia's palm frond," he stated, nodding to the maid. "They mean business. They want our land. *My* land," he added, defiantly slapping his chest. "Delgado land."

That's how I knew that Papa and I were family. Our mutual love for the farm. It was in our blood. The sugar coursing through our veins was pure cane. We weren't even that close, genetically I mean. After all, my father was only a sort of third cousin of Papa's, hardly related at all, by Filipino standards. Nevertheless, it was like we fell from the same tree. And yet, Papa's own kids, Boy and Wing, seemed indifferent to the farm. Wing wasn't so bad. I think she just took it for granted. She didn't know what she had. Boy, however, detested it. He wanted nothing more than to move to Manila, where he was frankly embarrassed about his upbringing on the farm. It was obvious to everyone. The maids secretly suggested that whatever cane farm blood Boy might have inherited from Papa was more than cancelled out by Mama's sugar-free city blood.

So when it came to the farm, Papa couldn't help but speak from the heart. And the other haciendaros could see how serious he was. They were just as wedded to the soil as he, but they were never equipped with his foresight. They weren't capable of turning the page to see where the story was going. Papa was the worrier.

"Cheer up, José. Let's talk about soccer. Spain's in the World Cup."

And just like that, the mood shifted, and life went on. The party progressed on schedule. Drinks were had and food was devoured. I noticed the music had gotten softer, and that's when Wing showed up to drag me back to my own generation.

"Someone brought lambanug," she whispered in my ear so the grown-ups couldn't hear. Lambanug is Filipino moonshine, made from coconuts, and it tastes like gasoline. The haciendaros would have nothing to do with it. After all, they could afford Tanduay. That left the poor, who couldn't, and the kids, who thought it was stronger than rum and rumored to be mildly hallucinogenic, or so I was told.

Sure enough, when we arrived poolside, the music had slowed and the action had already started to heat up. After each taking a bowl of ubé ice cream to sustain us through the show, Wing and I grabbed a spot close enough so as not to miss anything, yet not too close to inhibit the older kids. The girls were especially skittish as they always necked with one eye open should one of their parents make an untimely appearance. There was a lot of contact going on on the dance floor. Unfortunately, just as things were really beginning to heat up, the plug got pulled. Literally. When Mama pulled the plug on the turntable, Barry White's already deep baritone fell through the floor, and ground to a halt.

Like cockroaches caught in the light of the refrigerator, kids went scurrying for cover in all directions to Mama's "Aye! Aye! What's this? Stop it. Stop this instant." Her hands covered her eyes so as not to see anything she'd have to discuss with Father Rivera later. However, in so doing, she managed to trip over a chair. If the lechon hadn't broken her fall, she might have been hurt. The maids rushed to help her up, but Mama shoed them away so as to contain the damage already sustained to her image. And she'd have pulled it off too, considering she'd just lain with a roast pig, had the apple from the animal's mouth not somehow been impaled on one of her high heels. Mama didn't notice it. And the maids were afraid to upset her. So off she went, the picture of grace, back to her guests, sporting the pig's apple on one heel. The men probably wouldn't notice. And the women might conceivably assume it was some kind of new fashion statement, or social grace from Manila, soon to turn up at all proper dinner parties.

Wing and I never imagined how painful it could be to have ubé ice cream shoot out of one's nose. But once we'd wiped the tears of laughter from our eyes, we agreed it was worth it. It wasn't every day we got to see the First Lady of Casablanca flat on her ass, hugging a roast pig.

Unfortunately, that brought make out madness to an end. No, the party wasn't over. The kids would find something else to do. Only, something not quite so wholesome as making out. Something bound to lead to trouble.

Once the music had stopped, the boys noticed the sound of a basketball being dribbled. It was coming from outside the gate, beyond the courtyard. The cane workers didn't have much in the way of parties on Saturday nights, but they did have a basketball, and like many things in the Philippines borrowed from America, they took great pride in their skills on the court. Oh it wasn't a wood-floored full court by any means. It was a simple metal backboard and rim bolted to a tree at the end of a patch of flat hardened dirt. Papa had donated the backboard, rim, and ball, to help keep the workers out of trouble, which it usually did. But sometimes trouble came looking for the workers nevertheless.

Boy Delgado wasn't the best basketball player among the haciendero boys but he was fairly good. What he really excelled at, though, was cheating. And how much could the workers protest when the boss's son decided to take advantage of his position?

Tonight would be different, though. A new ingredient had been added to the stew, a wild card.

"Hey, guys," shouted Boy to his friends. "You hear that?" The sound of the bouncing basketball stood out against the silent turntable. "Sounds like a challenge to me."

Playing against the cane workers was nothing new for the boys. But a belly full of rum and a group of pretty girls to show off for certainly sweetened the pot. The boys quickly filed out the gate after Boy, and the pack of giggling girls wasn't far behind. Wing and I tagged along reluctantly. This game didn't interest us as much as the one on the dance floor, but right now it was all we had. It never occurred to me that Johnny might be there.

And at first, he wasn't. At least I didn't see him. It had grown dark by then and the court was lit only by a floodlight hanging from the tree that held the backboard.

The game began innocently enough. The haciendros kept their shirts on while the cane workers went shirtless so that teammates could be easily discerned on the dim court. The workers were, as always, shoeless, but I'm not sure the dress shoes worn by the haciendero boys provided any advantage. They only played four to a team, as the court was rather small. Even at that, there was quite a bit of bumping and jostling around, the dust from the packed dirt court flying. The lean workers were noticeably outweighed and getting shoved around the court, but calling fouls was generally discouraged. I think it was some sort of macho thing. The haciendros also seemed more skilled at the game. But the speed and stamina of the workers, from toiling in the fields, seemed to make up for their size and ball handling skills. It wasn't long before the cane workers had built a sizeable lead over the half-drunk haciendero boys. At one point per basket, it was already nine to two in favor of the workers, on their way to 21.

One of the workers named Speed took particular joy in beating the haciendros. He was on the small size, tanned almost black, highlighting the flashing whites of eyes, teeth, and nails, akin to a wild panther. He was only able to build their lead, though, with the help of another worker, the largest boy on the court, aptly nicknamed Tiny.

Sensing an embarrassing defeat, Boy did what Boy does best. He began cheating. At first it was simply a matter of bending the rules. He would take extra steps without dribbling the ball, and call the workers out of bounds when they weren't. Other than a few verbal protests early on, the workers accepted Boy's rule bending as part of the game. Nevertheless, while their lead was slowly melting, they still appeared to be on their way to victory. It was soon twelve to seven.

Most of the hacienderos' cheerleaders didn't even understand the game of basketball. But even they could see it wasn't going well. Having hung around Papa and his friends enough, I'd learned pretty much all I needed to know, certainly enough to know that Boy was cheating. Still, it didn't seem that big a deal to me. After all, it was just a game. At least that's what I thought. Things soon turned serious.

Frustrated at their inability to turn the game around, Boy stepped up the cheating in a physical way. He began blatantly pushing and using his elbows. His teammates quickly caught on to the new strategy, and soon it began to look more like a hockey game than basketball, full body slams leading to bloody noses, and limps beginning to show on the workers. This was all taken in stride by the workers, a sign of their position in life, and soon the hacienderos had overcome their scoring deficit and taken the lead, to the cheers of their adoring fans.

The score was soon 19 to 14 in favor of the hacienderos. But they couldn't seem to finish things off as Tiny stepped up the pace, using his size to stifle any scoring attempt they could muster. He was just too big to be intimidated, even by Boy's blatant fouls. That's when things got ugly.

Out of shape haciendero lungs gasping for air, and frustrated by their inability to finish the workers off, Boy saw the only path to victory was to take Tiny out of the game. So as Tiny went up for a rebound, Boy used his shoulder to cut his legs out from under him, and Tiny went down hard on the back of his head. He only blacked out for a minute or so. But he remained woozy and was clearly out of the game. To most, the whole event was taken as just a matter of tough luck, all part of the game.

That is, to all but Speed. No, even Speed didn't counter with any physical threats, but visibly enraged, he turned to the darkness at the end of the court and shouted, "Hey, Cano, is that how it's done in the States?"

I didn't know to whom he was speaking. And when I tried to see into the blackness at the other end of the court, all I saw was a vague shape. But no response came to Speed's question.

"Do you have another player, or do you forfeit?" demanded Boy, bent over out of breath, and prepared to call it a night.

"I don't know if this guy counts," Speed replied, pointing to the darkness with his lips. "I don't know if he's on our team or not."

Boy looked to the other end, annoyed that he might have to continue the game. "Well, does he *sell* cane, or does he *cut* it?" Then, looking about to the other haciendero boys with a chuckle, "Unless he's got a deed to one of our farms, he's certainly not on *our* team."

They nodded in agreement, gathering together on the court, closing rank.

Speed turned back to the mysterious figure in the dark. "Well, Cano? Do you have a deed to some land I don't know about? Maybe back in the States?"

No reply from the darkness.

"Oh, that's right," Speed continued. "I forgot what the maids told me. They seem to know your whole story, how no one wanted you stateside. Even your stepmom. All she gave you was a one-way ticket back here. Back where you came from. Isn't that right?"

Met only by continued silence from the darkness, Speed stepped up the pressure. "And your daddy drank himself to death. Poor boy." Finally stepping closer to the target of his assault, "So she sent you back to the Philippines, your real country, to this farm, where I hear your real mom worked as a maid, and like you, was sent away as well. So tell me," he continued, advancing into the darkness himself, "unless the maids over at Casablanca have a deed to this farm, seems to me you're one of us."

Boy was growing impatient. He wanted to end the competition and get back to the rum. "Well? Do you have a team, or not? I don't plan on spending the whole night wallowing in the dirt with you people."

Even the cheerleaders had grown bored. "Really. Can we just go now?" from one of the girls.

Speed's attention returned to the subject of his sermon. "So? Are you on our team? Or are you going be an outcast the rest of your life?"

Something inside me knew it was Johnny even before he emerged from the shadows. Just the whole sense of intrigue. Sent back to a farm in the Philippines where his mother used to work, by a stepmother in America that didn't want him, after his father drank himself to death. These were major pieces to the puzzle, the puzzle I'd been handed the first time I saw him. And though they only served to wet my appetite, they offered a significant start. There was no denying that. Like when you fit jigsaw pieces together and start to make out a face. I could already see Johnny's face. His blue eyes.

That's when the darkness broke, and Johnny emerged. And he was beautiful. A face chiseled more on the Hispanic than the Asian, more like the hacienderos he would play against than the cane workers he would join. I looked over at Wing who apparently shared the same cloud I found myself on each time I'd seen Johnny. I felt my palms sweating again when Johnny approached the court, peeling off his shirt to take Tiny's place on the worker's shirtless team.

When Wing's elbow informed me that she'd caught me staring, I tried to claim it was the small tattoos on each of his shoulders that held my attention, one of the American flag, and the other of the Filipino flag. I tried, anyway. But clearly that wasn't it. It was Johnny. It was his chest, his muscular arms, and the ripples covering his stomach headed down to his narrow waste. He looked like Michelangelo's David. His jeans, however, kept me from making any other comparisons to the statue.

The hacienderos made a few comments about the tattoos. "Hey Boy," began one of Boy's friends, "you're employing Americans in the fields now? Be careful. He might start a union."

"He's not American," Boy replied. "His daddy was supposedly an American GI. Got some Pinay knocked up. Took him back to the States. But the old man killed himself with booze, and the stepmom sent the mistake back where he came from."

I couldn't believe what I was hearing. Sad enough if it was true, but that Boy would talk that way right in front of Johnny as if he weren't there. I looked at Johnny and wanted to cry. This wasn't the first time I was ashamed to be related to Boy Delgado.

Johnny didn't seem to mind the taunts. He matter-of-factly walked onto the court and said, "Y'all talk more than a flock of preachers at an AA meeting. Is this a basketball game, or some kind of soap opera?"

I picked up on a southern accent, from the States. And not the dumb hillbilly Gomer Pyle sort either. It was subtler than that, with just enough of a southern drawl to take my breath away.

You hardly ever heard words between the cane workers and the haciendero boys, except maybe a "good morning sir" or a "yes sir." Certainly nothing close to sarcasm. And the hacienderos were somewhat taken aback.

"Whoa, with that chip on his shoulder, maybe he really is American," began one of Boy's friends. Then half kidding, "You better watch out for this one, Boy. He could be trouble."

Boy responded by rolling his eyes upward. "Well, let's see if he plays basketball like an American."

"You mean, by the rules?" added Johnny, noting Boy's fondness for breaking them.

"Ooooooh!" chanted Boy's team in unison, acknowledging the insult.

Boy couldn't think of a quick come back, so he just decided to get back to the game. "Your ball," he said, throwing it smartly at Johnny's head.

Johnny didn't even flinch, catching the ball easily with one hand. He passed the ball to Speed and the game resumed. It quickly became apparent that Johnny had indeed picked up some skills in the States. The gap in the score was closing quickly. The workers, carried by Johnny, soon come from behind to tie the score at 19.

At least that's what they said the score was. I couldn't really concentrate on the game. I was too busy concentrating on Johnny. It wasn't long before his shirtless torso was gleaming with sweat, only accentuating his sculpted muscles. He reminded me of a thoroughbred racehorse with his long black mane tossing about the back of his neck as he ran. And like a racehorse coming out of the final turn, I found myself cheering for him, louder with each point scored. This only served to rouse the other girls who'd long before lost interest in the game, drawing stares of disbelief that I would cheer against their home team haciendeos. Even Wing found herself being tested, torn between her allegiance for her brother and her obvious infatuation with Johnny.

Unfortunately, once the score was tied, things began to get ugly again. It was like a warning to Boy to pull out all stops and resort to all manner of cheating to prevent Johnny and the workers from taking the lead. Competitive jostling turned to blatant shoving, and elbows began to fly again. That held the workers off for a while, but when Johnny scored the go ahead point bringing them within one point of an upset victory, all semblance of order separating the game from a brawl had ceased. The haciendeo boys held nothing back, throwing punches, tripping from behind, and clotheslining workers with outstretched arms to the front of the neck.

All this was met without retaliation from the workers. This was nothing new to them. They knew better than to allow themselves to be provoked into biting the hand that feeds them. They knew their place.

That is, all but Johnny. Johnny had yet to learn his place in the world. Johnny had an American flag tattooed on one shoulder. And when Boy tried the same move on Johnny that took Tiny out of the game, the gloves came off. As Boy cut Johnny's legs out from under him during a rebound, Johnny made sure to come down on something soft to break his fall. Something soft like Boy's back. And just to make sure that Boy would break his fall, Johnny wrapped one arm around Boy's neck, driving Boy hard into the ground beneath him, his face in the dirt. Boy came up swinging.

Everyone expected that. Anyone that knew Boy knew he wouldn't let a cane worker get the better of him. But there was one thing they didn't expect, one thing foreign to the hacienderos and perhaps the whole town of Bais for that matter. Johnny, a cane worker, swung back.

No one had seen a cane worker lift a hand to a haciendero before. Yet Johnny never thought twice about it. In return for a glancing blow from Boy that caught Johnny in the ear, Johnny landed one squarely to Boy's jaw, and Boy went down. When that happened, everyone froze. Gasps of surprise could be heard from the girls. The cane workers all took a step backward. Boy, flat on his back, shook the stars from his eyes. Johnny held his ground, standing over Boy like a storm cloud, fists clenched.

I was as surprised as anyone. Like the others, I'd never seen a worker raise a hand to a haciendero. But Boy deserved it. In fact, Boy'd had it coming for years. And for the first time, someone had the guts to stand up to him. I looked at Johnny standing over Boy, and I melted. I saw someone avenging the wrong done to Tiny, all the workers for that matter. I saw someone doing the right thing.

I guess Boy expected someone might see it that way too. So he scrambled to his feet, and without taking the time to dust off his barong, launched himself at Johnny. Johnny was more than ready, and in fact, was clearly getting the better of Boy when the other haciendero boys jumped in. Even against two or three, Johnny held his own, but when they all came at him, it was more than he could handle. I got scared and looked over at the other cane workers, but no one was coming to Johnny's aid, not even Speed. He was on his own. They were going to hurt him. I started to cry.

And that's when I heard the first gun shot. I didn't know where it came from. Did one of the boys have a gun? Had someone shot Johnny? I quickly tried wiping the tears from my eyes to find the source of the shooting. But then more shots rang out and I dropped to the ground in fear. Even the boys had stopped fighting, looking at each other, to see if anyone'd been hit. The girls were screaming. As the gunfire continued, everyone ran for cover. Everyone except me. I lay on the ground, frozen with terror. I suddenly felt a firm hand on my back. Then two hands roughly rolling me over. I instinctively recoiled, bringing my hands up to protect my face.

"Don't shoot!" I pleaded.

"Don't be a ninny," someone replied, pulling me up by my wrists. "Run for cover!"

My legs wouldn't move. And they started to give way, when the person who'd pulled me up threw me over his shoulder and started running. I screamed for help. Then, "Where are you taking me?" I shouted at the kidnapper.

"Just saving your life, you little idiot," he replied.

Curiosity overcame fear, and I opened my eyes just enough to see over whoever's shoulder I'd been thrown, only to find myself staring at a tattoo of the American flag.

Then it was gone as I flew through the air, landing on my back on a pile of straw inside the barn next to the basketball court. Johnny stood over me, and with a sense of déjà vu, I looked up at him and noted, "You always seem to be saving me."

"Bad habit, I guess," he quipped, peering out the open barn door to see what was going on. "But you're just such a cute kid, I can't help myself."

At those words, I guess I'd forgotten about the shooting, because I could feel the blush running through my cheeks. Johnny thought I was so cute that he couldn't help himself? Maybe I'd been shot and gone to heaven after all. Yet something he said pulled me back to Earth.

"Kid? I'm not a kid," I protested.

"If you say so, your Highness," he replied, without turning around.

"My name's Lisa," I replied indignantly. And when I looked up at him, I could see through the opening in the barn door clear up to the watchtower. It was a tower supposedly built to keep an eye out for fires in the cane fields. But now it looked more like a prison guard tower as I saw Captain in the bird's nest shooting a rifle.

"It's Captain. Captain's shooting at something. Or someone," I shouted to Johnny. And the shots were frighteningly loud. It's not like in the movies at all. Real gunshots are so loud they rattle your brain. But at least these weren't aimed at us. Even in the dark, I could see Captain's silhouette in the flashes of gunfire. He was shooting toward the pen where the cows were kept. There didn't seem to be anyone firing back. And as suddenly as the shooting had started, it abruptly ceased, gunfire replaced by the chirping of crickets. And by the decree of crickets, the battleground had magically transformed back into the farm, like nothing had happened.

Only after finding out the details of the shooting was I able to absorb what had happened, put everything back into proper perspective. What I later learned was that a small band of communists had tried to rustle some cattle. They were spotted from the watchtower and Captain opened fire, no questions asked. He even killed one of them before the others scattered, running off to the hills again. No police ever showed up. There was never any inquiry of any kind. This was the farm. And on the cane farms, the hacienderos were the law, the police, the judges, and the executioners. By taking a life, Captain had saved a couple of cows and scared off a pack of communists, for the time being anyway.

As reward, Captain was given a couple of days off, sufficient time for the hero to answer all the adoring maids' questions and start the tsismus rolling, which quickly spread from one farm to the other, until the whole island was put on notice that the Delgados would not tolerate communist thieves. The family of the young man killed came for the body and had it buried in the town cemetery, a sad little place overrun by weeds, crooked makeshift headstones sinking into the muddy earth. The immediate family and the priest were there. But no one else attended the brief ceremony. They would not honor a communist thief, out of respect for the hacienderos.

Chapter 3

By morning, it was as if nothing out of the ordinary had happened, as if people were shot and killed all the time. No big deal. I know that might sound weird. And thinking back, at the time, it probably seemed that way to me as well. But when you're young, you still think everything is supposed to make sense. And when the world around you doesn't stand up and say, hey, it's not supposed to be that way, well, you assume that's just how it goes, just part of life on the farm.

Wing never knew about Johnny carrying me to the safety of the barn. I didn't want to anger her again by seeming to steal her crush. It wasn't my fault he always seemed to be saving me. But I wasn't in complete denial. I mean, I knew I was attracted to him. I wasn't that thick. But I wasn't in love with him. There was a difference. He was just a cane worker after all. Nothing could happen. And I'm sure Wing felt the same way. So let her have her crush. It was just a game, something to do, something to keep us entertained during the slow days of summer. We were only 14-years-old for God's sake.

Now don't get me wrong. It wasn't every day on the farm that something exciting happened. I can see how I might be giving you that impression, what with all the parties, fights, and guns. But that's only because I've been skipping the boring stuff. In fact, more often than not, that's exactly what the farm was. Boring. Most days, at least for us kids, we'd wake up with nothing planned, and that's exactly what would happen. Nothing. But that was just the point. No responsibilities. No worries. Just time. Time to bounce around from one thing to another, on a whim, the way a stray dog walks down a road, drifting from one side to the other, following his nose toward whatever scent grabs his attention.

On a typical day, I'd wake up with an empty head. I'd lay on the cool white sheets of my bed, staring up at the ceiling, with what little attention I had, focused on a small lizard slowly making his way from one end to the other. I didn't suppose he had any plans either. It was too hot anyway. I was reluctant to move for fear that any physical exertion would cause me to break out in my first sweat of the day. And it was too early for that, too early to start sweating already. No, I'd just lay there, my gecko and I. And with my eyes momentarily occupied, my other senses would begin to kick in. I'd hear the maids and the houseboy outside my window happily dividing up chores. I didn't have any chores. There really was no reason for me to get out of bed. I could even have had the maids bring me breakfast in bed here at the Casablanca Hotel. It was truly paradise.

On the other hand, I really had to pee. I tried to let my mind wander again, but soon I could think of nothing else. I really had to go. There, darn it, the mood was broken. It looked like I was going to have to get out of bed and start sweating after all.

So Wing and I got back into our normal routine, which, in fact, was no routine at all. It was more like, what do you want to do today? I don't know. What do *you* want to do? During the week, one of our favorite pastimes was hanging out at Mama's dress shop. Actually, it was more like a dress factory. Papa had given Mama a small building on the farm, by Casablanca, and encouraged her to manufacture dresses. She would pay the wives and sisters of the cane workers to sew dresses, which Mama could then bring to Manila on one of her frequent trips, to sell in a small shop she shared with a couple of friends. Mama's shop in Manila was more like a little place she could go and have coffee with her friends, a hobby. The factory, on the other hand, served two purposes. It gave Mama something to do to keep her from moaning about her boring life on the farm, all the while clothing and feeding many of the families on Bais.

This whole thing may have been no more than a hobby for Mama, but for the women back on the farm these were real jobs. The pennies they made for each dress they sewed meant food on the plate for their kids. Looking back, some might see it as a sweatshop, or slave labor. But in a country with no welfare system, Medicaid, or food stamps, it often meant the difference between life and death.

So while some might say Mama was taking advantage of the poor, the poor looked at her as a savior, a Godsend. After all, it wasn't like some of her friends, whose corrupt relatives in government agencies intercepted clothing donated by charitable organizations across the world and sold them to the poor at a profit. Not that Mama wouldn't have done that, given the chance. But Papa would have been furious. And that's how Mama was. She had no real conscience of her own. It was never a matter of right or wrong. It was only fear that kept Mama in check, fear of Papa, and God.

Wing and I loved to hang out at the factory, modeling the clothes. We'd even get to pick out our favorite fabrics and have dresses custom made for us in whatever style we chose. And the women in the factory could copy any famous designer dress we liked, as long as we could bring them a picture of the dress. Wing and I each had a closet full of designer knock-offs.

Hanging out at the dress shop was something we could do during the week. But on the weekends, there were more options for entertainment. We'd often tag along when Papa and his friends went golfing. Sometimes they even let their wives play. *That* was entertainment.

Now this was no fancy Manila golf club, mind you. This was Bais, where half a dozen hacienderos got together and agreed to clear a small piece of jungle none of them would miss, to make room for a golf course. And that was it. No one else played there. I don't think anyone else on the island even had a set of clubs. It was out in the middle of nowhere. The barefoot caddies in jeans and T-shirts would drop their cigarettes and scramble out to greet them, jumping at the chance to earn some tip money. The caddies might sit there everyday for a couple of weeks with no pay waiting for one of the hacienderos to get the urge to golf, because the few pesos they would earn in tips was more than others on the island might earn in a month. In fact, so as not to lose all their caddies, the hacienderos would feel guilty if they didn't play golf at least every couple of weeks.

After dropping the golfers off at the clubhouse, the drivers would park around back and talk tsismus or sports while cleaning the cars for the second or third time that day. The ladies of the clubhouse would run out with homemade snacks, junk food and drinks for the golfers to buy, which they would, if only out of obligation to support the enterprise.

Papa was playing with Ron Fanlo that day, a foursome including Mr. Fanlo's wife, Girlie, and Mama. That's really why we went, to giggle at Mama's attempt to play golf. Mr. Fanlo came out of the clubhouse ripping open a bag of Twinkies. He left the clubhouse workers behind with their usual good-hearted snickering in homage to his infamous nickname.

"Hey José!" shouted Mr. Fanlo to Papa. "How's your back? Or is it your shoulder? Which excuse will it be today?"

"Ha ha," Papa replied, only half smiling. "I don't need excuses when I golf with you, Ron. They're reserved only for golfers who can beat me."

Mr. Fanlo turned toward me in a conspiratorial whisper. "I'm not sure, but I think I've just been insulted. Now my honor is at stake. You know what that means?"

I shook my head, no.

He pulled me in closer by the elbow. "There's only one thing I *can* do. I'll have to cheat."

He pushed me away with a chuckle. This was going to be fun.

Despite the early hour, as we strolled out to the first tee, you could already feel the sweltering humidity of a summer day in the Philippines. Best to play golf early in the morning. Especially for the poor caddies. No one used golf carts in Bais. Too expensive. Besides, that would defeat half the purpose of golfing to begin with, to provide jobs for the locals. Dragging a set of golf clubs around for half a day in the sweltering heat was just about the best paying job on the island. In fact, we actually figured out one time that, on an hourly basis, one particular caddy did indeed have the highest paying job on the island. That was Mama's caddy.

No, it wasn't that Mama was the biggest tipper. Mama didn't tip at all. Papa took care of that. And Papa made sure Mama's caddy got the biggest tip. There was good reason for that, and it had nothing to do with trying to impress anyone. The reason was obvious. After all, Mama was the worst golfer in the Philippines. The poor guy lucky enough to carry Mama's clubs would spend most of the day crawling through the snake-infested jungle searching for Mama's golf balls, which could never manage to stay on the actual golf course. And he had to do all that while enduring Mama's condescending tone directing his search, always in the wrong direction. Perhaps it's the natural thriftiness of the Pinoy people not to waste golf balls and simply break out a new one every time one got lost. That, and the doggedness of the caddies who always seem to find the darn things, no matter how thick the jungle.

Mr. Fanlo tee'd off first, cigarette dangling from his lips. "Watch this José. In the hole," as he swung his club, contacting the ball with a solid ping sound. Well, it was nowhere near the hole. But it was straight. He couldn't complain.

As Papa prepared to take his turn, Mr. Fanlo conveniently decided to have a coughing fit. Papa waited patiently for silence so that he could concentrate, but each time he was ready to swing, Ron would start up again.

"You know, that smoking of yours is going to kill you," said Papa as he finally hit the ball amid a particularly distracting gagging sound from Ron.

"No, it's actually very strange, José. It only seems to bother me when I play golf."

"So I've noticed," answered Papa. "And only when it's my turn," he added.

"Yeah, it's funny that way, isn't it?"

Despite all of Ron's distractions, Papa's shot surpassed Ron's.

Girlie, shooting from the ladies' tee, hit a ground ball. But even though it never left the ground, it went straight and rolled pretty far.

Now it was finally Mama's turn. Wing and I elbowed each other to make sure we were watching. In fact, if one wasn't watching when Mama hit the ball, one might get seriously injured. One never knew where the thing might go. So as Mama approached the tee, everyone else took a few steps back and behind her. Not that it was necessarily safe there either, but playing the odds was the best you could do. Even Mama's caddy knew he wasn't getting paid enough to risk bodily injury. So after handing her the proper club and pointing her in the general direction of the hole, even he hightailed it for the safety of the crowd behind her where, like a herd of water buffalo, we were all jockeying for an interior position, protected from the outside threat.

Her swing was surprisingly good, almost perfect, the men agreed, whispering to each other. Now if only it had made contact with the ball. That was the amazing thing. How such a beautiful swing could entirely miss the ball.

"Where is it? Did anyone see where it went?" asked Mama, looking up the course with one hand shielding her eyes from the sun.

We all looked at each other, hoping someone else would break the news. When she turned toward us for an answer, her caddy proved once again why he was the highest paid man on the island. He surged forward, pointing off down the fairway.

"Fantastic shot, Dai (the Filipino term for ma'am). Right down the middle." The rest of us began clapping. Not for the phantom shot, but for the caddy who managed to surreptitiously sweep up her ball with her tee as she squinted down the course, striding straight down the fairway like a hunting dog to reach the spot where her ball was to land before anyone else could see him actually place it there.

"I think my shot's beaten all of yours," noted Mama to the crowd.

"Seems so," coughed Ron, as the herd broke up.

Wing rolled her eyes at me as we followed the crowd, trying our best to suppress any errant giggles.

I always enjoyed walking the golf course, taking in gorgeous views of the surrounding mountains, including huge Mount Talinas, the island's volcano. And the mango trees scattered about the course were tremendous. Hanging from each tree were thousands of little brown paper bags up to one hundred feet in the air, placed by the locals around each individual mango to protect them from insects and small animals. They dangled in the breeze like Christmas ornaments waiting until they were ready to be harvested, the proceeds split between the hacienderos and those crazy enough to climb up and pick them.

They found Ron's ball on the fairway, sort of. Actually, it was about two inches above the fairway, nestled on top of a heap of water buffalo dung. That, in itself, would not normally represent a problem, however, this particular heap of dung was still warm. It was still warm because the source of the dung was happily grazing only a couple of feet away.

"Play it as it lies," reminded Papa, insisting that the ball not be moved unless Ron wanted to count a penalty stroke. Ron defiantly approached the ball, intending to play it. The water buffalo, a full-grown bull, had other ideas, picking his head up and stamping his foot when he picked up Ron's scent. Ron, of course, not the confrontational type, sent over his caddy, who, stripping off his red shirt and waving it in front of the water buffalo's nose began drawing the beast away from the ball. Unfortunately, he soon had the creature's full attention, as it began to charge the caddy in earnest. The boy barely made it to the tree ahead of the water buffalo, scampering barefooted up the trunk like a monkey.

Wing and I, along with the wives, headed in the opposite direction, to the edge of the woods across the fairway. The men, of course, stood their ground. And Ron, five iron in hand, approached the dung. Noticing how close Papa had remained, combined with the direction of the breeze, Ron saw his opportunity and took it. Making sure his swing got a little more under the ball than usual, Ron smacked it, and half the pile of dung at the same time, making sure part of the brown spray made it's way to Papa's white shirt. Noting the splatter on Papa's shirt more so than the ball's trajectory, Ron couldn't help but note, "That was a crappy shot."

Papa swore he would get revenge as he moved on to find his own ball, blotting spots of dung off his shirt with a hand towel.

For the rest of the morning, we all did our best to stay upwind from Papa and his malodorous shirt, which grew more and more pungent with the heat of the day. It grew so hot, in fact, that Mama had soon gathered her own little entourage. One local girl appeared with a portable chair for Mama to sit on between shots. And another would stand over the queen seated on her throne, holding an umbrella to shield her from the sun. Not only did the girl hold the umbrella, but she would continually pump it up and down to create a breeze for her royal highness. The locals had certainly mastered the fine art of earning tips. Anything they could imagine doing that would garner the favor of the hacienderos, and their money, was done.

One particular caddy that Papa always used earned more than tips. When faced with a particularly difficult shot, the men would often drop a ball so that Papa's caddy could take a swing himself. They were so impressed by the boy's skills with a golf club that they would observe his swing, which club he used, and where the ball landed, to gauge their own shot, subtracting a few yards, of course, in the knowledge that none of them could hit the ball as far themselves. Out of respect for the boy's natural ability, as much as his work ethic and good nature, the hacienderos had all agreed to fund an education for him all the way through college. Earning the whopper of all tips, this boy's life, and that of his whole family, would be inevitably changed for the better. He'd earned a chance to learn a profession, a chance to leave the island for greater opportunity. He'd earned a future, which was never taken for granted among the poor in the Philippines.

Anyway, Ron continued to cheat, picking up and moving his ball to his advantage, and taking extra shots when Papa wasn't looking. And Mama continued to send her caddy into the jungle to battle venomous snakes and alligators in pursuit of her ball.

Oh, and Papa did finally get his revenge. In areas, wild chickens overran the golf course. In fact, when he came across one particular hen sitting on his golf ball, which she'd mistaken for one of her eggs, it gave Papa an idea. He gathered her real abandoned egg, shaped remarkably like a golf ball, and placed it in his pocket for future use.

And when finally he came upon one of Ron's balls before Ron, Papa slyly replaced the ball with the egg.

"It's over here, Ron," shouted Papa, fighting back a devilish grin.

Taking Papa's word for it, Ron neglected to check the "ball" for any marks identifying it as his. He didn't notice Papa taking several steps back, or signaling the rest of us to do the same. So when his club made contact with the egg, a delicate cracking sound was followed by a stream of yellow yoke and slimy egg white gracefully following the arc of Ron's club and ultimately landing across his face and on his head. Everyone burst out laughing before Ron even knew what hit him.

The realization showed on his face, simultaneously with the oozing egg, as Papa declared, "The yolk's on you, Ron."

The grown-ups could be so corny.

Chapter 4

And so the summer went, Wing and I filling our life of leisure one day at a time with whatever entertainment presented itself. It was a couple of weeks later that our next big adventure began. It started with a typical breakfast at Casablanca. The Delgados and I all sat around the table out on the veranda, the large lazy Susan spinning wildly as everyone chose their favorites from the wide selection of breakfast treats provided by Lou and the maids. Each serving dish was covered by a little screened umbrella to keep the flies off. Hortensia stood guard as well, armed with her palm frond fly swatter.

Papa was experimenting with a new homemade blend of coffee. Coffee was one of his hobbies. He'd obtain various exotic beans and blend them together in various proportions, searching for that ever-elusive perfect cup of java. It was actually quite humorous watching Papa's face as the first sip touched his lips. More often then not, the experiment resulted in disappointment and, not uncommonly, Papa couldn't help but spit the concoction onto the ground in disgust.

Coffee wasn't Papa's only vice. There were always five or six bottles of vitamins and medicinal herbs standing about his breakfast plate, like sentries warding off the effects of aging. Papa single-handedly kept the mail order vitamin companies in business, all in an effort to thin his blood, lower his cholesterol, shrink his prostate, cleanse his bowels, and generally live forever. Mama, on the other hand, as if to balance Papa's yin with her yang, ate only sweets and lard. Extra molasses and butter on everything. Yet anything green or even resembling a vegetable was never permitted anywhere near her plate. The kids lived on mangos. The delicious oval fruits were piled high on the table, and we each ate three or four before even noticing anything else to eat.

Hortensia brought Papa the week-old newspaper just arrived from Manila. He glanced over at the headlines and froze, his coffee cup suspended in mid-air. I thought he was having a stroke. And when I saw the tremor start, coffee trickling down the side of the cup, I was about to scream. Only when he spoke, did I see it was shock. Shock from the news.

"They've killed him," Papa mumbled.

I looked around the table to see if anyone knew who he was talking about. "Who? Who did they kill?"

Papa slowly lowered the newspaper to the table, and deliberately exhaled through pursed lips, as if releasing pressure. When he inhaled again, it was through his nose, eyes closed. I thought maybe it was about some relative of the family's. Everyone else just sat and stared at him. I couldn't take it anymore.

"Papa. Who? Who is it?" I repeated.

Papa just looked up at the sky. "Aquino."

"Who?"

"Benigno Aquino."

Wing and I just looked at each other for any sign of recognition. Mama just kept eating. But Boy was even worse.

"Who cares?" he groaned, reaching for another mango.

I've never seen a human being turn the shade of purple I saw rise in Papa's face. He reminded me of Mount Talinas. And Papa was about to erupt.

He started to speak, but stopped himself, placing his hands flat on the table in an attempt to retain control of himself.

"Benigno Aquino was the only hope this country had," he began, quietly and deliberately. "The only political force capable of rescuing the Philippines from the Marcos regime."

I knew how to add two plus two. I no longer needed to know who **they** were when Papa said **they**'d killed him. "Is that why they killed Aquino?" I asked.

Papa was still staring at his son in disbelief, but I think my probing was helping to diffuse the situation.

"They tried everything else," Papa began. "Aquino was an extremely charismatic senator. He was certain to succeed Marcos to the presidency, until Marcos had him falsely imprisoned back in the early seventies, canceled the elections, and declared marshal law."

Wing was beginning to glaze over, as the discussion clearly seemed to concern politics. Boy and Mama never even looked up from their breakfast. It was different for me, though. Like a bloodhound given the scent, I wouldn't stop until I'd had the whole story.

"Then what happened?" I asked.

"Well, he'd been in prison nearly eight years when Marcos allowed him to leave for the States in need of heart surgery. He stayed away three years, but was coming back last week."

I didn't understand. "Why? Why would he come back?"

Papa looked at me. "Why? Because Benigno Aquino was a patriot. This was his country. We were his people. He couldn't desert us."

"So what happened? How did they kill him?"

Papa threw the newspaper across the table for me to see the front page. I struggled to keep my breakfast down when I saw it, a full-page close-up of Benigno Aquino's face as he lie in his coffin. For the wake, the family had requested that the body not be cleaned up in any way, so the world would see the brutality of what had happened. He lay there in the same blood-stained clothes he'd had on when they carried him from the airport tarmac, his face battered, bloodied and swollen.

"They wouldn't even let him touch Filipino soil," Papa lamented. "Marcos sent his military goons to escort him from the plane, where they gunned him down in cold blood."

I didn't know what to say. I couldn't understand how something like that would be allowed to happen. "He can't get away with it, can he? Marcos, I mean. Isn't someone going to do something?"

Papa smiled. "Oh sure, something will be done all right. Marcos himself will demand an official investigation, led by political friends of his, of course. And the truth will be officially buried. There will be some rallies and protests. But they will be squashed under the military's thumb, like ants. Remember, we've been under martial law since Aquino's arrest ten years ago."

"Why marshal law?" I asked.

"Marcos has so mismanaged and robbed our country," Papa began, "that his own people were getting fed up. The only way to control them, to keep order, was to strip them of their rights, their freedom, and have the military maintain order. So he announced there was a communist insurgency threatening the country, declared martial law to allow him greater powers in quelling the insurgency he himself had created, and placed Aquino, the leader of the opposition, under arrest. Not only did martial law grant him greater powers, but it suspended the political process, leaving Marcos as President until further notice. And from the look of things, that's no time soon."

"Will they come here? The military? And control the communists?" Wing asked. So she had been listening after all. At least to anything that might directly affect her small world.

Papa burst out laughing. "Here? Send the military here? That's funny. The communists are only truly a problem out in the country. Marcos isn't interested in what goes on out here. He's too busy protecting his palace and his gold back in Manila from regular citizens fed up with watching him rape their country. Marcos only talks of the communists as an excuse to invoke martial law and have his generals, instead of the courts, control the people. He may have sewn the seeds of communism with his own greed, but those seeds have taken root out here, where the farms are. Communism is *our* problem. Marcos won't be sending any troops out here. They're too busy at the palace guarding Imelda's shoes."

"José! Stop making fun of poor Imelda," interrupted Mama. "As first lady, she does a lot of entertaining and needs all those shoes."

Papa ignored her. I looked at Mama and thought, at least she was consistent. Mama was an idiot.

Boy took advantage of the break in Papa's speech to change the subject. "We're planning a trip to Salama beach."

Typical. Papa's talking of politics and communists. Boy's going to the beach. At first Papa just stared at him wondering how any son of his could jump from the assassination of the only political figure capable of saving the country, to planning a trip to the beach. But knowing his son as he did, Papa just gave up and addressed Boy's statement.

"Who's we?" he asked, interested in Boy's guest list.

"Everyone. The guys, a couple of their girlfriends..." and then, as if to add some legitimacy, he included Papa's own spies, "Wing and Lisa."

Wing and I looked at each other. We knew we only got invited as a ploy to convince Papa to let Boy have his friends at the beach house. We knew they didn't really want us to go. On the other hand, we loved the beach and we found the older kids' antics entertaining. We looked over at Papa with our best "please, please, can we go, can we, can we" faces.

"OK," Papa agreed. "But take Hortensia. I don't want you wrecking the place. You'll need two cars. Captain's new boy, what's his name, uh, Johnny can drive the second car for you."

Wing and I locked eyes with each other. This Johnny seemed to be everywhere.

"Johnny?" complained Boy. "Does he even know how to drive?"

"He had his driver's permit in the States. I'm sure that's good enough for the back roads out to Salama," Papa assured him. "Why, you don't like him?"

"We've had our differences," admitted Boy.

"Good. Maybe, along with your sister and cousin, he'll help keep you out of trouble."

Boy shot us both a threatening glance. Wing and I stuck our tongues out at him. The deal was done. We were going to the beach. And Johnny was coming. It didn't get any better than that.

Two hours later, after a quick visit to church, and the Aquino assassination behind us, the caravan was assembled at the courtyard. Boy with five friends squeezed into the Toyota. Johnny drove the old VW van with all the provisions, Hortensia, Wing, and me.

"Hey, Hortensia. Did you remember to pack your bikini?" I shouted, knowing full well that Hortensia's ample physique would hardly flatter a bikini, and except for her head and hands, like one of the nuns, no part of Hortensia had seen the light of day since she was a child.

Not one to be outdone though, Hortensia replied, joking and blushing at the same time, "What bikini? I thought Salama was a nude beach."

"Eeewww!" yelled Wing. "Gross! Can we just start driving before I puke right here!"

It was easy to see that Boy wanted nothing to do with us when the Toyota flew out the gate to the farm in a spray of gravel, leaving the old van behind gasping for air as Johnny tried to get the creature rolling. Johnny probably would have been an adequate chauffeur, given an automatic transmission, but we all soon got used to the periodic grinding of gears after he got offended by my suggestion that I thought he was supposed to be using the clutchy thingy to the left of the brake pedal.

The drive to Salama beach brought the journey of Marco Polo to mind as the path degenerated from paved to gravel to dirt roads, passing from one chicken-infested town to another. Scores of small smoky Japanese motorcycles with passenger sidecars turned to human-powered pedicabs, tricycles pulling people behind them.

I'm sure Boy and his friends had the air conditioning on full blast as our poor van couldn't remember what working A/C was, the dust from the road finding its way into our open windows. Wing and I were constantly leaning between the forward seats to fool with the radio. Johnny kept futilely searching for a station that would play anything close to southern rock, while Hortensia periodically searched for a religious station, all prayer, all the time.

The sun beating on the white dirt road was blinding. We almost didn't see the commotion ahead when Johnny abruptly brought the van to a stop. As the dust cleared, we saw the Toyota surrounded by a crowd of angry villagers. We quickly saw that they weren't just angry. They were clearly communists. No smiles. Even in a traffic argument, there were bound to be some Filipino smiles. But not so with the communists.

They were shouting and rocking the car as if they might turn it over. Some were waving machetes. Boy and his friends stayed locked inside the car. We wondered why they didn't just step on the gas and speed away. It wasn't like Boy to be worried about possibly injuring one of the villagers in the path of the car. But as a couple of the angry men jumped from behind the car onto the trunk and hood, we saw what the problem was. There was a small cow wedged under the car. Well it was a calf, but it wasn't that small. It was still a cow, after all. It was plenty big enough to stop the car by raising the wheels off the ground when it got wedged under the front axle of the front wheel drive car. Boy must have run over it while it was sleeping in the middle of the road. Had it been standing when hit, the Toyota would have been totaled in the collision. Instead, judging by the frantic waving at the villagers by the cars inhabitants, everyone appeared to be OK... at least, for now.

Johnny turned to us in the back seat. "What are they jabberin' about? What do they want?" Johnny's skill with the Filipino language was still limited, especially the Visayan dialect spoken out in the country. After all, we spoke mostly English on the farm.

Even *my* Visayan was limited, Tagalog being the favored dialect back in Manila. I poked Wing in the ribs with my elbow so she would serve as translator.

"They're angry!" she shouted. Wing shouted when she was frightened.

"I can tell that much," moaned Johnny. "Is it the cow? Is that the problem?"

Hortensia was praying in the back of the van, her eyes locked shut.

"They want a new cow. They want the dead calf replaced," explained Wing.

Johnny turned around to face Wing in the back seat. "They want us to give them a cow?"

Wing nodded.

"Well, don't just sit there. Hand me the spare cow we brought along. It's wrapped in the beach towels," ordered Johnny.

With a surprised look on her face, Wing turned to look behind her. If it weren't for the gravity of the situation, I would have burst out laughing at her gullibility. But I was too scared. Of course, that wouldn't stop me from retelling the story many times later at Wing's expense.

The villagers looked like they were going to break in the windshield when Johnny asked, "Why doesn't Boy just pay them? How much can a cow cost?"

"I don't think they want money," I replied. "I think it's more than that. Cows are like members of the family out here. They don't want money. They want revenge."

At that moment, they smashed the rear window of the car with a rock. It shattered, but the safety glass didn't give way. They still couldn't get at the car's occupants. Johnny swung his door open and started pounding on his horn to get their attention. It seemed to be working. The mob had been so preoccupied with their captives that they hadn't noticed us. When we saw the angry crowd turn our way, Wing and I looked at each other. We weren't sure this was a good thing. But their stares lasted only a moment as they ignored the distraction and went back to their business with Boy's car. Hortensia continued to finger her rosary as her lips moved in silent prayer.

"There must be something else they want," said Johnny, looking about the van.

"Don't look at us," Wing and I said in unison. "They're not my type," I added.

Just then, the villagers had managed to yank Boy's door open. They were dragging him from the car. Johnny suddenly grabbed something and bolted from the van into the street. I wondered for a moment if Captain had provided Johnny with a rifle for just such an emergency. Whatever it was, we heard the thud of its weight on the roof of the van. Johnny stood one foot on the front seat of the van and one foot in the window of the open driver's door so as the reach the van's roof. Then we heard a boom.

The villagers' heads all turned in our direction once more. There were more booms. Johnny had their attention. But they weren't running. Then we noticed the rhythm to the booms. And the singing. It wasn't a rifle. It was Johnny's boom box. The volume was turned all the way up. And the air was filled with Lynyrd Skynyrd's "Gimme Three Steps."

I don't know what made Johnny think of using the boom box as a distraction. But it was working. While three of the attackers held onto Boy, the others all started walking toward us. Among us, I guess only Johnny knew the power of music, the universal language. I thought I even saw some communist smiles as the crowd began to surround us. Johnny's face suddenly appeared in the windshield as he motioned to Wing for an interpreter. But Wing was frozen with fear. I tried pushing her, but it was no use. She wasn't leaving the car. Seeing the look on Johnny's face, I couldn't just sit there. I thought I might know enough Visayan dialect to help. So I swallowed my fear and climbed through the window of the van onto the roof with Johnny.

Over the music, Johnny shouted in my ear. "Tell them we'll trade. The boom box for the cow. We give up the box. And they give up Boy and the others."

I'm not sure how much actual Visayan I used. It was more a blend of Tagalog and English, or Taglish as we called it, but I guess it was enough to get the message across, as the villagers began nodding their heads in agreement, and reaching their arms out for Johnny's prized boom box.

Johnny looked pleased with himself as he removed his Lynyrd Skynyrd cassette before handing over the stereo.

Big mistake. Apparently the traditional Filipino folk music on the radio wasn't part of the deal. The communists quickly dropped the boom box, held out their arms, and began chanting, "Rock and roll! Rock and roll!"

Johnny didn't need my translation. He pulled the cassette from his pocket, gave it one last kiss, as if he were giving up a child for adoption, and tossed it to the angry mob. Like seagulls at a clambake, the villagers swarmed the scene, fighting over the ransom. They climbed all over each other attempting to claim the prize as their own. Amid the confusion, Johnny jumped off the van and organized Boy and his friends to lift one front corner of the car enough so that they could roll it off of the calf.

Despite our near death experience, I couldn't help but feel sorry for the baby cow. I apologized to God for taking the poor thing's life and hoped it hadn't felt any pain. And just then, as if in answer to my prayers, the goddamned thing stood up, shook off the dust from the road, and walked away as if nothing had happened. I rubbed my eyes in disbelief. Either I had a direct line to God, or more likely, the beast was in on the villagers' scam from the start, playing possum so its owners could squeeze the accused murderers for whatever possessions they might have on hand. It was hard to imagine such an innocent looking creature could be so devious. Just another communist plot, I guess. Nevertheless, we'd survived the ordeal intact, making our getaway amid a cloud of dust and grinding gears, hastily resuming our pilgrimage to Salama beach.

It seemed this summer on the farm was providing more adventure than most. Communists and guns were playing a much larger role than expected for a child's summer vacation. Yet when you're young and feeling immortal, I suppose danger seems more exciting than frightening, and every day left you wondering what was coming from around the next corner. I was looking forward to Salama.

Chapter 5

In those days, the beach house still seemed big to me. It's really just one great room on stilts with a large balcony overlooking Salama beach. But back then, everything seemed big. It's not until you've been away for a while, matured a bit, and returned, that you suddenly notice how small everything becomes. The house you grew up in, your school, your hometown, your friends, your dreams. Everything shrinks over time. But not your first loves. Have you noticed that? Not your first loves. They do just the opposite. The briefest crush, really no more than the flash of a firefly on a warm summer's eve, only seems to thrive and grow amid your mind's fertile imagination.

The sand at Salama was a soft black velvet. The dark volcanic residue contrasted sharply with the ocean water, aqua and crystal clear. Thinking back, it's the clarity I recall. That's something you don't appreciate until later, how waters once so clear can grow muddy over time, how colors, once so vibrant in childhood, tend to take on reality's various shades of gray as we grow. Life becomes complex, and even a trip to the beach becomes messy.

The beach house was really more of a hut than a house. There wasn't even any electricity. Without air conditioning, we usually slept out on the balcony. The breeze helped keep the mosquitoes off. But they weren't the only creepy crawly things at the beach house. The bugs at Salama were huge. I remember Wing used to make me turn the water on in the shower for her, because the giant cockroaches would scramble out of the drain to keep from drowning. She imagined they would carry her off to their lair to be eaten.

Then there was the toilet. Instead of sitting on it, we used to stand on the seat ever since that time our friend Mary got poked in the butt by a rat. I suspect the rat was more surprised than she was. But Mary certainly won the screaming contest. For Wing and me, that rat would live forever in the Salama toilet. Poor Mary, though. I don't think she'd ever sit on another toilet in her life, Salama or otherwise.

Days at the beach were spent snorkeling and tanning. My wardrobe, as Wing's, was essentially a wad of bikinis stuffed into a small duffle bag along with sunglasses and various tanning oils. The boys normally liked to go fishing, but once they'd grown older, and there were girls to impress, the fishing gear seemed more likely to be left behind. Instead, there was a small Sunfish sailboat at the beach that we all used for exploring other nearby beaches. Normally a one-man vessel, one time we had up to twelve kids on that boat. It wasn't very fast, overloaded that way, and hovered more under the water than above, but we all had a ball getting around.

Johnny, of course, like Hortensia, had to stay behind, at the beach house. I still had some trouble thinking of him as just one of the help. I don't know if it was because he looked and acted more Cano than Pinoy, or maybe just because he'd saved my life a couple of times. But that's the way it was. Besides, just hanging around the beach house wasn't much of a job. It sure beat cutting cane.

Wing and I found a nice flat boulder to work on our tans while watching the older kids look for trouble. It didn't take them long. All the ingredients were there. Young Catholic girls hunting for mates, and bored young privileged boys from families with money. Just throw in a double dose of testosterone as catalyst and stand back. It was only a matter of time before the boys found a cliff they could dive off of, where surviving the fifty-foot plunge to the water below depended on correctly timing the incoming surf.

"Think anyone will kill themselves?" I asked, eying the dangerous mating ritual on the cliff as I waited for Wing to pass the suntan oil.

Wing didn't even look up from her task, committed to making sure she would tan evenly. "Nah. They're always doing things like that."

"Well, if anyone gets killed, don't tell me. OK? I just hate when that happens." I turned my attention back to the ocean, a beautiful shining blue. Just like Johnny's eyes.

"You're thinking of him, aren't you?" accused Wing, staring right through me.

"Who?" I asked, playing dumb.

"Who? Johnny. That's who." Wing wasn't buying the innocent routine.

"What? You think you can read my mind?"

"Of course I can. Ever since we were five, when you first started coming to the farm."

She had a point. Wing did have a way of getting inside my head. Ever since we were little. On the other hand, maybe it was part of herself she saw in me. Or any generic 14-year-old girl for that matter. Who wouldn't be thinking of Johnny?

"So what if I am? Aren't you thinking about him?" I asked.

"Of course I am. But that's different. He's mine. I claimed him," as if he were a new pair of shoes we'd both spotted at the same time.

I knew that was ridiculous. And I was going to say so. But then I caught myself and reconsidered. What was the point?

"And what is it you plan to do with him?" I asked. "You're going to marry a cane worker? Your family would disown you." I lay back on my beach towel. Point made. Discussion over.

Wing wasn't ready to concede, however. "And what about you? Don't tell me you don't like him too."

"Yeah, but not to marry him or anything. I just like to look at him."

I wonder if it's a sin to lie, if you don't know you're lying? I don't think that counts, does it? Well, apparently, as long as I didn't know it was a lie, Wing, the mind reader, couldn't see through it.

"I guess you're right," Wing admitted. Then she poked me in the ribs. "Get up. Let's make a pact."

"What about?" I asked, rising to my elbows.

"About Johnny. Let's agree, since neither of us can really have him, that he'll be out of bounds for us both. All thoughts of pursuing him must stop. All pretending to be helpless or making of googoo eyes must cease. Any romantic acts shall be strictly limited to haciendero boys." She then spat on her hand and held it out for me to shake.

Seemed like a no-brainer to me. As I said, I knew nothing could really happen between a cane worker and either one of us. And I never was pursuing him. Romantic thoughts would be hard to stop, though, especially now that Johnny was forbidden fruit. Nevertheless, I didn't think a dirty thought here or there would be a sin, so I spat in my palm, shook Wing's hand, and immediately started thinking about him.

I guess that's when we heard the scream. I felt my stomach jump into my throat as I looked up at the cliff and saw the girls looking over the edge, eyes wide, hands over mouths. There'd been an accident.

Scrambling from our beachfront position to the bottom of the cliff, we found Boy's bloodied body on the rocks below. I guess it was even before the shock had a chance to hit that I noticed how angelic his face looked in death, practically smiling. As if he knew God had forgiven him all his sins, and the gates of heaven lay open before him. No one from up at the top of the cliff could have appreciated that smile.

Nor, for that matter, could they hear the quiet laughter Boy was trying to suppress as he began to lick the ketchup, turned fake blood, from the corner of his mouth. The other boys wanted to kill him after diving off the cliff themselves to check on the body, only to discover Boy'd fooled them all. He then tried to get them in on it, to confirm his untimely demise to the girls. I think even Boy's friends knew there was something seriously wrong with him, mentally, that is.

"Asshole!" had become the word of the day. Boy's pleading for forgiveness fell on deaf ears, perhaps due to the blatant lack of sincerity implied through his fits of laughter.

So instead, opening the bottles of lambanug moonshine they'd brought along seemed like the appropriate way to break the mood. And it didn't take long. The lambanug, combined with afternoon sun and empty stomachs, definitely shifted gears. Even Wing and I took a few sips after Boy's prank. I'm sure Wing must have really been shaken, thinking she'd actually seen her brother's dead and broken body on the rocks that day. And even though Boy'd never been a favorite of mine, the world probably a better place for his early departure from it, I would have dreaded bringing the news back to Papa. Yes, we all needed a drink that day.

And the drinking continued into the night around a bonfire at the beach. Wing and I lay on our backs, looking up at the stars, calling out the names of lambanug-induced animals we thought we could see. We were even too out of it to notice the courting rituals of the older kids, a pastime we would normally relish. And when Wing and I managed to drag each other off to bed, sleep came quickly.

Morning, however, did not. My dreams seemed to go on forever. Dreams of Johnny, of course. He always seemed to be saving me, like some kind of knight in shining armor. That was the nice part. But the rest, the rest was more of a nightmare. I dreamed that Boy died again, but for real this time. The farm was overrun by communists. And they were burning it to the ground. I was searching for Papa, but couldn't find him. Then Yaya was there. She was fighting with someone, which was nothing new for Yaya. Only this time it wasn't just words. They were physically exchanging blows. She looked so old and frail. Too much so to be in a brawl. And Father Rivera. He was there too. But he was hiding from something, and wouldn't come out to help. And then, finally, Johnny appeared, to save the day, of course. I thought the dream would end happily. Until someone pushed Father Rivera from where he was hiding in the shadows. He had a knife. And he was going to stab Johnny in the back.

That's when I woke up. It took a few moments to catch my breath, only to be greeted by my first lambanug hangover. At least that was the excuse I gave for not going to the beach that morning. Between the nightmares and the headache, I was wiped out. I thought

I would just stay behind and lie in bed for a while counting the geckos scampering across the ceiling.

That is until I smelled the food. It smelled like adobo, our traditional Filipino chicken dish, but I couldn't be sure. We'd had some the night before. Lou had packed it for us to bring along. But I thought we'd finished it. And frankly, in light of my hangover, my queasy stomach had hoped we had. Nevertheless, the thick scent kept me from getting back to sleep, so I decided I might as well investigate and see what was going on. After all, I thought everyone had gone to the beach already.

I don't know what I was thinking. I'd forgotten all about the help. There was Hortensia and, yes of course, Johnny. But that wasn't all. There was the beach house caretaker's family. While the kids and I were around, it was as if they weren't even there. They seemed to sort of hover just out of sight, always there to make sure we had everything we needed, to clean up our messes, but never in our way. Like little elves, they would come out only when we couldn't see them, to magically provide all the comforts of home, as the spoiled rich would expect.

They were all rather embarrassed when I came upon them around the old stove in the hut at the back of the beach house. It was actually more of a lean-to, lacking walls entirely, the smoke from the wood stove making its escape up around the edges of the roof. It never occurred to me that the caretaker's family was actually allowed to live in the beach house when we weren't there. Our visits only served to displace them to the hut at the back of the house.

The smell of the adobo actually seemed to seep into my head and massage my lambanug headache. The caretaker's wife had made a soup from our leftovers that Hortensia had given her. She rose to apologize for waking me with the smell of her cooking and asked if there was anything I needed. Some aspirin would have been nice, but I didn't imagine she had any sort of medicine. So instead, I just sat down for the company and listened as she told her life story in broken English to Hortensia and Johnny.

She had two small children, three and two years old, and appeared to be about 30 years old. I later learned she wasn't much older than me. Hardened by poverty, I wondered if it wasn't so much premature aging as forming a protective shell, a shell impervious to things that would gouge and scar one of the soft pampered rich.

Although I now know the story of her life was not so unique, at the time, I was both shocked and disgusted to hear it. I sat wide-eyed and speechless, learning of things I hadn't imagined could happen to a young girl. Sent to Saudi Arabia alone at the age of 12 to serve as a maid, sending her pay home to the Philippines to support her family, she'd been beaten and raped by her employer with no legal recourse and no way of getting home. Rather than being imprisoned or executed for being promiscuous, as some Muslim countries are famous for doing, she was mercifully sent home at the age of 14, pregnant. Already appearing to be about 20 years old, the two years in Saudi showing in her face, she quickly married in the Philippines. And after laboring at various jobs for two years to keep food on the table, and having a second child, her face reflected 30 years of hard living. She was only 16 years old. It just didn't seem possible to me. She'd already been through so much. While she was nursing her babies and struggling to survive, I was nursing moo cows and working on my tan. I felt like such a retard.

Hortensia held the baby while Johnny shadowed the active two-year-old wandering about the grounds. It was kind of nice seeing him playing with the little one. Until then, I'd only seen him fighting or dodging bullets. Apparently, even the Cano warrior had a soft side. I guess we women find that kind of thing sexy, a man playing with small children.

"Where's your husband?" I had to ask.

"He works in Manila," she replied, tending to the kettle hanging over the open fire. "We don't see much of the money here, but every bit helps. We don't need much. And thanks to the Delgados, we're allowed to use this fine house."

Even though I knew she would receive a small gratuity when we left, enough, sadly, to support them for six months, I felt terrible knowing that we kids had displaced them from the house they'd been using, just so we could go to the beach and get drunk. I thought of asking her and her kids to stay in the house with us, but I knew she wouldn't do it. Besides, the haciendero kids would all freak out.

The adobo smelled wonderful now, but when I peeked in the pot, it was only chicken bones inside. She'd made a soup just from the bones we'd left behind the night before. Then I saw her add something to the pot. It was a pork chop. It occurred to me to wonder where she'd gotten a pork chop, but then I recalled Boy had dropped one on the ground while barbequing the day before. It got full of sand so he threw it in the trash. Apparently, she'd pulled it from the trash, washed it off, and was now making a meal out of it. One man's trash...

For the rest of the afternoon, I stayed with the help, though hardly at ease with the situation. I felt like a voyeur, like a journalist gathering research for some kind of sappy documentary about the invisible poor. Johnny was much too preoccupied with the two-year-old ball of energy to notice the more than passing looks from the boy's mom who was actually just about Johnny's age. Like Wing, maybe I was just being jealous, but I certainly noticed. And soon the little boy's mom noticed I noticed. I guess it was just one of those things we women do.

Nevertheless, my increasing discomfort was soon relieved upon hearing the return of the beachgoers. I thanked her for her hospitality and ran off to grill Wing on the events of the day. Wing, however, seemed more interested in Johnny as he helped unload their supplies from the van. And I soon noticed they'd all been at the lambanug again. Despite good-natured denials all around, I'd learned how easy it was for a sober person to tell when others weren't. It's like watching Disney cartoons. When you're stoned, Goofy has a deeper philosophical side. But when you're straight, Goofy's just, well, goofy.

After dinner that night, the bonfire was burning again at the beach and the lambanug was flowing. But soon the well was dry. And that's when Boy shifted gears. Producing a cigar box out of nowhere, Boy revealed his stash of pot. He'd soon lit up a couple of joints and began passing them around. Wing and I didn't want to seem like babies, so we did our best to conform. We gave the older kids quite a laugh when, taking our first puffs, the burning smoke caused such a coughing spell, the other kids scrambled away from us, thinking we might barf on them. Well, so much for pot. I guess it's an acquired taste.

An hour later, it seemed as though we would survive another night, until Boy, never satisfied, never knowing when to quit, pulled something else from his little bag of tricks. I'd never seen anyone pop pills before. And frankly, even the older kids seemed uncomfortable with the whole idea. But Boy, always at the cutting edge of what's wrong with the world, produced a bag full of pills and began passing it around to the guests. Some of the boys took them, looking uneasily at one another. Most of the girls politely passed. Then the bag came to Wing and me.

"What is it?" I asked, pulling a pretty colored one from the bag. Wing's eyes were wide, wondering whether to stay or run.

"No big deal," replied Boy, as if in answer to my question. "It'll just take the edge off."

I never knew I had an edge. And even if I did, I'm not sure I wanted it removed. Looking at the faces around the fire, it seemed to me, probably Boy was the only one with an edge that needed removing. I guessed an edge was that thing that kept you from enjoying life or appreciating the warmth of friends around a bonfire at the beach. Those were the things that Boy's edge kept him from enjoying, all those things that the rest of us naturally loved. But Boy couldn't be happy until the edge was gone. And he'd spend the rest of his life looking for ways to do just that.

"No thanks," I said, politely placing the pill back in the bag as Wing passed it on.

Boy frowned at us. "You have to."

Wing and I chuckled, "What do you mean?"

Boy was serious. "I said you have to."

I looked at Wing to see if her smile had left her face as mine had. "Why?"

Boy grabbed the bag from the next kid and threw it back in our laps. "Because if you don't, you'll tell on me. I don't want Papa on my case when he hears what we're doing."

"We won't tell," stated Wing.

"I don't trust you. Just have one, then I won't have to worry about it. You'll have as much to hide as the rest of us."

"But we don't want to," said Wing, looking at me for confirmation.

"We're too young," I tried.

"Too young? I've been taking these since I was your age," he countered, shaking the bag in our faces.

"Where'd you get them?" I asked.

"That's none of your business."

I later learned where the cane worker, Speed, got his nickname, as well as his spending money.

"Take one," Boy insisted.

A few of the other kids shook their heads in disapproval, seeing that Boy was getting out of hand. "Boy, leave them alone. They're just kids," protested one of his friends.

Boy turned on him, furious. "Shut up! Who the hell asked you? This is my beach. At my beach, it's my rules. If you don't like it, you can get lost!" he snapped.

The group was cowed into silence. Not that they were afraid of Boy. They just knew that when he got moody, there was no reasoning with him. Kind of like a two-year-old throwing a tantrum.

One of the girls with babysitting experience tried changing the subject. "Hey Boy, where's the music? Why don't you put on some tunes?"

Boy wouldn't have it. Ignoring her, he turned his icy stare back to Wing and me.

We looked questioningly at each other. And question silently answered, we turned back to Boy. "We don't want to," in unison.

Boy stood up, approached us, and grabbed the bag. Pulling out two pills at random, he shoved one into Wing's hand and one into mine. "Take them."

"We don't want to," repeated Wing.

Boy slapped her in the face. Wing recoiled more in shock than pain. I looked to the other kids, who were looking to each other for someone to step forward and stand up to Boy. But none did. What a pathetic bunch, I thought.

Someone finally shouted, "Cut it out, you fucking asshole!" I looked about to see who it was and saw that everyone was staring at me. It was *me*. *I'd* said it. I couldn't believe it came out of *me*. I guess when he hit Wing, something snapped. And despite my fear upon realizing it, there was no taking the words back.

Boy turned on me amid a few snickers from his friends. "What did you say?"

Looking straight into his eyes, with unusual calm and deliberation, I responded, "I'll say it slowly so you can understand me. Cut— it— out— you— fuck— ing— ass— hole." I guess it turns out you could say I was kind of spunky for a kid. Maybe too spunky. Boy's friends were laughing at him. The laughing stopped, though, when he pushed me backwards off the log I was sitting on. I landed flat on my back, the wind knocked out of me, gasping for air. Boy stood over me, menacingly.

His friends finally approached him to try and broker a ceasefire. But that only made him crazier. Grabbing a heavy branch from the fire, Boy waved his friends off. He then pointed the glowing end of the hot poker at my face. "Swallow the pill," he ordered.

I held the pill tightly in my closed fist. I like to think I kept my fist closed with the intention of fighting back, of landing one between Boy's eyes, or better yet between his legs. But I'll never really know. Because that's when I heard the pump action of the shotgun.

I'd only heard that sound once before, when Papa had to shoot a rabid dog that wandered onto the farm. But it's a sound you don't forget. It's a decisive sound, a no fooling around, the party's over, everyone out of the pool, kind of sound.

"Drop it," from whoever held the gun.

I guess the order was intended for Boy's burning poker. But my fist apparently heard the same demand and took the opportunity to drop its pill into the sand.

Boy whirled about to find himself facing the wrong end of a shotgun. And who would be at the other end but Johnny? Who but

Johnny could bring such an abrupt end to such a pleasant evening, a civilized conversation between relatives?

"I said drop it," he repeated, with icy calm.

Boy's eyes averted only momentarily to confirm his hand still held the burning poker. His brain, however, was still trying to process the scene in which 'the help' was holding him at gunpoint. "Have you lost your mind?"

Johnny didn't waiver. "No, I can't say as I have. But yours just might end up splattered all over the sand if you don't drop that branding iron and leave these kids alone," he said with a jerk of his head, indicating Wing and me as the kids to whom he was referring. Given the circumstances, I let the 'kids' comment slide this time.

"Where did you get that gun?" asked Boy. He seemed to be wondering if he was imagining the whole thing. Maybe it was the pill he took. He tried to remember which kind it was.

"Where do you think?" replied Johnny. "I wasn't sent along just to wipe your nose. Your daddy insisted I bring this to protect these kids. I just didn't think I'd have to protect them from *you*."

"Well, you don't. So why don't you run along back to the help's quarters where you belong? Here's a couple of pesos. The caretaker's whore will keep you busy all night for that." Boy reached into his pocket for some money and threw it at Johnny. "Don't worry. I'm sure it's enough. That's about what your mother used to charge down on Mabini Street."

I wasn't really paying all that much attention to what Boy was saying. After all, how much trust do you put in the word of a person who buries cats alive? Besides I was too busy staring at the gun. Not until later, lying in bed, would my mind come back to Boy's words about Johnny's mother. Were they just a spoiled bully's taunts? Or were they more pieces to the Johnny puzzle?

In any event, that would have to wait for later. Because in response to Boy's words, Johnny calmly placed the gun down on the ground and put Boy to sleep for the night with a single fist to the jaw. None of Boy's friends even tried to intervene. Just like when Papa shot that rabid dog, no one came to help it. No one would even touch it. They just looked down at it in curiosity, lying there, still foaming at the mouth, everyone taking the chance to see up close what moments before represented a frothing monster.

Without another word, Johnny went back to the beach house to sleep. It was a little scary how, only 17 at the time, Johnny handled that rifle so calmly, dealing with the whole conflict in a mechanical, matter-of-fact, fashion. No show of emotion. No doubt. Just action. Decisive action, just like the pulling of a trigger on a gun. If you pull the trigger, the gun fires. There's no discussion or debate between those two actions. And Johnny would have done it, too. I could tell he was capable of it. It frightened me a bit to wonder what Johnny's childhood could have been like.

In the morning, Boy would wake up on the beach next to the burned out bonfire. At first, he wouldn't remember why his face hurt. Then it would come to him. Then he would come up with his story, his version of events, in case Johnny, Wing, or 1 tattled on him. He would tell Papa how he caught Johnny trying to sell us drugs. And how he, Boy, had come to our rescue and saved the day.

Chapter 6

For a while, each day at breakfast, I waited for the bomb to drop, to hear the fallout from the events at Salama. Yet nothing happened. In fact, no one ever mentioned anything to Papa. Johnny didn't want to cause any trouble. Boy wasn't sure his version of the events would be believed. And Wing and I didn't want to gain a reputation as narcs and get shunned by teenage society. So instead, the tension I felt each morning at breakfast faded a bit each day and soon was forgotten. The whole mess turned out to be just another one of those close calls, merely another life-threatening event your parents never find out about. You know, like, 'How was the beach, kids?' 'Fine.' 'What did you do?' 'Nothing.' Versus, 'How was the beach, kids?' 'Well, after we almost got beat to death by an angry mob of communists over a cow, we went diving off a cliff and we all thought Boy was dead. Then everyone got stoned, except Wing and me, but that was only because Johnny knocked Boy unconscious instead of shooting him.'

Looking back now, I wonder, if one of us had said something at the time, would things have turned out differently? Somehow I doubt it. I believe in destiny. I think God plans on stuff happening, and it does, even when you see it coming. We're all kind of like deer caught in the headlights. You can see the car bearing down on you, yet you can't seem to get out of the way.

It was torture trying to sit still in church on Sunday. Father Rivera's mass was yet another rambling, endless epic about guilt. Like a dentist performing a root canal, he would drill and drill, digging deeper and deeper, until he finally hit the nerve. Then he would drill some more, like a marksman, aiming to destroy it. Only this time, I was immune to it. Sure I could hear the endless drone of the drill, but I didn't feel a thing. Not this time. I was fully anesthetized. Like some kind of Zen Buddhist monk, my mind had left the confines of my body, levitating over the room, free of its earthly trappings, silently repeating its mantra, over and over. "Johnny, Johnny," despite my promise to Wing. Call it puppy love or childhood infatuation. It didn't matter. When you're 14 years old, you don't know what it is. And you certainly can't control it. To the contrary, it controls you.

Johnny was right there, in the church. I didn't really expect to see him. Not that the workers didn't attend. Of course they did. After all, the church was built for them. At least that's what Mama said at the ground breaking, the day the Delgados started construction. Mama herself put the first shovel in the ground. Never mind they almost had to cancel the ceremony when she broke a fingernail. With Hortensia's help, she was able to pull it together long enough to dedicate the church to all the workers on the farm and their families. Well, that's the way it was presented anyway. Yet, despite the childlike good nature of the people, naivety is not a Filipino trait. Everyone knew the church was built for Mama. She was devoutly religious, harboring a lot of well-deserved guilt, and hoped to buy her place in heaven by donating a church to the poor. Of course, that didn't mean she had to sit with the people she'd built the church for. That would be crossing the line. No, not Mama. She even had her own special pew built that no one else was allowed to sit in. She'd had extra soft upholstery added for her bony ass. Everyone else, of course, sat on those hard benches like some sort of sacrifice to God.

Mama was afraid of God. One might wonder what someone who builds churches has to fear from God. But it all makes sense to me now. After all, when you're guilty, you *should* be afraid of God. And for certain sins, you should be scared shitless.

I hadn't expected to see Johnny, because he'd seemed such an angry rebel, an outsider. He had that whole American independence thing about him. Yet there he sat, not only in church, but right between Captain and, who'd have believed it, Yaya. Yaya was in church, as if hell had officially frozen over. What was that all about? It seemed the more I learned about Johnny, the less I knew. For each question I'd answered, three more were asked. I saw there'd be no rest for me that summer, not with all this intrigue going on right in front of my nose. And I wasn't going to stop pulling that thread until I'd unraveled the whole sweater.

Thank God, Father Rivera finally ran out of gas and everyone was free to go. Before leaving I took another look in Johnny's direction just in time to see him get a kiss on the cheek from Yaya and a handshake from Captain. The handshake was no big deal. Captain shook a lot of hands. But a kiss from Yaya? What secret power did Johnny possess that could melt the iron maiden? The only things I'd ever seen come from Yaya's lips were spit and foul language. But a kiss? Only in a church could one witness such miracles.

I hadn't planned to run into Johnny. Not in a premeditated way. It was more like an involuntary, temporary insanity, stalking sort of thing. Without thinking, I'd quickly positioned myself just outside the church door so that Johnny would have to walk right past me to leave. I had my hair up in a ribbon and I'd worn my best dress, so white it could blind you in the sun. Well apparently that's just what it did, because Johnny walked right past me without so much as a nod hello. Being just 14 years old, however, I had yet to develop the sense of pride that would keep me from scurrying after him. If I couldn't attract his attention, I would simply have to grab it. I caught up to him and jumped into his path. Not exactly subtle or ladylike, yet effective. If he didn't notice me now, he'd have to knock me down to get by. He didn't… knock me down, I mean.

"Hey kid," he began, stepping around me, "you're hurting my eyes." He'd put his hand up to his brow as if to shield his eyes from the sun.

"My name's not kid," I corrected him. "It's Lisa. And stop making fun of my dress," I added, catching up to him.

Johnny stopped walking, and for the first time, he took a good look at me. I felt like a pair of shoes on display in a store window, marked half off. I managed an embarrassed smile, hoping to make a sale. I may have looked like snow, in my white dress, but I hadn't expected to melt the way I did when Johnny returned the smile with a gorgeous one of his own. And then, as if I'd passed some sort of inspection, he said, "OK, OK, Lisa it is," then continued on his way.

Well at least I was sure he knew my name now, I thought, ever the optimist. "Where are you going?" I asked, trying to keep up with him.

"It's my day off," he answered, without stopping. "Going for a swim."

"Cane workers aren't allowed to use the pool." I felt terrible the moment the words left my lips, but I figured, being new around the farm, maybe Johnny didn't know all the rules yet.

Sure enough, I could tell I'd offended him when he stopped, glaring at me, and said, "Oh don't you worry about that, little Darlin'. I can assure you, the only time you'll find me near that pool is if master wanted it cleaned."

"Master? What do you mean, master?" I asked.

"The Delgados," he replied. "They're the masters. I'm just one of the slaves." Then he began walking again.

I couldn't tell if he was serious, so scurrying after him, I took the bait, and said, "You're not a slave. No one's forcing you to work here."

Without stopping this time, he replied, "You think so, huh? Where would I go? Ain't no other jobs around here."

"Well, that still doesn't make you a slave. You're free to leave anytime you like."

"By God, you're right," he began with a note of sarcasm. "I'm free to go starve to death anywhere I want. I'd have no job, no money, and no family. Sounds like a plan to me."

I didn't know what to say to that. But I hadn't planned on getting into an argument. So, hoping to change the subject, "Well, if

you're not going to use the pool, where are you going to swim?" I
noticed we were approaching the horse corral.

"Got my own private swimmin' hole."

Johnny then grabbed a bridle from the fence, opened the corral
and marched straight toward Thunder, the only horse on the farm.
Now, I knew how to ride. I'd ridden other horses. But not this one.
This was Thunder. He was Papa's horse, and even Papa'd never
ridden him. In fact, as far as I knew, no one had ever ridden him. Not
that plenty hadn't been permanently maimed trying. He was the
meanest animal I'd ever seen. Wing and I thought he must have been
possessed by the devil. Even Captain begged Papa to get rid of him.
But Thunder was a magnificent black stallion, and Papa thought he
was the most beautiful thing in the world. So he kept him, just for
looking at, not for riding.

"Johnny, stop!" I shouted. "He'll kill you!"

Johnny ignored me. "Who, Thunder? Aw, he's just a big
pussycat."

I watched in awe as Johnny put the bit and bridle on Thunder.
Not only did Thunder not kill Johnny, he didn't even bite his hand
off or kick him in the head or anything. So when Johnny hopped up
on the monster, bareback, and trotted over to me, I was dumbstruck.

"You know," Johnny began, "with your mouth wide open
catching flies like that, you remind me of a big mouth bass I once
hooked back in Alabama."

"But how did you do that?" I asked, finding words. "No one's
ever ridden Thunder."

"Oh, he's not so bad." Then patting Thunder on the neck, "Let's
just say old Thunder and I have an understanding."

"Does Papa know you ride him?"

"Course he does. His idea, matter-of-fact. Soon as I saw this
beauty, I asked if I could take him for a run. I expect Mr. Delgado
was just hoping to have a good laugh at my expense when he agreed.
But when he saw how Thunder and I got along, he asked if I'd take
him out for some exercise whenever I had the chance. Even wanted
to pay me. But I couldn't take his money for the privilege of riding

this fine animal. We didn't have nothing like this back home." He gave Thunder a hardy pat on the neck.

I didn't know what to say.

"Well Darlin', you comin' swimmin' or you gonna stand there all day catchin' flies in that pretty little mouth of yours?" he asked, from Thunder's back, offering a hand down to me.

I couldn't believe I was about to get on Thunder, but something about Johnny holding his hand out to me said everything would be all right. So I took Johnny's hand, and he swung me up onto Thunder's back right behind him, white dress and all, like some kind of runaway bride. I wished I could have enjoyed putting my arms around Johnny more, but I was too scared, having seen what Thunder was capable of, too busy holding on for my life. Things eventually calmed down though as Thunder happily headed toward Johnny's swimmin' hole.

I could see there was a slight breeze as we approached the edge of the fields and the sugarcane waved to me as if in greeting. Just the sight of my precious cane calmed me enough to resume my conversation with Johnny.

"You said if you left here, you'd have no family. Well, it's not like you have family here, is it?" I asked, knowing I was out on a limb, probably prying a bit too much.

"Captain's my uncle."

Just like that. As if it were no big deal. I think, being raised in the States, Johnny simply had no appreciation for the importance of family and the role it plays in determining one's destiny. In the States, anyone could become pretty much whatever they wanted to. Not so, here in the Philippines. I mean, I wouldn't call it a caste system or anything, but it was close. A great deal of where you can go, in the Philippines, is determined by where you come from. A person's family and its connections are a person's best assets. Nepotism rules. Long live nepotism.

So Captain was Johnny's uncle. This was huge. I couldn't hide my surprise as my eyes almost popped out of my head. "Captain is your uncle?" I had to hear it again just to make sure I hadn't misunderstood.

"Sure," he replied, way too matter-of-factly for me.

That's it. Forget the beautiful ride by the sugarcane fields. Forget the Sunday dress. You could even forget Johnny's eyes. I'd shifted to detective mode. "No, really. How is Captain your uncle?"

His answer was anything but what I'd expected. I thought for sure his mother would have been some distant hardly related eighth cousin I'd never heard of from Captain's extended family. I never expected the connection to be right here on the farm, and such a prominent one at that.

"My mom was Captain's sister."

I didn't even know Captain had a sister. And if there was any truth to what Speed and Boy had said, she was a maid right here on the farm. Johnny's mother had worked on the farm. I needed to confirm that though.

"And she worked on the farm?" I asked, tentatively, afraid to scare him off with my prying.

"Where else would Yaya's daughter work?" was his reply.

Yaya's daughter? Wait a second. Captain was Johnny's uncle and Yaya's son? Johnny's mother was Captain's sister and Yaya's daughter? And, then it finally hit me. Oh my God, and leaping lizards Batman. Yaya was Johnny's grandmother? That explained the church scene. It must have been a very special occasion, the return of her grandson. And Johnny's mother must have been the daughter of Yaya that was banished from the farm to become a hostess in Manila. That must be how she met Johnny's dad, the American GI.

As my brainteaser had me so distracted, I hadn't seen where Johnny was taking me. We'd passed the first set of cane fields and come to the edge of an unfarmed area in the middle of the second, a sort of oasis amid the cane, overgrown by wild bamboo and coconut palms. It stuck out like a cowlick on the head of the farm, an obtrusive wart marring an otherwise smooth complexion. But there was a purpose for this blemish. It remained unfarmed for a reason.

"Stop!" I shouted.

Johnny was caught by surprise. "What!?" he yelled in reply, causing Thunder to rear as he yanked back on the reins.

"You can't go in there."

Johnny reluctantly turned Thunder, looking about for some sign of communists or maybe a venomous snake.

"Why not?"

My response came without any sense of embarrassment or apology. It was a sober and serious reply. "The dwarves."

Johnny stopped. "The what?"

"The dwarves."

He turned to face me. "What are you talking about?"

I looked him right in the eye. "You don't know what dwarves are?"

"Course I know what dwarves are. Short people. Midgets. What's that got to do with anything?"

"This is their land," I pointed. "We can't be here."

Johnny looked back at the awkward patch of unfarmed land, then to me, confused. "Wait a second," he began. "You mean a bunch of dwarves own a part of the Delgado farm? I don't get it."

"They don't own it. They just live there. We can't go in."

Johnny couldn't hide the beginning of a smile. "Because dwarves live in there."

"Right."

"So, these dwarves, are they some sort of lost civilization like your Tasaday Indians, or did Barnum & Bailey's circus take a wrong turn?" He was making fun of me. He was laughing.

"I'm serious. It's their place. They live in there. And if you upset them, they'll guarantee we have a bad crop of cane this year."

Johnny began a full belly laugh. "So, you mean, if we upset the great and powerful little dwarf gods, they'll take revenge by spoiling the crops? No problem. All we have to do is toss a virgin into a volcano to appease them. Well, we got the volcano," he said pointing up to Mount Talinas. "And you're still a virgin, ain't you?" His laughter had him doubled over gasping for air.

"Johnny, please." I punched him in the arm. "That's why that field lies unplanted. So as not to disturb them."

"Since when?"

"Since forever. No one's ever tilled that field. Even before the Delgados."

"So how do they know what would happen if they did? Hmmm?"

Damned Americans. No faith in anything except what they can hold in their hands. Things are a little different here in the Philippines, being mostly Catholic believers in saints and miracles, with a pinch of Pacific Islander idol worship thrown in for good measure. I must admit, though. I'm sure the whole thing sounded awfully weird to an outsider. But, no matter. I couldn't risk the cane crop. Ever since I was little, I'd been told the stories of the magical dwarves that lived in the field. How they could make wonderful things happen if you were nice to them by staying out of their field and leaving them baskets of food once in a while at the edge of it. Or, if you didn't respect their privacy, they could put a spell on you, ruin your life, or even take it from you.

Johnny finally yielded, allowing me to divert him from the field. Thank God. He was still giggling when he agreed to go around it. But that was OK with me, as long as we went around. I started to calm down, that is, enough to realize I was off by myself, away from Casablanca, with a boy I hardly knew. Not that I was worried. Maybe it was the fact that he'd already saved my life a couple of times. Or maybe it was just that 14-year-old girls in the Philippines were unaware of the dangers of the world, of men, and bad people. It's the innocence of baby seals that allows them to crawl right up to club wielding fur traders.

I don't know what the Delgados would have said, knowing I'd wandered off with one of the cane workers. I didn't want to know. But it wasn't the same. I mean, Johnny was, after all, Captain's nephew, Yaya's grandson, for God's sake. That had to count for something. No, I had nothing to fear from Johnny, nothing bad anyway. But what about something good? Somewhere, deep inside, I felt a hint of uneasiness, but the kind that comes with excitement, with adventure. Like starting a journey, a new ship launched at sea. Somewhere at the pit of my stomach, I felt I was taking those first baby steps toward the future, *my* future. I looked up at beautiful Johnny and hoped maybe this time he'd notice me as more than a little girl. Maybe this would be my coming out. *Our* coming out.

I'd seldom gone beyond the dwarves' field. So when we came to the next treed area, I was in unfamiliar territory. But following my trusted guide, we soon came to the most beautiful place I'd ever seen. The coconut palms cleared to reveal a natural pool at the base of a waterfall. The water cascaded off the top of a 30-foot rock formation to land in a 50-foot wide pool of sparkling water, all framed by exotic foliage and palm trees. It was a hidden tropical paradise. It could have been a postcard for tourists back in Manila.

"Wow," was all I could say, hopping down from Thunder's back. I can be real profound sometimes.

"You like it?" asked Johnny as if he were showing off a new car or something. "This is my swimmin' hole. Or sometimes I just come here to think."

Johnny hitched Thunder to a palm tree, as I slipped my shoes off to cool my feet in the water.

"What do you think about?" I asked, looking up at him, hoping I could crack that shell he seemed to keep about himself, get him to open up.

He was skipping small flat stones off the water's surface.

"Oh, just about life. Where I've been. Where I'm going." He threw the last stone from his hand and sat next to me.

I thought I would start at the beginning. "So, where *have* you been?"

Johnny got this far off look in his eyes, but didn't say anything. I knew I'd have to be more specific. Then I said it. I'd like to think it was more than just the detective in me, that I was more than just some nosey reporter.

"Johnny, tell me about them."

"Who?"

"Your parents. They seem like such a mystery."

Johnny looked at me, weighing my sincerity. Then, deciding I'd passed muster, "Not much to tell really. Being Yaya's daughter, my mom worked as a maid on the farm, of course. When she was 18, she was sent away to work in Manila."

"Why was she sent away?" I interrupted.

"I don't know. Maybe there wasn't enough work for her here. Or maybe the money was better in Manila. I don't know. Anyway, she got a job as a hostess near Clark, the American Air Force base. That's where she met my dad."

"What does a hostess do?" I asked, naively.

And just as innocently, Johnny responded, "I guess they show you to your table in a restaurant?"

"That seems pleasant enough."

"Yeah. Well anyway, after my mom died, my dad took me back to the States. I even remember getting on a big plane. I was five years old."

I had to slow him down. He was skipping too much. "Wait. How did your mother die?" I hoped I wasn't being too ghoulish.

"I don't know. I just remember she got sicker and sicker until she couldn't take care of me anymore."

"But your dad did. Your dad took care of you."

"Right. He loved us both. He made sure my mom was comfortable during her last days and he even left the Air Force to be able to take care of me. As soon as he was able to get the right papers in order, he took me home with him to Alabama. He had a ranch there. That's where I learned to ride. It was a dream come true, growing up on that ranch."

"But?" I asked. There was always a but.

"But I didn't know I would have a new mom when I got there."

"You mean your dad met another woman right away?"

"Well, not exactly."

"What do you mean, then?"

"He was already married."

It took me a few moments to add two plus two. I was only 14, after all. And Catholic. "You mean, he already had a wife back in the States before he met your mom?"

Johnny shrugged his shoulders. "Welcome to the military. And boy was she a bitch."

"The evil stepmom?"

"Cinderella had it good. I guess she didn't appreciate my dad bringing home a bastard for her to take care of. She already had a daughter of her own. And with my dad leaving the military, the ranch wasn't enough to make ends meet. Soon what little money they had dried up. So when my dad died—"

"Whoa. What happened to him?"

"I guess you could say my stepmom killed him."

"She murdered him!?"

"More like poisoned. First with hate. Then booze. She was so angry about me and his leaving the military that she drove him to drink. So by the time I was 15, he died of a bad liver. She killed him all right. God, I hated her."

"So you ran away, to come back here, to family?"

"Not directly."

"What do you mean?"

"As soon as my dad died, my stepmom wasted no time trying to get rid of me. She kept kicking me out of the house, but the cops kept bringing me back. They even arrested her once for abandonment. I pretty much stayed with friends from school or lived on the street."

"Lived on the street? That's terrible. How did you survive?"

"Oh, I managed. Hunger can be a powerful force. I fell in with some rough characters, did some things I wasn't proud of, and eventually earned quite a reputation proving myself over at the juvenile detention center just so no one would mess with me."

"You mean you were in prison?" I asked, dumbstruck. I'd never even *seen* anyone who'd been to prison, let alone spoken to them.

"Well, only juvenile. I mean, I never made it to the big time," he laughed.

I couldn't even imagine myself in a place like that. "So how did you get back to the Philippines?"

"I wasn't given a choice. One day after I was caught shoplifting something to eat, the cops brought me home, but my stepmom told them I was an illegal alien and should be deported."

"What? But your father was American. So you're an American too. Right?"

"She said my dad wasn't really my dad and that my immigration papers were falsified."

"And they believed her?"

"I'm here, ain't I?"

"But it's not true, is it?"

"All I can say is my dad was the only dad I ever knew. He raised me and loved me like a dad. As far as I'm concerned, he was my dad. But the immigration people believed her. They said they found family of mine in the Philippines and were fixin' to send me to be with them."

"Wow. Just like that."

"I wanted to go. The Philippines sounded exciting, like an adventure. And a real family sounded too good to be true. I just didn't know they were slaves."

"Hey, I told you. They're not slaves."

"You know what I mean. Anyway, it's still better than what I had in the States. It's nice to have family. Captain and Yaya are good to me."

I found myself comparing Johnny's life to mine, how my mom and I didn't really get along, and how I wished I could stay on the farm instead of living in Manila. But I realized any similarities were really just the imagination of a spoiled 14-year-old girl. I wasn't an orphan. I never had to steal food out of hunger. I sure as hell never went to prison and got deported. No, maybe the drama queen in me wanted to feel that my life had been more exciting than it was, that I'd done my share of suffering. But that was just schoolgirl fantasy. Johnny won that contest hands down. I'd never suffered a day in my life. I was never sent away, shuffled around like Johnny. I always had family and friends around me, a home, even the farm. The farm was like an anchor to which I could always cling when things tried to change too fast. And God, of course. I always had God. Johnny didn't. I don't think he believed in anything. And why should he?

I turned to speak to Johnny, but he was gone. While contemplating the ways of the world, I hadn't noticed him slip away. The prisoner had escaped the interrogation. He hadn't gone far though. In fact, no sooner had I noticed his clothes piled on a boulder ten feet from me than I heard the splash from the pool, the waterfall's reflection in the surface of glass shattered by the less than perfect entry of Johnny's dive. A flock of wild parrots took flight as

Johnny voiced his relief at escaping the summer heat in the cool water.

"Ahhhhhh," he half moaned and half shouted like a pressure valve releasing pent up steam. He shook the drenched hair from his face and called to me. "Come on in. It's like goin' to heaven."

Of course just being in that paradise with Johnny, it was as if I was already there, in heaven, that is. "I can't," I shouted in disappointment.

"Why not?"

"I didn't bring a bathing suit."

"So what? Neither did I."

I looked back at the pile of clothes, then back to Johnny again, clearly blushing. "You're not naked, are you?"

"Why don't you come on in and find out?"

I'm sure he didn't mean it in a sexual way. I don't think he even saw me as a woman... yet. He was just playing with me. And yet, the nuns at school wouldn't have allowed me to take any chances. *My* clothes were staying on. Unfortunately, I never imagined how much a drenched Sunday dress could weigh. So by the time I made it out to the point where I couldn't touch bottom anymore, I only had time for one brief gasp and sputter at the surface before going down like an anchor. Yet, before I even had a chance to panic, my savior was there once again, pulling me toward the surface. I was only able to catch a quick gulp of air before going under again as my Sunday best began to drag us *both* under. Any panic I might have felt at the time was quickly replaced by wonder at the speed with which Johnny was able to remove my dress, deftly sliding it from my shoulders. Still under water, I tried to imagine where he'd picked up that particular skill. Nevertheless, in just a pair of panties, I quickly bobbed to the surface. Parents all over the world would have been proud as I'd been sure to wear clean underwear just in case of an emergency. In fact, I'd worn my cutest pair, a sort of Brazilian cut with a touch of lace. The nuns would not have approved. In addition, being only 14 at the time, without too much reason to wear a bra, the heat of summer had convinced me to go without. Putting everything in perspective, I wasn't concerned. At least I could swim and breathe now. I would just have to stay modestly submerged form the neck down. I looked about just in time to see Johnny's cute naked butt as he tossed my dress onto a rock to dry in the sun. That was followed, as Johnny turned to re-enter the water, by a brief view of what I'd only before seen during diaper changes on baby boys, or on bulls at the farm. Johnny's was thankfully somewhere in between. I prayed my blush had subsided by the time Johnny made it back to where I was treading water.

"Isn't that better?" he asked, paddling up to me.

"Except that I'm naked now," I replied, the Catholic girl inside getting the better of me.

"Not quite," answered Johnny. "You've still got your cute frilly underwear on."

My arms reflexively came across my chest wondering what else he'd noticed. I may not have needed a bra, but that didn't mean I had nothing at all to hide. I meant to respond to Johnny's commentary on my undergarments, but by the time I'd found my tongue, he'd already headed toward the waterfall. I followed, doing the breaststroke, literally.

I watched Johnny approach the waterfall, and then, at the last second, dive under it, without coming back up. By the time I reached the falls myself, I'd grown concerned about his disappearing act. Then I heard Johnny's voice.

"Come on through." He was on the other side.

I dove under the falls and came up behind them only to discover there was a cave or grotto on the other side. It was fairly large, about the size of my bedroom back in Manila. A beam of light shone through a small opening at the top of the cave. The warm spotlight bounced off the back of the waterfall, refracted by droplets of water, and reflecting the colors of the rainbow shimmering off the wall at the back of the cave. The constant motion of the light made the cave wall seem alive. And combined with the different shades of moss growing on the damp rock, it was quite a light show, almost mesmerizing, not too different from what I'd imagine tripping on LSD would be like. That is, had I known what LSD was at the time.

I was so distracted by the beauty of the light show that I hadn't noticed Johnny's bare bottom standing next to it. In fact, before I realized what I was doing, I'd emerged from the water myself to stand next to him in my wet clinging panties, completely forgetting I had nothing covering my recently arrived breasts. I sometimes forgot they were there.

Johnny was staring at something on the cave wall. It was some sort of graffiti. "I can't believe it," he began.

"What?" I asked, looking at the heart drawn on the cave wall, complete with cupid's arrow and set of initials.

"Those are my mom's," Johnny replied solemnly. She used to tell me about this place when I was little, how Yaya and the whole family hid out in this cave through the Japanese occupation during World War II. My mom was born right here in this cave. L.S. Those are her initials. Linda Saporo."

"Wow. And who's J.D.? Who's the other set of initials?"

"Must be my dad. That's funny. I never knew he even came to the farm. Anyway, his name's the same as mine. Johnny Dillinger."

Dillinger, I thought. Sounded like the American gangster. Standing there looking at the initials of the two deceased lovers, my whole body shook with a chill. Forgetting our nakedness, Johnny instinctively put his arm around my shoulders. His warmth felt good. That's when it occurred to me that the lovers' initials were the same as ours. Johnny Dillinger and Lisa Salonga. What were the odds of that? I looked up at Johnny.

"Those could be our initials, you know."

Johnny quickly dropped his arm from around my shoulders. "Don't be silly, Kid. See the moss over it. Those were there before you were born. Besides, who could love someone as ugly as you," he added, before punching me in the arm and diving back into the water.

I lingered a moment, rubbing my arm where he'd hit me, before turning to follow him. I didn't care how much he joked about it. I could tell. This was fate. And it wasn't just silly Filipino superstition, either. I knew it in my heart. Johnny and I were soul mates. Only Johnny didn't realize it yet.

I only briefly gave my now broken "hands off Johnny" pact with Wing any thought at all, and then, throwing the lovers' legacy one last look, I dove back into the water to emerge on the other side of the waterfall. I saw Johnny, but I decided I was mad at him for calling me a kid again. So I swam right past him and emerged from the water to stretch out on a huge flat rock and catch some sun. I still had just my panties on but I didn't think Johnny seemed to care one way or another anyway. Why did he keep calling me a kid? I lay on the rock face up, then arched my back and stuck out my chest just to see how big my breasts were. I must admit I didn't think they were that small when I looked over at Johnny to see if he'd noticed. To my great satisfaction, apparently he had. He was staring at me from the water. In fact, he was so drawn to my chest that he didn't even notice me notice. Perfect. I arched my back a little more and my perky new friends seemed to grow another size. I looked back at Johnny through the corner of my eye and he was definitely caught in the headlights. I didn't know when I'd have him like this again, so now that he'd swallowed the hook, I thought I'd better reel in some line. I slowly got up and walked to the water, doing my best supermodel impression, shoulders back, hips rolling. Johnny looked away, trying to pretend he hadn't been staring at me. I walked down into the water to where he was standing chest deep. Don't ask me where I found the courage. Believe me. There was no thinking involved when I took his face in my hands and kissed him on the mouth. I saw fireworks against my closed eyelids. And in his weakened state, brought on by my secret womanly powers, Johnny didn't pull away. That is, not until I slipped my tongue between his lips. I mean that's what Wing said all the older kids did when they kissed. But I guess I'd overloaded his circuit, because he gently, yet firmly, pushed me away and fell back under the water as if to douse the fireworks in his head.

"We'd better get going," he suggested when he came back up for air, which was fine with me. After all, I thought I'd accomplished quite a lot that day. In fact, the true measure of my success was the amount of time it took Johnny to come out of the water. I think he was waiting for whatever had poked my leg beneath the surface of the water during our kiss to subside before coming out. Like I said, Johnny and I were soul mates. He just didn't know it yet.

Chapter 7

Nothing happened. We put our clothes back on and left. I think Johnny was a little freaked out by the whole "she's only 14 years old, what was I thinking" thing. And I never got any closer to Johnny that summer than that time at the grotto. I think it was just a timing thing. He wasn't really interested in a little kid, and I was afraid to pursue him. I wasn't really sure what I'd have done even if I'd caught him. It wasn't like I was planning on anything happening anyway. I didn't even know what "anything" was. I was only flexing my newfound girl muscles. I still had no idea what to do with them. Poor Johnny.

Of course, he didn't have to endure me all that much. After all, just because it was *my* summer vacation, didn't mean it was *his*. It seemed, in fact, that I hardly saw him at all. Maybe he was right when he implied he was just a plantation slave. Captain and the Delgados certainly seemed to be getting their money's worth out of him. Lucky for Johnny, it wasn't just sweating in the cane fields. He worked at many other chores as well, from scheduling the other workers to ordering, buying, and more often repairing, equipment. I don't know if he got those jobs because he was bright and eager, or because he was the foreman's nephew. In any event, Johnny seemed to be learning everything there was to running the farm. Maybe Captain was grooming his eventual replacement.

I wasn't as busy as Johnny. With no schedule and no responsibilities, Wing and I bounced around the rest of the summer from one thing to the next, with no concern for tomorrow. We were convinced, after all, that nothing would ever change. Summers would remain forever carefree, and the farm would always be there, our own little world, steadfast and protected. I never suspected that I wouldn't be back for three years, that a separate outside world would conspire to keep me from my own little El Dorado. And worse, without me there to watch over things, the farm itself would be forever changed, never so separate as I had believed it to be.

There were still a couple of weeks left before Wing and I would have to head back to Manila for school. We were hanging around the kitchen while the maids were preparing dinner, in hopes of overhearing some new tsismus. It had been a while since we'd picked up any juicy gossip. We knew the best gossip came out when the maids forgot we were there, so we took our usual seats inconspicuously at the table in the corner of the big kitchen. That's where Lou did the baking. She had already started working on dessert. It was called Food for the Gods. It had the consistency of brownies, but was made with dates and walnuts. Oh, and about half a ton of sugar and a whole ton of butter. It seemed like there was a whole stick of butter in each small square serving. Whenever Wing and I helped serve them to guests who declined because they were dieting, we always assured them they were fat and sugar free. When they tasted how good they were, they didn't believe us anymore. But by then it was too late. They couldn't stop eating them.

"It's nice that Linda's boy, Johnny, is here with family," Lou began.

I kicked Wing under the table to be sure she was listening. Tsismus about Johnny. This was too good to be true.

"I still remember the day poor Linda was sent away," reminisced Hortensia, thinking of Johnny's mother. "We were both barely 20 years old. It was Christmas Day when Mama told her she had to leave. Imagine. Christmas Day no less."

They all shook their heads in disgust. Wing and I didn't see it coming, but sometimes the best gossip hits you when you're not looking. The maids were so preoccupied reliving the past that they completely forgot Wing and I were in the room. That's when Lou dropped the bombshell.

"And by Cinco de Mayo, little Johnny was born."

It didn't set in at first. In fact, it almost slipped by me entirely. Math was never my strong suit. I mean, I could do it. I just wasn't the fastest horse in the stable. I could certainly count to five, though. Five months. That's when I couldn't help but elbow Wing in the ribs. She let out a surprised little squeak.

"Hey," she whispered. "What was that for?"

I grabbed her by the elbow and pulled her close so I could whisper in her ear. "Johnny's mom, Linda, was sent away from the farm on Christmas. Johnny was born on May fifth." I don't know why I thought that would explain my excitement. Wing wasn't the fastest gecko on the wall, and she was even worse at math than me.

"So?" came her reply.

I grabbed her elbow again. She winced from the pain of my grip. "So Johnny was born only five months after leaving the farm. His mom must have already been four months pregnant."

Wing was so thick. "So?"

"She didn't meet Johnny's American dad until she left the farm. He can't be Johnny's real dad. I think Johnny's real dad is someone from the farm."

"What do you mean, like one of the cane workers?" asked Wing in disbelief.

I shrugged my shoulders in reply and then decided to raise the ante. "His father could still be alive. He could even be one of the neighboring hacienderos, you know, like "The Case," I kidded, just to make for more juicy gossip.

"No!" blurted out Wing's whisper as she punched me in the shoulder. "Seriously, is that possible?"

I thought I would play with her a little. "It could be someone who was at the party the other night. Maybe Ron Fanlo or Scooby Montero." I couldn't hold back a giggle.

Wing almost fell off her chair and Lou couldn't help but notice the commotion. "What are you two flies on the wall up to?"

Our cover was blown. "Nothing," we replied in unison.

"Nothing, huh?"

Quick to cover, I joked, "We were just remembering Hortensia at the beach in her bikini."

Hortensia didn't appreciate the other maids' giggles. "I don't have a bikini and you know it."

The opportunity was too great. I couldn't let it go. "That's right. I forgot. It was a nude beach."

"Aye!" yelled Hortensia, launching a wet dish towel at our heads.

After running from the kitchen giggling, we plopped ourselves in the hammocks on the front porch of Casablanca to catch our breath before dinner. They were burning cane after harvest. The air was thick with sweet smoke, making the entire landscape slightly hazy, just enough to mute the summer glare, all soft and dreamlike. That's how my memories of the farm would always appear to me, airbrushed and flawless. Even the mosquitoes had fled, thanks to the smoke, soon followed, however, by the rats, droves of them driven from the burning fields. The maids were good about keeping them from the house, but still, Wing and I always kept our feet up off the ground.

We weren't expecting guests for dinner, but I was always glad when any of the hacienderos showed up to speak with Papa. It was good old Mr. Fanlo as well as Scooby Montero. While the maids went to inform Papa of their arrival, the men waited on the porch with Wing and me. Ever the jokers, each grabbing one of us by the cheeks to shake the cuteness out of us, I could see serious matters deepening the sun-weathered lines in their faces. And most telling of all, they weren't accompanied by their wives. Something was definitely up.

"How are you, Mr. Montero?" I said.

"Mr. Montero?" he replied. "Where? Is my father here?" he added, looking about as if he were in trouble.

"No, no. I meant you," I responded, playing along.

"Me? People call me Scooby," he reminded me, as if I didn't know.

"Just trying to be respectful."

"Oh, well, in that case, it's Your Highness, to you," he said straightening up and looking down his nose at me.

Mr. Fanlo came to my rescue. "She meant respectful of your age, Your Lowness. Stop flirting with the teenagers. You might hurt yourself."

The chuckling died out when Papa emerged from the house, all faces growing serious.

"When?" began Papa, getting right down to business.

"Last night," answered Ron. "The whole family."

"Any witnesses? Do we know who took them?" Papa continued.

Scooby jumped in. "Witnesses? No. Do we know who took them? Of course."

"There are never any witnesses because they fear for themselves if they point fingers," added Ron, matter-of-factly.

Wing had already tuned them out, as the topic didn't appear to involve her. I, on the other hand, sat up with interest, smelling intrigue.

"Scooby, will you pay?" asked Ron.

"Never!" interrupted Papa. "If you pay them the ransom, it will only encourage them. Soon they'll be kidnapping everyone. And they won't stop with maids or houseboys."

"What are you saying?" asked Scooby, a skeptical eye to Papa.

"What am I saying? I'm saying if they find they can make money kidnapping, they'll kidnap more. And before you know it, they'll realize the price they can get for family of haciendero would dwarf what would be paid for the hired help."

"They wouldn't dare," boasted Scooby.

"It's only a matter of time," stated Papa. "They grow more and more bold every day."

"I blame Marcos for all of this," moaned Ron. "Marcos and his martial law. Things are really getting out of hand in Manila. The people have nothing, and they're tired of hearing about how many pairs of shoes Imelda Marcos has, or which movie stars attend her parties. There's talk of a coup."

"That's no excuse for what's happening here," complained Papa. "We give these people jobs. We pay them well. We take care of them. Who built them a school and a hospital? Not Marcos. We did. If we weren't here, they'd starve."

The others nodded in agreement.

"And don't tell me they should have their own land," he continued. "It's hard enough for one of us large landowners to compete in today's market. You think subdividing the land into tiny plots and distributing them among people without the skills to manage them will help them to a better life? Nonsense. And most people know it. It's just a few agitators, criminals really. Kidnapping for ransom. Do they think we will stand for it?"

I couldn't believe my ears. I'd heard of it in Manila, kidnapping family members of famous politicians for ransom. Even *I* could see that as long as the ransoms were paid, the kidnappings would continue. But here? In Bais? I couldn't believe it. This wasn't Manila. Everyone knew everyone here. Everyone grew up together. I wouldn't have been surprised if the kidnapped maid wasn't related to one of the kidnappers. Would they really harm her or her family? It all seemed so implausible, like a bad soap opera.

My thoughts broke up as I felt Papa's eyes bearing down on me. I saw the concern on his face as he looked from Wing to me and back. He didn't have to say it. I knew he'd be sending us back to Manila ahead of schedule. He wouldn't be responsible for anything happening to us.

"So what's the plan?" asked Scooby, looking from Ron to Papa. "We can't just do nothing."

Ron looked to Papa. Everyone looked to Papa, their unofficial leader, for advice on such matters.

Papa was silent for a moment. I saw the change in his face as the words made their way to his mouth. Initially, I read a worried look, a look of concern, concern that the old ways were gone, that the world had become a different place. That look was followed ever so briefly by sadness. I doubt the others even picked up on it as their eyes darted about uneasy with the silence. I saw it, though. I never took my eyes from Papa's while he was thinking. How else would I be able to read his mind? I'm sure I saw a tear collecting at the corner of his eye, only to retreat unnoticed, blinked away in an instant as Papa's face changed once more. The sadness was gone. The worry, too. Replaced by outrage, outrage that someone would try to take his world away, outrage that they thought he would let them. Soon the outrage melted ever so slightly, finally replaced by determination. Then, looking from Ron to Scooby, he spoke. "We must hunt them down."

Ron and Scooby looked at each other with apprehension. But Papa gave them no chance to protest.

"We must hunt them down like the animals they are. Arm your best men. Question everyone. No one can keep secrets in Bais. They'll talk. And we'll hunt them down."

The others quickly took on Papa's look of determination, resigned to the facts. They must all take action. And like soldiers sent to action, they were gone.

Papa turned to Wing and me. "Pack your things. You're going back to Manila."

I'd seen it coming. Wing, however, who'd tuned out the whole boring conversation, was caught off guard. "What? Why? Summer's not over yet."

Papa ignored her, knowing that I'd explain everything. "Day after tomorrow." Then, a smile trying to break through. "But first, it looks like we'll have to have your barbeque early this year. Tell Lou we barbeque tomorrow."

I had trouble sleeping that night, thoughts of kidnappings and manhunts racing through my head. But maybe more so, thoughts of the farm and change. It felt as though something was being taken from me. But I wasn't sure what it was or how to stop it.

The next day, Wing and I were already packed by the time folks started showing up for the barbeque. It was tradition to have a barbeque at the end of summer, the day before us kids were sent back to Manila for school. There was quite a bit of murmuring about the barbeque being early this year. Serious faces and talk of kidnappings permeated the normally joyous event. Well, joyous for the grown-ups anyway, already savoring thoughts of peace in the absence of school-bound offspring. For the kids, it was a mixture of excitement to get back to the big city and loathing to go back to school.

All the usual suspects were there, including the Fanlos, Monteros, and Arroyos. And always ready to enjoy life, all talk of kidnappings and martial law soon faded, replaced by boasting of sports, farming, and family. The San Miguel beer and Tanduay rum began to flow, and soon a party was under way.

Never missing an opportunity to spoil a good time, we soon found Boy and some of his friends conspiring to sneak out after the barbecue to attend the cockfights in town. And never missing an opportunity to be sure we didn't miss an opportunity, Wing and I soon had plans to follow them.

The kids were all pretty well-behaved and low key so as not to draw any attention to their plan. For just that reason, the grown-ups should have suspected something was up. But I guess the good food and rum had clouded their vigilance. So as soon as night fell, Boy stol— uh, borrowed, one of the pickup trucks, and with a bunch of his friends in the bed of the pickup, headed for town. As usual, he wouldn't give Wing and me a ride. Something about us being babies and cramping his style.

Town wasn't far though. So Wing and I, not ones to go down without a fight, took our bikes and started pedaling after the truck. There was just enough moonlight for us to avoid the millions of potholes in the old road to town.

"Hey Wing. You think the capré is out tonight?" I kidded. The capré was our Filipino version of the boogeyman, a giant that hid among the trees alongside the road at night. He would come out when he got hungry, to eat children. I loved anything that would scare Wing.

"Shut up," came Wing's simple reply, trying to sound more indignant than scared.

"Just asking," I replied. "I mean, isn't this just the kind of situation he likes? I mean, two kids out in the dark, far enough from home that no one would hear their screams?"

"I said shut up." Wing tried to maintain her cool. But I noticed she'd begun to pedal faster in hopes of reaching town before the monster could get her, before he could skin her and eat her young succulent flesh.

"Hey, wait up!" I shouted, as I pedaled to keep up. Then, unable to resist, "I think I heard something."

"You're such an asshole," from Wing, as her pedaling became frantic and I could detect whimpering through her gasps for air.

I felt bad about it, but there was only one thing I could say to Wing at that point. "Wing!" I screamed. "It's the capré! He's right behind us! Save yourself!"

I caught up to her only after she'd reached town. She sat on the ground next to her bike, exhausted, still gasping for air. I knew she was mad at me, and yet, for just a brief second, when she looked up, I'm sure I recognized a look of relief on her face, relief that I too had escaped the clutches of the capré. It didn't last, though. If not for her still being out of breath, I'm sure the punches she threw at me might have done some damage. As it was, though, the only thing that hurt was my belly, from laughing so hard.

Town wasn't much to look at. It was just one dirty patched-up road, with a few ugly buildings scattered on either side, including a rusted-out gas station, and a small restaurant at the back of a grocery store. Well, to call it a restaurant was being kind. It was just four wooden tables with mismatched vinyl table clothes thrown together in a back room with harsh fluorescent lighting and a fly zapper for entertainment. Town seemed somewhat deserted, but that was only because of the cockfights that night. Everyone was packed into the big barn at the edge of town where the fights were held. The few stragglers, most simply too drunk to find the barn, looked up as Wing and I walked our bikes over to the barn. Everyone knew who we were and nodded respectfully as we passed.

Neither Wing nor I had ever been to the cockfights before. In the bigger cities, like Manila, it's an organized sport, just like horse racing and boxing. It's held in large arenas, professionally organized, attended by huge crowds. This wasn't Manila.

You could hear the excited shouts coming from the barn even before we could see it. But the real experience hit you when you went through the door. The noise was deafening, staccato shouts in the native Vizayan dialect hammering your ears. The stench in the air seemed to be a combination of unwashed human and barnyard compost. And the smoke. Everyone in Bais smoked. You could hardly see through it in the dimly lit barn.

"Eeewww. It smells like chickens," proclaimed Wing, covering her nose and mouth.

"Duh," I replied. "These are cockfights, after all. What did you expect?"

The crowd was packed around the ring. The outermost spectators were standing on benches and crates. Wing and I couldn't see the ring and we weren't strong enough to push our way through the crowd. I thought we might never see the fights until I noticed the people up in the hayloft overhead. We managed to find our way up the ladder and squeeze out a spot on the hay among the loft-dwellers. The smoke was even thicker up in the loft. And with all the smoking, I couldn't help but wonder if anyone would even know if a fire broke out.

Looking down on the crowd, we could see everything. In front of the people on benches and crates, people were standing, packed like sardines. In front of those, people were squatting or sitting on the dirt floor. And at the center of the pushing and shoving, shouting, smoking, drunk, sweaty crowd, sat the focus of everyone's attention, the ring.

I don't know why I thought it would be bigger. I mean, how much room do two chickens need? It was maybe six feet on each side, bound by chicken wire about three feet tall.

Wing interrupted my survey with an elbow to the ribs. "Look, it's Boy."

She was about to shout to him, when I grabbed her by the arm to stop her. My spying tendencies had kicked in and I shushed her, pointing at Boy with my lips. Something was up. He was back in a corner, away from the crowd. He was with Speed, the cane worker. I never thought I'd see those two associating with each other. But the reason became clear when I saw Boy exchange some money for the bag in Speed's hand. Now I knew where Boy was getting the drugs, and how Speed got his nickname.

Wing looked at me, eyes wide. Not the sharpest pitchfork in the barn, even she knew what was going on.

"What should we do?"

"Let's tell Papa," I replied.

"No," Wing said, after a brief pause to think.

"What do you mean, no?" I asked, surprised at her answer.

Once again, we were faced with the problem of how to deal with Boy. Do we tell Papa? Do we report Speed and get him fired? And what good would it do anyway? Boy would just deny everything.

"It wouldn't do any good," said Wing, resigned to the facts. "Besides, we're not even supposed to be here. Mama will kill me if she finds out I went to the cockfights."

I knew what we had to do. I knew it didn't matter what Boy or Mama would or wouldn't do. I knew we had to tell Papa. We just had to. It was the right thing to do.

But we didn't. Once again, we didn't listen to the little angels on our shoulders. Instead, we listened to the other guy, the one with the horns, the one who came up with one excuse after another to keep us from doing what we knew was right. God, I hate that guy.

I don't know if things would have turned out differently. I don't know if telling on Boy would have done any good. But I know now that I would never fully forgive myself for not trying. I should have tried.

The cockfights were starting. There was a certain amount of pushing and shoving as people attempted to get a look at the contenders being brought to the ring. I didn't think chickens could get that big. Well, they weren't chickens. They were roosters, after all. But still. They were huge.

Even from the distance of the hayloft, I could see the reflection of something metallic and shiny coming from the cocks' legs. I asked someone next to me what it was.

"Those are razor knives," answered a much too familiar voice.

I turned toward the voice to find Yaya sitting right next to me. Uh oh, I thought. Busted. I elbowed Wing in the ribs and when she turned to see Yaya, she actually screamed in surprise. We sat there wide-mouthed and blinking as Yaya took a long drag on her cigar with one hand, a bottle of lambanug in the other.

"What?" she said in reply to our stares, finally breaking the awkward silence. Then, like some kind of pirate, she spit on the floor of the loft, took a big swig from her bottle, and belched, loudly.

"What are *you* doing here?" I asked.

Wiping her mouth with her sleeve, "You think I have no life of my own? You think I live only for you brats?" At that, a couple of friends with her laughed with toothless grins to match Yaya's, one of the old women beginning to cough and choke from laughter. Yaya shoved the bottle of booze at her to clear her throat, which her friend unceremoniously grabbed.

"I guess we're in trouble, huh," I said, lowering my head in guilt.

Before she could answer, her friends began poking her to get her money ready for betting on the fight. Yaya reached down the front of her dress and pulled out a small roll of pesos. Handing the money off to her friends, she turned back to Wing and me to see the look of shock on our faces.

"What now?" she frowned. "Never saw anyone place a little wager before?"

"Gambling's a sin," stated Wing.

Yaya took another swig of lambanug before replying. "Yeah, and the Virgin Mary got knocked up."

Wing and I covered our mouths in shock.

"OK, OK," Yaya continued, "I'll make you a deal. Mums about the gambling to Father Rivera, and I won't report you two for breaking curfew to hang with us sinners." With that, she spit into the palm of her hand and held it out to us to seal the deal with a handshake.

I looked at Wing, who eventually nodded her head to take the offer. I took Yaya's hand by the fingers, avoiding the handful of spit.

"Deal," stated Yaya. "I hate giving Rivera the moral advantage," she added, holding out her bottle of booze to us.

Carried up in the moment, I actually went to take it until Wing slapped my hand away. Well, at least now we knew where Yaya went on the weekends. One mystery solved.

Anyway, getting back to the razor knives, Yaya explained how they were taped to the cocks' legs, the left leg, to be exact. Apparently Filipino chickens were all left-handed, or footed. Go figure. I knew the birds were going to fight. I mean, it was a cock *fight* after all. But I figured there'd be some pecking and clawing. I didn't know they'd be armed with blades like some kind of gang members. I was beginning to see this wasn't going to be a friendly little fight. No Marquis de Queensbury rules.

"One of them might get hurt with those knives," Wing pointed out.

Yaya chuckled at Wing's, uh, joke. "Of course they get hurt. That's how you know who wins. The first one that dies is the loser."

Wing was horrified that they would fight to the death.

"The first one?" I asked.

"Sure. They'll both die, of course. From the wounds."

"The wounds?"

"Oh yes. Very bloody."

I looked at Wing. Wing looked at me. Very bloody. How nice. That's just what we wanted to hear.

Money was flying all around the barn as soon as the cocks were brought out, everyone betting on their favorite, one man recording the wagers with pad and paper. The people of Bais didn't have much money. But what little they did have was surely changing hands that night at the cockfights.

As they prepared to release the cocks into the ring, all eyes were on them. Well, not quite all. As I scanned the room, taking in the excited frenzy, I noticed a few pairs of eyes on Wing and me. Through the smoke and darkness, I couldn't tell who they were, but they certainly seemed interested in our presence. I didn't make too much of it, as we were certainly out of our element, and that in itself must have been entertaining to many of the town folk. Still, more than a few of the hairs on the back of my neck said otherwise.

It started with feathers. They flew everywhere. Wings flapping. Birds lunging and jumping. The squawking and shrieking could barely be heard over the cheering of the crowd. Then there was blood, a lot of blood, red blood on white feathers, the left-handed birds striking over and over with their razors. I could see some of it spraying onto the faces of the front row spectators, grinning and laughing maniacally as they leaned in even closer for a better look. I wanted to run, but my body wouldn't take me, suddenly unable to move. I wanted to shut my eyes, but they wouldn't close, glued to the slaughter taking place down in the ring. Both birds were bleeding profusely, now more red-feathered than their original white. And the more blood spilt, the slower the birds moved. The slow motion effect only emphasized every brutal blow. Looking for any way to end the slaughter, I began to wonder how much blood a rooster actually contained? They both began to stagger. I couldn't tell one bird from the other, let alone which one was winning. Soon one stopped striking and slumped to the ground, the imminent loser my guess. A cheer went up from the crowd. I thought it was over. But not just yet. All eyes stayed on the remaining cock, staggering about the ring, which seemed to know he had one more obligation to fill. To be declared winner, the remaining bird had to peck the loser on the head two more times before dying himself. And then, like a true champion, only seconds after that second and final peck, the winner went down for the final time amid the cheers of the bloodthirsty crowd. I didn't even have time to feel the vomit rise in my throat.

I had no idea if anyone amid the madness of the crowd even noticed my retching into the hayloft. When my convulsions abated sufficiently to allow me to raise my head, my watering eyes cleared just enough to make out the back of Wing's head, right next to mine, similarly bowing in homage to the puke gods, just as mine had done moments before.

Well, someone certainly noticed. Yaya was laughing, poking her friends to look at us as she took a puff of her cigar.

"There. You happy now?" I groaned to Wing, wiping my mouth with the back of my hand.

"Hey. Don't blame *me*," Wing moaned. "This was *your* idea," she added, turning her head back to me, causing her ponytail to drag through the puke-ridden hay.

"*My* idea? Who forced you to come? Did I pedal your bike for you?"

"Don't get pissed at me cause you got sick."

"You got sick too," I chastised.

Wing sat up, smelling her puke-stained ponytail. "Yeah, but I only got sick cause you got sick."

"What are you talking about?" I demanded. "You puked because of all that blood, just like I did."

"Not."

"What do you mean?"

Wing explained. "Well, *you* puked because of the blood. *I* only puked because I saw *you* puking. You know I can't stand the sight of someone puking."

She was right. It was the weirdest thing, but Wing had to puke whenever she saw someone else puke. In fact, one time I faked it so well, I got her to puke by herself. She got really mad when she realized I was faking. Then I almost really did puke from laughing so hard.

Anyway, we found ourselves outside the barn, gulping fresh air as soon as our rubbery knees would carry us. The whole cockfight barely took a minute. It just seemed like forever. I mean, we knew birds would get hurt. It was a fight, after all. But the blood, it was all just way over the top.

Unable to ride just yet, we began walking our bikes out of town toward home. The taste of vomit still lingering in our throats, we began to joke about the whole thing, trying to turn it into just another one of those quirks of living in the Philippines, another beauty mark adding character to that less than perfect face.

The road seemed darker on the way home, the trees leaning in to nearly block out the moonlight. A slight breeze moved leaves and small branches overhead. I thought I heard something.

"Shush," I said, coming to a stop.

"What now?" asked Wing, stopping alongside me.

"I thought I heard something."

"Oh no. Don't start that again," declared Wing, pushing her bike again.

I grabbed her by the back of the shirt, halting her progress. "No. I'm serious."

"Come on, Lisa. Cut it out." She pulled my hand from her shirt.

At that moment, there was a loud snapping sound, a twig breaking amid the trees alongside the road. We both heard it that time, grabbing each other by the hands. There was someone, or something among the trees. The first to see the dark form, Wing began to shake. I looked at her, only to see her eyes go wide and her jaw drop open. Her mouth was saying something, but no sound was coming out. I finally read her lips, which were forming one word over and over.

"Capré."

I turned to find the monster, but couldn't. "Where? Where?"

Stepping backward in slow motion, Wing was able to raise one pointing hand. I looked and finally saw something. But what? A shadow? There, against a tree. It was something very dark, almost black, with two gleaming eyes. It was on fire. No, not fire, just smoke. Wait a second. It was smoking a cigarette. A capré with a cigarette? I dropped Wing's hand and took an angry step toward the creature.

"Who's there?" I demanded. Wing was grabbing at my shirtsleeve trying to save me from certain death. "Who's there?" I repeated.

The thing took a step out from the trees into the moonlight, revealing itself.

"Speed!" I gasped with relief. God, he was dark. "What are you doing in the trees?"

Pausing to first take another drag on his cigarette, "Just having a smoke." He attempted to blow smoke rings in the air.

We weren't amused. "You scared us to death."

Then Wing, with a nervous giggle, "Yeah, I thought you were a capré."

Without breaking a smile, Speed raised his hands in imitation of claws. "Maybe that's just what I am."

I guess he was making a joke. Wing was certainly relieved to see Speed instead of the capré. I wasn't so sure myself. Instead, I found those hairs on the back of my neck standing again. "Let's go," I urged Wing with a nudge. Wing waved goodbye and we started up the road. After just a couple of steps, I turned back to check on Speed, but he was gone.

Wing was rambling on about something or other but I couldn't hear her over the alarm going off inside my brain. Something wasn't right. But I didn't want to scare Wing and have her fall apart on me again.

"Let's ride," I said. "It's faster."

Wing obliged without a fight and we were off.

We never saw what hit us. Unable to make it out in the dark, the wire booby trap strung across the road knocked us from our bikes like a giant hand. Thrown on our backs in the middle of the road, we hadn't had time to catch our breath when they were upon us.

Hands. Lots of hands. And rope. They gagged us and tied our arms and legs. I couldn't see their faces. They wore masks or hoods. It was so dark. Someone shoved something into my pocket and then the hands were gone. As I lie in the middle of the road, I could hear them dragging Wing away, her gagged screams growing more faint with distance. What about me? Why weren't they taking me? Why only Wing? The answers to my questions would come later. But my thoughts were soon interrupted.

I'd been blindfolded and could barely hear a thing over the pounding of my heart in my ears. And yet, I suddenly heard that unmistakable sound again. I'd first heard it when that rabid dog showed up, then more recently at the beach. A shotgun. There can be no more distinct sound in the world than the metallic pumping of a pump-action shotgun. It makes a statement that's not to be fooled with. And there's no debating a sound like that. You do what it says, or you get out of the way. But I couldn't. Blindfolded and bound in the middle of the road, there was nowhere for me to go. Nowhere to hide. Realizing I was about to be executed, a quick final Lord's Prayer, ingrained from years of Catholic schooling, went through my mind.

"Though I walk through the valley of death—"

The gunshot came from so close to my head, I guess it was what they'd call point blank. I didn't feel a thing. I opened my eyes to finally see what heaven looked like, but all I saw was darkness. No clouds. No angels. No chocolate.

I was beginning to wonder if maybe it was, you know, that other place, when I felt the blindfold pulled from my eyes. Ringing still in my ears, I looked up from the road to see her standing over me. An angel? Hardly. Not unless *my* angel smoked cigars, which she abruptly yanked from her mouth to spit in the road. She then unceremoniously slipped her sawed off shotgun back into the holster beneath her dress.

"Yaya?"

"Who were you expecting? The Lone Ranger?"

"What are *you* doing here?"

"What does it look like I'm doing? I'm saving your ass." She walked over to untie Wing, trussed like a roast lechon, at the edge of the woods.

"Is she OK?" I asked.

"She's just fine," answered Yaya.

"But the gunshot. You shot someone?"

Yaya gave me a look of indignation. "You bet your ass I shot someone."

"But who? Who were they?"

"Don't know. They wore hoods. But whoever they were, one of them's carrying a buttload of buckshot."

I was a little shaky standing up. Then I remembered that something had been shoved into my pocket. I pulled out a folded piece of paper. The note was short and sweet.

"José Delgado. Ten million pesos for your daughter or she dies in one week. Will contact you then." Now I understood. They never wanted me at all. Only Wing.

I was helping Wing up from the road when Yaya called to us from the pedicab she'd hired to follow us home.

"Let's go. Leave your bikes. I'll send someone for them in the morning."

Wing and I gratefully crowded into the little cab on either side of Yaya as the driver pedaled for the farm.

"Thank you, Yaya," Wing whimpered as the tears finally came, reflexively hugging the woman that raised her.

"What are you thanking me for, you silly child?" asked Yaya placing her arm around Wing's shoulders to comfort her.

I turned to her, incredulous. "Yaya. You saved our lives. You shot someone, for God's sake."

Yaya spit in the road, put her other arm around my shoulders, smiled, and put it as simply as she could. "I'm the Yaya. It's what we do."

That one drew a chuckle, even from Wing.

Back at the farm, I didn't think I'd get to sleep that night with so many things to think about. But maybe that was just it. There were too many things all running around my head. And unable to focus on just one, I fell instantly asleep, exhausted.

No, they never found any buckshot in Speed's butt. And believe me, Yaya made sure they checked, after we told her how we'd seen him earlier that evening.

They *did* find Scooby Montero's maid and her family. And, as suspected, it *was* communists that took them. They're not communists anymore. They're not anything anymore.

Our bags were already out on the porch when we awoke. Back to Manila. It all seemed so abrupt. Not the way summers were supposed to end. Yet there was no way we could stay. Things had become too dangerous. Imagine that. The farm. Too dangerous. It didn't make any sense.

Breakfast was unusually silent. Everyone just sort of pushed their food around their plates with nothing close to appetites. As soon as we were excused, I ran to say goodbye to Johnny, but couldn't find him. He must have been out working in the fields, probably didn't even know I was leaving. Otherwise I was sure he would have been there to see me off. Or so I rationalized, ignoring the reality that he hadn't even spoken to me since our, uh, swim, a couple of weeks earlier. Well a girl can dream, can't she?

Giving up on Johnny, I went to bid farewell to my other summer love, but Molly Moo Cow wasn't there either. That was strange for Molly not to be in her stall. I wondered where she could be. Was *everyone* avoiding me?

My thoughts were interrupted by Wing shouting for me to get in the van or it would leave for the airport without me. I was certainly tempted to call that bluff.

The entire flight home, and for weeks after that, I felt hollow inside, like something was missing. No, not just missing. Taken. Or better still, stolen. My summer. The farm. Johnny. Even Molly.

Well Molly wasn't exactly stolen. You see, there was always plenty of food at those end of summer barbeques. And yet, I still hadn't figured out just exactly what veal was. God I was stupid.

Chapter 8

As much as I feared change at the farm, I prayed for it back in Manila. It just doesn't seem fair that while we're preoccupied trying to change the things we hate, the things we love the most seem to go and change on their own while we're not looking. But revolution is a funny thing. I compare it to our Mount Talinas volcano. It just sits there, all quiet, pretending to be innocent, while the people have no idea what's boiling and churning just beneath the surface. Then one day, seemingly without warning, **boom**, it erupts and makes a mess of everything. I always thought, no matter what happened in Manila, things would stay just the way they were at the farm, awaiting my return. I just never thought I'd be away three years.

Even back in Manila, I spent most of my time at Wing's house, if for no other reason than just to get away from my mother. I'd grown tired of being polite to all the applicants she'd lined up to replace my dad. And besides, I didn't like the creepy way some of them looked at me.

Papa came and went, but spent most of his time back at the farm. Mama only spent summers at the farm, and even then, under protest. And yet, in Manila, we never saw her anyway, as she was always out attending teas and luncheons with her socialite friends. No, we were pretty much on our own. That is, except when we were at school. And Catholic school in Manila was no piece of cake. Kids in Catholic school didn't really need parents. The nuns offered plenty of discipline to go around. They were pretty much the meanest people we knew. We blamed it on the heat. How anyone could walk around all day in stifling 90-degree heat, dripping with humidity, wrapped in black burlap habits, was beyond comprehension. We imagined that inflicting pain on others was just their way of forgetting their own miserable plights. There was certainly no shortage of excuses for a good whacking with a metal-edged ruler, whether it be chewing gum, personal grooming, skirt length, swearing, or boys.

But then there was Sister Angelina, our one saving grace, a beacon of kindness, shining from the oppressive depths of hell that Catholic school had come to represent. She was young. Very young. We didn't really know how old she was, but she could have passed for one of us, a student. And just like us students, you could tell the other sisters hated her. She was too energetic, too optimistic, too... uh... happy, all those things a nun wasn't supposed to be. We called her Angel, for short, of course.

"Come on you guys," she implored the class. "This is your country I'm talking about."

I felt bad for her. No one was listening. They were all dreaming of boys and where they might meet them after school. Did I fail to mention there were no boys at Catholic girls' schools? All the more reason to spend all day dreaming about them.

Finally, one of us whined in response, "Yeah but what's the government got to do with us? It's not like we've got any say."

"Really," chimed in another. "This martial law stuff is really putting a damper on my social life," she added with a flip of her hair and a giggle.

Angel wasn't easily defeated. "But that's just my point. You *do* have a say. Or you did, until President Marcos declared martial law. We're a democracy. You've got elected representatives in government looking out for your interests. When Mr. Marcos declared martial law, he took their power away. Your power. The people's power."

"People Power!" someone in the back shouted. The whole class laughed. Then a low chant began to the rhythmic pounding of desks, slowly growing in volume. "People Power. People Power." Angel couldn't help but smile. That is, until—

"What's all this commotion?!" came an icy shout from the classroom doorway, immediately followed by the sound of a ruler smacking the doorjamb. Hearing that familiar shrill voice, the room went silent, backs straight, eyes ahead. Sister Mary Alice, or Malice, as we called her for short, of course, was the school principal.

Angel wasn't easily cowed. "Why good morning Sister Mary Alice. Everyone kindly greet your principal."

The class moaned the customary greeting in unison. "Good morning, Mali—, uh, Sister Mary Alice."

The scowl on her face unchanged, Malice continued, "I repeat. What's all this commotion?"

"Political Science, Sister. We're learning about our government," Angel replied, smiling defiantly.

The whole class stared at her, wide-eyed, for challenging Malice with her smile. We'd never seen a teacher get spanked with a ruler. This was going to be good.

"Sister Angelina," began Malice, "what about our government incites our students to riot with chants of, what was it, People Power?"

"We were discussing the power of the people provided through democracy," Angel smiled proudly.

Malice was not impressed. "You mean the power to disrupt and reap havoc, as your class is doing to my school?"

"Well, not exactly. You see, school is not a democracy. So you're correct. The right of students to have political representation does not exist," Angel began.

Malice nodded smugly in agreement, sure to make icy eye contact with each of us.

"But outside of school," Angel continued, "the people must always maintain that right. In fact, it's their duty. If the government presumes to usurp the powers bestowed upon the people in a democracy, then the people must fight to maintain that power at all costs. Even if it calls for revolution. To do less, would be, well, unpatriotic."

I'm not sure how many of us understood Sister Angelina's speech, but we all sat wide-eyed, anticipating Malice's response to calls for revolution.

Fortunately, Malice didn't understand her either, revolution apparently representing a concept foreign to her order of the church. With brows furrowed and head cocked to one side, like a poodle watching television, she brought the discussion to an end.

"Good. School is not a democracy. Remember that, children." And with a crack of her ruler to the palm of her hand, she was gone.

As always, the departure of Malice brought with it a combination of sighs of relief, and a general mumbling about witches and devils.

"Class. Class," shouted Angel above the drone. "Let's get back to work." But before she could proceed, a girl from the front row named Clara, probably the only one who ever fully paid attention, raised her hand, waiving it like a flag until she was called upon.

"Yes, Clara. What is it?"

"Sister Angelina, are you a communist?"

A general silence fell over the class. Like me, most of the class had already had some exposure to the Filipino version of communism. We couldn't imagine Sister Angelina to be one of *those* people. Sister Angelina stopped in her tracks, seemingly speechless.

"Why would you think such a thing, Clara?" she asked.

"Well, you're talking about revolution and overthrowing our government. Isn't that what happened in Russia and China?"

Angel smiled. "Very good, Clara. I see you're thinking. That's wonderful."

Many of us sat in stunned silence. Angel was a communist?

"However," she continued, "revolution and government overthrow does not a communist make." She let that sink in just long enough to be sure no one understood it, then continued.

"You know of the American revolution, right? Is America communist?" She didn't give anyone a chance to reply incorrectly. "Of course not. The overthrow of a nonrepresentative and unjust government doesn't mean one plans to replace it with a communist one. It doesn't mean one is in favor of forcibly redistributing wealth and land from the rich to the poor. As well, maybe you don't know this, but true communism outlaws religion. Do you really think I would support such a thing?"

Murmurs of agreement among the class seemed willing to accept the idea that Angel was no communist.

She continued. "No, but that doesn't mean one should stand by as elected officials strive to become dictators." She was talking about Marcos. I'd learned enough at the farm from Papa to recognize a rat by its description.

We endured many more lessons about revolution and freedom. But political science wasn't the only thing we were taught in Catholic school. We were taught all the basics, like how to be good girls, to keep our legs together, and how marriage comes before children.

Of course, we weren't all A-students. One of the older girls from school, Mary C, for Catherine, wasn't an A-student, if you know what I mean. So when we noticed she'd stopped coming to school, we started asking her classmates questions. The reply was a familiar one. She'd gone to Mabini Street to become a hostess. Most of my classmates assumed this was where people without high school diplomas got jobs.

I, on the other hand, suspected this wasn't just about a job. As was the case with Johnny's mom, I assumed she'd gotten pregnant and was forced to leave school. So when we heard Boy Delgado was going over to Mabini Street with some friends, our curiosity got the better of us and Wing and I begged to go along under the pretense that we could report back to the class on Mary C and her "new job." In addition, my naive hope was to find the restaurant where Johnny's mother used to work.

* * * *

I should have known better. Anything involving Boy had to be just plain wrong. Boy had picked up in Manila pretty much where he'd left off at the farm, that is, looking for trouble. And Mabini was as good a place as any to find it.

Despite the declaration of martial law, for those of means and connections, travel was pretty much unimpeded. The police knew everyone and which families they came from. While those without connections could end up in prison simply for being on the street after dark, we kids from good families never got hassled, and instead were simply written passes by the first policeman that stopped us. In fact, we never even got stopped on our way out to Mabini, as the police all knew our car and just waved to us as we drove by.

The change in surroundings as Boy's van drew closer to Mabini was a gradual one. Street by street, the difference was so subtle as to not draw notice, yet, had one fallen asleep at the beginning of the journey and only awakened at the end, the change was so striking as to suggest you'd entered another country.

Messy. That's the first word that comes to mind. Not like a teenager's bedroom. Not that kind of messy. More like a dictionary sort of definition of messy. Disordered. The usually busy and already overcrowded streets of Manila had taken on an almost chaotic character, where even the most basic rules of the road had been tossed aside. Traffic could be going in three different directions on the same one-way street. Instead of following any sort of rules of the road, the air was continuously punctuated by staccato horn honks announcing, "look out, here I come, ready or not." Small dirty children weaved in and out of traffic on foot selling cigarettes by the stick. The homeless to stretch of sidewalk ratio had soared, and with it, the ever present pungent smell of urine. Neon soon became the signage of choice, tacky signs with missing letters announcing both pawnshops and porn shops. No sign seemed complete without the word nude on it, at least once.

"Hey Boy," called Wing from our position at the back of the van, "I think you're lost."

Boy's friends laughed, then Boy replied. "I thought you wanted to see Mabini Street."

"Exactly," Wing agreed. "You must have taken a wrong turn somewhere. The neighborhoods just keep getting worse and worse." Wing pointed out the window, for my benefit, at a sign reading, "Nude, Nude, Nude, XXX, Live Young Girls."

"Well this *is* Mabini Street," announced Boy, making one final turn onto a crowded street full of open doorways laced with teenage girls in miniskirts or short shorts, bikini tops, and cartoonishly-high heels.

Wing and I looked at each other, wide-eyed. Where were the nice restaurants with those "hostess" jobs?

As it turned out, the rumor that Mary C even went to Mabini turned out to be a mean-spirited lie. You see, Mabini Street was just another example of what being from the wrong side of the tracks could mean. Girls from good families like mine or Wing's or Mary C's, girls from private Catholic schools, didn't end up at Mabini Street. Only those from families without connections, the poor, and banished maids, would find their way to Mabini.

And it wasn't about abortion either. *That* was almost unheard of, *certainly* unheard of among young Catholic schoolgirls. If you were to check the menu of life's options for Catholic schoolgirls in the Philippines, you wouldn't find abortion anywhere. Now, I didn't say it didn't happen. But it certainly wasn't on the menu. It was more of an a la carte sort of thing, a rare delicacy, an acquired taste, requested in whispers, at the suggestion of older individuals already destined for hell. At the time, I'd never even heard of it. And I know, even if the possibility were raised, none of my schoolmates would have chosen such a path. Oh, there were plenty of things Catholic schoolgirls did which would send one directly to hell. Do not pass go. Do not collect $200. But abortion wasn't one of them. I think maybe it had to do with the unwritten rule that doing bad things to yourself or even to other adults was just so common that we knew there wouldn't be enough room in hell for all of us. Yet for those that would harm a child, the devil could always find room at the inn, and for harming a baby, you'd probably get your very own private room, or even a suite, complete with hot and hotter running brimstone.

No, Mabini wasn't about abortion. Mabini was a place to get work, the kind of work that only one with no other options would take, work that a young, uneducated, unskilled young woman, cast out from her family, would take. And it was usually the last job she would take, sort of a one-way ticket.

No, Mary C was probably just on an extended vacation until her baby was born. She wouldn't be allowed back at Catholic school. But she wouldn't end up at Mabini either.

Johnny's mom, however, wasn't a Catholic schoolgirl, like us. She was a maid. She was from the farm. She was pregnant, in need of work, and soon to have an additional mouth to feed. If they'd issued a casting call for Mabini Street, she'd have presented the perfect resume. She could have been the Mabini Street poster child.

Boy parked the car and we all got out. I hadn't even noticed until then that there were no girls in Boy's crew that day. I guess it hadn't seemed important at the time we got in the van. But now, Wing and I felt like some sort of aliens. Sure there were plenty of girls on Mabini, as I've already mentioned. But they were all there to "work." Their uniforms were very different from ours. Now that's not to say there weren't plenty of Catholic schoolgirl uniforms on display. They just came from a different tailor. Micro-short skirts, tight, cleavage-revealing blouses, and heels, heels reaching for heaven. No, there was no mistaking any of these girls for actual Catholic schoolgirls.

Wing and I felt as though we'd fallen into some kind of alternate universe. Wing had unconsciously grabbed my arm out of insecurity. We were so distracted by our new surroundings, we'd almost missed the fact that the boys were headed into one of Mabini's fine establishments. I quickly pulled Wing by the arm that was locked to mine and tailed the boys into a place called The Landing Strip. Under the flashing neon sign was another that read "Welcome, Clark Air Force Base." I remembered the fact that Johnny's "dad" was in the Air Force, stationed at Clark. I wondered if this could be where Johnny's mom had gone to work. It had been a long time, but maybe one of the other hostesses would remember her.

I didn't realize that just about every door on Mabini Street had a sign welcoming the soldiers from Clark. As we ran through the filthy door to The Landing Strip trying not to lose the boys, the cheap photos tacked about the rotting doorway of young girls in various stages of undress hadn't escaped my notice, even the little red stars in the photos, covering the girls' strategic points.

Once inside, we were hit with a barrage of senses, only intensified by the darkness of the club. We were blind for a moment, before our eyes could adjust from the sunlight outside. I don't know which hit me first, the pounding bass beat from the blaring music, or the smell. But I can definitely tell you the smell made the greater impression. It was the unforgettable combination of smoke, sour beer, and urine, all refusing to be drowned out by the sharp odor of cleaning ammonia. Wing was making gagging noises. I wanted to let go of her to be sure she wouldn't puke on me, but my instincts kept us clinging to each other in the dark.

As our eyes adjusted to the darkness, we found the boys crowding up to the bar ordering drinks. Scantily-dressed young girls seemed to appear out of the darkness, drawn toward the boys, like moths to a porch light bulb. Boy and his friends were yukking it up, toasting to the good life, as the girls draped themselves about the boys' shoulders like cheap coats.

Wing and I hadn't made it up to the bar when a mostly toothless bouncer grabbed us by the arms and turned us toward the door.

"No freelancing allowed," he said, preparing to toss us into the street. "If you're interested in work, come back later tonight when you can audition with the boss."

I didn't like the way he said "audition." It sounded too much like something that would be done *to* me instead of *by* me. I yanked my arm free, and grabbing Wing's arm, began a tug of war with the bouncer.

"We're not here for jobs," I insisted. "We're here with those guys." I gestured toward boy's troop.

The bouncer stopped, but didn't let go of Wing.

"Hey! You guys!" he shouted to Boy and his friends over the music. "You bring these girls in here? What's the deal? Are you buying or selling?"

Boy turned around. For a moment, I could actually see him considering his options, until one of his friends elbowed him jokingly in the ribs.

"No, no. It's not like that," explained Boy, chuckling. "The goofy one's my sister."

Even the toothless bouncer took on a look of confused repugnance at the idea that someone would bring his little sister into a place like that.

"But you can have the ugly one," added Boy, referring to me, before turning back to his drink.

The bouncer took another look at me, but didn't care for my "touch me again and I'll kick your nuts off" look. Besides, the whole "bring your little sister to Mabini street" thing had so weirded him out that he simply turned and walked away in disgust.

Like battered wives going back once more to their abusive husbands, Wing and I, with no other choice, returned to the "protection" of our herd at the bar.

I soon noticed that some of the herd were missing. It seemed that each time one of the scantily clad sluts approached the group of boys, she would peel one away from his friends and, hips asway, lead him, as though by a leash, through a door at the back of the room.

Boy saw me eying the mysterious door. "So you want to be a hostess, huh?"

Something about the smirk on his face made my skin crawl. But curious about Johnny's mom, and maybe the girl from school, I said, "Maybe."

Boy almost choked on his drink.

"But where do the hostesses work?" I added.

As luck would have it, one of the girls had just come back out to reel in another one of Boy's pals. "They work right here," said Boy, pointing at the girl with his lips.

I turned to watch a pair of hot pants in six-inch heels lead the boy through the back door. "No. Wait. *That's* a hostess?"

"Sure. What'd you think?" responded Boy.

I didn't know what I thought. But I wasn't thinking these were the elegant women that would show you to your table at a fine restaurant. Then again, maybe this was just a really sleazy restaurant, thus sleazy hostesses. "But where's the restaurant?"

Boy's face contorted in confusion. "What restaurant?"

"You know, where the hostesses bring the customers to be served," I replied.

Boy's eyes opened wide. "To be served?"

"Sure. Is it in the back? Through that door?" I asked, indicating the unmarked porthole at the back of the room.

Boy's face seemed to light up in comprehension. The look of confusion was replaced by one of smug satisfaction. I could just make out one of Boy's evil smirks penetrating the dim light.

"Yeah. The *restaurant's* in the back, through that door." He gave a little chuckle to his friends. "Why don't you have one of the hostesses take you to the *restaurant,* where you can be *served*?"

I had no idea what they were laughing at, but I didn't see the harm in just seeing the restaurant out back. "Come on, Wing. Let's go see." A girl in a Catholic schoolgirl miniskirt hiked up to—, well hiked up as far as it could, offered to show us the way, wearing a smile I could only describe as wicked.

Wing didn't move. "No, that's OK. I'm not hungry." I could tell she was afraid. But as usual, Wing's fear only made me more brave. Or reckless. One or the other.

Boy gave the hostess a handful of pesos. "Be sure to tell us how you liked it when you come back," he shouted, as the girl led me away, holding me uncomfortably close by the arm.

I shouted back in answer to Boy. "I just want to take a look. I'm not going to eat." I didn't know what the Boys were laughing at.

And as we approached the door, the hostess whispered in my ear, "But I have a little something you really must taste." Then looking me up and down, "I feel like eating something myself."

Passing through the door at the back of the bar, my eyes took a moment to adjust, as the back room was even darker than the bar. This time, smell was definitely the first sense to check in. The odor of cleaning ammonia had gotten even stronger. Piercing the jolting smell of the ammonia were scattered giggles from girls, and moans from men. The hostess and I walked down a hallway lined on either side by small cubicles, each maybe six feet by four. A crude cushioned bed nearly filled each cubicle. Several were screened off by what appeared to be shower curtains. Those were the ones from which the moans and giggles came. Occasionally I could make out a pair of feet from under the drawn curtains, some high-heeled girls, some men with their pants down around their ankles.

I bumped into my hostess before realizing she had stopped in front of one of the open cubicles. Before I could ask where the restaurant was, she'd pulled me into the little room by my hand and drew the curtain. The space was so small it only took a nudge from the girl to send me falling backward onto the mattress.

And before I could even get back on my feet, the hostess had whipped off her tank top in one smooth well-practiced motion. I remember briefly hoping that my boobs ended up just the size hers were, but I can assure you there was never a moment that I wanted to touch them in any way, despite such an offer from the hostess when she noticed my brief distraction. So when she reached for the zipper of my skirt I knew it was time to go.

"But you haven't had anything to eat yet," the hostess teased, forcing me back down on the mattress with one hand, lifting the front of her skirt with the other, and licking her lips.

I'd had enough.

"Believe me. There's nothing on the menu here I want."

And without thinking, my leg instinctively went up and shoved her through the curtain. The hostess fell backward into the curtain behind her which had opened to one side, granting me my first view of two people making love... uh... scratch that, having sex. When my hostess fell to the floor, I could see the naked backside of the man in the booth across the hallway, rocking back and forth, pants down around his ankles. His hostess was sitting on the waist high mattress, her legs wrapped around the man's back. She was trying to close the curtain with one hand, giving me the middle finger with the other, all while her angered face continued to emit phony groans of ecstasy. The man didn't even notice, or care, that he'd been exposed. I guess he was preoccupied.

Strange, but the last thing I can remember, before bolting from the room, was the tattoo at the top of the man's butt. It was the Virgin Mary. That's right, the Virgin Mary tattooed on the man's butt. And each time the man clenched his butt cheeks in pleasure, Mary seemed to grimace in pain. Go figure.

Anyway, without another thought, I ran from the back room, grabbed Wing by the arm, and dragged her out of the bar into the street.

"What's wrong with you?" Wing protested, tugging at her arm.

I was hyperventilating and couldn't speak yet.

"Was the food that bad?" she continued.

Still gulping air from my doubled-over position, I looked back up at Wing, and couldn't help but start laughing.

"What?" demanded Wing, assuming, correctly I might add, that I was laughing at her. "What's so funny?"

"No food," was all I could get out at first, between gulps of air.

"What do you mean, no food? The restaurant had nothing for sale?" Wing frowned and raised one brow in disbelief, and when I couldn't immediately reply, added, "I'm going back in to see for myself."

I was just able to catch her by the elbow. "No. They've got plenty for sale all right. Just, not food."

A blank look came over Wing's face. But as I explained the whole episode to her along with the realization of what exactly being a hostess on Mabini Street entailed, her eyes went wide and her hand covered her gaping mouth.

If nothing else, this confirmed that Mary C, from school, certainly wasn't here. Every fiber in us knew that this was nothing a girl from our school could be involved in. There would always be better options for girls from privilege. Always.

But what about Johnny's mom? Just a maid, cast out, with nothing? Where could she go? All I could think of was the anguish expressed on the Virgin Mary's face. The tears of laughter running down my face instantly morphed into tears of sadness, tears for Johnny's mom, tears for the girls still back in the bar, tears that such a thing as this even went on at all.

And speaking of Johnny's mom, she died there on Mabini Street. Of what? Well, it would have been too long ago to be from that brand new incurable disease going around in the eighties. They didn't even have a name for AIDS back then. But it could have been any number of things. Working on Mabini Street, I put my money on alcoholism or drug abuse. How else could a girl make it through the day? After all, I barely made it through five minutes. I couldn't imagine being one of those hostesses.

Both Wing and I were still sniffling on the steps outside the bar when the boys finished their business and came out patting each other on the backs. Boy saw us there, crying, let out a maniacal laugh, and walked right past us, back to the van. Wing and I pulled ourselves together and followed, afraid they might leave us behind. We didn't say anything on the ride back. We just wanted to get home.

Chapter 9

That wasn't the last adventure with Boy Delgado that summer. In fact, thanks to Boy, over the next three years, Wing and I learned quite a bit about all that's wrong with the world. Like what? Well, we learned what a drug addict was, from pot, to pills, to cocaine and heroin. And we learned what someone addicted to drugs would do to get a fix. We knew Boy was stealing from his own parents to pay his junkie. For three years we watched Boy descend into drug addiction, stealing to feed his habit.

And, speaking of addiction, for three years we watched President Marcos steal to feed *his* habit. Power. He wanted more of it. And he didn't want to give it up. Elections were generally suspended during martial law. Even when elections were sporadically held, they were just a sham to appease public opinion. Votes were bought, ballet boxes were stuffed, and vote-tallying officials were bribed.

We weren't allowed our summers at the farm. Due to the communist situation and the kidnappings, the farm remained off limits to us for the next two summers. So we stayed in Manila, where it was safe… to learn about heroin and prostitution.

I missed the farm terribly, as if it were my own addiction. I'd gone cold turkey for going on three years. Three years without fields and forests, farm animals, and the smell of cane burning. Just smog, concrete, and sweaty crowds of people. I was suffocating in the city.

And as if from the hot sun hitting the endless pavement, the city itself had become a pressure cooker, the lid tightly screwed on, as the political climate was coming to a boil. The people were at the end of their rope with Marcos's oppression. Political rivals were being deported. People reporting government corruption were disappearing, and the people were getting fed up.

I suppose I'd witnessed the beginning of Marcos's downfall three years earlier, that morning at breakfast on the farm with Papa, seeing Benigno Aquino's assassination all over the front page of the newspaper. That was Marcos's biggest mistake, giving the people a martyr, someone to rally around. Now the Church was forced to take a side. Along with Cardinal Sin, the Church began, subtly at first, then openly from the pulpit as well, and through the media, to criticize Marcos and his cronies. And with Manila being greater than 90 percent Catholic, things quickly began to heat up.

It was my last year of high school. We thought we were all grown up then. Not that you could tell. It was still Catholic school, run by the same nuns. We even wore the same uniforms. Yes, I'm afraid it was still all girls, all God, all the time. I didn't know if I could take it much longer.

We still had Malice to deal with. But to make up for that, Angel seemed to be taking on an even greater influence in our lives. She had really gotten involved in the whole political scene.

"You heard Cardinal Sin," she shouted. "It's up to us to assure a fair election."

Many of my classmates were less than enthusiastic.

"Couldn't we just go shopping?"

Angel was persistent. "Not this time, ladies. We're finally having elections and you know Marcos will be up to his old tricks again. But this time we must stop him from cheating, from stealing this election."

"Borrrrrring," the reply from one girl polishing her nails.

"Maybe you'd prefer to spend the day in Principal Mary Alice's office instead," offered Angel.

The girl scrambled to put her nail polish away and sat up straight. "Reporting for duty Sir, uh, Ma'am. Anything for my country."

A few of us girls had been "volunteered" by Angel to help monitor ballot boxes. After all, the Church had put a lot of effort into supporting Cory Aquino's challenge to Marcos for the presidency. This was no time to lose the election due to ballot tampering. Cory Aquino was Benigno's widow. The people practically forced her to run as the spiritual representation of her martyred husband, the only one with any chance of defeating Marcos in the new elections mandated by our allies, including the United States. She initially feared for her life, but being devoutly religious, she placed her life and the future of her country in the hands of God.

Cardinal Sin and the Church supported her candidacy not with money— that wouldn't have been allowed— but by organizing support for a political campaign, and galvanizing the people on a spiritual level. Well, the people were us.

"I am not chaining myself to a ballot box," insisted Wing, dropping her end of the rusty chain as if it had cooties.

"But what if someone tries to take it and steal the votes, or stuff the box with phony Marcos votes?" I implored, as the church's vote monitors wrapped the chain around my waist along with the others.

"Exactly," answered Wing. "If someone steals the box, I don't want to be attached to it."

She had a point. But we were banking on the hope that ballot stuffers were not the same as kidnappers, and wouldn't steal a box with people actually attached to it. At least that's what I told myself, as I heard the padlock click about my waist.

Wing groaned when she saw the lock close, taking her place on the floor next to me.

"Some friend you are," I chastised. "What good is it to sit here with us if you're not chained to the box."

She was lying on her back, relaxing, with her hands behind her head. "Well, someone's going to have to go for help when Marcos's goons drag the rest of you off with that box."

Again, she had a point.

"Hey Lisa," Wing added as an afterthought, "What happens when you have to pee?"

Everyone chained to the box looked at each other. We hadn't thought of that.

As it turned out, none of our efforts mattered. As the votes across the country were slowly tallied by hand, everything went just as expected. Aquino would get the votes, but the count would go to Marcos.

The elections were stolen and everyone knew it. Votes were bought with cigarettes. Ballot boxes were stuffed or stolen. Vote counters were threatened or simply bought off. Marcos had it all arranged from top to bottom. We never had a chance. The people, that is. Not a chance. All of us cried when we heard. All the volunteers. All the people who believed in righteousness, that good would prevail over evil, that there was a God. And in the Philippines, that meant just about everyone. I like to think that even those induced to support Marcos cried with us. They knew what they did. They were Christians who believed in God too, after all. They must have cried if for nothing but their very souls.

Cardinal Sin and the Catholic Bishops pointed to unprecedented tampering and called on the faithful to resist evil. Soon news media around the world ran headlines reporting massive fraud. The world was watching us. We couldn't go down without a fight. We didn't know how. But we would. Not with guns or fists. It wasn't our way. But somehow, with God's guidance, we wouldn't allow this to go unchallenged.

That's when Marcos made his next mistake. On a tip from informants that his own Defense Minister, Juan Ponce Enrile, and Armed Forces Vice Chief of Staff, General Fidel Ramos were not loyal to him, Marcos ordered their arrests.

Enrile and Ramos were not naive. They knew that even if they weren't murdered in prison, they would never see the light of day again. They knew they were cornered and had no choice but to resist.

That's when Radio Veritas interrupted its broadcast to announce that Enrile and Ramos had broken their allegiance with Marcos and barricaded themselves, along with loyal troops, inside the Ministry of

Defense. They, and their supporters, would hold their positions until they were killed.

Marcos, of course, appeared on government television assuring the public that an attempted coup had been thwarted. Cardinal Sin, as Archbishop of Manila, publicly offered to mediate, in hopes that a peaceful resolution could be reached. But he knew that wouldn't suffice. It would take more than words. That's when the Church went to work. Radio Veritas, our Christian station, was broadcasting information and instructions to the people. All the faithful were implored to go out into the streets to block the movement of any hostile troops attempting to reach the Ministry of Defense.

Being just stupid kids, Wing and I had never seen a war up close. We figured we'd be back in time for dinner. Our folks wouldn't even know we'd gone.

By the time we got there, there were already thousands of people surrounding Camp Crame, Ramos's headquarters, where he, Enrile, and their small loyal force had moved to make their final stand. Priests and nuns seemed to be directing the crowds. People had barricaded the streets with trees, telephone poles, and sand bags. Apparently, the Church didn't fool around.

Everyone had their transistor radios tuned to Radio Veritas, which was receiving anonymous telephone calls with information about troop movements, requests from Enrile and Ramos, and instructions from Cardinal Sin. The people had delivered food and supplies to the rebels. And in true Filipino fashion, where there were crowds and food, there were picnics. In fact, the whole place looked like one huge picnic, like they were waiting for some sort of rock concert to take place. And everyone seemed to be having a great time. That is, until we felt the rumbling. Sitting on the street, everyone could feel them before we could hear or see them. The tanks, that is.

No one said there would be tanks. Just the vibration in the pavement brought the people to their feet. Initially there was just an apprehensive buzz spreading through the crowd. We weren't really sure what was happening. But when the first one came into view at the end of the street, panic ensued. Some people immediately bolted from their position surrounding Camp Crame. Those that remained were all turning this way and that, looking to each other to see who would be next to flee.

Wing clutched my arm. "That's a tank," she noted, as if she were teaching a course on military weaponry.

"I can see that," I replied.

"Let's go," said Wing, tugging on my elbow.

My brain was more than happy to comply, but my legs wouldn't move.

Wing continued. "We are *not* staying here to be run down by tanks. My parents will kill me."

As the distinctive diesel smell of the tanks began to reach us, all of Angel's remarks about democracy and the power of the people were running through my head. Still young, I had yet to come to grips with my mortality, with the idea that I could actually die. I was thinking this thing we were doing was bigger than all of us. This was no time to turn tail and run. Then again, those tanks looked awfully big as they approached us. The crowd compressed itself together out of some instinctive tendency to protect the herd. Everyone was looking about for some sign of leadership.

"Lisa, please. Let's go." Wing was being squeezed up against me.

I'd decided to stay. I'm not entirely sure why. Was it for something I believed in? Or was I just caught up in the moment? I don't know. But I didn't have to drag Wing into it.

"Go ahead, Wing. Go home. Really. You don't need to stay just because I am." I tried to pry her hands from my arm.

"I can't," she said.

"What do you mean? I'm serious. I won't hold it against you. This is crazy. I know. Go home."

"I can't."

I turned away from the oncoming tank to look at her face. "What do you mean, you can't?"

Wing was shaking. "My legs. They won't move."

Our discussion was interrupted when we got shoved from behind. I thought someone was pushing us toward the tanks until I saw the crowd to my right part. A stream of black habits emerged, spreading out in front of the crowd like an armored shell. The nuns had situated themselves between the tanks and the crowd. And who but Sister Angelina would be right in the middle as three monstrous tanks came to a halt right in front of her?

I felt Wing bouncing up and down next to me.

"What are you doing?" I asked her.

"I have to pee."

"You know, you're really pathetic."

I was rolling my eyes at her when the middle tank decided to scare the crowd by revving its engine. It was like a hundred lions roaring. Thick black smoke billowed from its exhaust, the hot air blowing our hair back and choking us as it entered our lungs. They were preparing to run us down.

Wing tugged on my arm again.

"What?" I replied through my smoke filled throat.

"I don't have to pee anymore."

I looked down to see a new puddle at our feet. Wing was so pathetic.

The nuns linked arms, unwilling to yield. Sister Angelina stood right in the middle, holding an image of the Virgin Mary framed by hand-picked flowers. But as troops armed with rifles came from behind the tanks to confront them, another nun arrived, unsteadily pedaling a bicycle, completely out of breath. When she practically fell off the bicycle and turned toward Angel, I couldn't help but gasp in shock. It was Malice. Sister Mary Alice came to join the resistance? Well, no, not exactly. I should have known better.

"Stop this nonsense this very instance," she lectured Angel. "This is no way for nuns to behave, fighting with the army. You're to come home with me immediately." She turned to go, expecting Angel to follow, as the troops began to laugh. When Malice bent to pick up her bicycle she noticed Angel hadn't budged. She dropped the bike and returned to Angel. "This is no place for nuns."

Angel barely acknowledged her, eyes staring straight ahead at the armed men. "This is exactly the place for nuns. With the people. Helping the people."

Malice was furious. "You want to help the people? Convince them to go home. Getting themselves killed doesn't help anyone."

Angel was making a scene, drawing the attention of the troops. And with Malice effectively taking their side, the troops sensed dissention among the ranks. Feeling they might take advantage and exploit that weakness, the apparent leader of the middle tank crew came forward, helmet tipped back, cigarette dangling from an arrogant smirk.

"You there," he addressed Angel. "Why don't you listen to the old penguin? She's lived a long life. Someone who's lived so long must be very wise."

Malice wasn't sure whether to be flattered or insulted. But she didn't want to lose sight of her goal. "Please, Sister Angelina," she pleaded. "Come home." This wasn't the Malice we'd all come to know and hate. She wasn't giving orders or threats. She was pleading. I began to wonder if there might actually be a heart buried somewhere deep under her habit.

Whether Angel was wondering the same thing or not made no difference. Her reply made her position clear. "No."

The armed man took a step forward to where the bullets strapped across his chest actually touched Angel's habit. He pulled the cigarette from his mouth and deliberately blew smoke in her face. Angel squinted and struggled not to cough.

"Please, please," implored Sister Mary Alice, "leave her alone. Don't hurt her. Let me talk to her."

"You'd better talk fast," the man replied, staring down into Angel's eyes.

Sister Mary Alice was frantic. "Sister Angelina. I'm begging you. Let the military do their job. It's not your place to fight them. Come home with me and we'll pray. Let's pray that this all comes to a peaceful end."

Angel would not take her eyes from the man to look at her. "I have no intention of fighting. And I *am* praying. All of us here are praying for a peaceful end to this. But I'm praying right here. We're not going anywhere. We're taking a stand."

Sister Mary Alice made the sign of the cross on her chest and began to cry. It was true. She *was* old. She'd seen many things in her life. She lived through the Japanese occupation of the Philippines during World War II. She'd seen much killing in her life. She'd seen the atrocities that armies were capable of. She touched the soldier's arm, imploring him with her eyes not to harm Angel.

The military man remained smug. After all, he had nothing to fear. With a smile on his lips, he removed his helmet and reached around Angel, placing it on her back as if to embrace her.

"Do not worry, old penguin," he assured Sister Mary Alice. "You see, I'm a lover, not a fighter." And with that, he lowered his helmet to Angel's bottom and pulled her forward, obscenely grinding his hips into hers. The image of the Virgin she carried fell to the ground and shattered among the flowers that framed it.

The crowd of nuns and churchgoers about her were shocked at the behavior of this man toward a nun. Yet, they were afraid, and no one took any action. No one except Angel, that is. Almost simultaneously, she spit in the soldier's face and did what any father would expect his daughter to do under similar circumstances. She rammed her knee up between his legs with every ounce of strength she could muster.

As the soldier doubled over in agony, his army mates sprang to attention, their trained reflexes kicking in to counterattack in the face of an enemy assault. However, once the initial reflex came and went, they could no longer help but snicker at their leader's misfortune. Getting kneed in the groin by a nun wasn't something they got to see every day.

I wasn't the only one who'd begun to think I'd made a big mistake joining the resisters. It appeared this wasn't going to be a picnic after all. Witnessing the confrontation between Angel and the soldier, everyone in the crowd looked to each other to see who would be the first to turn and run. I'm sure some of us were simply frozen with fear. But most, I would say, stood their ground in support of the nuns, firm in the knowledge that God would watch over all of us.

The soldier, doubled over from the pain in his groin, didn't care who was watching over the one responsible for his discomfort. He no longer saw the black and white habit. He no longer saw the cross about her neck. He only saw red. Red fury. And without a thought for how many commandments he might be breaking, he raised the butt of his rifle and struck Angel in the head. He didn't mean to kill her. But he didn't mean not to either. And by the way she collapsed to the ground, we were certain that that's what he'd done. I don't know who screamed louder, Wing, or me, as our own legs buckled and we fell to our knees.

The screaming wasn't over. The next one was louder than both of ours together and shook us from our state of shock like a bucket of ice water. It was a scream from somewhere so deep in the soul that it didn't even sound human. I looked toward the source just in time to see Sister Mary Alice launch herself at the offending soldier. Her black habit engulfed him like some sort of angel of death, as she clawed at his eyes, saliva flying from her screaming mouth like a rabid dog. She'd completely snapped. Sister Mary Alice, the strict disciplinarian seconds before, advocating nonviolence and retreat in the face of danger, had just thrown herself into hand-to-hand combat with an armed soldier.

It was over before any of the stunned crowd could react. Malice collapsed on the ground next to Angel after suffering a similar blow to the head. We couldn't really tell, but for all appearances, they'd both been killed.

The crowd surged forward in response to the brutality inflicted upon the two nuns. Those of us in front, seeing the troops ready their weapons, knew it wasn't going to end well. Someone had to stop this.

Don't ask me how it happened. I don't remember. But still in shock from the sight of my two teachers crumpled on the ground, blinded by tears, I found myself standing out in front, facing the crowd with my hands raised.

"Stop!"

I didn't think they would. I didn't think anything. And I didn't know what I would say next. I just did it. Something inside of me snapped and made me act. The funny thing was, the crowd actually listened. They stopped. At least for the moment. Everyone was looking for a leader, starving for someone to just tell them what to do. They just hadn't expected it to be a 17-year-old girl in a high school uniform. Well, neither did I. And I had no idea what to do next.

"They've killed two nuns!" someone shouted. "We cannot allow it. If we charge them all at once, they can't kill us all. God will protect us." There was some grumbling of support for the idea, but no one quite ready to pull the trigger. The troops, on the other hand, were perfectly willing, as they raised their rifles.

I didn't know what to say. I didn't have the words. Another voice from the crowd rang out.

"Let's do it! It's now or never! God's on our side! They'll go to hell for killing the nuns!" The crowd surged a step forward toward me.

Someone sent words to my mouth and out they came. "Then let them go to hell! Let God take them! But not us. Not by our hands. Don't do this," I pleaded. I knew I'd taken my last shot. I didn't have any experience at crowd control. I didn't even know how to relate to these people, the masses, people who'd suffered the effects of the Marcos regime. Until the recent events at the farm, none of this had ever touched my life. Though I hadn't realized it until then, I wasn't one of them. I was just another spoiled rich kid. Marcos's evil had never touched me. I didn't know hunger. My family had no trouble earning a living. No one I'd ever personally known was jailed or killed by Marcos cronies. And I think they could sense it. They must have looked at me in my private school uniform and thought, who was I to advise them? What did I know about what was at stake here? Maybe I was just a plant by Marcos to keep them under control. Maybe I was a Marcos crony. I saw the way they began to look at me. They were about to run me over. I was losing them. I knew it was going to take something else. Someone else. One of them.

Then it started. Someone lunged out from the crowd. I heard the soldiers cocking their rifles. I covered my face and head with my arms, preparing to be trampled by the crowd, or shot by the soldiers. I prepared to die.

It seemed like a lifetime waiting for the inevitable. What was taking so long? Why wasn't I dead already? I opened one eye and saw the crowd right where I'd left them. Why hadn't they moved, followed the lead of whoever had lunged forward? Where had that person gone? I heard scrabbling at my feet and looked down to see a man gathering the flowers from Angel's shattered image of the Virgin. What was he doing? Why was he gathering flowers at a time like this? He quickly stood up and began handing the flowers out to all the nuns and young girls at the front of the crowd. He was quietly saying something to each of them as he did so. He finally turned to me, holding out the last flower.

"Give it to the soldiers," he said.

I was staring at the flower. Why did he want us to give them to the soldiers? I looked up at him to ask that very question. That's when I saw his face. I should have known. My life was in danger. Who else would it be?

"What are you doing here?" I asked.

It was Johnny.

Chapter 10

It had been nearly three years since I'd been to the farm. Three years since the summer of the mysterious Johnny, all the intrigue that surrounded him, and oh yes, that silly schoolgirl crush I'd had on him. I didn't know how he happened to turn up at the rally. And I really didn't expect him, under the circumstances, to explain it all as we stood facing a wall of army tanks. But there was one thing I couldn't help but notice, despite the madness of the situation I found myself in.

God, he was beautiful. He'd filled out since I'd last seen him. The gangly 17-year-old had grown into a 20-year-old man. Pounds of muscle, earned slaving at the farm, had appeared in just the right places. Even his beautiful boyish face had morphed into that of a virile young man. Testosterone was a beautiful thing. The gorgeous blue eyes remained unchanged, though. And as mine stared into his, I thought, for the briefest of moments, that I'd seen something in his gaze I'd never seen before. Could it have been more than his usual protective look of a big brother, of a babysitter watching over the child in his care? Could I have detected something more this time? Maybe he'd noticed some changes that had taken place in *me* over the past three years. I was 17 now. Maybe *I* hadn't noticed the subtle changes in myself over time. But surely a man would notice the difference between a silly young girl and a woman. After all, I suppose I'd filled out as well. The little bumps on my chest had certainly come into their own, cleavage and all. And somewhere I'd found hips to match. I'd even started using some make-up when not at school, lipstick accentuating my already full lips. In fact, I'm not even sure he recognized me until that moment when our eyes locked. That shared gaze that seemed to go on forever actually only lasted a couple of seconds, as there wasn't any time to lose.

"Go on. Give them to the soldiers," he repeated gently, now face to face.

In my trance, I'd forgotten to wonder why anymore. Instead I walked right up to one of the soldiers with his rifle drawn and placed one of the little flowers right in the open barrel of the gun.

Apparently it was something Johnny'd remembered as a child when he first went to the States toward the end of the Vietnam War, the flower children trying to pacify the National Guard. I don't know how successful the plan was back in the States, but here in the Philippines the effect was immediate. The troops had no desire to shoot their own people. All devout Catholics, they certainly had no intention of shooting nuns. And, of course, being not much more than boys themselves, a flower from a pretty girl was, after all, a flower from a pretty girl. The soldiers' stares quickly transformed from nervous anger to tentative smiles. Soon, despite the barking of their leader, they'd lowered their rifles and brought the flowers to their noses, infectious grins breaking out as they began to joke with each other about whose came from the prettier girl. Even those who'd received flowers from the nuns couldn't hide embarrassed little smiles. After all, these were Filipinos. And, like I said, except for the communists, we all love to smile.

And that's how it went. All around us, as men set up roadblocks to slow the advance of the tanks, women, children, and nuns confronted the troops head on with smiles, hugs, and flowers. Although most of the troops held their ground, unwilling to go AWOL, many actually took part in the spontaneous sprouting of picnics breaking out all about the grounds surrounding Camp Crame where the rebels held out.

Yet it wasn't over by any means, as more and more troops reported to the area, and Marcos plotted how he would snatch the rebels from their hide out. He was already speaking with the Air Force, planning an aerial assault. And I overheard a soldier's radio squawking something about orders to shut down the propaganda coming out of Radio Veritas. Yet, on the ground anyway, things seemed to be at a standoff, for the time being.

Angel and Malice weren't dead after all. Just really bad headaches when they regained consciousness. There'd been an awful lot of praying for them on their behalf. In the face of so much prayer, the saints couldn't let them die. I suggested Wing accompany them to the hospital, giving her an excuse to gracefully bow out of the mayhem and head home after the hospital. I saw the thanks in her eyes for the reprieve and she promised to tell my mom I was OK.

Through her tears of concern for the two nuns, I don't think Wing even noticed that it was Johnny urging us to hand out the flowers. And if she'd had second thoughts about leaving me behind, and turned back to me to say so, it would have been too late anyway. I was already gone. It wasn't a conscious decision on my part to follow him. I just did it. Like when two powerful magnets come close enough together, it's too late for one to just turn and go the other way. Instead, they're irresistibly drawn together and practically impossible to separate.

"Where are you going?" I asked him, struggling a bit to keep up.

"You'd better go home," he replied without slowing. "I think you've seen enough action for one day."

"But I want to help," I said, tugging at his arm.

Johnny stopped and turned. At first it was the same old Johnny, looking at me as if he were preparing to scold a disobedient child. But as soon as our eyes met, I saw his expression change. I could tell he saw it immediately. He could see I wasn't a child anymore. I was a woman. And looking back at him, I saw something else. Something unfamiliar to me. It was a look I'd never seen before in a man. I don't know how to explain it. It was a confusing mixture of possessive protectiveness tempered with surrender. Like wanting to hold and shelter something you had no power over, yet worse. As if that thing had power over you. That's what it was. I saw some sort of surrender in his eyes, an acknowledgement of this power I held. Held over him. That was new to me. That feeling of power over a man, just because I was a woman. It was confusing to me. And in the few seconds it all took place, I didn't have time to analyze it. But I instinctively knew it was a power not to be abused, to be thrown about frivolously. It came with responsibility. And more, it didn't exist in a vacuum either. For as I saw that look of surrender in Johnny's eyes, I felt something I couldn't deny. And that was the spell it cast on me. Oh I knew I'd always been attracted to him since first sight. But it was that look from him now that ended my schoolgirl crush. That look of surrender. And with it, he'd captured me. You see, it goes both ways. Seeing this beautiful man surrender to me, I knew it wasn't just *him* under *my* power, but *me* under *his* as well.

"OK. Come on," he said as he turned and continued walking.

"Where?"

"To the radio station," he replied without slowing.

"Veritas?"

"Didn't you hear that soldier's radio? They're planning to shut the station down."

"So? Why's that so important?" I asked.

"You're what, a senior in high school now?"

I was impressed he knew my age. "Yeah. So?"

"Haven't you learned the importance of the media? Of information? How information is power? Marcos is already broadcasting his victory over the rebels on the government run station. Only Radio Veritas is broadcasting the truth, that the rebels, backed by the people, stand firm. And more than that, Veritas is reporting troop movements and relaying information between the rebels and the people. The rebels are calling in to the station to get their message out and instruct the people on how best to help."

On our way to the station, I listened to Johnny's lecture on propaganda and the media, on how communist and fascist governments control the people through the media. I learned what Johnny was doing in Manila. He was going to college. And he'd picked up a particular interest in Sociology and Political Science. I didn't have a chance yet to find out how he'd managed to be going to college, what with being a "slave" and all, when we arrived at the radio station.

When we got to the station, there wasn't any sign of troops yet. And I certainly didn't want to be there when they arrived.

"We'd better hurry, Johnny. Let's just warn them and leave, before the troops show up."

Johnny felt the same way as he impatiently kept poking the up button as if to summon the elevator faster.

It seemed like a lifetime had passed by the time the elevator deposited us on the tenth floor of the building that housed Radio Veritas. An extremely nervous Father Manolo, well known as the anchor of the Christian station, looked up from his microphone when he saw us enter the studio. I think he instinctively already knew the danger he'd placed himself in, aiding and abetting the anti-Marcos rebels. Seeing that we appeared to be harmless, he threw us a nervous smile and indicated we should take a seat while he wrapped up his current broadcast. Afterward, he removed his headphones and wiped the beads of sweat from his forehead.

"Thank God. I thought it was the military when I saw the door open," he said, relieved that it was otherwise. You could see the tension dissipate as he leaned back in his chair, still somewhat shaken by our intrusion.

Johnny didn't want to waste any more time. "That's why we're here. We heard on one of the troop radios that orders have been given to shut you down."

Father Manolo smiled. "Well I knew they'd come eventually. It was just a matter of time."

Johnny wasn't one to give up so easily. "But we've got to stop them. You've got to remain on the air."

"And how do you suppose we stop them? Counting the two of you, there are only three of us. We can't fight them."

"Call for help. Broadcast it. Tell the people to surround the station. We can't allow our only source of information and communication to be shut down."

Father Manolo explained. "The people are needed over at Camp Crame. I knew they'd shut me down eventually. But I thought if I kept a low profile, kept the crowds away, it would take some time for the military to recognize I was an important target. I didn't think I'd have even as much time as I've had."

The Father was a man resigned to the fact that his contribution to the fight would be limited. He'd known it was only a matter of time. And like the good martyr, he'd serve the people until he was silenced, until the microphone was ripped from his hand. He'd planned all along to go down with the ship. Only then would he feel he'd given his all. And if things got ugly, if he were hurt or killed in the process, so be it. He wasn't afraid of death.

As Johnny pleaded with the Father to call for help, I'd wandered over to the window to take in the view. "We're too late," I said, looking down at the street.

Johnny ran to the window. "What do you mean?"

"They're here. The troops," I answered, pointing down at the ants swarming about the entrance to the building.

Father Manolo, seeming almost relieved that his path to martyrdom was nearing its conclusion, joined us at the window. "You two had better go. There's still time to get out before they catch you with me in the studio."

Johnny turned to me. "You'd better go, Lisa. I'll stay with Father Manolo."

Father Manolo objected even before I had a chance. "Stay here? For what purpose? Do you plan to single-handedly fight off armed troops? Don't be ridiculous."

Johnny wasn't easily dissuaded. "I'll help barricade the door. I can at least stall them. Every minute helps." Turning back to me, "Go, Lisa."

I didn't understand the plan. Johnny wasn't making any sense. Staring back into his eyes, there was one thing I knew I did understand. "I'm not leaving without you."

Johnny froze. "Lisa, please. Don't be silly. You're not a kid anymore. Don't act like one."

If the situation wasn't so desperate, if I'd had the time, I'd have been furious at Johnny's comments, suggesting that I was acting like a child. Who the hell did he think he was? But there wasn't any time. So I let it go and calmly repeated my decision.

"I'm not leaving without you."

I could tell he was angry with me. He was gritting his teeth, squeezing his hands into fists, no, not to punch me, but to keep himself from spanking me.

"I can't just give up like this, Lisa, I've got to stay." He was ready to pull his hair out.

"Then so am I."

* * * *

I imagine the whole country had their radios tuned to Veritas when Father Manolo resumed what would be his last broadcast.

"This is Father Manolo at Radio Veritas." There was a pause for a deep breath. "I'm afraid I must announce that this appears to be my final broadcast."

I'm sure people throughout the Philippines, ears glued to their radios, were looking at each other, mouths open in astonishment.

"Government troops are entering the ground floor of the building as I'm speaking to you. And I'm pretty sure they're not here to compliment me on my coverage of the events unfolding before you. On the contrary, it's abundantly clear that they're here to silence Radio Veritas, the voice of the people."

There was a brief pause.

"We've disabled the elevator, but I can hear them storming up the stairwell. I don't know how many there are, but it won't take many to get the job done. I am, of course, unarmed. I have no use for weapons. I have no intention of fighting anyone. I am confident the Lord will protect me. And should he choose to bring me home, I'm not afraid to die, not in the line of duty, doing God's work."

Over the father's broadcast, one could clearly hear that the troops had arrived. There were shouts, demanding to be allowed in. They were pounding at the door which Father Manolo had no intention of opening. Instead, he continued his farewell address, sounding completely calm and deliberate.

"It sounds as though my guests have arrived. I hope they'll forgive my lack of hospitality, but I still have a few things to say to you. Don't worry about me. I am not afraid. I shall be content to die for this great country of ours, for what's right, for the people, and in the name of God. You must all carry on the fight. Not with your fists, but with your voices and smiles. Do not despair. You are not alone. Now let us pray."

With that, over the sounds of troops smashing down the door, Father Manolo recited the Lord's Prayer. "Our Father, who art in heaven—"

He was soon interrupted by a crashing sound, and shouts from the invaders to cease broadcasting. After the microphone was yanked from his hands, only garbled sounds of the father resisting could be heard over the noise of the troops filling the studio. Apparently he'd been able to reach for one last button as the Filipino national anthem began playing, sung in the traditional Filipino dialect of Tagalog. Over the chords of the national anthem, could be heard the sounds of troops smashing equipment. Distinctly absent, was the voice of Father Manolo. Ultimately, there was one final crashing sound, followed briefly by screeching audio feedback, then silence, deafening silence.

* * * *

Listeners throughout the Philippines tapped and shook their radios in disbelief. Radio Veritas had been silenced. It's been said the whole country cried at that moment, the moment when the voice of the people was silenced. The people felt lost amid that silence, as everyone in their homes, their cars, or even with their transistor radios surrounding Camp Crame, suddenly felt alone. They didn't know what was going on. They didn't know what to do. Johnny'd been right about the importance of the media. The only live media left was the government-run stations on both radio and television, but no one had any interest in propaganda about a small insignificant band of rabble about to be squashed by the mighty Marcos authority. They knew in their hearts that such reports were ridiculous. The cat was out of the bag. They'd already been made aware of just how big a movement it was, that the government was teetering on collapse. But now, without Veritas, without a way to get the message out, the revolution was in danger of fizzling.

That's why, after hours of radio silence, a little before midnight, when a small and shaky voice resumed broadcasting for Radio Veritas, that small spark lit up the whole country with renewed hope.

Father Manolo hadn't been hurt. But he was taken into custody when the troops destroyed the radio station. But it wasn't Father Manolo who'd resumed the broadcast.

"Hello? Test, test. Hello? I hope someone can hear me," the frightened high-pitched voice began.

Across the country, people were turning up their radios to hear what was interrupting the steady hiss of the ominously silent Radio Veritas.

The little voice continued. "I don't think I'm doing this right. Did I press the right button?"

"Go ahead. You're on," came another voice a distance away from the microphone.

"It's on? You mean people can hear me? Oh shit! Oops. Sorry. What should I say?"

There was a muffled sound as a hand covered the microphone, and a brief garbled discussion took place.

"OK. Here goes. Hello everyone. For Radio Veritas, this is Lisa Ro—"

"No, no, no," interrupted the other voice. "Don't give them your full name. And put your headphones on."

"Oh. OK, Johnny. Eh hem. This is, uh, Lisa, for Radio Veritas. We're back on the air."

That's right. No bullshit. It was me.

I guess when I made it clear to Johnny that I wasn't leaving without him, he did the only thing he could to protect me from the troops. He took me by the hand and we left by the back stairway. We tried to get Father Manolo to see the futility of staying, but he wouldn't hear of it. So we ultimately took his advice to save ourselves.

But by Johnny's determined stride, I knew this was only a temporary retreat. He had something else in mind. And as we entered the University of the Philippines, I was able to catch my breath enough to start asking questions again. Besides his other coursework at the University, Johnny was taking a class in communications. And as part of that class, he had been volunteering at the college radio station. After learning the basics of operating the station and broadcasting, he even served as disc jockey once a week on his own show which he called, what else but, Rebel Yell, a commercial-free hour dedicated to southern rock music.

When we got to the station, no one was there. I guess everyone had gone to the rallies at Camp Crame and elsewhere. Johnny had a key and unlocked the darkened office. It took a while to get things up and running by himself, but it was only a matter of time before we began broadcasting in the name of Radio Veritas. I was enlisted as the announcer mostly because I didn't have the technical know how to do anything else. Besides, Johnny knew exactly what needed to happen and relayed instructions to me from the engineer's booth through my headphones.

"I'd first like to ask that everyone pray for the safety of Father Manolo who valiantly kept Veritas on the air as long as physically possible, until Marcos's troops literally smashed the station to pieces.

Please bear with me as I'm new to this, and to be honest, I have no idea what I'm doing. But my faithful engineer is telling me we need to start with a few announcements.

First of all, I can't tell you where we're broadcasting from, for obvious reasons. But I will give you a phone number where you can reach us with any information that needs to be disseminated. I would just ask that anyone familiar with that number and knowing where it's located, please be cool and don't blab it around, as I'd rather not get arrested, or shot for that matter."

We didn't think anyone other than students would know where the number came from. And maybe we were being reckless with our safety, but we took the calculated risk that any college student familiar with the phone number at the college radio station would be a supporter of the insurgency.

The phone began ringing instantly and didn't stop for a couple of hours. The first few calls were calls of gratitude for our carrying the Veritas torch and prayers for our safety. But it wasn't long before things got serious.

I saw Johnny's eyes grow wide and he started waving to me frantically.

"Who?" I asked, always forgetting which button to press so the audience couldn't hear me. "No really. That's not funny." I saw a look on Johnny's face that made it clear he wasn't fooling around. Next thing I knew, I could hear him putting the caller on the air with me. "Uh, hello?" I began. "General Ramos?"

"Yes. Hello. This is General Ramos. Am I on the air?"

I looked to Johnny who nodded his head in confirmation.

"Uh, yes sir, you're on the air."

"Hello Lisa." I almost freaked out when I heard General Ramos say my name. That was so cool. But I somehow managed to pull it together. The general continued. "I'm calling to appeal to all my colleagues in the military to join us in attempting to take our country back. Mr. Marcos has been allowed to pillage this country and its people long enough. To line his pockets with gold. To buy Imelda's shoes. I appeal to your loyalty to me as your commander, to the military, and to your country. Now is the time to join forces and do the right thing."

The general went on to address particular officers by name in personal appeals asking for their assistance in this time of need. He also gave specific tactical instructions on how best to support the insurgents. That was to be only the first of many calls from General Ramos throughout the night.

Other callers, I remember, did not rank quite so highly in importance. There was a call from someone looking for someplace that would take an order for one hundred pizzas to be delivered to the crowds gathered outside Camp Crame. There was a call from a pizza place looking to fill the order. There was even a request for the song "Free Bird," by one of Johnny's favorites, Lynyrd Skynyrd.

But mostly they were calls relaying troop movements, and calls directing people volunteering to aid the insurgency where they were most needed. I took a call from a former US Special Forces member on how best to make a barricade out of a bus by flattening the tires and turning it on its side. Instructions on how to handle tear gas by staying low, covering the face with a wet towel or shirt, and neutralizing the canister in a bucket of water, were particularly appreciated.

It was a very long night. I thought it would never end. But after the initial barrage of calls making up for the time lost while Veritas was down, the stretches between calls grew longer, and finding myself alone with Johnny, I began to wish morning would never come. We had turned off all the lights so as not to attract the attention of any patrolling troops that might be seeking the new source of Radio Veritas. Feeling a bit ripe from the events of the day, and more than a little hungry, we each took an improvised shower in the office water fountain, broke into a candy machine down the hall, and feeling a bit renewed, ventured out onto the 20th story balcony outside the studio to catch some fresh air. There was a balmy breeze, and the view of the city lights under the starry night was phenomenal. We could see some of the smaller crowds of people manning various barricades set up throughout the city to impede the troops. More than one bonfire could be seen burning amid the city streets. Periodically, we could hear the thumping of government helicopters overhead.

Maybe it was the events of the day. Maybe it was the idea that, at any moment, government troops could break down the door and drag us away. Maybe it was just being alone with Johnny again. Maybe it was the stolen candy. I don't know. But what ever it was, I was all wound up. It was 2 a.m. and I was wide-awake.

Like new parents listening for the stirring of a sleeping newborn, we kept one ear out for the studio telephone. And with the other, Johnny and I caught up on things since we'd last seen each other. Nervous and awkward at first, it had been three years after all, that was quickly overcome by our, what I assumed to be mutual, attraction.

He was just getting to the part where he proudly told me how Captain had given him greater and greater responsibility on the farm and how he could pretty much run the place himself if he had to, when he creased his brow and abruptly stopped.

"What's is it?" I asked. "What's wrong?"

He stared at me silently for a bit while I tried to read his mind.

"None of it matters," he said.

"What do you mean? It sounds like you're doing really well. Remember when you thought you were just a slave?"

"Is it really that different?" he began. "No matter what I do, I'll never be anything more than the hired help."

"But you're going to college. Now you can do anything you want."

"You think that's how it works? Maybe in the States. But not here. Not in the Philippines."

"What do you mean?"

"I'm not like you. I'm from the wrong side of the tracks. I'm not from the right family. No one will ever give me a real chance to be anything but the help."

I never thought about it before, but he was probably right. I felt terrible for him. I wanted to take him in my arms and make everything all better. "Even with college?"

"Sometimes I think college makes it worse," he continued. "I mean, it's not that I'm not thankful for everything the Delgados have done for me. They've been wonderful, paying for everything. I guess they saw promise in me. But I never wanted to be some kind of charity case like one of those golf caddies back in Bais. It's just that it's given me a taste of something I can never really have, seeing all these college kids from well-to-do families following their dreams."

Maybe I couldn't really relate to someone from the other side of the tracks, but I thought I knew Johnny. No, not as if I'd known him for years. Not like that. It had only been one brief summer, after all. But I'd looked into his eyes. I'd seen it. And I knew it. He wasn't one to give up so easily. Not Johnny. Johnny was a fighter. And I wasn't going to let him off so easily.

"So why do you stay?" I challenged him. "Why don't you just go back to the farm?"

I could tell I'd hit a sore spot, which was right where I'd been aiming. I guess it was OK for *him* to talk about giving up. But when *I* suggested it, he seemed offended.

"I've got my reasons," he muttered.

"What reasons?"

"You wouldn't understand," he answered. And before I could walk away, now myself offended, he grabbed me by the hands and continued. "I didn't mean it that way," he pleaded. "Not like you're stupid or something. It's just, just that, I mean, coming from your family, I don't think you can really relate to what it must feel like being poor, with all its limitations, its lack of opportunity. That's why I'm here, at college. I'm not just studying Business Management and how to run a cane farm. I'm taking advantage of everything else they have to offer here that I'll never get another chance to experience. I'm taking all sorts of courses in Philosophy, Sociology, and Political Science. This isn't the only country that's ever had class struggles. I've learned about propaganda and the value of mass media, passive resistance, even revolution. You know Marx and the communists weren't all wrong. And I know your family would disagree, but I'm not sure land reform is such a bad idea."

I had to interject. "You think my family would disagree? That's the understatement of the century. Don't you dare say any such thing in front of Papa. You'll give him a heart attack. That is, if he didn't kill you first."

I had to admit that three years ago, none of this would have made any sense to me. I didn't know I was rich or privileged. I didn't even know there were poor people in the Philippines. I was an idiot. But that was before. I'd seen a few things since then.

I didn't have to say anything. I just squeezed Johnny's hands and looked into his eyes. I think he knew I understood now. And with that knowledge, standing hand in hand on the starlit balcony, looking into each other's eyes, I guess he couldn't help himself. He bent his head to mine, and kissed me. No, not like he might have three years ago, on the forehead, like I was his little sister or something. Not this time. This time it was on the lips, at first soft, then harder, like a man would to a woman. And as he did, my entire being went into that kiss. The world around me was forgotten. The rich. The poor. My world. His world. The revolution going on all around us. It all melted away as I felt my lips part and our tongues meet, our separate worlds melding into one. Not mine, not his, but ours.

Soon we were no longer holding hands as I reached up around his broad shoulders, and his powerful arms encased me, crushing my body to his until I couldn't breath. It didn't matter. Who needed air? I was already in heaven. Not dead, but alive, like I'd never been alive before. And when Johnny's hand found it's way to my breast, it was electric. There was an ache I'd never known as his lips nuzzled my neck and his warm breath sent ripples down my body.

I don't recall him opening my blouse or even removing my bra, but when he gently took my breast in his hand and teased the nipple between his teeth, I saw stars behind my closed lids, and found myself short of breath. I began to feel a warmth between my legs I'd never known before. And it seemed to spread downward, melting whatever muscles were holding me up. Johnny caught me in his arms and gently laid me down on the floor of the balcony. As his lips went back to my mouth and neck, I could feel his hardness against my thigh, that same hardness that only briefly touched me three years prior, in the water outside the hidden cave. Only this time, he didn't pull away, but instead, pressed harder against me. And it felt right, more right than anything I'd ever known. Without thinking, I reached down between his legs. I wanted to take it in my hand. And when I did, I felt Johnny tense up in surprise, but only for a moment, as he just as quickly surrendered to my touch. My inexperienced hand was taken aback by his size. And from what I'd heard about where it was supposed to go, I couldn't imagine how it could possibly fit. Not that I was concerned. After all, my brain wasn't running the show anymore. My body was. And judging by the reaction my body was having, it seemed to suggest all systems were go, and accommodating Johnny's ample size wasn't going to pose any problem at all.

I didn't know what was going on in Johnny's mind, or whether, like me, everything was now running on autopilot. But I guess my hand between his legs was all the signal his body needed to advance things to the next level. I don't even remember him removing the rest of my clothes, everything but my panties. And all I remember about undressing him was, realizing, like an idiot, why I couldn't get his pants off. I finally figured out that I'd have to remove his shoes first. Serves me right for not reading the manual.

I wanted him so badly. I wanted, no, I **needed** him. Inside me. I needed him so badly that I thought I heard ringing in my ears. I had no idea you could get ringing in your ears just from being horny. But I did. I could hear it. Johnny must have heard it too, because he suddenly stopped what he was doing, and his head jerked up as if listening for something. That's when we both heard it together. The telephone. It was the fucking telephone. I couldn't believe it. I was sex-crazed out of my mind and about to lose my virginity when the fucking telephone rang with some kind of life and death call concerning the damned revolution.

Johnny and I briefly looked at each other, wanting to remember the moment, not wanting to lose our place. But we knew it couldn't wait. We just had to get that phone. I don't know who groaned louder as we disengaged and Johnny ran back inside the studio to answer the call.

"This had better be good," I remember him saying as I found myself alone on the balcony, on my back, catching my breath.

Apparently it was indeed a matter of life and death. Word on the street was that additional troops were headed toward Camp Crame. But this time they had orders to storm the compound and take the rebels dead or alive. The people were only there for passive resistance. They knew they'd have no chance fighting an armed military. And yet, reports of people getting hurt, not killed, but hurt, were starting to flow in. It was usually a matter of rifle butt versus civilian head. And it was the head that always seemed to get the worst of it.

General Ramos made several more calls appealing to military officers to join him or it would be the blood of brother Filipinos they would be spilling.

Before we knew it, it was about 5 a.m. and we sadly reported that troops were advancing with tear gas. We could hear the cries from people over the telephone. Ramos had to cut off his final call to me, saying, "I cannot talk any longer. We are about to be attacked."

I knew there were people all over the city clutching their rosaries and holding high their images of Christ and the Blessed Virgin. When the phones grew silent I played the national anthem one last time. It was 5:45 a.m., and, while waiting for the sun to rise, all I could do was urge everyone to pray.

Johnny and I could see troops down in the street below our building. We didn't know if they'd discovered our position, where we'd been broadcasting from. They might have been preparing to storm the building any minute. But there wasn't anything we could do about that now.

Johnny did answer one final call. "Don't broadcast this one," he said to me.

"What do you mean, don't broadcast this one?" I asked, confused.

"It's for you. It's personal"

"What? Who is it?" I asked.

"It's from your house. It's your yaya."

"My yaya?"

"Yup. And she's pissed. She was hollerin' at me."

"What does she want?"

"She says for you to go home."

* * * *

I didn't go home. The soldiers didn't storm the radio station. And I don't know when we fell asleep. I guess it was from complete exhaustion, combined with the feeling that we'd been defeated, that Marcos would almost assuredly crush the small band of rebels at

Camp Crame, along with any unarmed civilians that might get in the way.

But what we didn't know was that while we slept, the desperate appeals by General Ramos, voiced through our broadcast, had indeed struck a chord with the military. After all, they felt a stronger allegiance to General Ramos than they did to Marcos. And they were Catholic. The very idea of harming unarmed fellow Filipinos, let alone defenseless nuns, rang as distinctly unchristian to them.

So when the final orders came to charge the crowd of people surrounding Camp Crame, they did so. Only not with clubs and bayonets, but with smiles. They moved into the crowd with knowing grins. And the screaming of women and children among the crowd soon stopped as everyone realized the troops were only pretending to strike them. Clubs didn't even come close. Bayonets were falling off guns. And the troops were laughing. Soon the crowd was too, as they embraced the soldiers, their fellow Filipinos.

From within Camp Crame, helicopters could be heard overhead. And like the crowd outside, the rebels assumed the end was near. The Air Force would make short work of them. But they also had underestimated the effect of Ramos's appeals. The Air Force had defected. And when the choppers landed inside the camp without firing a shot, and the smiling pilots emerged, they were engulfed in a sea of tears and friendly embraces.

It all happened so quickly. Marcos was in the middle of a live television broadcast over channel 4 reporting that the rebels were about to be crushed when television screens all across the Philippines went black. By the time they came back on, channel 4 was under the control of the rebels and Marcos had already fled the country.

As the bright sun of a new day lit up the balcony outside the college radio station, I awoke in Johnny's arms. I wasn't yet aware of the final turn of events that had taken place after we'd surrendered to sheer exhaustion and dozed off. All I knew was that it felt right, me in Johnny's arms, that is. I didn't want to move or do anything that might wake him and spoil it.

So when the phone began ringing again, I cursed it. I didn't know it was good news. I didn't know we'd won, that we'd awoken to a new government, a new Philippines. There'd been a successful, virtually bloodless revolution, something only possible in the Philippines. Our new president, Mrs. Corazon Aquino, would be inaugurated soon thereafter.

Chapter 11

Marcos may not have survived the revolution. But my virginity did. I know, I know. It was all so romantic. Revolution. That starlit night on the balcony, all to ourselves, overlooking the city. Clothes peeled away. The heat of our bodies feeding off each other. We were so close. I could practically hear the violins playing. And then that damned telephone. My country and its pesky revolution just couldn't wait. Like a newborn baby, it was only concerned with its own needs. But what about mine? Johnny had me right where I wanted him. And I was ready. He was the one. The time was right. But it wasn't to be. The moment had come and gone.

What about the next day, or the day after that, you might ask? Well just because I'd practically single-handedly overthrown the evil Marcos regime and freed my country from the yoke of oppression didn't prevent me from being grounded for a whole month for staying out all night without letting anyone know where I was, especially on a night when the air was filled with the sound of tanks and the stench of tear gas. Fruitless pleas over the telephone to Papa couldn't get him to change my mom's mind. Even the maids, who usually took my side and normally would have covered for me in the event of any unexplained absences, supported the ruling by not letting me sneak out. I think my yaya, the one who recognized my voice and called the radio station, was even more upset than my mom.

I guess by the time the month had passed, so had the moment. It was practically impossible to even find Johnny again. He'd become so involved in the post-revolution politics that he didn't seem to have much time for me. The massive white-hot flames of revolution made our little game out on the balcony seem like the lonely little candle on a baby's first birthday cake, snuffed out in a breath of laughter. I felt like his head had been turned by another woman, like he was cheating on me. I know it sounds crazy. But I guess that's how love makes you. Crazy.

Besides, I figured this revolution stuff would eventually cool off. Maybe I'd finally get to go back to the farm again this coming summer. Then we'd both be there, away from Manila and its politics. Then we'd have our chance, Johnny and I.

Sure enough, I did get to return to the farm that summer. I told my mom that it couldn't possibly be any less safe than Manila, and she fell for it.

After being away in Manila so long, the ride to the farm from the airport was like diving into the cool aqua ocean after baking in the sweltering heat of the sun. The fresh air, the lush foliage, the happy waving locals. The sweet smell of cane from the car window hit me before I could even see the farm, like the sight of water to someone lost in the desert, like heroine to a junkie. I was so excited when the driver opened the door for me at Casablanca that I almost fell out of the car. I was back. Back on the farm. And it was still there, just as I'd remembered it.

"Aye, Lisa!" shouted Hortensia, running from the kitchen, smiling, arms open wide. Her maid's uniform could barely contain her overabundant flesh as it strained to break free during her sprint toward the car. Frozen with joy at the sight of her, I couldn't escape before her bear hug engulfed me in her ample bosoms. "You're finally here. Come. Come. Lou's prepared a snack. You must be starving. Look at you. Skin and bones." Then she stopped in her tracks, held me at arms length, and looked me up and down. An expression came over her as if maybe she'd mistaken me for someone else. Then, putting her look to words, "Where is she? What did you do with her?"

"Who?" I asked.

"Little Lisa. Where is she? What did you do with her?" She was shaking me by the shoulders. That's when I realized I was looking down at her. I didn't remember being taller than Hortensia.

"*I'm* Lisa," I said, catching on to her little game. "It's me, Hortensia."

"Impossible," she replied, wanting to play a little longer. "My Lisa's just a little girl. You can't be her. You're a grown woman. What did you do with her?"

"It's been three years Hortensia. Did you expect me to stay a baby?"

Finally she smiled, still looking me up and down. "Well, one can dream." And she put her arm around me, guiding me to the kitchen. It felt wonderful as the scent of fresh baking hit me. I didn't even mind so much when she suddenly grabbed one of my boobs and asked accusingly, "And what do you think you're going to be doing to the poor boys with these?" I was home.

It wasn't long, however, until the first haciendero social, where I began to notice that things had changed. Of course things in Manila were different. We'd just had a revolution after all. But this was the farm. I never thought the farm could change. Well, I guess it wasn't the farm itself. The land didn't care who was in charge in Manila. The cane still grew straight toward the sky the same way it always had. It was the people. The mood. Sure, they were all glad Marcos was gone. It wasn't that. It was the anticipation of, what now? When would the other shoe drop?

"To Marcos!" they all toasted in unison, drinks raised.

"May he enjoy his vacation in Hawaii," added Scooby.

"I wouldn't go that far. Just so long as he doesn't come back here," said Chica-ting.

"I don't know," began Ron, with a frown on his face. "I worry about them." The others looked at him, shocked that he might somehow feel bad for Marcos. But they soon got the joke when Ron added, "I'm just not sure they'll have enough room in Hawaii for all of Imelda's shoes."

I loved to hear them laughing.

But as usual, Papa had to ruin it with reality. "But now what?" he asked.

"What do you mean?" answered Chica-ting.

"Well, the communists are still here. They still want our land. And I believe this "revolution," as you call it, will only embolden them. They believe the time for land reform is here.

"Always the worrier," began Scooby. "Aquino won't give our land away. She knows that dividing us into small farms run by people without experience would only cripple the whole industry."

"Don't be so sure," Papa replied. "Unlike Marcos, Cory Aquino was actually elected. This isn't martial law anymore. The people expect her to do their bidding. And land reform is all they talk about. They believe they've won the lottery, and they're already planning on what to do with the winnings, the money they'll get for selling our own land back to us."

There followed an awkward silence as Papa's words settled in. But it wasn't too long before Ron broke the ice.

"So you think Spain will win the World Cup?" And just like that, it was the good old days again.

Certainly Mama hadn't changed, still desperately trying to outdo all her neighbors with jewelry and a new designer gown. Wing was still Wing. She came to steal me away to where the kids and the music were. That's where I noticed that time on the farm had moved on without me. First of all, Wing and I were no longer little kids eating ice cream on the sidelines. On the other hand, it seemed we were still on the sidelines as I could recognize the little brothers of haciendero boys I used to ogle, asking girls I didn't even know to dance. I'd only been away three years, but somehow, at the ripe old age of 17, I felt as though I were over the hill. Even Wing confirmed my suspicion by filling me in on whom she'd dated during my summers away, the lost years, as we referred to them, those years when a girl was 15 and 16, when Wing and the slightly older boys realized they were so different yet irresistibly drawn to each other. But I hadn't been there. I'd missed it all. I looked around and felt like a spinster. The boys I'd remembered, college boys now, hardly even attended the socials anymore. On the bright side, at least Boy wasn't there to cause any trouble. Oh he was there, at the farm I mean, just not at the social. In fact, we almost never saw him anymore. And we, Wing and I, were probably better off not knowing what he was up to anyway. It couldn't possibly be anything good.

But there was someone else I almost never saw anymore. Someone I wanted to see. Someone I'd missed desperately. Johnny wasn't hiding. But he was busy. Busy practically running the farm for Captain. But busy with something else as well. Something Papa wouldn't appreciate.

I sat there feeling like an outsider, watching the kids dance, like I didn't belong there anymore. So I left the party and headed to the barn to go see the cows. I didn't have a calf this summer. I guess I was too old for that. And I hadn't forgotten what happened to Molly Moo Cow three years prior. Even to this day, I can't eat hamburger. Yet I still find it somehow calming to be around the gentle creatures with their big noses and floppy ears. I had just discovered a newborn calf in need of petting when I was interrupted by someone returning some farm equipment to the barn. Initially frightened, as I wasn't expecting company, fear instantly turned to excitement as I recognized the familiar drawl coming from the barn door.

"You were playing with some silly calf the first time I saw you."

"Johnny!" I shouted, turning and running at him. I know I didn't imagine his initial smile as I jumped into his arms, wrapping my arms around his neck and my legs around his waist. I was about to plant a wet kiss on his mouth when I felt things turn chilly. Unwrapping me from his body, Johnny deliberately held me at arm's length and shook my hand, looking nervously about.

"How are you?" he said coolly, as if greeting an old business acquaintance.

Maybe I'd been mistaken. Maybe this wasn't Johnny after all. Just some other gorgeous hunk I'd mistaken for the boy, uh, man of my dreams, the one I'd had all picked out to father my children. Or maybe it *was* Johnny, but his body had been taken over by aliens from outer space. Or maybe I was just losing my mind.

"What's wrong?" I asked.

"What do you mean?" he replied.

"You're shaking my hand."

"Oh. I'm sorry," he answered, letting my hand fall self-consciously.

The way he dropped my hand, I felt like some kind of leper. I took a step back. "You're sorry?" Wasn't this the man I'd spent a night with tearing each other's clothes off? The man I'd consented to lose my virginity to? That the act was never consummated was merely a formality. What had changed? What was wrong?

"I'm sorry for being so forward," he continued.

"Shaking my hand is being forward?"

"Not just that," he began. "The whole thing. That night at the radio station. Even our little swim a few summers back." I was impressed he even remembered that. But then he continued. "I've given it all a lot of thought. It wasn't right. There's no way anything could possibly work out between us."

I was on the top of the world, finally running into Johnny after all these months. But just then, when he said what he did, I thought I'd fallen off the highest mountain peak into the deepest canyon on Earth. And that's a long way to fall, all the way from the top to the bottom. Why would he say such a thing? I couldn't find words.

Johnny filled the silence. "We're from two different worlds, Lisa," he began. "You're from the haves. I'm from the have-nots. Your family owns this farm and everything on it, including me. They would never allow a relationship between us. And if they found out, they'd probably have me shot. Or at least fired."

I couldn't believe it. What had happened to him since we last met? What had they done to him? Why was he saying these things? He was a man. I was a woman. What more did it take? It was right for us to be together. I felt it from the beginning. I took his hand in mine again. "Johnny, none of that matters. As long as we're in love, everything will work out." I know it sounded pathetic. And so did Johnny.

"You know that's a bunch of baloney," he began. "You've been reading too many fairy tales. Think about it. I've got nothing. What will you do when your family disowns you? Come to live with me in my little hut while I go to work in the cane fields all day? Be serious."

"If that's what it takes," I heard myself say. "I love you. And I love this farm. Would that be so bad, being here, with you?"

"Don't be ridiculous."

I felt like I'd been slapped in the face. Why? What did I do wrong? Why didn't he love me? Maybe he found me ugly. Maybe my boobs weren't big enough. Maybe he didn't even like Filipino girls. Maybe he wanted a blonde American girl.

"I can dye my hair blonde."

Johnny stared at me like I was speaking a different language. "Come again."

"I can dye my hair blonde. I can get a boob job."

"What are you talking about?"

"If it's my looks, I can change. Just tell me what you want me to be." I know. I know. Pathetic and desperate.

Johnny just continued to stare. "You've lost your mind."

I continued to blather on, tears starting to fall. "What's wrong with me? Why don't you love me?"

Seeing the tears, Johnny went to take me in his arms, but then held back, not wanting to encourage me. "It's got nothing to do with you," he began. "It's just the way things are. You can't marry a cane worker. Now grow up."

Grow up? So that was it. I was too young for him. He still saw me as just a child. "So you still think I'm too young for you. You think I'm too inexperienced? Not worldly enough for you? Is it because I'm a virgin? Would you rather I were a whore?"

"Shut up!" I thought he was going to slap me. "Just shut up!" I took a step backward. But Johnny followed me, taking my hands in his. "I'm sorry," he said. "I didn't mean to yell. But you're not listening to me. It's not about you, Lisa. It's me. I'm the problem."

"What do you mean?" I asked, wiping my tears with the back of my hand.

"I'm poor," he said. "I have nothing to offer you."

"I don't care about that."

"You say that now. But your family does. They'd never permit it. They'd make us miserable. And in the end, you'd leave. You'd go back to them."

I couldn't imagine doing such a thing. But to be honest, I couldn't think that far ahead. I wanted Johnny. That's all. I couldn't even consider the consequences. So when he said what he did, I couldn't accept it. It couldn't have been true. He was just saying it to get rid of me. I wasn't pretty enough, old enough, good enough, something enough, anything enough for him. I just wasn't enough. He didn't love me. That's all there was to it.

I slumped down onto a pile of hay, hugging my knees. Johnny sat down beside me. He mumbled something about being friends that I couldn't quite make out over all the noise in my head. At the time, I guess I hadn't really heard anything Johnny had said. I really had made it all about poor insecure me. I hadn't heard Johnny's concerns about social and financial status. I hadn't seen them as his own insecurities. Beautiful Johnny, strong and fearless. It never occurred to me that he had any insecurities of his own. Concerns over being the breadwinner, the provider, for his woman. It's a guy thing, I guess, to provide, to conquer, that we women can never fully understand. Like a guy trying to understand a woman's love of flowers or need to mother everything. I think we're just wired differently. So when Johnny laid his own insecurities bare, exposed them plain as day, that he felt *he* wasn't good enough for *me*, I couldn't see it. I turned everything around and made it all about me. And it was pathetic.

Fortunately, the scene was interrupted by someone at the door. "Hey Cano. You coming? We're going to be late." It was Speed. And, yes, he still gave me the creeps. He stood at the door impatiently awaiting Johnny's reply. I did, however, see a brief look of surprise on his face, seeing me lying on the hay next to Johnny. That look alone made me stand up, brushing the hay from my jeans. But it wasn't until I saw the smile on his face that it even occurred to me what thoughts might have been going through his twisted mind.

"Oh, excuse me," Speed continued in a suggestive tone. "The boss's niece, no less. You never cease to impress me, Cano." He couldn't resist adding a wink.

I was embarrassed. We hadn't even done anything, but it didn't matter. And just having someone like Speed even touch upon any relationship I might have with Johnny made me want to take a shower. Johnny saw how I felt and spoke up.

"Whatever you're thinking, Speed, you're not even close. So you can wipe that smile off your face."

"Oh, I don't know," responded Speed. "You've come up from nothing to practically foreman. Then you come back from college and I find you in the hay with the boss's niece. Maybe you think you're a haciendero now."

I think Speed hit a sore spot, because even though nothing was going on between Johnny and me, it was the very fact that Johnny was anything but a haciendero that was preventing it.

"Shut up, Speed."

"Hey, hey. Calm down brother. I'm just saying—"

"Well stop saying," interrupted Johnny, visibly getting angry.

"No problem," said Speed, holding his hands up in a defensive posture. "Peace, comrade. Let's just go. Everyone will be waiting already."

Johnny turned to me. "I've got to go, Lisa. I'm sorry. I didn't mean to upset you."

I didn't like the idea of Johnny hanging around with Speed. "Where are you going?" I asked, my eyes narrowed at Speed.

Johnny hesitated, looked at Speed, then stammered, "Um, I, uh, can't say."

I didn't like the sound of this.

Speed smiled slowly. "Go ahead. Why don't you tell her about the meeting? Maybe she wants to come along."

Johnny froze at the thought, and cast a menacing look at Speed. "She can't come."

Never the one to cooperate, I took that as an invitation. "Why not?" I asked, with a pinch of indignation. "Is it an all boys club? Gambling? Drinking? I'm a big girl."

Speed saw his opening. "Yeah, Cano. She's a big girl. Let her come."

Johnny ignored me and approached Speed, pulling him aside. He spoke in a hushed fashion so I could barely hear. "Are you crazy? You want the Delgados to know about our meetings?"

Speed smiled at me. "It's obvious she likes you. Don't you trust her? She won't rat on you. Besides, we all heard about her contribution to the revolution. Why wouldn't she see the value in our cause as well? Maybe we can get some of the enemy to see the light. Divide and conquer."

"But she's a Delgado, she's—"

"I'm not a Delgado," I interrupted. "But I'm also not anyone's enemy. What are you talking about? Why can't I hear about it?"

Johnny turned to me. "No, you're not a Delgado. But you're family. And no, I don't consider the Delgados enemies, but your Papa can't know about our meetings. He'll kill us."

I almost laughed at the idea. But I saw the seriousness in Johnny's face. Now I needed to know. "What are these meetings about?"

"Lisa, you can't know about—"

"Oh, let her come. She won't rat on us. Will you kid?"

So now Speed was calling me a kid. "I'm not a kid. And I can keep a secret."

Speed was smiling.

But Johnny wasn't. "Lisa, I don't want you involved. You can't—"

Speed interrupted. "You heard her. She's a big girl. She can make up her own mind."

That sounded just about right to me. I glared at Johnny, challenging him to say otherwise.

"Lisa, please—" Johnny began.

"No." I cut him off. "I'm coming."

Speed held the door open. "Shall we, your highness?"

My indignation at not being taken seriously as an adult had gotten the better of me. And I was already upset with Johnny, still reeling from our recent conversation. How else could I have found myself siding with Speed over Johnny? I took Speed up on his invitation, walked past Johnny and out the door.

Life is certainly a kind of road we follow. Sometimes the road only leads one way and there is no choice. Other times you come to a fork and must choose the right road to take. Then there are times when you come to that fork and you think you're choosing, but you're not. Instead, you're being chased. You're letting someone choose which road to chase you down. And that's always the wrong road. I was chased down a road once before, with Wing, on our bikes. Looking back, it was no coincidence that we happened to see Speed on *that* road as well.

Chapter 12

The last time I entered the barn in downtown Bais, there was a cockfight going on. The barn was the same, but there was a different sort of struggle taking place. There were a couple of dozen people ranging from cane workers, to unemployed young men, to obvious communists. You could smell the discontent in the air, a noxious bitter smell. They were all arguing about something when I entered with Speed and Johnny. Suddenly it was as if someone hit the mute button. Mouths froze in mid-sentence. All eyes were on me. All except some of the cane workers who actually ran to escape by the back door.

"Whoa! Whoa! Stop. It's OK. She's cool," shouted Speed, laughing.

"Are you crazy?" shouted one of the cane workers.

"She's Delgado," from another.

"You'll get us all killed," stated one of the communists, looking even less happy than usual, if that were even possible.

"I tried to tell him," said Johnny. "He wouldn't listen."

Speed just smiled, those white teeth gleaming. "Come on guys. Don't you trust me? Would I do anything to endanger our cause?"

That calmed them a bit. But the apprehension was still thick.

Speed continued, bringing me forward. "Don't you know who this is?"

"She's Delgado," someone shouted.

"Well, not technically," answered Speed, "but I admit she is family."

"Same thing," shouted another.

"I know. I know," continued Speed. "That's not the point. This is Lisa Salonga."

The faces in the crowd looked at each other blankly. My name didn't seem to change any minds.

"Lisa Salonga," repeated Speed. "The revolutionary."

I turned to look at Johnny. He looked just as bewildered as I.

Speed forged ahead. "Remember the voice that kept the revolution alive that night when Marcos shut down Radio Veritas? This is it," he proudly announced, nudging me out in front of him.

There were a few nods of understanding. Yet not everyone felt relieved. "But what's that got to do with us? Overthrowing Marcos is one thing. Getting us some land is another."

"It doesn't hurt to have someone on the inside," said Speed.

"She'll tell Delgado. She'll get us all shot," shouted one of the cane workers.

"I don't think so," said Speed, placing an unwelcome arm about my shoulders. "She's, uh, how do I put it, a good friend of Johnny's." I thought I saw a wink accompany his oversized smile at the words "good friend."

I looked over at Johnny, who shrugged his shoulders at the suggestion. Finally, I couldn't stand being talked about like I wasn't there. "What, exactly, are we talking about?" I asked.

"Something you're the expert at," answered Speed. "Revolution."

Confusion registered in my furrowed brow. "But the revolution is over. Marcos is gone. Aquino's been elected."

"That's where you're wrong," Speed began. "On the contrary, it's only just begun."

"What are you saying?"

"I'm saying, despite the new president, nothing has changed. Not for us."

"What else do you want to change? What do you want?" I asked.

I'd never seen Speed smile so widely. He patted me on the back with such bravado I almost fell over. Then taking me by the shoulders, he pulled me close, too close, and said one word.

"Land." There was a cheer from the crowd. "That's why we're all here," continued Speed, turning and gesturing to the crowd. "We all want our share." And another cheer from the crowd.

It finally hit me. My eyes went wide. "You want the Delgados' land?" I turned to Johnny for confirmation.

"Well, not all of it," answered Speed. "And not just from Delgado. We only want a portion, from all the haciacenderos. Just our fair share." There were nods of agreement from the crowd.

"How is that fair?" I asked. "It doesn't belong to you."

"That's just my point," continued Speed. "None of it belongs to us. And the way the current system works, it never will. That's why it'll take a revolution to correct the situation."

I couldn't believe Johnny would be a part of this. I turned to him in disbelief. I knew it was true when Johnny had trouble looking me in the eye. Then my fears were confirmed.

"Speed's right," began Johnny. "None of us will ever have anything. Not even if we slaved two lifetimes. There needs to be a radical change in the way things are done. College helped me understand that."

I couldn't remain silent. "College? You mean the college the Delgados paid for? And that's how you repay them? By trying to steal their land?"

The crowd began to look unnerved by my protest. Maybe Speed had miscalculated. Maybe I would tell José Delgado after all, just as they'd feared, and get them all shot.

"Lisa, you don't understand," he continued. "They would be compensated by the government. Things can't go on the way it is. The people are realizing the plight they're in, and see the revolution as a chance to set things right.

"Compensated by the government? Sure, but at what rate? And how would they be able to continue to compete in the world market on smaller farms?" I was beginning to sound like Papa. I know he'd have been proud.

"Look. Maybe Speed was wrong to bring you along. Maybe you'll never get it. But these people are right about one thing. If you mention any of this to the Delgados, blood will flow." Johnny looked at me, pleading for nothing more than my silence. He was right about that, all right. I'd seen first hand what Captain was capable of. And I knew how the hacienderos were when it came to their land.

I began to feel sorry for them. They only wanted a chance, or as Johnny would say, a shot at the American dream. Only this wasn't America. There was no dream. No dream of becoming a haciendero. No chance of owning land. No way out of the hole they'd been born into. No, I wouldn't expose them. I couldn't. It might have gotten them killed. On the other hand, Papa would have killed *me* if he'd known the secret I was keeping.

I stayed for the rest of the meeting. I heard what they had to say. And no, the communists didn't win me over. Along with Speed, I still found them creepy. But the others, the cane workers and the unemployed, they actually started to make sense to me. They didn't want to steal anything. They didn't hate the hacienderos. They only wanted to come up with a fair way to have their chance, for them and their families. Despite their lack of education, they actually held some rather intelligent and sophisticated debate on the issue. Johnny made sure of that. He practically ran the meeting. Yet it was only Speed who was capable of bringing the communists back in order when their angry protests and demands stepped over the line.

By the end of the meeting, I wasn't as concerned about not telling Papa. After all, they were only talking of spreading the word, the idea that they deserved a fair break. They would have leaflets printed up and try to increase their numbers so their voices could be heard without fear of being seen as just a few troublemakers that could be stamped out. Once they'd gathered enough supporters, they could stage open rallies. They would work for change through the government. There wasn't to be any violence. Surely Papa couldn't deny them the right to think and speak.

I would attend more meetings. Not that I was having second thoughts about Papa's stand on the matter. But I found it exciting to see people working together to change society. To improve it, as they would say. Oh, and did I mention, Johnny would be there. I still didn't buy his excuses for dumping me, that he was too poor, that he was from the wrong side of the tracks. I was sure it was because he still saw me as just a kid, or that my boobs weren't big enough. But who knows? Maybe if I hung around long enough, eventually I wouldn't seem like such a kid to him, or at least my boobs would grow some more, and Johnny would come around. He'd realize we were meant for each other.

Unfortunately, there was just one problem. Apparently not everyone at the meetings believed in the concept of nonviolence. Not everyone was as patient as I.

I was in the kitchen, the heart of the farm, when I heard about it. I was just hanging around enjoying the scents, and trying to pick up some new recipes. Well, I was paying the price of admission, after all. They had me peeling about a million pounds of onions.

"But everything's been so nice and peaceful lately," began Hortensia, stirring a saucepan. "Has been since the revolution. Since we got rid of Marcos. Why can't they just trust in President Aquino and the Lord to do the right thing?"

"They'll never be happy until everyone's a communist," answered Lou, dragging a new sack of rice from the pantry.

"And they think kidnapping innocent people will accomplish that?" Hortensia asked. "She's just a maid. Never harmed a fly. She doesn't have any land for them."

"But her employers do," answered Lou. "The Fanlos. And if they pay the ransom money, the kidnappers will buy more weapons and soon the communists will take all the land themselves without waiting for the government to steal it for them."

"Aye, it's terrible. What can be done to stop them?"

"I say cut their balls off. That'll take the fight out of them." I hadn't seen Yaya enter the kitchen.

"Yaya!" the others all protested in unison. "How do you say such things?" followed Hortensia.

Yaya sat down at my table and began to light a cigar. "Well you asked what could be done to stop them. It's good enough for cattle. Why not communists?"

Nothing Yaya said anymore shocked me. I never knew when to take her seriously or not.

"Never mind her," answered Lou. "I told you she's going senile."

"Hey!" protested Yaya.

But Lou interrupted her. "And put out that disgusting cigar. There's no smoking allowed in my kitchen." Yaya may have been in charge of all the maids, but it was definitely Lou's kitchen.

Yaya complied by extinguishing the lit end of her cigar in that leather palm of hers and placing it in a pocket of her smock for later. Not to be completely cowed, though, she concluded by spitting on the kitchen floor. The others ignored it. "I suppose we don't have to cut their balls off. Too messy. Easier just to shoot them."

I wondered if Yaya knew about Johnny's meetings. Not that he had anything to do with kidnapping anyone. I was sure none of the people at Johnny's meetings had anything to do with kidnappings, but there were communist representatives there after all. Seems to me she wouldn't be too happy about that. Anyway, I hated to even think about this kidnapping stuff. I thought I'd seen the last of it since the revolution. I thought, with our new government, things could go back to the way they used to be. This wasn't Manila after all. It was the farm. My farm. The farm I'd grown up loving. There weren't supposed to be any kidnappings at the farm. Why did things have to keep changing?

Hortensia tried to change the topic of conversation from kidnappings, only seeming to follow my own train of thought. "So Yaya, how's Johnny doing?"

Yaya sat up straight, assuming a more stately posture whenever she spoke proudly of her beloved Johnny. "Oh, you know Johnny. He's just perfect."

I couldn't hold back a smile of agreement, though I'm not sure Yaya and I were thinking of exactly the same thing.

Yaya had the floor, and continued to expound on Johnny's virtues. "Have you seen the way he runs this place? Captain might as well retire already. He's getting fat now that he has Johnny doing his job for him."

The others chuckled, Lou adding, "I'd like to think I had something to do with that."

"But it's true," said Yaya. "Johnny knows all there is to know about cane farming. And going to college only added to his qualifications. The other cane workers now all look up to him."

"He's practically a haciendero," added Hortensia, meaning to compliment.

But apparently, Yaya didn't take it that way, as a compliment. "Haciendero," she muttered, with another spit on the floor. Then, more loudly, "He should *be* a haciendero." Then after a pause of stunned silence, "Who's going to run this place after José Delgado passes? Who?! Boy Delgado?!" Another spit.

Hortensia was shocked. "Yaya! You can't talk that way."

"Says who?" answered Yaya. "That boy's good for nothing and everyone knows it. Just like his mother."

"Yaya!"

"Don't Yaya me. Like two peas in a pod. Never wanted to be here. Only interested in dress-up and playtime in the big city. Not a drop of cane sugar in their blood."

Lou spoke up. "Well, that's certainly true of Mama. But Boy's a Delgado after all. He must have farming in him somewhere."

"The only thing Boy Delgado can grow is marijuana," answered Yaya. Then turning to me, "Lisa here has more farm dirt under the nail of her pinky finger than Boy has in his whole body."

I instinctively checked my nails to make sure they were clean, but I knew what she meant.

"Well, then it's a good thing that Boy will have Johnny to run things for him," chimed Hortensia, thinking she'd solved the problem of world hunger.

I could see the smoke rising from Yaya's ears. "You think Johnny will be a slave to that fool? Boy Delgado's got no one's respect, and he'll surely be the end of this farm. You mark my words. Unless a miracle happens where the sky falls, the lamb kills the wolf, and the poor become rich, Boy Delgado will be the end of this farm." She punctuated her prophecy with a spit to the floor, as the others stared at her in silence. They were all a superstitious bunch and prophecies made them uncomfortable.

So when Lou's largest cooking pot fell from its shelf and came crashing to the floor, they were all sure it was a sign from God. Making the sign of the cross on their chests, muttering prayers, and clutching their rosaries to ward off evil spirits, it hadn't occurred to any of them, as it had to me, that it was probably just a rat from the fields looking for a snack from Lou's kitchen. Yaya, always with impeccable timing, recognized her cue to exit the kitchen, vindicated. I thought I saw a rat scamper out after her, and wouldn't have been surprised if, once outside the kitchen, it jumped back into Yaya's pocket, a job well done.

* * * *

Johnny's meetings had become quite popular. Initially trying to see the good intentions in it all, I remember one meeting where I began to wonder just where it was all heading. We were in the barn, the same one where the cockfights had taken place.

Johnny and Speed were down in front, as usual, running things. Until that point, the meetings were mostly attended by cane workers, with a handful of communists who were sometimes unruly. But now, as I looked about the barn, it seemed the ratio had flipped. Over time, more and more communists had begun attending, and encouraged by their numbers, had grown more and more disruptive.

"Enough talk!" they shouted. "It's time for action!"

"This is a big change we're advocating," began Johnny. "It will take time. We must be patient."

"Patient? At this rate, I'll be dead and gone before there's any change. The only land I'll ever get is an unmarked grave in the squatters' cemetery." There were nods of agreement among the communists.

"I say we act! Let them know we're serious!" shouted another.

Speed, smiling, acted the peacekeeper. "Now, now. Let's calm down. What exactly are you suggesting?" he asked, pretending he didn't already know the answer.

"They have something that's ours. Our land. I say we take something of theirs." The crowd turned to each other, nodding in agreement.

Speed continued. "What would you have us do? Take their maids?"

The heckler grew louder. "The hell with that. We've taken enough maids." I hoped that "we" referred to the communists in general, and not to this group in particular. "They don't care about their maids. We have to hit them where it hurts. Take something, or someone, they really care about." The hair on the back of my neck stood up.

"Whoa now," interrupted Johnny. "What are we talking about here?"

"We're talking about justice!" came a shout from the crowd.

"Kidnapping innocent people?" responded Johnny. "You call that justice?"

"No," answered the voice in the crowd. "But, we're not talking about innocent people anymore. No more maids. I say we take the guilty. The family of the haciendero. They're the beneficiaries of crime and therefore guilty by association."

"Crime? What crime?" Johnny replied.

"Shush, shush," interrupted Speed. "Let's all calm down."

"Calm down?" asked Johnny. "He's talking about kidnapping. He'll get us all killed."

A heckler shouted back. "Oh, is little Cano Johnny afraid to die? I thought America was the land of the brave. You weren't afraid to die in front of Marcos's tanks. What's happened to you? Have you become a Delgado?" I guess they'd gotten so used to my presence at their meetings, they spoke as if I wasn't even there.

Johnny shouted back. "No, I wasn't afraid to die standing up to tanks. But I wasn't kidnapping anyone either. Would you have us lower ourselves to behave as Marcos did? With violence?"

A brief contemplative pause was quickly shattered by one of the crowd. "I do! The time has come. It's time for violence."

I looked back at Johnny to see the shocked expression on his face. And right next to him stood Speed, smiling triumphantly. I was reminded of the cockfight. No the ring wasn't red with blood. But there was no doubt that a battle had been waged. A battle of words, instead of razor blades. And, in the end, it was Johnny's feathers no longer white. He stood alone, frozen, merely waiting for Speed to peck him three times on the head. A feeling familiar to me from my first cockfight resurfaced, and I ran outside just in time to puke.

Looking back, I guess that was the point I was supposed to run to Papa and spill the beans, foil any such plot in its infancy, before any damage was done. I'm not sure why I didn't. Was it fear for Johnny's involvement and what the hacienderos would do to him? Was it fear for myself, that the members of the meetings would seek revenge against me for turning them in? I don't really think it was any of that. I think it was guilt. I was frozen by it. Guilt that I'd somehow taken part in all of this. Guilt that I'd already let it get as far as it had. I don't think I could have handled the look on Papa's face when he found out I'd been attending these meetings all along. No, that I couldn't bear. I was weak. I might just as well have converted to communism. So to avoid confronting my own involvement, my guilt by association, I froze. I didn't go to Papa.

But that didn't stop me from speaking to Johnny. It seemed as though every time in my life that I'd felt threatened in some way, Johnny'd always been the one to come to my rescue. I didn't think it would be any different this time. I guess I was wrong.

"Johnny, things have gotten out of hand. We have to stop them," I urged.

I could see Johnny was torn, unsure. It wasn't the Johnny I was used to, always confident and decisive. "It's just a few radicals," he began. "I don't believe the vast majority would ever support kidnapping anyone. I'll talk to them."

"But it doesn't take a vast majority to kidnap anyone," I countered. "It only takes one or two. And you heard the way they talked. Johnny, I'm scared."

I'm sure Johnny saw how upset I was. I'm sure he could see the tears I was holding back. That was the part where he was supposed to take me in his arms and tell me how he would take care of everything, how there wasn't anything for me to worry about, how he would make it all go away. I ached to feel his arms around me, to hear those words. Yet for the first time, it seems, I didn't get what I wanted. Johnny didn't drop everything to catch me from falling. Maybe the world didn't revolve around me after all.

"You're overreacting. It was just some idle threats," he said.

"I don't know about that. Is it a chance you want to take?" I implored.

"But we've come so far. We've gotten a lot of people finally working together to bring about change through the political process," he argued, as if he were back in some college political science class.

"Kidnapping? Is that the political process?"

"No. Of course not. There are always going to be a few nuts. Let me talk to them."

"They won't listen," I implored.

"Then I'll stop them," he stated, looking me firmly in the eye. I thought I could see a glimmer of the old Johnny in his eyes.

I guess it was just enough for me to let it slide for now. After all, Johnny'd never failed me before. He'd always been right about everything. I had no reason to start doubting him now. No reason at all, except for the little voice in the back of my mind screaming itself hoarse, screaming for me to grow up, to stop letting everyone else tell me which path to take, to follow my own heart. I was a fool.

Chapter 13

I never thought about typhoon season until that year. I mean, sure, we had a typhoon season every year. Some years we got hit, some years we didn't. Just a matter of luck, or lack of it. But as kids, we just never thought about it. Kids don't worry about such things. How could a little rain hurt anybody? We certainly never concerned ourselves with preparation. And if a big one did hit, it became a game, a game of watching to see how far over the palm trees would bend, of moving your bed around to dodge newly discovered leaks in the roof, of losing electricity and fighting over flashlights and candles, of trying to decide whether the howling wind sounded more like a jet or a train.

Reassuring smiles and jokes from the grown-ups only served to encourage our delusion. It never occurred to us that it was just a mask they put on to keep us from getting frightened. But they knew, the grown-ups did. They knew what a typhoon was capable of. At some point in everyone's life, a time comes when you're old enough to comprehend, to recognize horror, to feel profound loss. That's the day childhood ends.

I never even remembered preparing for typhoon season before. But it was something the grown-ups did every year, almost by instinct. A certain time of year, the sky takes on a slightly different hue, the air a subtly altered scent. Maybe the livestock becomes a little jittery, nothing obvious, and certainly nothing children can detect. But the grown-ups can feel it. They feel it in their bones. It's time. Time to clear away unnecessary debris, time to patch up roofs, maybe shore up some less than secure doors and windows, some less than vertical walls. Just subtle things. Not as if a storm were actually coming. I mean we usually didn't know that until the last minute, when one of the hacienderos would pick it up on radar and spread the warning. That's when the last minute panic would set in. By then it would be too late to shore up a barn leaning too far to the left. No, that's when it was time to gather. Water, candles, your children, and ammunition for the rifles, for afterward, in case things got out of hand. Things can get out of hand after a typhoon.

Papa and Captain oversaw the clearing and repairing. The maids handled organizing and gathering. For something I never even noticed before, it was pretty clear that everyone seemed to be involved. Everyone but Mama and Boy. Mama couldn't be bothered. The whole idea that a storm might blow away her impatiens was so inconvenient to her, she couldn't bear to think about it. And Boy, no one saw much of Boy those days. He'd drifted further and further from the family, and closer to his own nefarious contacts, his own little underworld.

"Where do those candles go every year?" asked Hortensia, searching through the kitchen cabinets. "It's not like we use them. Do they just melt into thin air?"

"Why are you asking me?" responded Lou, discovering a stash of batteries. "Do you think I add them to the stew?"

"I wouldn't be surprised, the way you keep your recipes so secret. I would keep it a secret as well if I were putting wax in my stew."

"Aye, Hortensia. Don't be ridiculous. Lisa, why don't you make yourself useful and check the barn for those candles. Maybe Yaya's been using them for some sort of witch's sacrificial right."

"Aye, Lou!" said Hortensia, making a sign of the cross. "Don't say such things."

"You never know," countered Lou. "The way Yaya and Father Rivera fight so, nothing would surprise me.

"Lou!"

I left the kitchen laughing. Not at the idea that Yaya might be a witch. That wouldn't have surprised me. No, it was the way Lou's teasing could get Hortensia so upset that amused me. They fought like sisters.

* * * *

I'd finished greeting all my animal friends in the barn and had just gotten on hand and knee to search some low shelves beyond the stalls when they came in. Boy had become so creepy lately that normally I'd have made a hasty exit before getting caught alone with him and any of his associates. But something in Boy's voice alerted me that I'd already heard too much and would be wiser to stay put, unseen.

"I'm begging you," whined Boy. "I'll do anything."

"No shit. I can see that." I recognized Speed's voice, always the fox calmly assuring the hen that he was there to help.

"So you'll get me something?" begged Boy.

"You know I always take care of my regulars," Speed replied.

Boy exhaled a sigh of relief. "Great. Great. When?" he pressed.

"As soon as we settle up."

"You know I'm good for it. I always pay up eventually. It's just been a little tight lately."

"Yeah, well, it's a little tight everywhere. I've got responsibilities too, you know. This stuff doesn't grow on trees."

I was pretty sure I knew what "stuff" he was referring to. There was no way for me to exit gracefully now, as my cramped knees pressed me further back into the shadows at the rear of the barn.

"But I need it bad, man," Boy continued, almost crying.

"I know you do," replied Speed with the compassion of a mother soothing her hungry child. "We all have needs."

"But my dad's taken to hiding the cash. I just need some time to find out where. Then I can get you your money.

There was a brief pause while Speed gathered the nerve to raise the negotiations to a new level. "What about your little sister?"

Until that point, my only concern was to escape the barn undetected. But now, I didn't care for this new turn in the conversation. My focus now was to hear it through, follow it to its dark conclusion.

"Wing?" asked boy, as if he had a number of sisters he might confuse her with. "What about her? She doesn't have any money."

"Why do you think everything's about money? There are other things of value, you know."

I could sense the smirk on Boy's face. "You, uh, you like my sister? You want a, uh, date? Is that what you're talking about?"

"Me? No. Not exactly. But I do have some friends that would like to get to know her a little better."

I'm not sure what Boy thought Speed was referring to. But I never thought that Boy's hesitation in replying was ever a matter of conscience on his part. I felt it was more out of shock, not at anything specific Speed might have been suggesting, but at the idea that Wing herself had any intrinsic value. The concept had never occurred to Boy before. If it had, I honestly believe Boy would have brought it up himself long ago. Yet no sooner had the concept sunk in than Boy jumped at the chance to cash in his newfound asset.

"Sure. Sure. Whatever you say. What do you need me to do?"

Why is it, I often wonder, that hell is supposed to be such a hot place, yet, in the presence of the devil, it's always a chill we feel. A chill to the bone, so cold that the blood freezes and slivers of ice stab at the heart.

What I'd just overheard left me feeling so weary, that I'm not sure I could have made it out of the barn even had the chance of escape presented itself. And yet I'd heard enough. I didn't think I could listen any more in silence, as I imagined Speed's pearly white grin salivating at Boy's willingness to go along with whatever it was he was suggesting.

That's why it was just as well that Johnny interrupted the negotiations when he entered the barn in search of some tools. Boy and Speed were quick to excuse themselves under Johnny's suspicious gaze.

Johnny was more surprised to find me curled up in a corner at the back of the barn, trembling.

"Lisa! What's wrong?" he demanded, dropping to his knees in concern. Looking back to where the others had just left, "What did they do?"

All I could do was shake my head, unable to find my voice.

"I'll kill them both," declared Johnny, grabbing a hammer and rising to go after Boy and Speed.

I grabbed him by the leg of his pants. "No. Don't."

Johnny knelt down again, taking me by the shoulders. "What is it, then? What's happened?"

The tears started to flow. "They haven't touched me. They didn't know I was here."

I saw some of the urgency leave Johnny's face, but his eyes held their concern. "Then, what? What did they do?"

I tried to compose myself, wiping my eyes and nose with my sleeve. "They haven't done anything."

I could see Johnny's concern turning to confusion. "If they haven't done anything—"

"Yet," I interrupted. "They haven't done anything, *yet*."

Once I was able to stop shaking, I relayed all I'd overheard to Johnny. While I didn't have any specifics as to what Speed intended to do with Wing, it was clearly something sinister. I just knew it. And with all the talk of kidnapping going on, I can't say that Johnny and I didn't consider such a plot. It wasn't, however, at the top of our list. We thought it would be something simpler, something more, uh, personal.

Johnny felt it would be useless to expose the, as yet, unhatched, plot. Without informants to corroborate the plan, or catching them in the act, chances were that no one would be brought to justice. He suggested that he continue attending meetings and disrupt their plans from the inside.

I felt a slightly different approach was in order. Warn Wing, tell Papa and Captain, and have Boy and Speed shot, by noon, if possible. I know, I know. A bit over the top, you're thinking. Well, sometimes the simplest approach is the best. Johnny and I were debating the very issue at the back of the barn when Wing walked in, looking for me.

"Lisa? Are you in there? Hortensia was wondering about the candles."

I didn't even hesitate before calling out to her. "Back here." I planned to tell her everything, despite the look from Johnny telling me it was a bad idea.

Wing found us at the back of the barn. Prepared to immediately spill the beans concerning the plot against her, I was momentarily taken aback when I saw the look on her face. She clearly hadn't expected Johnny to be there. "Oh."

"Wing, I overheard Boy and Speed talking—"

"What are you two doing in here?" she interrupted. Then, before I could answer, "No, no. Never mind. I don't want to know."

It took me a couple of seconds to comprehend what she was suggesting. Then, seeing her looking back and forth between Johnny and me, I saw the light. "No, no. We're not doing anything." Johnny and I stood up.

But Wing was still impressed by the straw clinging to the back of my pants. "Yeah, right. I can't believe this."

I actually had to chuckle a bit at her suggestion. "No, no. We weren't— I mean, nothing happened. It's Boy and Speed. They—"

Wing wouldn't let me speak. "You don't have to laugh at me. It's not funny. I thought we had a deal. We shook hands, with spit and everything."

Johnny gave me a confused look, but this was no time to explain. I figured I would just ignore her comments and come right out and say it. "Wing, they're planning to do something to you."

"What are you talking about?" Wing replied.

"Boy and Speed. They're planning to—"

"Don't," interrupted Johnny, still hoping to gather more evidence.

"Yeah, don't," continued Wing. "I'm not an idiot. You don't have to make up a load of nonsense just to cover your tracks."

"Cover my tracks?"

"That's right. All this time I thought we were more than just cousins. We were best friends. We made promises to each other. I thought that meant something. You lied to me."

"I didn't, well, we haven't done, Wing, just listen to me for a second. This is more important than—"

"I don't want to hear it. Your word obviously means nothing. OK, the joke's on me. I hope you're happy." Wing turned to walk out.

Johnny looked at me in confusion. He had no knowledge of the pact that Wing and I had made concerning him. And even if he had, he wouldn't have seen how in the world I'd broken it. He didn't know that he and I were madly in love with each other, or at least that I was madly in love with him, and that we were going to live happily ever after, together.

And frankly, except for our brief little swim, and that close encounter on the balcony the night of the revolution, I don't think I'd broken the pact. At least, not technically. I mean, just wanting something isn't the same as having it. Am I splitting hairs here? And when did Johnny become so important to Wing? Did she have her own crush on him? Did I just not see it?

Anyway, Wing was walking away. "Wing," I called. "Stop. This is important."

"I don't want to hear your excuses," she replied, without turning around. "I won't believe a word you say."

"But Wing, this isn't about Johnny and me," I shouted. "I'm trying to warn you about Boy. He's—"

"What?" interrupted Wing, turning to shout back at me. "Is Boy sleeping with Johnny too?"

It took me a moment to even attempt to follow her train of thought. By then, she'd turned and left the barn.

"Don't worry. I won't let anything happen to her," Johnny assured me. "I promise."

And I believed him. I didn't run after her. Is Boy sleeping with Johnny too? Yeesh. It never occurred to me that those might be the last words ever spoken between us.

* * * *

But they didn't waste any time. The ransom note was found the next morning. They must have taken her during the night. And I wanted to kill myself for not getting word to her in time. I should have persisted. I should have forced her to listen. I shouldn't have let Johnny dissuade me from telling her all I knew. I blamed him as much as myself. And I swore I'd kill myself if anything happened to her.

The note demanded 20 million pesos. That was about a million dollars. To be brought into the mountains and left at a predetermined spot. She would then be returned, unharmed.

Word had already gone out and all the haciend/eros were on their way over to Casablanca. I went to speak to Johnny, to blame him, to curse him, to force him to get Wing back. He knew these people. He had to go to them and make them free Wing. I looked everywhere for him. But he was nowhere to be found. That was odd.

By the time I'd given up looking for him, the haciendros had arrived and the meeting was beginning over at Casablanca. Everyone was there, even Boy Delgado. This was the first haciendero meeting I'd ever seen Boy attend. I found that rather ironic, seeing as I was sure he shared some responsibility for Wing's disappearance. I took my usual place at the back of the room. I was the only woman there. This was apparently men's work. There was no room for frantic mothers or crying maids. This was the war room, a place for level heads to discuss strategy, to plan how best to win Wing's freedom. And I was one of them. Calm and level headed. That's the only thing that frightened me. My cousin and best friend in the world had been kidnapped. Her life was in danger. Yet there were no tears, no emotions at all. Not from me. In this time of crisis, I'd become one of the warriors, calmly assessing the battlefield, weighing how best to achieve our goal, the return of Wing.

"José," began Ron Fanlo, "the animals will have their ransom money by tomorrow."

"Twenty million pesos?" asked Papa. "I don't have that kind of money."

"Of course you don't," answered Ron. "But *we* do," he add, looking around the room at the other hacistanderos. "Together. We'll all pool our resources and have the money gathered by tonight." All the heads around the room nodded in agreement.

I could see the change come over Papa's face, from fierce leader to humbled friend. "I... I don't know what to say." Then putting his arm around Ron's shoulders, and gesturing to everyone in the room. "You all honor me with your support. I thank you all from the bottom of my heart. I cherish your friendship. And I will never forget this." Many stood to pat Papa on the back.

"We are all fathers," answered Scooby Montero. "We can only imagine what you're going through. And we stand with you, shoulder to shoulder. None of us would think twice, no matter which of us stood in your shoes." Again, heads around the room nodded in agreement.

Papa paused a moment before I saw his expression change once more, back to fierce leader. "Well *I* would. Think twice, that is." The others looked at him, confused. "Yes. *I* would think twice. I cannot accept your offer."

"What?" began Ron, in surprise. "José, please. Take our money. Together we can do this."

"Yes, we can," answered Papa. "Together. But not this way. We cannot deal with terrorists. You know my feelings on this. If we give in to them and reward their behavior, we'll only regret it when they come for the rest of our children. Who wants to be next? You, Chica-ting?"

Chica-ting looked about the room in disbelief. "But José. It's your daughter. Are you saying we don't pay for her release?"

"That's absurd," added Scooby. "You don't mean that, José. Please. Take the money. Let's go get Wing."

Papa was resigned, his face drained of all emotion. "I cannot permit it. If we give in to them, they'll take all our children. No. We must stand strong and united in this."

There was silence in the room as all the hacienderos looked to each other, speechless. Finally Ron found his mouth. "José, what are you saying? Are we to sacrifice your only daughter? Are you saying we sit here and do nothing? Not respond at all?" All eyes were on Papa.

The silence was shattered by a firm knock at the door. All eyes instinctively turned toward the sound. Yet, whoever it was knew better than to interrupt such a meeting by entering without permission. They would wait until given word to enter. All eyes turned back to Papa, who now had an eerie satisfied smile on his face.

"Who's at the door, José?" asked Scooby.

Papa continued to smile. "Even before I called this emergency meeting, I gave orders for inquiries to be made concerning the identities of the kidnappers. I believe the report is in."

I tried to imagine the fate of these kidnappers. There would be no trial. Captain and his rifle would be appointed judge, jury, and executioner. But what about Boy? What would they do when his involvement was revealed? I assumed there'd be some special treatment. But I don't know. Papa's honor was at stake among the other hacienderos. He couldn't let Boy off with just a slap on the wrist.

"But who are they? Who's responsible for this?" shouted Ron.

My eyes involuntarily glanced over at Boy.

"Lisa," Papa began, looking to me by the door at the back of the room.

"Me!?" I thought, feeling like I'd been hit by lightening. And for a brief second, as all eyes turned to me, I felt the blood rush from my head, until Papa finished.

"Would you ask Captain to come in?" he finished.

I don't know how I found my legs to stand up and open the door. I didn't have to look for Captain. He was right there, waiting for his cue. He marched into the room, his rifle in hand. He wasn't alone. One of the cane workers was with him. The cane worker's hands were tied. His mouth and nose were bleeding. Captain kicked him behind the knees and he fell to the floor. There were murmurs of surprise throughout the hacienderos.

"Captain's been making some inquiries," began Papa. "So Captain, tell us what our friend's had to say under, uh, questioning."

"Why?" answered Captain. "I haven't cut his throat... yet. He can speak for himself." Captain kicked his prisoner in the butt.

All eyes turned to the cane worker, bloodied and breathless. But when he took too long in responding, Captain put the barrel of his rifle to the man's head.

The worker's discomfort aside, I eagerly anticipated the demise of Speed, the local group of communists, and even Boy. The secret would be revealed, sparing me the trouble.

When the words came through bloodied teeth, Papa was shocked. I could understand how hearing his own son's name in connection with all this was the last thing Papa expected.

In disbelief, Papa made him repeat the name. But it wasn't until the cane worker repeated the name that I heard it right. I was so sure of what I expected he would say, that I didn't hear the actual name that came from his lips until he repeated it for Papa.

"Johnny," groaned the cane worker. "Johnny Dillinger."

I heard it that time. But I was too shocked to react. My brain couldn't make it fit into any sense of reality.

"He's been leading meetings between the cane workers and the communists," continued the informant.

"I told you he was trouble!" shouted Boy. "And now he's taken my sister. I say we hunt him down."

That's when I passed out.

Chapter 14

It was all just a dream. Wing taken by kidnappers for ransom. And Johnny accused as the ringleader. Imagine. I'd have to think back to what I'd eaten before going to bed. Whatever it was, I'd never eat it again. But at least it was over. I was waking up. I'd get dressed, run into Wing's bedroom, jump on her and give her the biggest hug of her life. She'd wake up stunned by my unwanted advances and throw me off her onto the floor, cursing that she wasn't gay and that I'd lost my mind. But that would be OK. I wouldn't mind. Then I'd run to Johnny and tell him all about my silly dream. We'd fall to the ground laughing so hard our bellies would ache.

Still half asleep, I felt a smile come to my face. It was time. Time to get out of bed and put my little plan into action. This was going to be fun. I finally forced my eyes open. But it wasn't the ceiling of my bedroom. I had the pattern of cracks and morning shadows all memorized. This wasn't them. Even my friend, the gecko, wasn't there. Where was I? That's when Hortensia leaned over me, holding a cold towel.

"How do you feel?" she asked with a motherly smile.

"Where am I?" I asked, afraid to move. But before she could answer, something in my gut made me change my question. "Wing. Where's Wing?" I asked, sitting bolt upright.

Hortensia looked puzzled, then resigned to breaking the news to me all over again, "Wing's not here. She's been—"

"Kidnapped?" I interrupted, already knowing the truth.

Hortensia just nodded sadly in agreement.

I then realized I was on the couch in Papa's den, just outside the meeting room. I jumped up and ran back into the room not wanting to miss any more of the meeting than I already had. But the room was empty. The meeting was over. I turned to Hortensia. "How long?"

"A couple of hours. You took a nice nap."

"But what's happening? What are the hacienderos going to do? What's Papa going to do?"

Hortensia hadn't been allowed in the meeting, but she knew enough. "They're gathering the money tonight. They're planning to drop it off for the kidnappers in the mountains tomorrow morning. In exchange, the kidnappers will free Wing, releasing her near the farm later that night." Then, with a smile, "Wing should be home by tomorrow night. Lou's making her favorite. Chicken adobo with raisins. Though I don't know why anyone would put raisins in adobo."

Ignoring Hortensia's dinner plans and concern about the raisins, I started to question her understanding of what the hacienderos intended to do. "But I thought Papa said— Well, I didn't think they were going to pay the kidnappers the ransom." I saw only confusion on Hortensia's face.

Then she laughed. "Not pay the ransom? Don't be ridiculous. Of course they are. This is Wing we're talking about." Then reaching to put the cold towel back to my head, "Maybe you hit your head when you fell."

"No no. I'm OK," I responded, holding off the wet towel. "It's just Papa said— Well, I missed the rest of the meeting. I guess they changed their minds." Then suddenly remembering why I passed out, "What about Johnny? They said he was involved in the kidnapping."

Hortensia's face changed from concern to anger. "That, I cannot discuss. Yaya might shoot me."

"Shoot you? Why?"

"She won't accept it. She says it's all a lie. I heard one of the workers ratted on him under, uh, questioning from Captain. But even if that wasn't enough, Boy confirmed it. He'd been hearing rumors about these meetings Johnny's been leading."

Somehow the idea of Boy's word confirming anything seemed unbelievable at best. That anyone would believe a word he said was practically comical. On the other hand, technically, Boy was telling the truth this time. Johnny *was* leading those meetings. At least, at first, back when they were peaceful. But toward the end, when the discussions turned toward violence, it would be unfair to say Johnny was leading anymore. The meetings were leading themselves. They'd taken on a mob's momentum, overtaking any one leader, and continued to surge forward in spite of any pleadings for calm by Johnny. The beast had gotten away from him, Johnny having long ago lost control of the reins.

But Yaya had to be right. He may have been at the meetings, but Johnny couldn't have been involved in the kidnapping. He told me he would protect Wing. And I believed him. He promised. And yet, she'd been kidnapped. Just as I'd warned him. We could have gone to Papa or Captain and stopped them. But Johnny talked me out of it. All for the sake of his cause, his dream that everyone could one day have a piece of land. Sure, it sounded nice, in theory. But in reality, it couldn't work. Of course it would be great if more opportunity existed for people to better themselves. But it made no sense to just take land from those that owned it, those with the experience, ability, and financial resources to work it, and hand it over to those who had no chance of success at farming a small plot of land, and many who frankly saw it as an organized way to lay claim to something that wasn't theirs. When would Johnny wake up and see it for what it was? If kidnapping teenage girls wasn't a clear enough sign, then what was? But where was he? Where was Johnny? I just prayed he wouldn't let any harm come to her. Not Wing.

That night, as I lay in bed, wide-awake, I made up my mind. I was going with them, with Captain and the men bringing the ransom money. Well, not exactly *with* them. They couldn't know I was there. If they did, I knew they wouldn't let me come along. But I had to warn Johnny. Whatever his involvement was, I knew Captain wouldn't let him get away with it. He may have been Captain's nephew and hand-trained successor to farm manager, but Captain's loyalty was to the farm and the Delgados. It always had been. And not to what he knew to be some illegitimate product of a financial exchange between an American GI and a Mabini hostess. Even if that hostess was Captain's own sister. I had to warn Johnny to stay away. There's no telling what Captain would do. At least until some kind of truce could be negotiated. And if that wasn't possible, he'd have to leave, the farm, the island, probably the Philippines. Otherwise Captain would hunt him down.

My sources in the kitchen blabbed where the ransom drop-off was to take place. It wasn't far. In the foothills before the mountains the communists called home at the base of Mount Talinas. I would leave before sunup, riding my bike, and get there before the drop-off time, then wait for the kidnappers and follow them, follow the money, to Wing, and Johnny.

* * * *

The road was dark. I'd forgotten how many potholes there were, and the tires on my bike managed to find every one of them. Watching the trees go by reminded me of the time Wing and I went into town to see the cockfights. Only this time, there would be no kidding Wing about the capré. It seemed the capré had already taken her. Now I was on my way to see that she came home. And to see that Johnny did not, at least not until the truth came out. The truth that he had nothing to do with Wing's kidnapping. At least that was the truth I was hoping for. It just had to be.

I ditched my bike in the bushes at the head of the path leading into the mountains and went the rest of the way on foot. I never feared for myself, that the kidnappers might welcome an additional hostage. I'd let my guard down. Maybe attending all those meetings rendered the kidnappers less fearsome. I almost felt as if I was one of them. I certainly deserved to share some of their guilt. At least I could have prevented the whole thing had I acted sooner.

It seemed as if no time had passed when I found myself in a small clearing at the foot of the mountains where the drop off was to occur. At least I'd gotten there before anyone else. The sun was just fully up when I found a good hiding place so that I could see anyone coming and going from the drop-off spot. Now it was just a matter of waiting.

I was just noting how active the mosquitoes were at sunup, when I heard the men coming. I was surprised at the number Captain brought with him. There were about a dozen, all loyal counterparts of his from the various farms about the island. And they were heavily armed. Sure it was a lot of money, but I thought the number of men and show of arms was a bit over the top. After all, they were just supposed to drop off the money and leave. Why all the heavy artillery? Something wasn't right.

I watched them leave with mixed emotions. On the one hand, I could relax that they hadn't discovered me, and now it was just a matter of waiting for the kidnappers to arrive. On the other hand, they were gone, and I'd be alone with my harebrained plan to follow the kidnappers right into their camp. I guess it wasn't too late to change my mind. I could have turned and gone home just to wait until Wing got there. But it was Johnny. I don't know why I kept letting him affect me so. I just had to know. Had he really sided with the rebels, knowing that they intended to kidnap Wing? Had he taken part in her kidnapping? No. It wasn't possible. I couldn't believe it. And sure in that knowledge, I had to go warn him. He had to know what Boy and the others had said about him, that he was their leader, the mastermind behind the kidnapping. He had to know that Captain would not rest until Johnny paid for his crime. And knowing Captain, that meant paying with his life. I had to get to him first. I had no choice.

My butt had fallen asleep sitting on the hard ground waiting, when I heard rustling amid the bushes a small way up the mountain. I peaked from my hiding spot just enough to see the kidnappers arrive. There were four of them. They looked about nervously, hoping there wouldn't be any trouble. They weren't happy about being chosen to go collect the money. I'm sure they knew there was a good chance they'd receive something other than money for their troubles. Something like a bullet between the eyes. They knew about

Captain's temper, and his views on justice. They'd come armed all right, but clearly they would have been overwhelmed had Captain and his men decided to stick around. Fortunately for them, it appeared that Captain had decided to play by the rules and trusted them to deliver Wing to the farm that evening. If not, they would have been severely outnumbered.

Not only had they underestimated the size of Captain's force, but they also hadn't thought about how much a sack carrying 20 million pesos weighed. They argued among themselves over who would have to carry it on the strenuous uphill trek back to their camp. I almost wanted to offer my assistance if it would get me to see Wing and Johnny sooner.

They finally started slowly back up the mountain and I waited for them to get just out of sight before venturing to follow them. They were making plenty of noise tramping through the brush, cursing each other as they took turns carrying the load of money. It wouldn't be difficult to follow them while remaining out of sight. I was just about to step out from my spot when the brush on either side of me began to move. I choked back a scream, thinking they'd somehow doubled back and surrounded me, just in time to see a dozen armed men emerge from the surrounding trees.

I guess I wasn't the only one with plans to follow the kidnappers back to their own camp. Apparently the hacienderos hadn't changed their plans after all. I should have known. Captain would follow the money to Wing, slaughter the rebels, and return with both Wing and the money. It was that simple. All in a days work for Captain.

Now what? Should I forget my plan and go home? That would have been the smart thing to do. Leave all this money and guns nonsense to the men. But then it hit me hard. What about Johnny? He didn't know what was coming. What if he was just there protecting Wing, as he'd promised me? I knew Captain would shoot first and not even get to the questions later. But what could I do? Could I get there before Captain and warn Johnny? I didn't see how, without being seen. Then it occurred to me that maybe Captain would delay his attack until nightfall and that would give me enough time to sneak into the camp. I had no way of knowing, but I had to try. I would follow Captain's men and hope for the best.

Despite the two teams of men making their way through the jungle ahead of me, I still wished I had my own machete, if not to cut through the foliage with, then to defend myself against some of the giant insects lying in ambush at every turn. I brought a small canteen with me, but I think I sucked it dry before we were even halfway there. So much for planning.

It was late afternoon when I practically tripped over one of Captain's men. We were there. And apparently they'd stopped just outside the camp. I backed up to hide among a small group of rocks until I could see what Captain's plan was. I hoped they would wait until nightfall, giving me at least a chance to get to Johnny.

But it wasn't to be. It seemed that Captain's men had spread out all over the place. My chances of sneaking into the camp unnoticed would be nearly impossible. Even worse, the men had somehow gotten behind me. I wasn't sure how it happened but now there were men in front of me toward to camp as well as behind me. Captain only had twelve men but they soon seemed to be everywhere. I pressed my body further down between the rocks to avoid being discovered.

That's when the shooting started. It was too late. There was nothing I could do for Johnny now. Bullets seemed to be flying everywhere. They were even ricocheting off the rocks where I was hiding. And from both sides. I was in the middle. It seemed as though everyone was shooting at *me*. I tried to convince myself that that was crazy. But it turned out that that was exactly what was happening. Captain and his men had walked into a trap. They were the men in front of me, toward the camp. The ones behind me were not. They were the rebels. Captain and his men had been surrounded. And I was caught in between, taking fire from both sides.

All I could do was shut my eyes tight and pray, for myself, for Captain and his men, for Wing, and for Johnny. I prayed to every saint I could think of, even Francis, the patron saint of pets. I know it sounds crazy, but I'd prayed to all the others and the bullets kept flying. I figured it couldn't hurt.

Well, I don't really think Francis had much to do with it, but eventually the shooting stopped. I didn't know if that was good or bad. Other than myself, I didn't know who was alive and who was dead. And from the first voice I heard, things didn't sound promising.

"I want Captain alive!" ordered Speed.

I wondered what that said about the others, the rest of Captain's men. I peaked from my hiding place and had to assume the worst. I could see a couple of bloodied bodies up ahead of me toward the camp. I recognized them as men recruited by Captain from the other farms. I'm sure the rest of them had met the same fate. They never stood a chance, surrounded and ambushed the way they were. How could Captain's plan have failed so miserably?

At least Captain was alive. I saw the rebels dragging him from the jungle into the clearing of the camp. When they pulled him to his feet, I saw he'd been shot in the thigh. His pant leg was soaked bright red. What was Speed going to do with him? Where was Johnny? Did he know about the ambush? How could he have allowed this to happen? Where was Wing? Was she already dead?

It didn't take long for all my questions to be answered as three of Speed's goons escorted Johnny and Wing, hands bound, into view. Johnny was angry. Wing was scared. But they were OK. Johnny appeared to be a prisoner. Despite all the bloodshed I'd just witnessed, at least it was some sort of relief to see that Johnny wasn't part of it.

"You crazy motherfucker!" he shouted at Speed, shaking off his escorts. "Why? You didn't have to kill them."

Speed turned to address Johnny. "I knew you wouldn't understand. I knew you were weak. Now you know why we had to restrain you, why you couldn't know what was going down. Chances are you'd have aided the enemy, come to your uncle's defense."

"You're damn right," answered Johnny. "We were supposed to be working toward a peaceful political solution. When did this become all about kidnapping and killing?"

"You see, that's just it," began Speed. "I always knew it would, while you choose to live in the theoretical world, a fantasy world.

You've lived in the States too long. You think anything's possible. But here, life's too short to wait for politicians. It takes men of action to get things done."

"Men of action? To kidnap teenage girls?"

"I knew your heart wasn't in it, but you knew about the kidnapping when you came along for the ride. If it was so against your lofty principles, you shouldn't have come. Sorry I didn't fill you in on our little ambush. But I knew you wouldn't have the stomach for it." Then turning to his goons, "Cut him lose. He can't do any harm now."

I couldn't believe what I'd just heard. Seeing Johnny tied up, I'd held out hope that he wasn't involved in Wing's kidnapping. But apparently he was, and willingly, as I saw Johnny free to move about. Wing received no such freedom.

"How did you know they'd follow the money?" asked Johnny. "I didn't think you were that smart."

"Neither did they," answered Speed, pointing with a jerk of his lips at a couple of Captain's dead men. "I must admit, I can't know everything. But I am smart enough to have friends in high places, friends with access to information I'm not privy to." Then turning away from Johnny, "Hey, Boy! There's a friend of yours here who wants to know how I knew about Captain's little mission."

Speed's supporters parted, allowing Boy Delgado to come forward.

"Boy! Thank God!" shouted Wing at the sight of her big brother, naively hoping he'd come to rescue her.

Boy ignored her. And seeing his lack of concern for his sister, I knew better than to believe Boy was here with good intention. I just couldn't believe it. Even for Boy. I mean, I knew he was an asshole. But this? Thwarting the plan to save his sister? And getting men killed in the process? I wouldn't have believed he'd have gone that far. I could see by the look on Johnny's face, though, that he wasn't surprised. I think he saw what Boy was capable of from the day he'd met him. Captain took the news like a knife to the chest.

"You!?" he spat. "You told them our plan? Our plan to save your sister?" I could see the veins bulging in Captain's forehead. "You little imbecile. You would destroy your farm, your family?"

"I don't give a shit about that farm or my family," answered Boy.

I could see Wing was no longer confused. She looked numb from the shock of it.

"But why? What do you gain by doing this?" pressed Captain.

Speed answered for him. "Twenty million pesos can buy a lot of candy."

Boy smiled stupidly in agreement.

"Candy? What are you talking about?" asked Captain, confused.

In answer, Speed pulled a small plastic bag of white powder from his pocket and tossed it to Boy who grabbed it like a five-year-old on Christmas day. "A small down payment," added Speed.

Finally Captain understood. Turning to Boy, "You pathetic loser. You're an insult to your family name, to José Delgado, and to God. You disgust me."

Preoccupied by his new candy, Boy ignored him, snorting pinches of cocaine.

"And you," added Captain, turning to Johnny. "I never expected much from Boy Delgado. But you. My own flesh and blood. That you would take part in such a thing. It could only have come from your father's side, some cowardly American GI knocking up hookers."

I could see Captain's words had hit home. Johnny started to say something but bit back the words. I had more than a few words for Johnny myself. I was disgusted that he'd taken part in this. I understood his involvement in the land reform movement. I understood his frustration with the system in the Philippines that offered so little chance for advancement. But this? Kidnapping and stealing. I couldn't believe I'd misjudged his character so. I was disappointed in myself. And I hated Johnny for that. For tricking me and proving what an idiot I was. I hated him.

Speed resumed his interview with Captain. "Don't you worry about Johnny," suggested Speed. "It's time you worried about me," he added, suddenly kicking Captain's wounded leg.

Captain was clearly in pain, held between two of the armed rebels, supporting himself on his one good leg. Johnny seemed to want to help him, but the coward didn't move. Captain's injury, however, didn't stop him from lunging at Speed, shouting, "You're a dead man! I'll kill you if it's the last thing I do!"

Speed laughed, easily dodging the wounded man's attack, as the two rebels let him fall to the ground. Standing over him in triumph, Speed responded, "You're not the boss anymore, Boss. I've taken orders from you long enough. Now it's my turn to give the orders. And I can assure you, killing me is definitely nowhere on your list of things to do, let alone last."

"What do you want from me?" demanded Captain, getting to his feet.

"Well, let me see," Speed began, looking at the palm of his hand as if checking his list. "You're already bleeding, so I can cross that off the list." He made a show of pretending to scratch that line off his palm. "What's next? Oh yes." He then took one of the rifles from his men and rammed the butt into Captain's bleeding thigh. Wing screamed as Captain dropped to one knee, an involuntarily moan escaping between gritted teeth. "That's it. Suffer is definitely on the list." He looked about at his men, smiling as he crossed another imaginary line from the palm of his hand. The men chuckled in response. Johnny didn't laugh. But he didn't protest either. He just stood there. That wasn't the Johnny I thought I knew. The old Johnny would have jumped between Captain and his tormentor and put a stop to it all. What was holding him back? I knew he wasn't afraid of Speed's goons. He didn't fear for his personal safety. That never stopped him before. And I knew he had tremendous respect for his uncle. They were more alike than Johnny knew. Captain's earlier chastisement must have really stung. Yet Johnny just stood there. I didn't get it. What made him weak? What power did Speed hold over Johnny?

"Leave him alone," whined Wing, crying.

Speed ignored her. Yet her words revived Captain. "You've got your money. Release the girl," he calmly insisted.

Speed smiled. "Oh, I don't think so. We're not done with her yet."

Captain's eyes narrowed. "And what do you mean by that?"

"That's none of your concern," answered Speed. "You're getting distracted. After all, we're not done with your list yet." Then, looking at his palm again, "Let's see. Where were we? You know, most of this is boring stuff. Why don't we just see what it says at the end of the list? Ah, here it is. It says, beg and plead for your life."

Even Johnny glared at Speed, trying to gauge the seriousness of Speed's threat. Wing stopped crying, unsure if she heard Speed correctly.

"No," refused Captain, calmly.

"That's too bad," responded Speed, taking the rifle back from one of his men.

"Speed," protested Johnny, seeing where things were headed, "don't do this." But it came out as a request, not a command.

"Am I going to have to restrain you?" asked Speed, turning to Johnny. "Is family more important to you than our cause?" He then nodded to a couple of his goons to be ready at Johnny's sides in case he decided to make trouble. Then, turning back to Captain, "Come on. Beg. It's the last thing on the list."

"I don't think so," Captain replied.

"You don't think so?" asked Speed. "Well, I think so." Speed raised his rifle, placing the end of the barrel to Captain's head.

Captain stared straight ahead in silence.

Johnny started to come forward, finally, but was quickly restrained by Speed's men.

"Stop it," pleaded Wing. "Leave him alone."

I wanted to jump up and start shouting as well. But I didn't see what I could do. They wouldn't listen to me. There wasn't any point. I didn't know what would ultimately happen to Captain. But I knew there wasn't anything I could do. I had to concentrate on Wing. I had to save Wing. I just had to stay hidden and wait for the right moment, probably after nightfall. I saw that I could no longer count on Johnny to help. I'd been so wrong about him. Apparently his cause was more important than the lives of Captain and Wing. It was going to be up to me alone to get Wing home.

I hoped maybe Speed was just bluffing. But I think I knew better. He couldn't let Captain go. Everyone knew Captain wouldn't quit until he'd hunted Speed down, if not for Papa or Wing, then for all the men who volunteered for this mission, trapped and gunned down. I'm sure Captain felt responsible for them. He would avenge them.

"Shut up!" Speed shouted at Wing. "I want **him** to say it. Not you." Then turning his attention back to his prey, "Come on, Boss. It's not so hard. Say it. Please, please, Mr. Speed, please don't blow my head off."

Captain held his silence.

"My patience is running out," stated Speed.

Speed's men easily held Johnny back as he appealed to Speed. "Speed, don't."

Wing was crying again. Even Speed's men were beginning to look nervous, as if finally realizing this wasn't a joke. Speed was serious.

"Go on. Say it," Speed insisted, obviously agitated. With no immediate response from Captain, he placed the end of the gun barrel between Captain's eyes.

I had closed mine to pray. I didn't remember doing it. But apparently I had. I couldn't watch anymore. But I could hear. I heard Captain's reply. And it wasn't the one Speed was looking for. It was calm and deliberate. I could hear every word. I'll never forget Captain's voice. "Fuck you. And may you rot in hell." I could hear Captain spit.

"No!" yelled Johnny, too late.

Then it came. My body felt the shock wave before my ears could identify the sound. But it didn't take long. After all, I'd heard that sound before. Yet, it's a sound you just don't get used to. Rifles. They're a whole lot louder than you'd think. I didn't want to open my eyes. But it wasn't up to me anymore. None of it was. The kidnapping, the ambush, the single gunshot. It was all out of my control. And it was the same for my eyes. They opened, just in time to see Captain's blood spattered body fall backward to the ground.

I screamed. I couldn't help it. It was out of my control.

Chapter 15

There wasn't anything else I could do. Watching Captain's lifeless body crumple to the ground, I froze in horror, but the anguish couldn't be bottled. My jaw dropped and out it came. So loud it hurt. Yet, miraculously, no one heard my scream. That's because I wasn't the only one screaming. And long after I'd closed my mouth, the screaming continued. It was Wing. Eyes shut tight, head flailing side to side, she screamed and screamed. And kept screaming, until Speed punched her so hard in the gut that there wasn't any air left to scream with.

"Shut the hell up!" he shouted. "You're ruining it for me. I've waited a long time for this. Let me savor it."

Boy Delgado looked up from his bag of cocaine with glazed eyes as if first noticing Captain's bloody corpse. "Hey, all right, Speed. I never did like that guy."

Johnny gave one half-hearted lunge in their direction, then stopped. It was too late. Johnny would not be saving *this* day.

"Let him go," ordered Speed to the men holding Johnny, so confident in Johnny's defeat. "He's harmless."

Harmless? Johnny? I couldn't make sense of it. How I'd been so wrong about him. So completely wrong. Johnny slowly walked over to Captain's body, kneeling to check the obvious. He remained still for a moment. I could only imagine what was going through his mind. Captain could be hard on a person. Yet he was the closest thing Johnny'd had to a father in a long time. And here he'd just witnessed his execution by a band of thugs. The Johnny I knew would have taken action. He'd have squeezed justice from their very throats, without hesitation, just as Captain would have. And he'd have done it despite the odds, without concern for himself. And if, overwhelmed by numbers, he'd fallen, then he'd have died with a clear conscience in the knowledge he'd done all he could.

But that's not what happened. This was a different Johnny from the one I'd known. This was the Johnny that wanted to steal Papa's farm, who let them kidnap poor Wing, and let them slaughter Captain and his men. When he finally turned to Speed, I thought for a moment he was going to say something, but then thought better of it, the words caught in his throat. What's done was done. He then stood up and calmly addressed Speed.

"When do we bring the girl home?" He said it as if nothing had happened. As if his uncle wasn't lying dead at his feet. And it chilled me the way he referred to Wing as... the girl.

Speed laughed. "Home?"

"Yes, home," replied Johnny. "We have the money. Let's bring her home."

"Not so fast," countered Speed. "They tried to trick us. They had no intention of letting us keep the money. To the victor go the spoils. I say we keep her."

"Keep her? What for?" Johnny looked sorry he'd even asked.

Speed seemed happy to reply. Staring sinisterly at Wing, "I'm sure we can find something to do with her." Then, eyeing Johnny, warily, "Why? What's she to you?"

"To me? Oh, nothing. It's just, you know," began Johnny, "if we don't bring her back, we'll never be able to get any more money out of them no matter how many people we kidnap. They'll know it's pointless to pay. It'll be all out war. That'll only set our plan back. We'll never see land reform. Our cause is more important than getting even with them. We need to win people over to our side. And that's going to take money."

Speed pondered Johnny's words. "You've got a point. Not that I wouldn't enjoy an all out war. It's just I'd rather improve our finances first. But we can't reward them for trying to trick us. They've got to pay for that."

Johnny thought briefly, then continued. "Then why don't we just demand a little more money, as restitution, before we release her. That way we save face, they get the girl, and we plan our next kidnapping."

Speed's pleasure at Johnny's plan showed in the smile on his face. "Not bad. I like it," he said, patting Johnny on the back. "Maybe there's hope for you yet." Then, putting his arm around Johnny's shoulders, "I was beginning to worry about you. Initially, you seemed a bit squeamish about all this kidnapping stuff. I wasn't sure you were going to work out. And then, your uncle had to try to be the hero. You do understand why I couldn't let you in on his ambush. I mean, I wasn't sure how you'd take it." He ruffled Johnny's hair and gave him a friendly punch in the shoulder. "But it looks like you're going to be just fine." Johnny just nodded his head in agreement.

It made me sick. How he'd convinced me not to tell anyone about the kidnapping while it seemed he was in on it the whole time. What a snake? He'd made a fool out of me. And now Captain and all those men were dead. I wanted to grab a gun and kill both Speed and Johnny, execute them, like they did to Captain. But I couldn't. I had to remain calm, and hidden, at least until nightfall. It was up to me to save Wing. There wasn't anyone else left. Over her crying, Wing hadn't heard any of the conversation about her. Speed may have knocked the scream out of her, but she could still cry over what they did to Captain, which is what she did until they dragged her away.

* * * *

It took forever for the sun to go down. I tried to keep myself preoccupied with a little game I'd made up between me and the mosquitoes. They would land on me and try to bite me, while I would try to smash them. I'd stopped keeping score, but I'm pretty sure the mosquitoes were winning.

I wasn't the only one passing the time with a game. Some of the kidnappers played cards around their campfire, gambling for cigarettes. I hadn't eaten anything all day and my stomach began to growl at the smell of whatever it was they'd cooked over the campfire. I was a little surprised that I could even think of food while people were getting slaughtered and Wing was held captive. It didn't seem to bother the mosquitoes appetite either, as I sat there being eaten alive, wondering how I'd gotten myself into this whole mess. Where had I gone wrong? And the same answer kept coming back to me. I'd trusted Johnny Dillinger. That's where I went wrong. Well, I wouldn't have to worry about that anymore. The hacienderos would make him pay for what he'd done. That is, if I didn't kill him myself.

Even after darkness came, it took a while for things to settle down at the kidnappers' camp. There appeared to be about 30 men in the group, and even after most had turned in, a few of them remained around the campfire for quite some time fighting over cards and cigarettes. Eventually, most of the men had run out of cigarettes, but they soon found something else to gamble over. It had something to do with Wing. I think it was over guard duty, who would have to guard her first. In the beginning, I thought they were trying to avoid it, the winner getting to go to sleep first. But it soon became apparent that it was just the opposite. Instead of avoiding guard duty, the winner got to go first. That seemed a little odd to me, why someone would want to be first on guard duty. Of course, that's only because I was an idiot. I hadn't learned to think like a murdering kidnapper yet. But there would be time for that later. It was still only evening, and they'd planned a long night ahead for Wing.

Speed had rewarded the four that had gone down the mountain for the money with a bottle of lambanug for their troubles. As if these men weren't evil enough sober, there's nothing like a little alcohol to fuel the flames of hell. They were having a good time and had no plans of leaving that bottle of lambanug until it was empty.

So I sat with my friends, the mosquitoes, patiently, until the lambanug was gone and all appeared quiet. That's when I finally got to stretch my legs and put my plan into action. I first had to check the bodies of each of Captain's men, looking for a knife. I knew the kidnappers had collected all their guns, but I was hoping they'd overlooked some kind of knife, as I would certainly need one to help free Wing. I was sure she'd be tied up in some fashion to prevent her escape. Not that Wing would have had the nerve to attempt it, or the sense of direction to succeed. It wasn't until the third body that I was able to find a nice-sized hunting knife in one of the men's socks. I'd never in my life imagined I'd be crawling through brush searching dead bodies in the dark. The flies, never to turn down a fresh meal, had already started without me. At least the bodies hadn't started to smell yet. If they had, I wouldn't have been able to keep even my empty stomach from heaving.

Now I had to find where they were keeping Wing. The kidnappers' camp consisted of scattered primitive lean-tos constructed of bamboo to protect them from the elements. Working my way around the perimeter of the camp, ultimately it was my ears, not my eyes, that found Wing. Her hands were tied behind her back and she was secured to one of the lean-to posts. I recognized the two men guarding her as two of those rewarded for carrying the money. Judging by the way they couldn't walk in a straight line, it was apparent they'd had enough lambanug to make trouble, but not enough to pass out and go to sleep. There was a fat one whose clothes looked several sizes too small on him, and a skinny one whose clothes looked several sizes too large. I didn't know whether it was just an optical illusion or whether they'd mistakenly worn each other's clothes. But it wasn't really their attire that concerned me. It was their conversation. They were discussing Wing's, uh, attributes.

"They're not *that* small," said the skinny one, pointing at Wing's chest.

Wing was attempting to avoid making eye contact as she stared at the ground, wishing she'd had many more layers of clothes on, and trying to twist her chest out of their view.

"Oh they're OK, but I like 'em big," stated the fat one.

"Oh, and you've had so many offers from the ladies that you could afford to be so choosy?"

"Well, I wouldn't say that. But a man's entitled to an opinion." He followed his remark with a loud belch.

"You know, we may have gotten to go first because we won at cards, but there are others in line. Our shift won't last forever. What do you say we take a closer look?"

Wing's eyes widened, as she pulled further at her ropes to turn from the ogling pair. Frustrated by her posture, Skinny yanked Wing by the shoulders to straighten her out and started to fumble with the buttons on her blouse. Wing didn't make a sound, but I could see the tears start to flow again. When he pulled her blouse open, she started to whimper and plead out of fear. At least she was wearing a bra.

"Shut her up," insisted Fat. "She'll wake the whole camp."

Skinny had to untie her hands to remove her blouse, but he was sure to tie them back to the post before stuffing the blouse into her mouth as a gag and tying it behind her head, successfully muffling Wing's protests. Wing's eyes went from wide to closed, probably resorting to prayer.

When Fat reached to remove her bra, Skinny stopped him. "No. No. Wait. Let's have some fun. Take it slow." He then reached to unsnap her jeans. Though I could barely hear it, Wing was screaming from behind her gag. The two men enjoyed themselves as they slowly peeled her pants down her legs. When they reached her ankles, they each grabbed one leg of her pants and slowly pulled them off, humming some strip-tease music for full effect. And I guess it worked, for soon the men were unsnapping their own pants as Wing shook her head back and forth silently screaming.

I wanted to scream myself, but who would hear me? Certainly no one that would put a stop to what was about to happen. I could tell this wasn't going to end well. But I couldn't just sit there and watch. How could I? This was Wing. How could I be a witness to her rape? It wasn't possible. I either had to do something to help, anything, or run away. Yet I knew running away wasn't really an option for me. I'd rather have taken her place than run away and leave her.

I remember when we were little, we'd get into all sorts of trouble. Whether it was picking all of Mama's flowers so we could play wedding, or bringing our calf into the swimming pool for a bath, we'd always taken our punishment together. We were a team. It wouldn't be right that one of us should receive a beating while the other just watched. It had become second nature that if one of us were hurt, the other would have to somehow take part. There was the time I'd broken my arm as a kid when I tried to ride that billy goat. The goat wouldn't have it, and tossed me off like a bucking bronco. I ended up with a cast on my right arm for most of the summer. But I wasn't the only one. Wing insisted that her arm was broken too. And when they told her she was crazy, and wouldn't give her a cast just like mine, she cut up an old shirt, mixed it with some plaster she found in the barn, and applied her own cast. She wore baggy long sleeved shirts around the grown-ups who took a week to discover what she'd done. Wing felt so bad when they removed her cast, because she could do things with her two arms that I couldn't do with my one, that she insisted on being my slave until my cast came off, even cutting my food for me at the dinner table. Wing could never abandon me in my time of need. And I couldn't abandon her.

No, I wouldn't leave her. I would stay, and fight. I had my knife, and I would use it. Just me against the two men. It didn't matter. I had to act. I was pretty sure, with the element of surprise, that I could kill at least one of them. As for the other one, I'd have to take my chances. There wasn't any time for contingency plans. I only had enough wits about me to wait just a few more seconds. By then they'd have their pants down around their legs. At least that would help immobilize them. And though it wasn't much of a chance, it would offer my best chance of success. Or survival. They were one in the same.

Just a few more seconds. It seemed like days. I gripped the knife firmly in my sweaty hand. There was no turning back. My heart was racing. I was ready to spring. Their pants went to their knees. One, two, three, now!

Wait! Someone else was coming.

"Hey guys. What's up?" came a third man's voice, entering the light of the fire.

Shit! A third man. That's all I needed. But then I saw who it was and couldn't believe it. It was Johnny. Was it really possible? Why was he there? Would Johnny save the day after all?

Fat and Skinny froze, pants around their knees.

"You got something to say?" challenged Skinny, waiting to see if Johnny was going to try to break up the party.

"As a matter-of-fact, I do," Johnny replied.

I thought that was a mistake. Johnny was losing his advantage, as I saw Fat and Skinny nervously start to pull their pants back up.

"Well, say it then," demanded Fat, getting ready for a fight.

Johnny remained calm. Then laughing and reaching to undo his own belt buckle, "I just want to know why you two get to have all the fun."

Fat and Skinny looked at each other, chuckled, and then began to lower their pants again. "Well, alright," said Skinny. But you go last."

At first, it didn't register. I wasn't sure what I'd seen or heard. It didn't make sense. It took a few moments for it to sink in. But I heard what I heard. I saw what I saw. Johnny would *not* be saving the day. He wouldn't be coming to Wing's rescue. He'd gone even beyond assisting kidnappers. He was unbuckling his belt, preparing to take part in the rape. Wing's rape. My Wing. That was the last conscious thought I remember. By that time, all reason had left me. It didn't matter that there was no way I could overcome three men. I would kill one and maybe injure another before they could stop me. But I wouldn't go down without a fight. I clutched the knife so tightly it had become a part of me, an extension of my hand, my body, my soul. I'd become that knife, sharp, cold, steel. And I was looking for a warm place to rest. Who would be the lucky beneficiary of my attention? Who deserved to be first? The answer didn't take any thought at all. It was obvious. Even the knife knew. And it was Johnny. We chose Johnny, my knife and I.

I think hate is a lot like fear. I find horror movies about things you know more terrifying than ones about things you don't know. Like the ones where the sadistic neighbor is out to get you, things that could actually happen, versus the ones where some corny alien from another planet shows up in town. The one that's actually possible, the one you're familiar with, seems so much more real. Well, it's the same with hate. People say it's easier to hate what you don't know. I disagree. I think it's easier to hate what you *do* know. We have expectations for people we know. Expectations to behave with a certain sense of decency, a decency we wouldn't necessarily expect from a stranger. I think that's why I chose Johnny. I expected more from him. And now, to see him taking part in this nightmare, I hated him a thousand times more than the other two men. I hated him for what he was about to commit. I hated him for his betrayal, for what he'd become. I hated everything about him.

Chapter 16

I never imagined how much blood the human body contains. Or how quickly that blood escapes when you grab someone by the hair, pull his head back, and cut his throat from ear to ear. But I do now. I stood frozen over his lifeless body, bloody knife in my hand, my own body splattered red from head to toe by what had pumped from his severed neck. I couldn't move. I could hear though. I could hear my own heart pumping in my ears. And I could taste. It was iron. From the blood. Some of it must have sprayed into my mouth. That brought me around. The metallic taste. I let go of his hair, dropped my bloody blade, and spit.

I felt someone grab me. I'd only killed the one. But I didn't care anymore. My strength was gone. I was trapped in another's arms.

"It's OK. It's OK," he whispered in my ear.

It was Johnny. He'd killed the first one, I think it was Fat, by strangling him with the belt he'd removed when he pretended he would take part in the rape. But that gave Skinny a chance to react. He'd hit Johnny in the back of the head with a fire log. When Johnny fell to the ground, Skinny was on his back, knife drawn.

It all happened so fast. My own knife was drawn, prepared to kill Johnny. But before I could make my move, Johnny made his. I was caught off guard. Confused. I don't know if I realized then that Johnny was trying to save Wing after all. I wasn't thinking straight. I wasn't thinking at all. But my body instinctively knew what to do.

My legs, my hand, my knife. Seeing a man about to plunge his knife into Johnny's back, I had no choice. I leapt from my hiding spot, grabbed the man by his hair, pulled his head back, and cut his throat from ear to ear. Then it came. And it was everywhere. The blood.

I remember the feel of Johnny's arms around me. Like a warm blanket, protecting me from the elements, the cold, the heat, the fear, the hate. Warm. Like a dream.

"Let's go. We can't stay here," he whispered, drawing me out of my dream. Then his arms were gone and he was cutting Wing loose. She couldn't stand. She'd been so frightened by the ordeal, that her legs wouldn't hold her. She simply lay on the ground in only her underwear, curled into a ball. Johnny knelt down and picked her up in his arms. "Come on."

I followed them. I didn't know where he was going. But I assumed it was away. Away from the camp and the kidnappers. Away from this nightmare. I wasn't really thinking. I was still looking at the blood on my hands and tasting the iron in my mouth to pay much attention. Yet, as we were about to leave the camp, something familiar caught my eye. I stopped.

Johnny turned and noticed I wasn't behind him. "What are you doing?" he whispered.

"Papa and his friends will want this," I said, as I heaved the sack containing the 20 million pesos over my shoulder. I don't know where I got the strength. I guess it was pure adrenaline. I'm sure Johnny must have mumbled something about leaving it behind, that it was too heavy, would slow us down, that it wasn't worth the risk. But, still in shock, I wasn't listening. I quickly caught up and we were out of the camp and into the jungle again. Me, Johnny, Wing, and the money.

We practically ran down the mountain and had already reached the bottom when I noticed just how heavy my load was and my arms gave out. Wing hadn't said a word, and she didn't look right, but fortunately, by the bottom of the mountain she'd found her legs, so Johnny could take over the job of carrying the ransom money.

Blindly following Johnny through the jungle in darkness, my mind kept coming back to the same thing. Finally, I found the words.

"You promised you would protect her," I accused Johnny.

"And so I have," he answered without turning around or slowing his pace.

Our conversation continued as we quickly made our way along the path. "But you were with them. You were in on it."

"Not this, I wasn't. I believed in a cause. But not through violence. I didn't know they were just a bunch of criminals, trying to steal what wasn't theirs. I was a fool. You don't believe I had anything to do with kidnapping, murder, or rape, do you?"

Yet I had. I was convinced of just that. "But you went along. When they kidnapped Wing."

"I promised you I wouldn't let anything happen to her. When they came to get her, it was so sudden. There were too many of them. I wouldn't have been able to stop them. I had no choice. So I went along, to stay with Wing."

It made sense. But it wasn't enough. I was angry. There was more to explain. "And what about Captain? They murdered…" The words got caught in my throat. "…murdered him right before your eyes. You watched his execution. How could you just stand there? Couldn't you have done something?"

This time Johnny stopped walking. He just stopped. I almost ran into him. He didn't turn around. "I couldn't." That was it. That's all he said.

"What do you mean? You could have tried. You could have fought back."

He still hadn't turned to face me. "There were too many. They'd have killed me too."

"So that's it. You were afraid," I accused. "Afraid for your own life. Captain was never afraid. He died trying to save Wing. He would have died trying to save any of us."

Johnny was silent, head bowed. "I know that."

I was ashamed of him. "But you didn't show him the same respect. Why wouldn't you do the same for him?"

Johnny turned and looked me in the eye. "Then who would have saved Wing?"

It hadn't occurred to me. He had a point. "You mean you let Captain die so that you could continue protecting Wing?"

"I had to," he replied. "I made a promise to you." There wasn't any anger or blame in his answer. Just sadness. Sadness at having to make such life and death decisions. He'd let one of his only relatives in the world die because he'd promised to protect one of mine.

I reached up to touch his face. "I'm sorry. I didn't mean to—"

"It's OK," he cut me off. "Come on. Let's go." He turned to continue down the trail. "Besides," he added, "you saved *my* life. We're even now."

I looked down at the blood on my hands. I did, didn't I? Without a thought for my own safety, I'd butchered a man to save Johnny's life. Spread the word. You mess with Lisa Salonga, you mess with your life. I was a bad ass. But that wasn't how I felt. I just wished the blood would go away. Yet Johnny was right. We both had faced difficult choices. And, in the end, we each did the right thing. I wanted to apologize to Johnny for doubting him. I wanted to thank him. He'd come through for me. Again. As always.

But before I could find the words, we'd come out of the jungle into a clearing. It was a full moon, and, emerging from the jungle into the open, I practically had to shield my eyes from the relative brightness of the moonlight. Without hesitating, we set out across the field.

"Shsh, quiet," Johnny said, stopping and turning to face the jungle from which we'd recently emerged.

I thought I could make out the sound of voices coming from the jungle. I wasn't sure. But Wing was. A look of terror came over her face, as she broke into a run across the field in the opposite direction from the voices. By then, I could hear them too. There was no mistaking the sound of Speed's men in hot pursuit. They'd discovered the bodies of Fat and Skinny, noticed we were gone, and come to hunt us down. Johnny and I took off after Wing.

There was about a half dozen of them. And when they emerged from the jungle, we were caught out in the open, with no place to hide under the light of the moon. Wing never looked back. She was running at full speed. But Wing was never very fast, and when

Johnny and I caught up with her, I thought she was going to collapse, whether from exhaustion or fear I couldn't be sure. Looking ahead about a hundred yards, in the middle of the clearing, I saw a small patch of jungle that might serve as a place to hide. Even from a distance though, it looked vaguely familiar and foreboding to me. I must have been distracted by the panic of being hunted, because as we approached, I finally realized what it was. I pulled up short just outside the tree line, grabbing Wing by the strap of her bra.

"Stop!" I shouted.

Wing looked at me, confused, but too tired to break free from my grasp. Johnny had already disappeared into the jungle, but immediately popped back out when he noticed we hadn't entered with him.

"What?" he demanded.

Wing looked at me, gasping for air.

"We can't," I answered.

"What do you mean?" asked Johnny.

"The dwarves," I replied. I thought that would be self-explanatory. "They'll curse us," I added, just in case.

Johnny looked at me as if I was a fool. "You and your damned dwarves. Well, the kidnappers intend to kill us. It's up to you. Cursed or killed?"

I didn't like my options. And Wing, looking back at the armed kidnappers, remembering her close encounter with Fat and Skinny, didn't take long to make up her mind. She darted into the dwarves' jungle and never looked back.

Seeing that I hadn't moved, Johnny gave me one last look, and said, "Well, say hi to the kidnappers for us. Wing and I will be breakfasting with the dwarves," and disappeared into the jungle. I was alone, that is, except for the pack of thieving, murdering, rapists rapidly approaching. I like to think that Johnny was just bluffing and would have come back out to save me. But I'll never know, because I wasn't waiting to find out. I made the sign of the cross, said a quick prayer, shut my eyes, and launched myself into dwarf territory.

It was dark again in the tree-covered jungle. I called out for Johnny. He wasn't far off. Anyway, the dwarves' patch of jungle was only about a hundred yards from one end to the other. But there was no point in heading for the other side. Speed's men would only catch us out in the open again. No, all we could do was find a place to hide and wait. Maybe they'd give up looking for us or help would arrive. More likely, we'd die fighting them when they found us in the jungle. But there was one thing I hadn't thought of. The obvious thing.

Speed's men were just as afraid of the dwarves as I was. And they wouldn't come in after us. We could hear the six of them spreading out, a man every 50 feet or so, encircling the small patch of jungle. They were going to wait. Wait for what, exactly, I wasn't sure. For us to starve? For new orders from Speed? For daylight, when maybe they'd have a better chance against the dwarves? Of course then they'd still get cursed.

So I sat in the dark, praying for help to arrive. Wing still hadn't said a word. I think she was in shock from her close call with Fat and Skinny. Johnny had given her his shirt to wear over her underwear. He and I sat silently for a while. I was thinking about how I used to be so sure about things. About how Johnny and I would somehow end up together. I didn't know how. I just knew we would. But now, with all his talk of social justice and his preoccupation with land reform in the Philippines, I wasn't sure where I fit in anymore. I know it was just the thoughts of a self-centered little girl. Yet there was something to it. How could I compete with "the cause?" It seemed, despite our silly little competition, it looked like neither Wing nor I would win the prize. Johnny, that is. It looked like his allegiance was to "the people." And I didn't like coming in second. Besides, "the people" didn't seem to be very nice. They kidnapped Wing, murdered Captain and his men, and now had us surrounded in the jungle, waiting to finish us off, that is, if the dwarves didn't get us first. Then, as if hearing my very thoughts, Johnny turned to me with a pained look on his face.

"I'm sorry," he said.

"About what?" I asked.

"Everything. I'm an idiot. I thought it could be done peacefully. That people could wait for change in the system. Change that would give them opportunity and hope. I should have known. They're no better than anyone else. They just want what doesn't belong to them. And they don't want to wait. They don't want to work for it. Earn it. They just want to take it. Grab it. Like children fighting over candy. I should have seen it coming. I just didn't want to believe it. I'm sorry I allowed this to happen. I'm sorry I let it involve you and Wing. Mr. Delgado's been so good to me. He put a roof over my head, gave me work, sent me to college, and this is how I repay him. I let them kidnap Wing. Now Captain's dead." He paused for a moment and I didn't know what to say. "I'm done with the whole thing," he continued. "No more revolutions for me." He bowed his head and held it between both hands as if it were going to burst. "I'm so sorry."

It's funny how only hours ago I hated him. He'd joined the enemy, those that would hurt Wing and her family, Papa's farm, everything I'd ever wanted to be a part of. I was only seconds away from plunging a knife into him to prevent just that. Yet now, I sat and stared at the same man, drowning in remorse, and I wanted to go to him, to hold him and say it was OK. Sure, he'd misjudged the very people he was trying to help. But *he* didn't make them bad. They did that on their own. Things wouldn't have been any different even if he hadn't gotten involved. Speed and the others would have been doing just what they did even without Johnny. The only difference would have been that Johnny wouldn't have been there to save Wing.

"It wasn't your fault," I offered. "They'd have done the same thing, with or without you." He didn't seem to hear me. At least, he didn't lift his head. "It wasn't your fault," I repeated, softly touching his shoulder. "You were only doing what you thought was right."

Johnny looked up. "But I wasn't right. I thought I could help them."

"So what's wrong with that? You know, you and Papa are a lot alike. He's always trying to help. Don't you see it? He gives people jobs. He helps them with schooling. He builds them churches. But he chooses carefully who to help. He only helps the good ones. You said once you felt like a slave here. Yet Papa sent you to college. Why? Because he saw promise in you. He saw you deserved a chance. Sure, he doesn't give out chances like that to everyone. Not everyone would know what to do with such a chance."

"Well he certainly didn't get his money's worth out of me," said Johnny. "It just doesn't seem right that it's up to Mr. Delgado or the other hacienderos to decide these things, who's worthy and who's not. It's like playing God."

I had to respond to that. "And who would you have make those decisions? The corrupt government officials that would give away Papa's land in exchange for votes in the next election? No. I think Papa's been doing a pretty good job. Papa loves his land all right. But he also loves his people. Filipinos. Take away his land and you take away his ability to help. You want to help people so much? Go ahead. Work for political reform. That's where change needs to occur. But don't take the farmers' land. That's not the answer. I think if I owned Papa's farm, I'd run it just the way he does. I'd fight to keep it in one piece, make it as successful as I could, and use it to help as many people as possible. What about you? If you owned Papa's farm. What would you do?"

Johnny didn't answer right away. He just looked at me seriously for a while. Then his eyes suddenly softened and he smiled. "That's exactly what I'd do." Then he let out a small laugh and added, "When did you get so smart?"

I narrowed my eyes at him, feigning insult. "I've always been smart. You've just been too stupid to see it."

We both laughed, but quickly hushed ourselves lest our pursuers decide to venture into the jungle and find us. Despite the fact that we sat in the dark, surrounded by people prepared to kill us, or worse, dwarves preparing to curse us, I felt a weight lifted after my little talk with Johnny. Maybe he wasn't a lost cause after all. Maybe there'd be room in his world for me yet. It just seemed a shame that being killed or cursed would be the price to pay for that knowledge.

The mood wasn't improved for long, though. I must have nodded off, my arms around Wing and my head on Johnny's shoulder, when I heard the first scream. My head jerked awake, unsure if it was part of a dream. But when I saw the look on Wing and Johnny's faces, I knew they'd heard it too. We couldn't all have been having the same dream. Before anyone could even find the words to ask what it was, there was another scream, this time from the opposite end of the jungle. Speed's men began to call to each other out of concern. The three of us sat in the dark, wondering what was happening out at the perimeter of the jungle. But judging from the shouts, it was something bad. And it was happening to Speed's men. At first they thought it was us, that the three of us were somehow picking them off, one by one. They just couldn't figure out how. And neither could we. Yet the screams continued, cold, blood-curdling screams, sporadically, throughout what was left of the night, each time, followed by the sound of Speed's men calling out to each other, running about the edge of the jungle, trying to make sense out of what was happening. To them. One by one. At first, we thought maybe Papa had sent reinforcements. But if that were the case, Speed's men would have seen them. We gathered our limbs close, climbing up onto some rocks as we wondered whether the men outside the jungle might have disturbed some kind of nest of poisonous snakes. Johnny was trying to see out where each scream came from. Wing was shaking. I was praying.

It seemed the night went on forever, as if dawn would never come. None of the three of us managed to catch another wink of sleep. Something gruesome was happening just outside the jungle. But whatever it was, it wasn't happening to us… yet. So we stayed put, waiting it out.

It wasn't until we saw the morning light begin filtering in through the jungle that we noticed the screams had stopped. We weren't going to let our curiosity get the better of us by venturing out of hiding to investigate. But soon the thought occurred to us that maybe the remaining men had been scared off by whatever it was stalking them through the night. It might have been just the time to make our escape.

We edged slowly toward the sunlight until Johnny silently raised his hand, indicating for Wing and I to wait. So Wing and I huddled together waiting, while Johnny went ahead to assess the situation. No sooner was Johnny out of sight, than Wing started shaking again. Clearly she'd come to see Johnny as her protector and was eagerly awaiting his safe return.

It didn't take long for Johnny to reappear, waving for us to come out. Wing practically ran to him as I brought up the rear, hauling the sack of money, and emerging at the jungle's edge to find Johnny standing over a body.

"What happened," I asked, running to Johnny and looking him over to see if he'd been hurt.

"I don't know," he replied, kneeling down to get a closer look at the body. Johnny looked confused. "He doesn't seem to be injured in any way."

Wing jumped back, apparently thinking the same thing I was, that he was merely sleeping, and at any moment he would jump up and get us.

Johnny looked at us like we were idiots. "No, no. He's dead all right." Then, looking back at the body again, "I just don't see why."

I recognized the man from the kidnappers' camp. Then stepping over him, "Well, I don't need to know why. Just as long as he's dead. Let's go." I pulled Wing by the arm.

"Look. There's another one," said Johnny, jogging over to another body lying in the grass about 50 feet from the first.

"Johnny, let's just go," I called.

"That's weird," he said. "Same thing. No blood. No wounds. Just dead." Johnny ran a little further along the edge of the jungle, stopped, and shouted to us. "They're all dead."

I felt a chill down my spine. I looked over at Wing. I knew just what she was thinking. That's because it was the same thing I was thinking.

Then Johnny just had to feed the fire as he came running back to us. "It's almost like magic." He went to carry the heavy sack of money for me. "OK, let's go." But when he tried to take the sack from me, I held back. "What?" he asked. "I thought you wanted to go."

"Wait," I said, pulling the sack away and opening it.

Johnny saw me going through the bag. "You're not going to count it, are you? There's no time for that now."

I ignored him, pulling out an armful of money. I didn't count it, but it must have been a couple of hundred thousand pesos. As the others watched, I ran just to the edge of the jungle and placed the money under a bush.

When I returned without the money, Johnny looked perplexed, asking, "What did you do?"

I walked right past him, taking Wing by the arm again.

"Lisa," he persisted, catching up with the still very heavy sack. "Where's the money?"

I continued walking. "You've got it, silly. In the sack."

"No," he said. "I mean the rest of it. The part you took into the jungle."

"Oh that. Don't worry about it."

"What do you mean? That was a lot of money. What did you do with it?"

I kept walking, but I knew he'd continue pestering me until I answered him. I couldn't look him in the eye when I replied, though. So instead, I looked at Wing, knowing she'd understand.

"It's for the dwarves," I said. He stood there, frozen in his tracks, with a blank look on his face. "Do you have a problem with that?" I challenged him.

He opened his mouth, but nothing came out when he first tried to speak. Finally the words came to him. "The dwarves?"

"Of course, the dwarves. Who else?" I answered.

"The dwarves?" he repeated. "But that was a lot of money."

"They saved our lives, Johnny. Seems a small price to pay." I looked at Wing who nodded in support.

Johnny stood frozen. Again, words seemed to escape him. Then, he suddenly turned and headed back toward the jungle. "I'm going back."

I ran after him, tugging on his arm. "Johnny, don't. Just be grateful. Let's go."

He ignored me. "That's just crazy. So much money. Thrown away in the jungle for nothing."

He just kept walking, dragging me along as I held onto his arm, Wing behind me, holding on to mine.

"It's not for nothing, Johnny. Leave it alone. Please."

I let go of his arm and stopped, not wanting to get any closer to the jungle.

"This is nuts," he said, as he went on alone to reach the edge of the jungle. I saw him stooping under the bush where I'd just left the pile of money. He stood up, scratching his head. He entered the jungle to check around the other side of the bush.

"Johnny, please don't go in there," I begged. "They let us go this time. They might not be so nice again."

Continuing as if he hadn't heard me, I could see the bush shaking as Johnny crawled all around it looking for the money.

I could hear him cursing in frustration. "Damn it. It was just here." Losing his cool, Johnny finally pulled the whole bush out of the ground. "It's gone," he said, looking over at me.

I quickly looked at Wing, who, without a moment's hesitation, dropped my arm and started running in the opposite direction.

"Wait for me," I yelled, turning to follow her. I glanced back just in time to see Johnny realize he was alone, grab the remaining sack of money, and sprint after us, never looking back.

Chapter 17

"What happened to your clothes?" asked Hortensia when Wing walked into the compound at Casablanca wearing only her underwear under Johnny's shirt. But when Wing just stood there, wearing the expression of a zombie, staring nowhere in particular, Hortensia wrapped her in her arms and rocked her as Wing hung limply in her plump embrace. Wing still hadn't spoken since her ordeal. So when Hortensia didn't receive an answer, she assumed the worst, started crying, and squeezed Wing all the harder.

"She'll be OK," I assured Hortensia, whatever OK meant, and not sure where I'd earned the credentials to make such a pronouncement.

But that seemed to make Hortensia feel better as I soon received my own Hortensia hug while she shouted, "They're home! They're home! They're both home!"

Soon all the maids were there, followed by Mama and Papa. Mama was the usual cold fish. But Papa wrapped his arms around both of us at one time and soon everyone was crying. I tried to show him that I brought back the sack of money, but he ignored it, escorting Wing and me into the house.

"What do I care about money," he said, hugging us even harder, "now that I have the family jewels back?"

The maids were left to haul in the heavy sack. It didn't take long before everyone was asking questions at the same time. They all wanted to know what happened, how we got away, what happened to the others. But Papa held them off until we'd been seated in the kitchen, a soothing cup of tea in front of each of us. I took a sip from mine, and could already feel the warm liquid washing away the events of the past couple of days. Wing just stared at her cup. I saw everyone looking at me, patiently waiting for some answers. I knew what they wanted to know. So I took one last swallow and just blurted it out.

"They're all dead." I saw everyone's eyes open wide in shock at the news. Then I saw the question return to their eyes, a question still holding out hope, hope that we weren't talking about the same people. "Captain and all his men," I added just to be clear.

The maids covered their mouths in shock, immediately began praying for the dead, and dreading the moment Yaya would learn of her dead son. Hearing of Captain's death, Papa looked like he'd taken his own bullet to the chest.

"Are you sure?" he asked, grabbing me firmly by the shoulders and shaking me.

I didn't mind though. I think I knew what he was feeling. I nodded my head. "I'm sure. I saw it happen right in front of my eyes."

Then Mama spoke up. "I haven't seen Boy around. I think he must have followed the men to help save his sister. Did you see him?"

Hearing Boy's name, I felt a foul taste rising in my throat. There were many things I wanted to say. But this wasn't the time or place for that. I would have that discussion with Papa, alone.

So I answered the question as calmly as I could. "Yes. I saw him."

The maids were shaken by the idea that Boy might have been with the rescuers who, I'd just informed them, were all killed. Mama's voice was shaking when she was able to get out the next question. "Did they hurt him? Was my Boy hurt?"

I unconsciously delayed answering just to see her suffer with concern over the animal she'd raised. "No. Boy's not hurt."

That's when Yaya finally appeared, the news of our return spreading throughout the compound. Seeing Wing and me safely returned, she nodded to me with a wink and a barely perceptible smile. Not one to beat around the bush, "Where's Captain?" she demanded.

The silence was sickening as all eyes turned to find someplace to look other than at Yaya. She looked into my eyes and right on through. I didn't have to say a word. She knew. Looking for her reaction, I thought maybe she blinked and took a slightly deeper breath, no more than as if she'd had a chill or maybe a hiccup. Then, without any other sign of emotion, she spit a squirt of chewing tobacco on the floor and asked me another question.

"Who? Who did it?"

"It was Speed," I answered. "Speed with several cane workers and communists, about thirty in all I think."

Yaya's eyes narrowed, as she was probably thinking of a fit punishment for Speed and his friends. The choices were few. Death or torture.

Papa nodded, his suspicion confirmed. "I should have known *that* one would be involved." Then looking at the shirt Wing was wearing, I saw sadness again. "And what of this Johnny Dillinger? I see it's true. He was involved after all."

Yaya's eyes flared at Papa, then holding a finger of warning in my face, she stated, "That's a lie."

I didn't need Yaya to threaten me. "No, Papa—" I began.

But Papa interrupted. "No?" Then looking at the shirt again, "He was there, wasn't he?"

"Yes, Papa. But—"

Again he interrupted me. "When Captain was killed, did he at least try to stop them?"

"Well, no, but—"

"I know you like that boy," Papa said, tenderly placing a hand on my cheek. "It's always been obvious. I did too. But now it's time to forget him. Even if he wasn't the leader, he went along with it. Now all those men are dead." He took his soothing hand from my cheek, made a fist, and pounded the table. "They must all pay for their actions."

"But Papa—"

He simply held up his hand, cutting me off, and stormed from the kitchen.

I didn't know what was worse, seeing Papa storm out of the kitchen with the wrong idea, or being left behind in the same room with Yaya. I looked over at Wing for help, but she was in another world, just staring at her cup. I turned back to Yaya.

"It's not like that, Yaya. Johnny helped us. And he would have helped Captain too if he could have. He knew people would blame him. That's why he didn't come back with us. He's hiding somewhere for now."

Yaya responded with just a small nod of her head that seemed to tell me she understood. She quickly turned and left the kitchen as if on a mission. I then tried running after Papa, to explain that Johnny was the one that helped us escape, that he only went along to protect Wing. But I wasn't fast enough. Papa'd already gone.

I guess Johnny was right not to return with us. He told me they'd be after him. So when we came within view of the farm, he sent Wing and me on alone. I asked him where he was going. He wouldn't say, telling me it was better I didn't know. But he told me he'd better lay low for a while, and if I'd put in a good word for him, he'd come back when things had a chance to cool down. Well, so far, I wasn't doing too well on my end.

I did eventually catch up with Papa. But he still wasn't ready to listen. I tried to explain it in a way that he would understand, why Johnny went with them, and why he didn't try to help Captain, but when I could no longer avoid mentioning the secret political meetings that were taking place, I saw Papa start to lose control. And finally, the topic of land reform sent him over the top. The conversation was over, and off he went to meet with the other hacienderos to discuss strategy on how best to dispose of the rebels.

Wing remained in la-la land. I sat with her and tried to bring her around, but I wasn't overly concerned about her staring into space, as she seemed to be eating and sleeping just fine. She just wouldn't talk. Once I even tried to snap her out of it by catching a cockroach and putting it on her arm. But without even turning to look at it, she crushed it with her hand and threw it at me. She sat there quietly while I ran around the room screaming until Hortensia assured me it wasn't in my hair. I promised Wing I'd get even with her when she got better.

But things got lonely without the old Wing. I began to wonder if Johnny would ever be allowed to return, and how he was surviving somewhere out in the jungle by himself. The time we'd spent together on the run from the kidnappers kept running through my mind, every word and look between us. How I'd gone from hoping that he would save the day, to hating him and wanting him dead, to seeing him, once again, come through in the end. His rebel days behind him, Johnny admitted how he'd made some mistakes, but only meant to make the world a better place. We'd both felt that way, only in the end seeing just how alike we were, finally agreeing on the best way to go about it. I felt as though we'd been on a journey those last three years. I couldn't speak for Johnny, but I felt that I'd ended that journey just where I'd started. Head over heals in love. Nothing had changed for me. I'd been weak in the knees since the first time I'd laid eyes on him. And now I missed him more than ever. If he couldn't come back, I would go to him. I had to.

I cornered Yaya in the kitchen one day gathering a sack of canned goods while the maids were out.

"Where is he?" I demanded.

Yaya didn't even blink. "Who?"

"You know who. Johnny."

"Johnny?" she asked, innocently. "What makes you think I know where Johnny is?" she added, grabbing a small sack of rice to add to the canned goods.

"Who's the care package for?"

Yaya looked back at me. "Oh, this stuff? It's for me."

"For you?"

"That's right. I'm trying to put on some weight. Just look how thin I've gotten. Must be nerves. I'm going to keep it in my room for when I'm too lazy to come to the kitchen."

"Really," I said, not fooled for a second. "I bet Johnny could use some of that stuff."

She finally put the sack down and looked at me. "Why so concerned about my Johnny, an evil man that would help kidnap your cousin."

"Yaya, you know I don't believe that," I replied. "He's made some mistakes, but he always meant well, and he would never do anything to hurt Wing."

Yaya looked at me, appraising the situation. "So why do you need to know where he is?"

It was a simple question. I tried to think of a complex answer. But when none came to me, I told the truth.

"I love him." It felt good to say it. It felt right. "I love him, Yaya. I miss him. I'm worried about him."

Yaya was smiling. It was an I told you so sort of smile. Like she knew it even before I did. It was only independent confirmation of a destiny she'd already seen.

"Poor child," she began. "You don't need to worry about Johnny anymore. He's no longer your concern."

Something about those words freaked me out. "What do you mean? Why? What's happened to him?"

Seeing I'd taken her words the wrong way, Yaya chuckled and touched my cheek with her hand. "No, no, silly girl. Don't worry. Nothing's happened to my Johnny. He's safe."

"Then why shouldn't I still be concerned about him?"

Yaya looked at me, unsure how to say what needed saying. Then, in usual Yaya fashion, she just said it. "He's leaving."

I was still confused. "I know that. He's already left. He's in hiding somewhere."

"No, you don't understand," said Yaya. "He's leaving. The farm. Bais. The Philippines. He's leaving."

I felt faint. The words didn't make sense to me. "What do you mean, he's leaving the Philippines? How? Where's he going?"

"There's nothing for him here anymore," she began. "The hacienderos want to hunt him down. He's got no family in Manila. I think it's time he went back."

"Back? Back where?"

"To the States."

"The States?" I was in shock. It made no sense. "Why the States? They didn't want him there. This is his home. His family's here."

"Family? What family?" chuckled Yaya. "It's only me. An old woman. No. He stands a better chance in the States. At least no one's hunting him there."

Then I saw her game and smiled. "Johnny's not going to the States. You made that up. So they'll stop looking for him."

Yaya didn't deny what I'd proposed but looked at me with a sadness that told me all I needed to know. It was true, all right. Johnny was leaving. To America.

"But how? Where's he getting the money?" I asked, trying to shoot holes in her plan.

"From a woman of means," she replied mysteriously.

"A woman?" I asked with a hint of jealousy. "What woman?"

"Me, of course. His grandmother."

"You? How would you get that kind of money? You didn't steal it, did you?"

"How could you even suggest such a thing?" Yaya asked, full of indignation.

"How then?"

"Gambling," she replied. "Cards, mostly. And dice. I've amassed quite a little gambling fortune over the years. And never spent a penny. Just saving for a rainy day. Well, now it's raining."

I was skeptical. "How much money could you have from gambling?"

"Have you ever seen me lose?"

"Well, no, as a matter-of-fact." It was pretty odd. All the years I'd watched Yaya play cards and dice, I'd never seen her lose. "How come?" I asked.

Yaya smiled. "That's easy. I cheat."

"You cheat?"

"Always."

"Yaya. How can you live with yourself? Taking all those people's money."

"It was for a good cause."

"What cause?"

"What cause? This one. Johnny. Your boyfriend."

"Yaya, you're such a liar. All those times you were cheating, you couldn't have known this would happen. You couldn't have seen all this coming."

Yaya just spit on the floor again and went back to packing Johnny's supplies. "If you say so."

Watching her continue to pack, I felt a sense of panic begin to rise in my throat. Johnny was leaving. How could this be happening? Just as I began to see a future for us. No, I still didn't have the whole difference in social class thing worked out yet, whether he'd be allowed to come live in my palace or I'd be forced to go share his shack with him, or whatever the options really were. But at least we'd cleared up our differences in the political arena. Oh yeah, and don't forget the fact that I'd pretty much become a woman, and he was still a hunk. What more did we need? I couldn't just give up now.

"Yaya, please tell me where he is."

She hesitated a moment, but stood firm. "I cannot."

"Why? Do you think I would turn him in?"

She looked right through me. Then answered. "No. I don't."

"Then why? Why not tell me?"

"That's easy," she answered. "I promised I'd tell no one."

And knowing Yaya, I knew she wouldn't. I felt defeated. I'd never see Johnny again. Then something struck me as odd. Johnny hadn't returned to the farm with us. He hadn't had a chance to speak to anyone at the farm. Not even Yaya.

"Yaya, how do you know where he is?"

Yaya smiled again. "It's a family secret. We have a place, a place to go when trouble comes, ever since the war. In fact," she continued, seeing the blank look on my face, "Johnny says you know of this place. And if that is so, my dear, then I guess you're family too." With that, she turned and walked away, leaving me standing alone in the kitchen, with Johnny's care package at my feet.

Chapter 18

It seemed farther the last time I went there. I didn't know where Johnny was taking me that time riding Thunder. But Johnny was with me. And when Johnny was with me, it seemed as though time stood still. This time I was alone. But I was on my way to him. To Johnny. And this time, I didn't need any horse. I walked on air. I was a bird in flight. Flying to Johnny. It didn't matter that I was hauling a sack of canned goods and who knows what else Yaya had packed. It didn't matter that Speed's men could be out there somewhere hunting me down. I was flying high above all that. And my feet didn't touch the ground until I'd passed the dwarves again and stood in front of the waterfall concealing the entrance to the hidden cave.

I felt sick to my stomach for a moment when I saw no sign of Johnny. Maybe I'd come to the wrong place. Maybe Yaya'd played a joke on me. Maybe he'd already left for the States. But then I figured, after all, there wouldn't be any sign if he were in hiding.

I was dressed in a T-shirt and shorts this time, instead of my white church dress, so I had no fear of being dragged to the bottom by my clothes as I swam under the falls to enter the cave. I knew, however, that if I attempted to swim with Johnny's care package, I'd sink like a rock. Johnny'd have to come out and retrieve the package himself. Besides, I was more interested in seeing Johnny than delivering his laundry.

It just never occurred to me that it might be someone other than Johnny waiting in the cave on the other side of the falls. So when, inside the cave, before I'd even reached the surface to take a breath, a strong hand grabbed a head full of my hair and yanked me out of the water, I was taken by surprise. The knife placed at my throat from behind was simply the icing on the cake. What had I gotten myself into now? I remember thinking how it would have been nice to see Johnny once more before dying. Then I thought that whoever had hidden in the cave to ambush me probably had already killed him. So I'd be seeing him soon after all. In heaven. It's amazing how many stupid thoughts your mind can squeeze into the few seconds right before you die.

Finally my executioner spoke up. "Who the hell told you where to find me?" It was a familiar voice.

Maybe it was the knife at my throat, but I got the distinct impression that Johnny wasn't very happy to see me. "It's good to see you too," I quipped, trying to keep my throat from moving unnecessarily.

"What are you doing here?" asked a surprised Johnny.

"Um, getting my throat slit?" I guessed, feeling the cold steel with each breath I took. "Was it something I said?"

"Oh, shut up," Johnny replied, taking the knife away. "I didn't know it was you. It could have been one of Speed's men, or one of the hacienderos. It could have been anyone. It doesn't matter. They're all out to get me."

"So tell me, sir, how long have you been having these paranoid delusions?" I joked to ease the tension as I turned to face him.

"You know, I could have killed you with this knife, just popping out of the water like that."

"Yeah, well, you didn't need the knife. Your smell alone could have killed me," I replied, holding my nose, suddenly aware that Johnny apparently hadn't brought any soap on his little camping trip.

He stood there in the rays of light coming from the opening at the top of the cave, a week's growth of stubble on his face, wearing the same pants he'd had on the day we left the rebel camp, minus the shirt he'd loaned to Wing. He reminded me of a lost puppy. I stood there, dripping wet, staring at him. Then I remembered something. How much I'd missed him, how I'd come to find him because I couldn't bear to be apart any longer, how I'd realized I loved him, and always would. I ran to him, wrapped my arms around him, and pressed my face to his chest. It felt so right, just listening to his heart beat. I thought maybe I had indeed gone to heaven. No. I'm exaggerating. It didn't actually feel like heaven. That didn't happen until a couple of seconds later, when Johnny wrapped his strong arms around me and squeezed. I just closed my eyes and savored it. That hug. Wrapped in each other's arms. Together.

I didn't want to move. I never wanted to leave his arms. I just wanted the embrace to go on forever. Let them find our dead and shriveled bodies just like that. In each other's arms.

But the mood was broken by the sound of Johnny's stomach growling. I hadn't appreciated the fact that he'd been out there for a week, living on who knows what.

I looked up at him. "Oh my God, Johnny, when was the last time you had a meal?"

"A meal?" he replied. "Well, I don't know if I'd call it a meal. But there's a mango tree not too far from here." He then pointed at an empty rusty can on the ground. "And those World War II rations I found aren't too bad."

I jumped back. "Johnny! Don't tell me you ate that. It must be forty years old. What was it?"

"I don't know. But it didn't kill me," he added, patting his stomach.

Then I remembered Yaya's care package. "I brought you supplies. A package from Yaya. It's outside."

His face lit up like a child on Christmas morning. And before I knew it, we were back in the water swimming toward the package I'd left at the water's edge. Even Johnny had to divide the package to make two trips so the weight wouldn't drag him to the bottom like an anchor. But we were soon back inside the cave opening the gifts. There was a little bit of everything, perishable items wrapped in watertight plastic. Canned foods, matches, even soap. And there were other things. Things that reminded me he was leaving. There was a picture of his mother, to remember her by. She was so young in the picture, about my age I thought. There was money, more than enough, I'm sure, to pay his way to the States. And there was a gun. In case someone had other plans for Johnny. Yaya had thought of everything.

Johnny sat holding the money in one hand and the gun in the other, feeling their weight, probably wondering which would prove the greater asset.

"You're really leaving?" I asked. The words came out more as a weak, squeaky little plea than I'd planned, like a small child being dropped at school by its mother for the first time.

"I have to," he replied, still staring at the money and the gun. He continued, the silence too much to bear. "There's nothing for me here. The haciendo want to hunt me down for organizing a rebellion and kidnapping Wing. The rebels want to kill me for stealing their prized possession, not to mention 20 million pesos. I was raised in the States. At least there I've got a chance. Here, I'll always be an outsider."

"What about family?" I reminded him. "Your stepmom had you deported. At least here you have family."

"Captain's dead," he replied without looking up.

"But there's always Yaya."

"Always? Yaya won't be here forever."

I knew in my mind that Captain and Yaya weren't the family I was referring to. It was me. I was talking about *me*. *I* was his family. Or at least I intended to be. Me and all the children Johnny and I were going to have. That's what I meant when I said he had family here. I just hadn't planned on saying it out loud. I didn't want to sound all needy and pathetic. I hadn't planned on it, all right. But it came out anyway.

"What about me? *I'm* here."

There, I'd said it. Now what? Does he realize he can never leave me? Or does he laugh at me? It felt like one of those nightmares where you find yourself standing in front of the class naked.

Johnny put down the money and the gun, looked over at me and smiled. I knew it. I knew he was going to laugh. I could see it coming. I was just sure of it.

Until he leaned over to me and kissed me. Not on the head. Not on the cheek. No, not this time.

On the lips. And not just a dry, tight-mouthed peck, a going to work Honey, see you later sort of thing. It was more of a hello kiss. The soft lipped, with just the right amount of wetness, open-mouthed, where've you been all my life, died and gone to heaven kind.

I don't know how long the kiss lasted. My brain had stopped working for the duration. It seemed my heart must have stopped as well, because when we parted, it was pounding so hard and fast, as if to make up for the lapse. I placed my head against Johnny's chest to see if I could hear his heart over the pounding of my own. And I heard something all right. It just wasn't exactly what I was looking for.

"I'm sorry," said Johnny, apologizing as the growling of his stomach continued to reverberate off the cave walls. "It's been that way for a couple of days."

He was so cute I couldn't get mad at him for breaking the mood. "That's OK," I said, looking toward the care package. "Let's have some dinner."

Johnny opened a few cans of food and set them down between us as though he'd prepared some kind of feast. He felt bad when he noticed I'd let him eat it all. But he was the one starving to death out in the jungle. Not me.

After he'd eaten, I went back to the sack of supplies and began to unpack. I imagined we'd gone on vacation and this was our hotel room. Or better yet, we'd just been married and we were on our honeymoon. It wasn't long before I'd placed some of Yaya's candles about the dim cave and lit them. But as I stood there looking for a place to stand his mother's picture, it wasn't so much like a honeymoon suite. It soon felt more like playing house. My mind was already imagining Johnny and I'd been married for years and were sharing a home. A home with dirt floors and no windows. Oh well. We were poor, but we were happy.

As I continued unpacking, I tried to ignore the money and the real reason we'd ended up in the cave. Even the gun gave me an idea.

"Johnny. I'm worried about the Japanese."

"Who?"

"The Japanese. They've taken over the island. We'll have to hide here until the war is over."

"The what? You've lost your mind."

I scrambled over to sit next to Johnny. Then taking his hand in mine, I placed my head on his shoulder. "I don't want our first child to be born in this cave."

Johnny stood up. "OK. Now you're freaking me out."

I looked up at Johnny, disappointed that he wouldn't go along with my little game. Soon my sadness began to show through, my sadness that he was leaving, that this was probably the last time I'd be with him.

Johnny saw from my face that this was more than a game. He came back and sat beside me again, putting his arms around me. "What is it?" he asked. "What's this really about?"

I looked up into his eyes. "I really wish that this was World War II, and we were stuck hiding in this cave from the Japanese, that there was no place else to go, that there was no option for you to escape to the States, that we were married, that I was having your baby, right here, in this cave."

Johnny wiped the tears that had started running down my face. "You know what I wish?" he began.

"What? What do you wish?"

"I wish I didn't have to leave, and I didn't have to hide in this cave, that my family owned a farm, and we could get married and live there together, with our children." He saw the beginnings of a smile come to my face. "That's better," he continued, "and I wish that all our kids looked just like you."

I couldn't help but smile. "Even the boys? I think that'd be a little weird." We both laughed. Holding each other, we put our foreheads together. "Do you really?" I asked. "Do you really wish we could get married? Don't tease about that."

Johnny stopped smiling, and, placing his hand under my chin, raised my face to look into my eyes. "Since that day you fell chasing after that stupid calf that got into Mrs. Delgado's flowers."

My eyes went wide.

"I know. I know," he continued. "You were just a kid at the time. But a boy knows when he's beat. I knew you'd grow up some day and then I wouldn't stand a chance. It was only a matter of time. I remember every second of every day I ever spent with you, and more than a few spent without you only wishing you were there. I tried to forget you, me being just a farm worker with no prospects, and you, practically a princess. I tried to be realistic. There could be no future for the two of us."

"But—," I didn't like where this was going.

"No, Lisa. It's the truth," said Johnny. "We weren't meant to be. Maybe this is all for the best, me leaving for the States."

I felt defeated. "When?"

"Now that I've got money for airfare, I guess I'll head out tomorrow, before anything else happens to stop me."

I silently cursed myself for doing Yaya's dirty work, for making it possible for him to leave.

Johnny put his arms around me to ease the pain. But it wasn't necessary. Because there was no pain. Just numbness. I couldn't feel a thing. I wondered if that was how criminals on death row felt during those seconds between receiving the lethal injection and the end. Only there was no end for me. I just remained numb. Even my mind went numb. I couldn't think of what to say, what to do. I didn't know what would happen when the numbness wore off. *If* the numbness wore off. I didn't know how I would feel later, the next day, a year from then, whether I'd still feel numb or whether I'd eventually follow the lead of my peers on death row and ultimately succumb, if from nothing else, then from the numbness itself.

I don't recall consciously deciding to make love to Johnny before parting for the last time. There was no plan, no premeditation. It all just happened. I remember telling him he smelled bad as I grabbed the bar of soap I'd unpacked and began to undress him. I don't remember Johnny removing my clothes. We bathed together, in the water at the entrance to the cave, still warm from the heat of summer.

I remember feeling that all was right in the world as we emerged from the water squeaky clean, without a stitch of clothing, and lay down together on the blanket Yaya'd packed. I remember Johnny's body, strong and hard, yet gentle, protective. I wasn't scared. In fact, it felt as though I'd never be frightened again. I'd been raised as Catholic as any, and I know it shouldn't have happened. Yet I didn't feel any shame or guilt. It just felt right. Everything about it.

I'd heard the first time's supposed to hurt. But I don't remember that. I just remember wanting it. Wanting him. Wanting him inside me. Then he was there. And we were one. And everything was going to be OK.

* * * *

In the morning, even before opening my eyes, I quickly prayed that it wasn't all just a dream. That I wasn't alone in my bed back at Casablanca. When I opened my eyes, the first thing I saw was a ray of morning sunlight hitting the wall of the cave, illuminating the heart with the initials of Johnny's parents. Then I remembered they were the same as ours. J.D. and L.S. Everything made sense now. All of it. Johnny and I were finally together. He said he wanted to marry me. We'd made love. And now that we were together, we'd be leaving for the States... together.

I wanted to wake him up and make love again. I knew then that making love is kind of like eating potato chips. You can't eat just one. I snuggled up against him, hoping he'd wake up and maybe continue where we'd left off last night. In fact, I hoped we could lie around all day making love. I didn't see any reason to leave the cave.

I felt Johnny stirring to my touch, and I quietly made my appeal. "Johnny, do we have to leave today?"

Johnny smiled as he turned to me. "Lisa, I really have to—" He stopped mid-sentence. "We?"

"Yes. Do we have to leave today? Can't we just stay here awhile before we head off for the States?"

"We?"

"Yes, we. Why do you keep saying it like a question?"

We were both fully awake. Johnny propped himself up on one elbow. "Because *we* aren't going to the States. *I* am. You're going back to the farm."

"What do you mean? I'm coming with you."

"No you're not. It's too dangerous. I don't know if I'll even make it myself. I've got to get to Manila, get a passport, and a plane ticket. Your family's probably already searching for you. That's all I need. Blame for another kidnapping. This isn't a game, Lisa."

He wasn't taking me with him. He wasn't taking me with him. I thought maybe if I kept repeating it in my mind, it would somehow start to make sense. But it didn't.

"What do you mean I'm not coming with you? Of course I am. We're in love. We made love. We're going to be married and have a houseful of children. We're going to die of old age within minutes of each other."

"Lisa—"

"No! Don't Lisa me." I'd had enough of this nonsense. I stood up and started packing. "Come on. Let's get your stuff packed. We'll have to go past the farm so I can get *my* things."

"Lisa, you're not listening."

"No, I'm not. Let's go."

Johnny grabbed me roughly by the arms. "You're not coming with me. Now go home."

I suddenly didn't feel very well. I thought maybe I was dying. My throat closed up. My chest felt tight. My vision was blurring. Simply fighting gravity enough to stand became overwhelming. I needed to lie down.

But Johnny was still holding me. "Go home," he repeated.

"But we made love," I said in a tiny voice.

"That's got nothing to do with it, Lisa. I'm sorry if I misled you."

I pulled away from him and looked away so he wouldn't see my tears. "No, no. That's OK. It was only sex. I knew there wasn't anything more to it."

"That's not true," he argued.

"Sure it is. It happens all the time over on Mabini Street."

"Lisa, don't talk like that. Of course there was more to it." He grabbed my arms again and tried to turn me to face him. "Lisa, I love you."

I wouldn't have it. I pulled free again. "Don't you dare. Don't lie to me. If you loved me, you wouldn't leave me. You'd either stay here with me or you'd take me along. I'm not stupid. I know about guys and sex. I know it's not the same as love. I'm not a child. So stop treating me like one. I'm not stupid."

"Lisa—"

I turned to leave. "Have a good life in America."

"But Lisa—"

"You should probably send Yaya a postcard once in a while. She'd like that."

"Lisa!" Johnny grabbed me hard and swung me around to face him.

I struggled. And when he wouldn't let me go, I slapped him in the face. "Don't!" I pulled away. "Don't ever touch me again." It was over. I was ready to go. Everything was perfect for one night. But all that was over. It was time to go home.

I heard him call my name one last time as I dove into the water to leave the cave. I didn't answer his call. And he didn't follow. It was over. Whatever it was. It was over.

Chapter 19

Pretty tough talk. That's right. But that's all it was. I was never going to see him again. But I knew it wasn't really over. And never would be. I'd think of Johnny until the day I died.

The next few days were all a blur. Every second Johnny and I'd spent together and every thought I'd ever had about him ran through my head. It was kind of like the way they say your life passes before your eyes just before you die. Only it was as if Johnny was my whole life. And I couldn't die. Or was I already dead? That's how I felt. Then again, maybe it was just the future that I mourned, the future between Johnny and me, our children that would never be born.

People knew something was wrong with me, but I just couldn't talk about it. There wasn't anything to say. Wing still hadn't uttered a word. And so now there were two of us. Two ghosts haunting Casablanca, taking some measure of comfort in each other's silence.

But it wasn't just Wing and me. Everything seemed different. Even the weather. Just something about the wind and the clouds, something subtle, something inexplicably foreboding. It seemed even the birds had stopped singing. All too cliché, I assumed it was just in my head, depressed over Johnny's departure. But it wasn't. The birds really had stopped singing. I should have seen it coming. More than one kind of storm was on its way.

It started with Boy's return. I'd already told Papa about Boy's acquaintance with the kidnappers. Everyone else bought Mama's line that he'd only been there to help free his sister. Well, of course, Wing knew better. But she wasn't talking. I don't think Papa believed Mama's claim, but he wanted to. He knew of Boy's drug problem and stealing, but the idea that he would participate in his sister's kidnapping and Captain's murder was a bitter pill. He said he would deal with Boy when he returned.

Well now he'd returned, with word from the kidnappers. He came running to Casablanca to warn everyone.

"They're planning an attack," he began, out of breath.

"An attack?" asked Papa, more interested in the news than Boy's return.

"They want revenge, for stealing their hostage and the money."

"Taking back my own daughter and money? They call that stealing?"

"Speed's really angry about it. Said it made him look bad in front of all the rebels. He wants revenge."

Papa stared at Boy. "And why do you know this? What were you doing there?"

"I was spying on them. They thought I was there for drugs. But I was only waiting to hear what their plans were. And now I'm telling you. They're planning to attack the hacienderos. And they're starting with Mr. Fanlo's farm. They've got a lot of rebels. I think you'd better send help."

Papa eyed his son suspiciously. "Mr. Fanlo's farm?"

Avoiding eye contact, Boy changed the subject. "I'm hungry. I'm going to see what Lou's got in the kitchen."

"Go see your mother first. She'll want to know you're OK," Papa called after him.

I knew that if Boy said it, it couldn't possibly be true. I tried to warn Papa. But I couldn't figure out why Boy would warn us about an attack on the Fanlo farm. And it wasn't until Papa'd sent his most loyal workers over to his good friend Ron that we all figured it out. Only then it was too late.

I was moping in the kitchen when Hortensia came back from Mama's church with last minute storm supplies. The sky grew steadily darker and the wind had already picked up quite a bit. In my fog, I hadn't even noticed everyone preparing for the typhoon.

"Where is everyone?" she asked.

"What do you mean?" Lou replied. "Papa's sent most of the workers to defend the Fanlo farm."

"No. I know that. But he didn't send them *all*. I don't see *any* of them. And what about the workers' families?"

"I guess they're at home preparing for the storm, just like us," suggested Lou.

"That's ridiculous," answered Hortensia. "The workers normally bring their families *here*, to the church, to ride out a storm. They're safer there than in their shacks. I've seen Tiny's family and a few of the families belonging to those men Papa sent to the Fanlo's. But I don't see any of the remaining men or their families. It seems kind of deserted."

"Then what do you think it means?" asked Lou.

"What does what mean?" interrupted Yaya, seeing the look on their faces from the doorway.

"The workers Papa kept on the farm are gone. And even their families haven't come to ride out the storm," answered Lou.

Yaya's face looked grim. "None of them?"

"Just Tiny" answered Hortensia.

Yaya's eyes went wide. "I'll tell Papa. Hortensia, go look for Tiny. Lou, gather the guns."

I followed Yaya out the door.

Papa seemed tired ever since Wing's kidnapping and Captain's death. Some of the workers had left with Speed at the time of the kidnapping. And with Johnny's banishment, Papa had to pick up the slack in the running of the farm. He just sighed when Yaya gave him the news. He saw it coming. It was only a matter of time. He raced to a telephone and picked up the receiver only to throw it to the floor in disgust.

"The lines have been cut. And there's no time to go for help," he said. "Father Rivera will take care of the women and children at the church. Bring Tiny here and gather the guns."

One step ahead of Papa since he'd learned to walk, Yaya didn't bother telling him that she'd already given those orders. She simply went to make sure they were being carried out.

"What is it? What's happening?" I asked him.

With one more tired sigh, Papa got up from his chair to leave, and answered my question in one word. "Betrayal."

Hortensia found Tiny tied up in the barn, but not before the shooting had already started. And it wasn't at the Fanlos'. It was at us. Hortensia and Tiny came running into Casablanca covering their heads from flying bullets.

So Boy, as usual, had done Speed's dirty work by getting Papa to send his men to the Fanlos' when the real attack was planned for the Delgados' farm. Boy's only loyalty was to drugs. And he would do anything for the one who supplied them. And that was Speed. Once again, Boy was nowhere to be found.

Instinctively grabbing one of the rifles Lou had piled in the kitchen, Tiny joined Papa at the windows on either side of the front door to Casablanca looking out at the entrance to the courtyard.

"There must be thirty of them out there," he said to Papa. They both peered out of the windows from a crouched position so as not to be an easy target. "Why don't they just charge us? We're only two men. We couldn't stop them all."

Papa laughed. "That's an easy one. They're cowards. That's why. They desire something that doesn't belong to them. But they have no desire to die for it. Not one of them."

"Besides, we're not just two men," added Yaya firmly, emerging from the kitchen carrying a shotgun in one hand, a rifle with a scope in the other, and two pistols tucked into her belt. "We're two men and a flock of angry women."

Yaya looked angry enough, but I didn't know about the rest of us. I mean, I was angry all right. But I'd never fired a gun before. I never knew how heavy they were, as I tried to balance the rifle in my hands. The long barrel of Lou's was dragging on the floor. Hortensia was holding the wrong end of hers. Wing, in her mute haze, just stood there with a pistol uncomfortably dangling from her fingers as if it were a dead rat. Mama was another story all together.

"Aye, no. I can't carry a gun," as if she might break a nail.

Yaya spit on the floor in disgust when she saw her motley crew of recruits. She had her job cut out for her as she instructed us in the basics of using a firearm, seeing how none of us had ever fired one before. I never knew there were so many different kinds of bullets, and you had to match the right bullets with the right gun. Then we had to learn how to load the bullets, aim the gun, and pull the trigger. It was all pretty confusing. Nothing like you see in the movies.

I think Lou and I got the hang of it, though. Wing wasn't paying attention, so I had to load her gun for her. And Hortensia kept pointing hers at whomever she happened to be talking to. We wished she would just stop talking so we could stop jumping out of the way every time she spoke to us.

There came a sudden explosion and I thought the house had blown up. Wing hadn't moved, but Lou and I dove for the floor while Hortensia dropped her rifle. I'd heard guns fired before, but never from inside a house.

"Take that you mother-fucker," Yaya stated calmly as she pulled the smoking barrel of her rifle back from the window. "I can pick those suckers off all day with the scope on this rifle. Got that one right between the eyes."

Hortensia, Lou, and I looked at each other uneasily, wondering if we'd actually be able to pull the trigger.

"Just be sure to make every shot count," ordered Papa. "We're outnumbered and we can't afford to run out of ammunition. Tiny, you'd better go take a position at the back of the house. I don't think they'll try to come over the rear retaining wall, not with that barbed wire on top. But we can't be sure. We'll call you back up front if we need you."

"Yes, sir," answered Tiny, turning to go.

"And Tiny," called Papa, "I want to thank you for taking this stand with us. I'm sure the others wanted you to jump ship with them."

"Sir, it was you and Captain that took me in and gave me work when my parents died and I had no one. I owe the two of you my life. The Delgados have always been good to my family and me. I would never desert them to join a pack of cowardly thieves. If they hadn't tied me up, I'd have stopped the others from going too."

Papa just nodded in acknowledgement as Tiny turned to take up his position at the rear of the house.

The battle was limited to sprays of bullets from the rebels answered by a shot from Papa, Yaya, and at the back of the house, Tiny, using just enough ammunition to keep the rebels from advancing. The wind had picked up considerably, and that was a mixed blessing. With the impending typhoon, it was just a matter of time before the rebels would have to seek cover from the weather. Unfortunately, the closest cover for them was the building we occupied, Casablanca. They would soon be forced to either retreat or charge.

Another explosion from Yaya's rifle filled the air. "They're inching forward," she shouted. "They've got good cover until they get into the yard itself."

"It will be a miracle if the handful of us can hold off all those men," said Papa.

"Oh, we'll hold them off all right," answered Yaya without taking her eye from her rifle scope.

"What makes you so sure?" asked Papa, trying to be realistic.

"Oh that's easy," replied Yaya. "Got no choice. And as soon as this one's over, you're going out to buy me some heavier artillery. A machine gun and some hand grenades would put an end to this nonsense in a jiffy."

Papa had to smile. Yaya had always been there to protect him and his family. Yet the idea of allowing her to store hand grenades under her dress just seemed a bit over the top.

I've never been able to get that smile of his out of my head. One of Papa's last, that was the smile he wore when a bullet crashed through the window hitting him in the chest. We all saw him get hit. At first, he just stood there, the smile slowly fading. Then he sat down on the floor beneath the window.

I ran to him, and knelt by his side. "Papa!"

He just sat there and looked at me.

"Papa! Say something!"

He looked down at his chest, confused. "I don't even feel it."

Yaya ripped his shirt open in front to see how bad it was. I saw blood on the back of his shirt and yanked it down.

"It went right through!" I screamed.

As if sensing a kill, the rebels launched a barrage of bullets at the front of the house as they came out of hiding to charge us.

I wanted to yell for Tiny, but I could hear him at the back of the house single-handedly fending off a group with ladders at the rear retaining wall.

"I'm all right!" shouted Papa. "It went right through. I think I'm all right. Fire on them! All of you!" He struggled to raise his rifle and began firing out the window himself.

Yaya didn't need her scope now. She was enjoying the fact that they'd come out into the open. But there were too many.

"Ladies!" she shouted to the rest of us. "Don't let me have all the fun! If any of you still remember where your triggers are, this would be the time!"

Lou, Hortensia, Wing, and I had frozen at the sight of Papa shot through the chest. His shirt was soaked with blood, both front and back. But he was alive. And he was shooting back.

"Come on!" I shouted, grabbing my rifle, setting an example for the others.

Wing still hadn't spoken a word, even when Papa'd been shot, but I could see tears rolling down her cheeks as she blindly fired her pistol out the window, reloading and firing again.

Hortensia screamed with fright every time she fired her rifle. We weren't sure whether she was shooting the rebels or they were shooting her.

Lou and I seemed to be doing OK. I don't think we were hitting anyone, but at least our bullets were helping to slow their advance.

And then, with a roar, the typhoon suddenly decided to come to our aid, peppering the rebels with bolts of lightening more numerous than our bullets, and sheets of rain so thick it would be hard to imagine the rebel rifles even functioning.

Tiny came running to the front of the house. "How's it going up here? The storm's driven off the attackers at the back of the house."

"Same here," answered Yaya.

Distracted by all the shooting, I hadn't even noticed that the typhoon had grown into a force greater than any guns and bullets.

"Tiny, help me up." I could hardly recognize Papa's voice, weakened by his wound. The bullet may have passed straight through, but not without damage. I noticed Papa's breathing wasn't right, and he was coughing up a little blood every so often.

"What happened?" asked Tiny, shocked at the sight of Papa's bloody shirt.

"I'll be OK," answered Papa. "The bullet went right through."

"Yeah, but right through what?" asked Tiny, helping Papa to the couch, not expecting an answer.

Papa sank onto the couch with a groan. "Tiny, we've survived the first round. Those cowards are gone for now. Probably retreated to the farm office. If we're lucky, the old thing will collapse on the lot of them and crush them like the cockroaches they are. Try to get the rest of these shutters closed before the typhoon finishes the job for them."

Between the cracks of thunder, tree limbs bouncing off the roof, and the gusts of wind pounding at the door, I couldn't be sure if it was Mother Nature or the rebels. I'd been through other typhoons, but as Tiny bolted the last shutter closed, I realized why I'd never recalled such terrifying weather before. I'd never seen it. That's why. The shutters were normally bolted shut way before the storm hit. We'd had them open this time only because of the attack, to allow us to spot the enemy. I remember as a kid how we felt frightened because we couldn't see what was going on outside during the storm. Well, now that I had, it became abundantly clear that, unlike children, typhoons were best heard and not seen.

And yet, I found myself praying the storm would never end, unless it had already destroyed the rebels, because I knew as soon as the storm was over, the enemy would resume their attack. And in Papa's weakened condition, our defenses were severely compromised.

"Will we really be able to turn them back when the storm is over?" I asked Yaya and Tiny.

"We won't have to wait until the storm's over to find out," answered Yaya, as she reloaded everyone's weapons.

"Aye, no," moaned Hortensia. "They can't even stand up in this wind. It must be blowing over a 160 kilometers per hour."

"They can't possibly attack in the middle of this storm," added Lou.

"But that's exactly when they'll attack," Yaya replied. "Right in the middle. As the eye passes over us."

"The eye?" I asked.

"The center," she answered. "As the center of the storm passes over, there could be anywhere from 20 minutes to a few hours when the sky turns blue, the sun comes out, and the rebels realize they'd rather spend the second half of the storm in here instead of the farm office."

"She's right," stated Papa softly, from the couch. "And I don't know how much strength I'll have left by then. We're going to need help."

"Help?" asked Hortensia. "Who is there to help us?"

"Fanlo," answered Papa. "We've got to get word to the Fanlos. As soon as the storm begins to let up, someone's got to go for help. Maybe they can get here before we're overrun by the rebels."

We all looked at each other, wondering who would have to brave the storm and get past the trigger-happy rebels to go for help.

"I'll get ready to go," volunteered Tiny.

"No," said Papa. "You're needed here. We'll have no chance of holding them off without you." He then motioned with his arm for me to come to him at the couch. "Lisa."

"Me?"

"You're the one. You've got to do it."

"Why me?"

"Tiny, Yaya, and I must stay to hold off the rebels. Lou and Hortensia don't know how to drive. And Mama, well, never mind."

I looked at Wing and she just shook her head no and laid her head on Papa's lap. I wasn't sure if she was afraid of the rebels or of not being present should Papa die.

"Why don't we all go? Everyone can fit in the van." I thought I'd solved all our immediate problems.

"You're not taking the car," Yaya replied. "It's stored at the farm office. We'll never get to it with the rebels there. You're taking the motorcycle stored at the barn."

"The motorcycle? Are you trying to send me for help? Or to kill me? Don't forget that tree." Captain used the small Honda dirt bike mostly to get around the cane fields checking on the workers. I remembered the first time Boy and his friends let me try to ride it. First I dropped it before I could even get on the seat. Then that tree just popped up out of nowhere. I wasn't out too long though, because they were all still standing over me laughing when I woke up. I'd since mastered the thing enough to get around. But it wasn't pretty.

"Will you just forget about that tree?" insisted Yaya. "We've got no choice."

So we waited. And waited. And the storm continued to pound Casablanca, the farm, and everything for miles around. We'd lost power long ago, and sat by flickering candlelight, listening to the shutters rattling, the monotony periodically broken as particularly forceful gusts of wind ripped clay barrel tiles from the roof and smashed them to the ground. Each time that happened, everyone looked at each other, silently praying the roof would hold.

I never thought I'd find myself wishing a typhoon would last forever. But the alternative was me getting on that stupid motorcycle, in a storm, and riding it past the rebels for help.

I was just beginning to believe my wish had come true when Yaya disturbed my praying with a tap on the shoulder.

"Let's go. The storm is subsiding." She'd bundled herself up in a rain poncho and boots, and stood cradling a shotgun in her arms.

I thought she was joking, as the wind continued to slam the house. Maybe I hadn't heard her correctly. "The storm is subsiding? What are you talking about? I won't even be able to walk to the barn in this wind."

"Oh, don't worry about that. We won't be walking. It'll be more like running... for our lives." She threw me a poncho and boots of my own.

"Seriously, what makes you think the storm is subsiding?" I asked, reluctantly adorning my raingear.

"I don't have to think," she replied. "I feel it in my bones. When you've been through as many typhoons as me, your bones will know too."

"You sure it's not just your arthritis?" I threw in, unable to help myself.

"It's good that this storm is taking so long. That means it's slow moving and the eye will last longer. You'll have more time to bring back help."

I watched as Yaya loaded a pistol for me and tucked it into the waist of my pants. I stood there feeling like one of those chimpanzees must have felt years ago just before being launched into space, people shooting at me as I rode a motorcycle through a typhoon. I just couldn't recall signing up for this.

Yaya reached for the door as I took one last look back at everyone. I took in everyone's nods of support like oxygen, as if I'd be holding my breath for the next hour or so. Only Wing stared back motionless. But that was OK. I knew her thoughts, as always. And she was much more frightened than I.

With Tiny's help, Yaya forced the door open against the howling wind. The last thing I heard before the sounds of the typhoon drowned out all else and the door slammed shut behind me was the sound of Hortensia reciting the rosary.

* * * *

It was black. It was wet. It was loud. Flashes of lightning were all that lit our path toward the barn. I was bent so far over fighting the wind that I was practically crawling on the ground, which was just as well, as I was sure I was going to have to dig my nails into the earth or grab a heavy stone just to keep from being carried off by the storm. I couldn't understand how Yaya, that skinny bitch, managed to remain Earthbound. I suspect it was only the weight of her shotgun that held her down.

I don't know how we ever made it to the barn, but Yaya held the door open just a crack so we could slip in without the whole door ripping off. I don't know about Yaya with her smoker's lungs, but I was gasping for air as I fell through the barn door.

"This is crazy!" I pointed out. "How am I going to ride a motorcycle in this storm?"

"The eye will be here any minute. Remember my bones? Besides, you don't want to go strolling past the rebels when the sun comes out."

"Yaya," I began, looking about the barn. "Where's the motorcycle?"

"Shit," answered Yaya, noticing it was gone. "Those thieves must have taken it.

Oh well, I thought. Too bad. Guess I'll just have to go back to Casablanca and sit tight. Maybe Lou could prepare a cup of hot tea. My happy thoughts were interrupted by Papa's horse, Thunder, jittery from the storm, nervously banging about his stall. While Yaya continued spewing profanities at the rebels and cursing their private parts, I wandered over to Thunder's stall to see what all the commotion was about.

I almost tripped over the lifeless body that blocked the stall gate from closing. He was wedged with half his body on the outside and half inside, his upper body and limbs stiffened in an apparent attempt to claw his way out of the stall, his lower body apparently mauled by the horse, shattered legs splayed in impossible directions. I felt that old nauseous feeling resurfacing.

"Um, Yaya," I called.

"What?"

"There's a dead body over here."

"Anyone we know?" she asked, matter-of-factly, as if a visitor were walking up the driveway. She found out for herself when she came over to see. It was one of the rebels. "Hey, chalk one up for old Thunder. I guess this one thought he'd steal Thunder along with the motorcycle." Then, nodding with her lips toward the mangled body, "I guess Thunder thought otherwise. That horse never did care for vermin. And he sure knows a rat when he sees one."

I gagged as Yaya began dragging the body from the stall. I thought I could hear bone-scraping bone.

"Old Thunder never lets anyone ride him, not even your Papa," she continued. "And he's Papa's horse. Imagine that."

"Except for Johnny," I corrected her. "He lets Johnny ride him." Just mentioning Johnny's name brought a lump to my throat. We sure could have used Johnny then. He'd always been the one to show up and save me. Now he'd up and left for the States. The nerve of that asshole.

"That's for sure," agreed Yaya. "That horse would do anything for my Johnny."

"He's not the only one," I murmured under my breath.

Yaya looked my way, suspiciously. "What's that supposed to mean?" she asked, depositing the body in a corner away from the stall.

I hadn't meant to say it out loud. "Oh, I just miss him," I offered, trying to cover.

"Well, we sure could use him now. But what did you mean when you said you'd do anything for him?" she asked again, in a suspicious tone.

I tried to look away, but I was too slow. She'd grabbed me by the chin and looked right through me the way she does. "Lisa."

I closed my eyes, trying to avoid eye contact, lest I turn to stone under Medusa's gaze. When I opened them to sneak a peak, I could see the beginnings of a smile curling the corners of her mouth.

"You did. Didn't you?" she continued, beaming. "You and my Johnny." She pinched my cheeks like I was a little girl. "I knew you had it in you. Thank the Lord." She then pulled me to her in a hug and kissed me.

She was right. We did it, Johnny and I. Nevertheless, my religious upbringing required that I protest her insinuation. "But I—"

"Was it good?"

"Yaya!" I'm sure I turned beet red.

"Come on. It's just us girls."

"Yaya! What difference does it make now? He's gone!"

I watched her go into the stall with Thunder.

"Yaya! Stop! He'll kill you!"

He went to bite her, but Yaya was surprisingly quick for her age, narrowly avoiding the loss of her hand to the horse's sharp teeth. In one quick motion, Yaya grabbed him by the bridle with one hand and the pistol from my belt with the other. Then, placing the gun to the horse's head, "Not if I show him who's boss."

"Yaya, what are you going to do?"

She just stood there with the gun to Thunder's head, staring him in the face, her eyes an inch from his. "Just letting him know who's boss."

Thunder tried to shake his head, but Yaya held firm. And when she cocked the pistol in his ear, he looked wide-eyed toward the sound and I could swear I saw the fear of God in his eyes.

"Yaya, don't." I hated that horse, but I didn't want to see him shot.

"That's OK," answered Yaya, speaking soothingly into Thunder's ear. "We have an understanding now, old Thunder and I. He doesn't hurt me, and I don't turn him into glue." She then led him out of the stall and turned to me. "Come on. Mount up."

"What?"

"Get on."

"Why?"

"You're going for help. Isn't that why we're here?"

"On Thunder? I don't think so."

"Come on. You know how to ride."

"Not on Thunder, I don't."

"Oh, he'll behave. We have an understanding now. Look, he's as gentle as a lamb."

I wasn't convinced. "Besides, even if I wanted to ride the devil himself out into a typhoon, it's too far to the Fanlo's by horseback. I'd never get there in time."

"But you're not going to the Fanlo's," stated Yaya.

"I'm not? Then where *am* I going?"

"To the cave. To get Johnny."

My jaw dropped. "Johnny? What are you talking about? Johnny's not at the cave anymore. He must be in the States by now."

"No. He's there."

"At the cave? No, Yaya, he's not. He told me. He was leaving for the States."

She just stood there looking at me as if I were an idiot.

"Why do you look at me that way?" I asked. "He told me he was going that very day I left him there."

"Don't be ridiculous," she replied. "Now get on this horse and go."

"Yaya, I don't understand."

Yaya finally turned from the horse to face me. "Did you make love with my Johnny or not?"

I gave up trying to deny it. I had to understand what she was talking about. "Well, yes, but—"

"Then he'll be there. Now just humor an old woman and mount up."

"But—"

"You young girls are such fools. You don't know anything. Why do you think I sent you to him with those supplies? You think I wanted him to leave? It's like a bee to honey. Now get your honey ass up on this horse and bring back our bee."

I looked up at Thunder. It was a long way up, and down, for that matter. I looked back at Yaya.

"Go on. Get up there," she ordered. "You're tougher than any stupid horse. Why do you think I chose you for Johnny?"

I stood there staring at her, trying to digest what she was saying. Yaya had chosen me for Johnny. I couldn't get my head around it. My mind was racing. I couldn't think straight. All I knew is that she was convinced Johnny was still here. And all I had to do was get up on that horse and go get him. Go get Johnny.

Thunder was a big horse. And I had no saddle or stirrups. I don't know how I got up there, but I somehow found myself on the back of the beast, Yaya handing me the reins. "Let's go, Thunder. Take me to Johnny."

Before she let go of the reins, Yaya grabbed both my hands and squeezed hard, looking up at me. "You can do this. You bring my Johnny home."

I looked down at her. And maybe it was just the way she looked from way up on Thunder's back. But she didn't look anything like Yaya. She looked small and frail, like any normal little old grandmother.

She opened the barn door and the wind blew it off the hinges. Rain slapped me in the face. Thunder reared in anger and I clutched his mane to stay mounted. He bolted out the door and before I knew what happened, we were out in the storm. Thunder was in full gallop. I lay on his back with my arms around his neck, holding on for my life. I realized my eyes were squeezed shut, and when I opened them, we were flying across the courtyard. To Johnny.

Chapter 20

Well, that was the plan anyway. Apparently Thunder hadn't gotten the memo. Somewhere in the middle of the courtyard, he decided he'd rather do his own thing. And he only had to dig in his front hooves with a dip of his shoulders to send me sailing through the air over his head.

I was still in a daze when I found myself in familiar territory, on my face in the mud with Mama's impatiens. I looked at my hands and saw that I'd somehow managed to keep hold of Thunder's reins. At first I was frightened. Frightened that he would drag me across the cobblestone courtyard, or worse, run off, leaving me alone in front of the farmhouse, at the mercy of the rebels.

But then I thought of Johnny. Yaya said he was still here. All I had to do was go get him. So I got mad. A typhoon raging all around, bloodthirsty rebels just waiting to get their filthy hands on me, Johnny, all but mine for the taking, and this God damned stupid animal decides to throw me face down in the mud. The nerve of him. I tightened my grip on the reins, jumped to my feet, and grabbed the overgrown piece of horsemeat by the bridle.

"Now you listen to me!" I shouted in his face as he tried to back away. "I've got somewhere I've got to get to. And this isn't working for me. So you can either—"

He lunged to bite me in the face. I don't know how I managed to avoid those big teeth, but now he'd crossed the line. And I'd had enough. I lost it. I just lost it.

"You mother-fucking sack of manure!" I jerked the bridle again, pulling his face close with one hand. With the other, I hauled back and slammed my fist, with all 105 of my pounds, into the tip of his nose.

His eyes crossed in pain, but he stopped pulling at the bridle. That showed him. I grabbed a handful of mane, half jumping and half climbing onto his back, pulled the reins around toward the courtyard gate, and kicked him in the ribs with all my might.

"Now let's go! And enough of this bullshit!"

I guess old Thunder got with the program, because he shot out of the gate from Casablanca and hurled us, together, headlong into the typhoon.

I was barely able to see through the weather to keep us heading toward the fields, and ultimately to the cave, and Johnny. Just as I found myself cursing Yaya and her bones for predicting the storm was about to let up, sure enough, the rain finally began to thin. The wind speed was pretty strong just from being on Thunder's back, but the gusts grew less frequent, and the sky'd gone from black to gray. Thunder flew through the fields. I was so worn out, it was all I could do to just hang on. I wasn't sure who was leading whom, but we seemed to be heading in the right direction. It was as if he'd understood when I directed him to bring me to Johnny. I grew so tired watching the world fly by that the last thing I remembered was passing the dwarves' place, wondering how they'd fared through the storm.

* * * *

I woke up to the sound of Thunder's whinny. We'd stopped. It seemed everything had stopped. The wind, the rain, everything. I found myself lying face down on Thunder's back. I opened my eyes and looked up to a blue sky. Maybe the whole storm had been just a bad dream, but this must have been the eye Yaya talked about. I didn't know how long I'd been asleep. I heard the sound of the waterfall. The cave. Thunder must have known the way. Then it all came back to me. Johnny! The rebels! Oh my God! The others back at Casablanca must have been under attack by now. I hoped I wasn't too late. Was Yaya right? Was Johnny even still there?

Without wasting any more time, I tied Thunder's reins to a tree, leaving my gun on a rock to dry, dove into the water, and swam toward the entrance to the cave.

When my head broke the water's surface inside the cave, I was disoriented. Something was different. Then I realized what it was. There was no floor. Just water. Apparently the water had risen during the storm, covering the floor of the cave and lapping at the walls. The place Johnny and I'd made love wasn't there anymore. Nor, for that matter, was Johnny. I knew it. He'd gone after all. So much for Yaya with her bees to honey theory. He was gone. Johnny was gone. All the strength left my body as I sank back under the water. Submerged in the darkness, I thought of the storm, the rebels, the people back at Casablanca. Were they already dead? And now, Johnny, off somewhere in the States. Everything seemed to be lost. Everything I ever cared for. What was the point? I felt weaker than I'd ever felt. My body felt so heavy, I didn't think I could make it to the surface again for air. I thought about not trying. Why not just let that very breath I took, realizing Johnny was gone, be my last?

But then I thought again of the people back at Casablanca. Maybe they weren't dead yet after all. I had to help. I could continue on to the Fanlo's. Thunder was fast. But not fast enough. No, that would take too long. I could at least go back to help fight. That's right. Why not? If I was going to die anyway, I might as well go down fighting. I felt my legs kicking toward the surface. I came back up for another breath, then turned and dove under the waterfall again.

I surfaced outside the cave to blinding sunlight, and swam toward where I'd tied Thunder. But when I got there he was gone. And so was my gun. Panic! Someone had my gun. And my only transportation out of the second half of the typhoon was gone. Had the rebels followed me, looking for Johnny? I'd only just emerged from the water when I got my answer.

"Looking for this?" said the voice.

It was by reflex that I raised my hands in surrender when I looked up into the sun, making out the silhouette of a figure on horseback holding my gun.

"Don't worry," he continued. "I plan to take you alive. Why waste a perfectly good bullet on such a pretty young thing?"

The horse moved a step closer, the mounted figure blocking out the sun and holding out a hand to me. I was about to spit on the hand that would take me prisoner, when my eyes adjusted to the light and the face came into focus. As I grabbed the hand, the strong arm above it wrapped around me and lifted me effortlessly onto the horse in front of the rider. I twisted around to face him and he wrapped me in a violent embrace, crushing my lips with his.

"Johnny," I gasped, catching my breath. "I thought you'd gone."

"I guess I couldn't go through with it after you bewitched me," he replied.

Yaya was a genius, I realized, smiling. "But where did you come from? You weren't in the cave."

"When the water started rising, I decided I didn't want to drown, so I swam out and tied myself to a tree in the jungle to ride out the storm. I woke up to the sound of Thunder's whinny and thought he'd escaped the barn to come rescue me, to bring me back to the farm." He followed that with a loving pat to Thunder's shoulder. Then he held up my gun, and shaking his head in disbelief, stuffed it back into my pants. "Better to head back and take my chances with your family than this storm."

"My family!" I began, remembering why I was there. "Johnny we've got to go. The rebels. They're trying to take the farm. They attacked just before the storm. It's just Papa and Tiny and the ladies holed up in Casablanca. Yaya sent me to get you. They may already be dead."

Suddenly all business, Johnny kicked Thunder into a full gallop, and we headed back to the farm.

"You know, when I found Thunder," he shouted over the pounding of hooves, "I almost left you stranded at the cave. Then I saw the gun. That's why I waited to see who was there. I never would have thought *you* rode Thunder. How did you manage that?"

"Oh, let's just say we have an understanding now, old Thunder and I."

I rode in front of Johnny, closing my eyes and leaning back into the warmth and strength of his body, his muscular arms wrapped about me as he held the reins. I felt as though I were back in a protective cocoon after being forced to spread my wings and fly on my own, dodging bullets and weathering typhoons. Our bodies molded to one another, riding as one on Thunder's back, racing toward the fight. During the ride back, I described to Johnny the situation back at the farm, how many rebels, where they were, how many guns and how much ammunition we had inside the house. I choked up trying to describe Papa's wound. I prayed he would still be alive by the time we got there.

The ride home always seems quicker, and the weather seemed to mirror my mood. As my apprehension of what I might find when I got there turned to dread of rejoining the gun battle, so the sunny sky turned to gray, and ultimately to black, the first strong gusts of wind announcing the return of the storm. The eye was about to close.

Thunder seemed to sense it as well, and eager to return to the security of the barn, seemed to find more and more speed each time I thought he was at full gallop. The rain resumed as the farm came into view. But the return of the storm was a mixed blessing. While I had no particular interest in being peppered by pellets of rain flying sideways like buckshot at 160 kilometers per hour, or better yet, struck by lightning, it was probably the noise and commotion of the storm that masked our approach from the rebels.

Sure enough, they'd emerged from the farm office and resumed their siege upon Casablanca. All their attention was focused on their prey and they had no idea that they themselves were being hunted from behind by Johnny. Despite my dread at approaching the armed rebels, I felt my heart dance in the knowledge that the targets of their siege were apparently still alive.

Johnny never hesitated in our approach, charging Thunder, unseen, directly at the rebels' backs. I didn't know if Johnny had any particular plan or if he was just going to wing it, when he suddenly pulled up on the reins, stopping Thunder a hundred meters behind the rebels. I looked back at him as he reached into my pants, taking my gun. He then had me shimmy around behind him. As I reached my arms around his waist to hold on, he handed me the reins. He then checked that both our pistols were loaded, and turned his head to me.

"No matter what happens, don't stop this horse until you're at the front door to Casablanca."

"You mean *we*. Until *we're* at the front door."

"OK. That works for me. But with or without me, you take this horse all the way to the front door. No stopping. No turning back."

I couldn't find words. I just nodded my head. And we kissed.

A pistol in each hand, Johnny kicked Thunder hard in the ribs with both heals, and we flew at the rebels as if shot from a cannon.

Between the rain, the wind, the thunder, and the sound of their own weapons, the rebels were caught completely by surprise. Thunder's hooves and Johnny's pistols were merely background noise. We swooped right down on them and Johnny had easily dispatched five of the rebels before the rest even thought to turn around. Their first reaction at the sight of Thunder bearing down upon them, Johnny's guns ablaze, was to scatter for cover. Before they could get very far, though, Johnny had emptied both six shooters making all 12 rounds count. By the time we reached them, 12 rebels lay shot dead. Well, 12 were shot all right. But only 11 were dead. The twelfth was only wounded. So when he heard the click of Johnny's empty gun, he saw his chance and drew a bead on Johnny with his own weapon.

I don't know what it was with Thunder having guns pointed at him. Must have been something in his childhood, a bad experience of some kind. I don't know for sure. But whatever it was, it sure pissed Thunder off. That's why he finished what Johnny'd started, rearing back on his hind legs and coming down hard with his hooves on the man pointing the gun at him. Now there were 12 dead rebels after all, 11 for Johnny and one for Thunder. Unfortunately, that still left about 20. And we were out of bullets.

It was time to get along to Casablanca. But before we could get Thunder back on track toward the house, the rebels, capitalizing on our predicament, began returning fire. Maybe there wasn't a sharpshooter in the bunch, but just like the broadside of a barn, Thunder was pretty big, and hard to miss. A bullet managed to find him in the shoulder and he went down. Johnny and I went down with him. I thought we were done for as I found myself falling to Earth amid a spray of bullets.

Face down in the mud yet again, I wondered what getting shot would feel like. We were defenseless. All they had to do was put a gun to our heads and pull the trigger. And yet, the shooting seemed to escalate, and I didn't know why. What was all the damn shooting about?

I didn't know where Johnny was. And I was just raising my face out of the mud to see why I wasn't dead yet, when someone grabbed me and threw me through the air like a rag doll. I'd thought when Thunder got shot and went down that he was dead. I should have known it would take more than one pesky bullet to finish off that horse. He must have simply brushed it off like a mosquito bite and got back up on his feet, because, sure enough, that's where I landed, right on Thunder's back. I turned around to see Tiny slapping Thunder's rump, sending the horse and me toward the house, before throwing down his spent pistol and raising his shotgun toward the rebels. He was standing over Johnny who lay motionless in the mud.

My first instinct was to turn back, to rescue Johnny, but then I remembered what he'd said. No stopping. No turning back. Not till I got to the front door of Casablanca. So I rode Thunder right up onto the front porch. I didn't stop. I didn't turn back. Not till I made it to the front door. It wasn't until I got there, and Yaya held the door open for me, that I turned to see Tiny fall, taking a barrage of bullets to the head and chest. He'd said he owed his life to Papa and Captain. And now he'd given it, protecting the farm and Captain's nephew. Well, I'd done as Johnny ordered. I didn't stop. I didn't turn back. Not till I got to the front door. Well, I was at the front door now. And Johnny was back there, alone, somewhere in the mud.

I turned Thunder on a dime, and when I kicked him in the flanks, he leaped from the porch back toward the rebels. I couldn't see much with the torrential rain now gusting at my face. I prayed good old Thunder would know where we'd left Johnny.

Yaya must have had six pistols on her, and six arms to handle them, as her seemingly endless spray of bullets from the front door managed to keep the rebels pinned down until I found the spot where Tiny's lifeless body lay. Poor Tiny. But where was Johnny? Damn it. I was just about to leap off Thunder to crawl through the mud looking for him when someone grabbed the reins from my hands and roughly joined me on the horse's back.

"I thought I told you not to turn back." It was Johnny.

"Until I reached the front door," I added, for completeness. "And that's just what I did. *Then* I turned back."

We were scrambling inside the front door to Casablanca before he could respond. And once inside, he decided it was a lost cause and changed the subject, taking me in his arms. I melted in his embrace, and with my head buried in his chest, I opened my eyes to see, off to the side, a smiling Yaya wink at me in approval.

You could say that with the loss of Tiny, bringing Johnny back only brought our numbers back to where they were before I went for help. But Johnny had taken out quite a few of the enemy on our return. Besides, Johnny's assault on the rebels had stunned them, putting them into disarray, at least temporarily, long enough for the typhoon, now growing in strength again, to come to our aid. The rebels seemed to have withdrawn to lick their wounds.

Johnny and Yaya took advantage of the cover provided by the storm to make a run to the barn to retrieve a secret store of ammunition Johnny knew of. Left alone with the rest of the ladies and Papa, I was finally able to get a good look at him since my return. He didn't look well. Pale, and barely able to keep his eyes open, his breathing had grown shallow. Wing sat mutely at his side. When I came closer, I noticed the handle of his pistol barely protruding from under his pillow. He no longer held it ready for battle, though I'm sure, in the event the rebels made it into the house, he planned to take as many with him as he could.

That's when, like the creature from the black lagoon, Boy showed up, just when I'd hoped he'd finally joined the rebels for good. It turns out Mama'd hid him in one of the bedrooms all this time. And now he was taking advantage of Johnny and Yaya's absence to make an appearance.

Catching us off guard, he stood there waving a gun in our faces, directing us all over by the couch with Papa. He seemed to be having some kind of attack, as sweat poured from his face and he twitched all over. He was apparently long overdue for some "candy." Mama stood beside him looking more concerned for Boy's state of health than for the fact that he held a gun on the rest of us.

"What's this all about?" demanded Papa, summoning what strength he had left to sound stern.

"Just lending a helping hand to my friends. They're out in the storm. They'd rather be in here, but you've been less than gracious," answered Boy.

Papa became incensed and struggled to get up, only sending himself into a coughing fit. He collapsed back onto the couch, unable to catch his breath, drowning in his own blood filled lungs.

"Friends?" he gagged. "You call that vermin friends? What about your family? You choose your junkie and his pack of thieves over your family?"

"My family? Mama's my only family," declared Boy. "And her only mistake was marrying you and landing us in this godforsaken place. I say let the workers have it."

Mama looked away with the tiniest amount of guilt over Boy expressing her true feelings.

"Besides," Boy continued, "what do you know about family? Mama never should have come back to you after realizing you were cheating on her."

An audible gasp came from Mama, covering her face with her hand, as if the words had escaped from her own mouth. Even Hortensia and Lou looked guilty, as if their secret was out. I looked at Wing who remained the unfeeling zombie, staring off into space. Papa squeezed the sides of the couch, writhing as if Boy were twisting a knife in his chest.

"And don't try to deny it," added Boy.

Papa seemed too weak to fight. "I won't deny it. It's true. But that was a long time ago. And none of your business."

"None of my business?" shouted Boy. "Why not? Why isn't it my business if you and some maid had a bastard who showed up here trying to take away my birthright?"

Hortensia and Lou couldn't restrain gasps. Even Mama looked taken aback.

"What are you talking about?" asked Papa, genuinely confused. "You've lost your mind."

At first I was confused. But then the story began to sound vaguely familiar to me. Johnny's mother. And I suddenly remembered back to my days as an amateur detective, when the evidence suggested Johnny's true father was actually someone from the farm. Was it Johnny that Boy was talking about? Was he suggesting that Papa was Johnny's father?

"Do you think I'm stupid?" shouted Boy. "I have ears. I've heard the rumors for years. About you and some maid. How she was sent away, only to have your baby."

"That's a lie!" shouted Papa, sending himself into another coughing fit, which left him gasping for air. When Papa was able to speak, he resumed quietly. "I guess I'm dying. There's no reason to hide anything. Yes, there was an affair. And yes, she was sent away. But there was never any baby. Not mine anyway. If she had one later, it wasn't by me."

Boy was unconvinced. "And I have eyes. You don't think I see the way you treat him?" And then he said the name. "That Johnny." Everyone else looked at each other, weighing the possibility in their own minds. "You treat him like a son. Your heir apparent."

So it *was* Johnny that Boy talked of.

"Johnny? That's ridiculous," answered Papa. "Before he got caught up in all this land reform nonsense, I treated that boy like a hard working young man trying to make something of himself. No more. No less. That's more than I can say for you. Hard work is something you wouldn't know the first thing about. And now, when this farm is under attack, he risks his life to defend it. While my own son is off hiding somewhere." Then, his eyes burning right through Boy, "And as to my heir apparent, that involves family. Something else you don't know anything about. Do you honestly believe I'd let any true son of mind, Delgado blood, be sent from this place? Bastard or not, I'd have raised him here, with me, as a Delgado. No, there was no baby."

I believed him. It's true. Papa would never have let even a bastard child of his be exiled from the family. That is, any child he knew of. I recalled the dates when Johnny's mom left the farm and when he was born. Was it possible Papa simply didn't know? That all this time it was kept from him?

"Nice speech," answered Boy. "But no one believes that. Everyone knows the truth. Tell him, Mama. Tell him what everyone knows. What he won't admit."

All eyes turned to Mama, her hand still over her mouth. You could see her eyes nervously bouncing about the room as if searching for a response, cobwebs, or more likely rust, gumming up the gears of her seldom used intellect. And yet, realizing she was in the spotlight, the lines came to her.

"Don't be ridiculous, Boy. There is no bas—" She had trouble even saying the word. "No bastard. You're Papa's only son. And don't let anyone ever tell you otherwise."

For a brief second, Boy looked confused, as if the rug were pulled out from under him. But then, slowly, as Mama would not meet his eyes directly, he thought he understood. His father was dying. There was no point in letting vanity endanger one's rightful inheritance. Oh, Boy never wanted the farm, all right. But he certainly had no intention of splitting the proceeds from its sale with a bastard half brother.

"Well, I'm glad that rumor can finally be put to rest," stated Boy, less than convincingly. When he pulled a lighter out of his pocket, I assumed he was going to celebrate with a cigarette, or maybe something more potent. But I soon saw I was wrong and that I'd never be able to predict Boy's behavior by using logic. Before anyone could even shout in protest, he'd lit the curtains on fire, and began pouring Papa's good scotch all over a pair of bookcases. He was going to burn the house down around us.

All the women looked to each other for what to do. But Papa didn't. Just as he'd never looked to anyone his whole life to know what to do, to do what had to be done. Before anyone realized it, he was on his feet, pale, out of breath, and unsteadily making his way to where Boy stood, preoccupied with the task of soaking the bookcases with alcohol. Boy was reveling in the sight of the curtains aflame and the thought that soon he would see the end of Casablanca and the farm, that he could finally go back to Manila, away from all this dirt and manure. He was just thinking how watching the fire at work would be easily as good as any drug induced high he'd ever experienced, when Papa came up behind him.

Had he been whole, Papa would have picked Boy up by the scruff of the neck and paddled him over his knee like a spoiled child. But Papa was far from whole, the strength gone from his arms, and lungs that should have been filled with oxygen, gurgled with blood.

Boy easily threw off the surprise attack, and could have just as easily escorted the now frail old man back to the couch. But when Papa went for Boy's gun, his grip was surprisingly strong, and Boy found himself struggling to maintain control of his weapon. I was about to join in the scuffle myself when the gun went off. I thought for sure someone was dead. I prayed it was Boy, and not Papa. But it turned out to be neither. The bullet simply went through the ceiling without finding flesh. Boy eventually managed to yank the gun from Papa's hands. I thought for sure he was going to shoot him then and there. Frankly, for a brief second, I think Boy thought so too. But then he looked at the wounded old man and thought there was no reason to waste another perfectly good bullet. So instead, he simply raised the gun and slammed the butt down onto Papa's head. Papa hit the floor like a sack of rice. He was still alive as the women surrounded him and dragged him back to the couch. I glanced back at Boy and thought, maybe hoped, I saw the briefest expression of guilt. Either that or he was just upset that Papa had interrupted the fun he was having with his fire.

Mama, of course, didn't say a thing, once again apparently taking Boy's side over Papa's, even as he lay unconscious at the hands of her son. The rest of us were in shock. We knew Papa was in serious trouble since being shot in the chest, though none of us wanted to admit he might be dying. But now, as he lay motionless, we couldn't help realizing how serious his condition was. Papa wasn't going to make it. The scene reminded me of a bullfight I'd seen once, where the bull was repeatedly stabbed in the back and drained of blood, just to take the fight out of him, before the matador'd even entered the ring. Papa'd lived life strong as a bull, and now it looked like he would go out like a bull, the blood slowly drained from him, continuing to lash out at the red cape.

What passed before me, seemingly in slow motion, actually only took a couple of seconds. Yet, before we could even absorb what had happened, the typhoon was in the room. Johnny burst through the door carried by the wind like a piece of flying debris. At the sound of Boy's gun, he came running straight for the house, thinking the rebels were upon us. Seeing Papa lying motionless on the couch, and flames beginning to engulf the room, I'm sure he expected his suspicion confirmed. What he hadn't expected, though, was Boy surprising him from behind with a gun before we could warn him.

And sure enough, like lemmings following one another over the cliff, Yaya burst through the door a heartbeat later, carrying the ammunition from the barn. Boy was fast enough to place Johnny between himself and Yaya before she could drop the ammunition and raise her gun. Yaya, as if using some previous training in military Special Forces, instinctively dove toward the dining table, turning it over to shield herself from Boy's weapon.

Boy shrank behind Johnny, his gun aimed at the back of Johnny's head. He backed up toward the couch, pulling Johnny with him, adding some distance between himself and Yaya.

"Drop the gun or I'll kill him!" shouted Boy, clearly dreading Yaya's skill as a marksman, particularly at such close range.

Yaya held her ground, her gun leveled at all of us, waiting for Boy to slip right or left into her line of sight. She calmly answered Boy without blinking.

"Go ahead then. You're going to kill him anyway."

Boy hesitated. I'm sure he hadn't expected that from Yaya. Not with him holding a gun to her prized grandson's head.

"I know you like to gamble, Yaya, but is this really a bet you want to take?"

Yaya spit on the floor, never blinking, the barrel of her gun never wavering.

"You're a bigger fool than I thought," she began. "I'll take those odds all day. In fact, I'll go one further and save two bullets in the bargain. I'll save the bullet you would have used to kill Johnny by killing him myself rather than give you the pleasure of doing it. I can also save the bullet you would have used on me if I laid down my gun, because, at this range, I expect the bullet I use to kill Johnny will go right through his head and take you with him on its way out the back.

I couldn't believe what I was hearing. Yaya was either the coldest son of a bitch ever, just plain crazy, or both. In any case, Boy took her at her word and knew he was in a spot. He had to up the ante, threatening Yaya with an even higher body count. He moved closer to the couch where the rest of us huddled.

"Drop the gun!" he shouted. "Or I start the executions. Johnny first. Then the others." He had placed himself among us, like one big happy family. He would have been able to finish off all of us before Yaya could even get off a clear shot.

Within easy reach, I thought of jumping him from behind but I couldn't be sure I'd be able to deflect his gun before he could get off a shot at Johnny's head. I felt paralyzed, then worse, as I thought of Boy's next move only seconds before he thought of it himself. He wasn't going to wait for Yaya to put her gun down. He would start the executions immediately. Johnny was to be the first, something Boy'd wanted from the first time they'd met. Now was his chance. And Yaya was in no position to stop him. What he did to the rest of us after that was irrelevant. At least he'd finally rid himself of his nemesis, this intruder who'd stolen everyone's respect, including Papa's, this interloper rumored to be next in line to the throne.

"Say goodbye, Johnny," chided Boy, roughly poking him in the back of the head with his gun.

I saw the look on Yaya's face as she too realized Boy's intention. He'd called her bluff that she would shoot them both. Her gun finally wavered, distress finally breaking through her unruffled demeanor. She saw Boy's checkmate, and there wasn't anything she could do about it. I'm sure Johnny knew the slightest movement on his part would only bring the bullet sooner.

Well, so be it. There wasn't anything to lose. I had to act. Every nerve in my body called for action, any action. There wasn't any thought involved. It was more like a reflex, like when your hand accidentally grabs a hot frying pan. You don't think about how hot the pan is before willing your hand to let go. Your hand just does it. Well, my hand was already in the fire. And without any conscious thought on my part, I lunged for Boy's arm, the one holding the gun. But before I could pull Boy's gun from the back of Johnny's head, I remember hearing the gun go off.

Time stood still in that split second following the shot. The last thing I saw was the anguish on Yaya's face before everything went red. Blood was everywhere. It covered my hand. It covered the back of Johnny's head. It was over. I was too late. I remember praying I would be next.

Chapter 21

A mournful wail could be heard over the screams. The screams belonged to Hortensia, Lou, and mostly myself. But Yaya stood oddly silent, looking confused. And the wail? The eerie wail sounded almost inhuman, more like some kind of beast having lost its child. Its favorite child. The beast was Mama. And when I looked down to see the crumpled body at my feet, it wasn't Johnny that I saw. It was Boy.

I looked up again to see Johnny still standing. He wasn't dead. He wasn't even hurt. The blood wasn't his. He was looking past me to someone behind me, to Wing. She stood there, holding the smoking pistol she'd taken from under Papa's pillow.

"You've killed him!" screamed Mama. "You've killed your own brother!" Then, the anger spewing from her mouth like flames, "You'll go to hell for this!"

Wing had been silent until that point. She'd neither screamed nor cried. And not because she was mute either. In fact, killing Boy seemed to have snapped her out of her catatonic state, for when Mama cursed her for what she'd done, Wing had no problem finding her first words since her ordeal with the kidnappers. She spoke softly, yet clearly.

"No, Mama. I'm not going to hell. It's Boy you ought to worry about. I, for one, pray that's not where my brother's gone. But he had to be stopped. Someone had to stop him. Someone… "

Wing looked down at the gun in her hand and dropped it to the floor, raising her hands to her face as the tears finally came. Johnny went to her, enveloping Wing in his arms as she sobbed into his chest. Papa, previously motionless on the couch, managed to reach a comforting hand to Wing's as reassurance that she'd done the right thing.

Wing was back. She'd clawed her way out of whatever dark place she'd been hiding in since the kidnappers, with Boy's cooperation, had taken and threatened her. I think she did it for Johnny, Johnny who'd literally carried her from that nightmare and brought her home. In shooting her brother, she had to choose between Boy and Johnny, which one deserved to live, and which to die. I don't believe the choice was a philosophical one, one she had time to debate. In fact, once, since that time, when Wing and I had the leisure, and courage, to bring it up, it became clear that Wing believed she hadn't made a choice at all. It was God. God made it easy. He made the choice for her, sending her to Papa's pillow for the gun, raising it at Boy, and pulling the trigger. Wing was right. Boy had to be stopped. Someone had to do it. But it wasn't Wing. It was God. At least that's how Wing chooses to remember it. I'm not so sure myself. I think it was Wing. Wing's not so weak as she chooses to believe.

But there wasn't any time to think about it all back then. The typhoon continued to rage, the house was on fire, thanks to Boy, and then there were the rebels. Looking back, I think when Boy set the curtains on fire, that was meant to be some sort of signal to the rebels, a signal that Boy had infiltrated our defenses and cleared the way for them to just walk through the front door. Because that's exactly what happened. If not for the storm pushing them from behind, you'd have thought Speed and his gang walked through the front door as if they'd arrived for Sunday brunch, as if they'd owned the place, as if the last thing they'd expected was a fight. Yet during the initial moment's hesitation by both sides, equally surprised to find themselves standing face to face, Speed immediately knew something about his plan had gone awry.

Yaya'd remained armed from her stand off with Boy. And Johnny had only to pick up the gun Wing had dropped at her feet. But Speed had earned his nickname in more than one way, and, quickly realizing he'd placed himself in front of a firing squad, he threw one of his comrades in front of him as Yaya and Johnny opened fire. Despite the rest of us frozen like deer in headlights, five rebels fell dead in a barrage of bullets from Johnny and Yaya, including the ill-fated comrade Speed used as a human shield. By then, the remainder managed to flee and take cover in the kitchen like naughty children having stirred up a hornet's nest. Speed only had time to dive behind the upturned dining table Yaya had previously used against Boy. The rest of us, as surprised as the rebels, ran in the opposite direction toward the back hallway and bedrooms. Johnny and Yaya held Speed pinned down from the entrance to the hallway.

That's when the negotiations began. And Speed wasted no time in demanding our surrender. "If you put down your guns and come out, we'll let you live," he began.

"I was just about to say the same thing," replied Johnny.

"We outnumber and outgun you at least two to one," continued Speed.

"Exactly," answered Johnny. "It was six to one when you began. You've lost about 16 men to our one by my count. I'd say it's you that ought to be surrendering, that is while any of you are left alive."

"I must admit, we've taken some hits by surprise," answered Speed. "But there will be no more surprises. We're all here together now, under the same roof, face to face. The farm is ours as the rightful owners. You yourself spoke of land reform, giving the poor man a chance."

Johnny was no longer unsure in the political arena as he once was. "True, I spoke of land reform. But I spoke of providing opportunity through peaceful reforms, not stealing at gunpoint, through kidnap and murder. That was all your idea." Then opening the debate to the ears back in the kitchen, "Is that how you understood things? When you stopped listening to me, and started listening to Speed, is this the path you chose? Living in the woods like animals, stealing, kidnapping, and murdering? Did you really think that was the answer? Do any of you even know how to run a farm? Do you have the business smarts and financial backing to support it? Who will cut your cane for you? Maybe you'll each take a piece of land. But it won't be a farm. You won't be able to compete in the world sugar markets. It's going to take more than stealing a piece of dirt to do that. Let the government help you. Sure, it's going to take time. But do it legally. No more killing."

We couldn't see the others back in the kitchen. And we couldn't hear them. But Johnny knew, as from the beginning, that they were not a unified force. They were a coalition, composed of equal parts communist and farm worker. Tiny had chosen our side from the start. Even if the communists were a lost cause, maybe the other workers could be brought around. I don't know about all the cane workers and all the hacienderos everywhere, but I knew the Delgados and their workers. The Delgados were good to the workers. They were fair. Could things be better? Sure. The workers just needed to know they had a chance, a way for them to work their way up the ladder. And that's what Johnny'd been preaching. But legally, through political reform, without bloodshed. He knew in his heart that that's all the workers wanted. It was Speed and the communists with their empty promises of quick unearned riches that led them astray. Well, now was Johnny's chance, in front of a captive audience, to win them back. If he could create dissention in the ranks, he could divide and conquer."

"Don't listen to him," answered Speed, realizing his life depended on keeping the loyalty of his mob. "They'll make him foreman, barking orders at you all day, working you to death. He'll practically be a haciendero himself."

"You know that's a lie," answered Johnny. "Sure, Captain was training me as foreman. But I always treated you fairly. I never overworked anyone, and you know it. Who helped organize our meetings back in the beginning? Who spoke of convincing the government to provide more opportunity?"

"Don't listen to his propaganda," interrupted Speed. "He's with them. He's with the hacienderos."

I don't know who was winning or losing this battle for the masses, but I never expected Hortensia to be the one to throw the most powerful blow. Her frightened, high-pitched voice rang from the back of the hallway in which we lay hiding.

"He's not with the hacienderos," she cried. "And he's not with you rebels. He's with God."

Silence followed, until Hortensia continued. "Just as God wouldn't have one man enslave another, he wouldn't have one steal from, kidnap, or kill another. It's something completely different that would lead one to do such things. And it comes in the form of that monster hiding behind that table. Denounce that monster. Listen to Johnny. He speaks for God in wanting to put a stop to all this madness. He speaks for God."

I glanced over at Hortensia, her hands held together in prayer, eyes closed, head bowed. It seemed Hortensia was wrong about one thing. It wasn't Johnny that spoke for God. It was she.

We're a religious bunch, we Filipinos. I just hoped the workers way back in the kitchen could hear Hortensia's words. I hoped they were listening.

Speed wasn't. Instead, he raised his gun to fire blindly at the hallway, hoping to get in a lucky shot at Johnny. But when he pulled the trigger, all that followed was a small clicking sound. Speed was out of bullets.

I briefly thought the battle was over. We'd won. Johnny could just walk over and finish Speed off. But I forgot about all the other guns and their bullets remaining in the kitchen just behind Speed. For all of Johnny's and Hortensia's words, there came no sign of surrender from the kitchen. It remained a standoff.

Speed may have been out of bullets, but he wasn't out of words. "It's your funeral then," he threatened. "No prisoners. And when you're all dead, we'll take this land just the same."

"That's right," came a groan from the couch. "It'll be over my dead body." It was Papa. When Speed and the rebels walked through the front door and everyone dove for cover, we'd forgotten all about

Papa left dying on the couch. Now all we could do was watch as he unsteadily got to his feet right in the line of fire. "I've had enough of this nonsense. No one's taking Delgado land."

Speed couldn't help but laugh from behind the dining table at the foolish old man, enjoying the prospect of watching his men finally put an end to José Delgado in a barrage of bullets. Yet as Papa slowly and painfully made his way to the table where Speed lay hiding, no shots were fired.

Speed stopped laughing. "What are you waiting for," he shouted to his men. "Finish him off." A muffled scuffling could be heard back in the kitchen, but still no shots. I don't know if it was Johnny's speech or Hortensia's, or even out of simple respect for a wounded old man. Yet this wasn't any old man. This was José Delgado. Well, whatever it was, no shots were fired as Papa slowly made his way toward Speed.

When Papa finally made it to the table, I thought I heard him mutter, "If you want to kill a snake, you have to cut off the head." And with that, he picked up Speed by the throat.

"Shoot him," yelled Speed to his men. He looked frantically about as he realized no one was coming to help him. Apparently the workers still had enough respect for José Delgado that they were preventing the communists from stepping in. They would let Speed and Papa duke it out.

But Speed had no intention of going quietly. His gun may have been useless, but his knife wasn't. I was just able to make out the gleam of his switchblade before he plunged it into Papa's side. Papa flinched, but he still held Speed's neck like a vise. Speed pulled out his knife and plunged it twice more into Papa's body. But Papa's hands didn't care. They only squeezed harder at Speed's throat. For this bull had finally managed to gore the careless matador. Despite being stabbed several times, his blood drained, the bull that catches the matador off guard with one of his horns only sees red, and doesn't rest until one of them is dead.

Deprived of oxygen too long, Speed's brain was soon no longer able to send instructions to his arm. His knife fell to the ground as his eyes began to bulge from his purple head. Papa's blood ran freely from his side, but he held Speed in his death grip. Only when Speed's grotesque twitching stopped, did Papa let the dead body fall to the floor.

And as Papa stumbled and fell himself, somehow still alive, a commotion could be heard back in the kitchen, followed by gunfire. At first, I thought they were shooting at Papa, but then two of the rebels came staggering out of the kitchen toward the front door. They'd been shot. I could tell they were communists because I didn't recognize them. Three more communists ran from the kitchen, shoving their wounded comrades out of the way as they ran over each other trying to escape out the front door. Johnny and Yaya held their fire, saving their ammunition to see what would happen next. A shout was heard from the kitchen.

"Hold your fire. We're coming out." It was the workers.

"Hold nothing," muttered Yaya to Johnny. "When they come out, we finish this."

"No, no. Stay cool," answered Johnny, eyes trained on the entrance to the kitchen. "Let's see what this is all about." Then, "What do you want?" he shouted to the remaining rebels.

"A truce."

"Truce, my ass!" shouted Yaya. "Surrender, or die!"

"OK. Call it surrender then. We give up. We never should have listened to Speed. Johnny was right all along. We want to work for change, not steal it. We never wanted to kidnap or kill anyone. Things just got carried away. It was Speed and those good-for-nothing communists. We're done with them. We want to come back and work at the farm. We want to see our families. We want to go to church and pray for God's forgiveness."

It was just as Papa'd said. He'd cut the head off the snake, and the body was lost without it. And Hortensia, she simply had to remind them that God was watching, which left them no choice but to do the right thing.

"Put your weapons down and come out," called Johnny.

The six remaining rebels, all workers, filed out from the kitchen, heads bowed in shame. Johnny and Yaya came out of hiding, guns drawn. They all stood for a moment, face to face, until one of the workers looked up and behind Johnny.

"The house is on fire," he said matter-of-factly.

"Don't fall for it Johnny," said Yaya, holding the workers in her sights.

"But, sir," the worker persisted, respectfully emphasizing the word sir, "the house really is on fire. We'd better help you put it out before it's too late."

It was true. In all the commotion, everyone had forgotten that Boy had set the curtains on fire, and now the fire had spread to the wall and ceiling. If something weren't done soon, Casablanca would be lost.

So the workers came back to work, helping Johnny fight the fire. Mama sat crying over Boy's body. And Wing and I went to Papa, though there wasn't much we could do. With his blood all over the floor, I didn't understand how he was still alive. Yet he began to tug at Wing's arm to draw her closer. She leaned in hoping to catch any last words her father might impart.

"Cigar," he whispered. "Be a good girl and get me one of my cigars."

Wing was taken aback. "A cigar? Papa, you're in no condition to smoke."

"I'm in no condition to be alive. Yet here I am. So don't argue with me. I keep a secret stash in my den."

Wing looked at me, but I didn't know where they were either.

"Papa, I don't know where—"

"I'll get it," interrupted Yaya from behind me, as she turned to go fetch one.

"So that's what's been happening to my cigars," groaned Papa, bringing smiles to both Wing's tear-streaked face and mine.

We sat with Papa watching Johnny and the workers battle the fire, listening to the storm rage and Papa wheeze. I'm not sure who was putting out the fire, the workers or the rain from the storm coming through shattered windows.

Yaya hadn't returned with the cigar and I grew concerned that what could have been Papa's last request, as silly as it was, might come too late. As I looked about the room for Yaya, I noticed Boy's body lay unattended and I wondered where Mama'd gone. So I got up and headed down the hallway toward papa's den. I hadn't quite reached the door to the den when I heard their voices. The tone of the conversation made me stop short of entering the room.

"Your husband still breathes in the other room and you talk as if he's dead and buried," Yaya was saying.

"A woman in my position has to be practical," answered Mama. "Mr. Delgado is dying. His son is already dead. What use would I have for a farm? I have no choice but to sell."

The bitch was already counting the money. What about Wing, I thought, imagining the Delgado farm leaving the family. But I wasn't kidding anyone. It wasn't Wing that would mourn the loss of the farm. It was I. I may be only a distant cousin, but there must be some Delgado blood in me, because at the mere thought of parting with Delgado land, I could feel that blood draining from my veins as surely as Speed's knife had drained Papa's.

"You never wanted anything to do with this farm," continued Yaya. "So of course you'd want to sell it the first chance you got. But you're forgetting something. There's another Delgado to consider."

"Oh, but Wing's just a girl," Mama replied. "What would she do with a farm?"

"You know I wasn't talking about Wing," answered Yaya.

"Well then, who—" Mama fell silent mid-sentence.

"You damned well know who," stated Yaya.

After a tense pause, Mama answered, "I have no idea what you're implying."

Yaya continued. "You can't just sell this farm out from under Johnny. No matter how you feel about it, you can't ignore the fact that he's as much Delgado as your son ever was."

"I can't imagine what you're referring to."

"I'm referring to José Delgado's son.

"Come now. You're not going to drag out that old rumor again, are you? Not at a time like this, when the poor man lay dying in the next room."

"It's precisely at a time like this, before he dies, that the truth must be heard," said Yaya.

"The truth? Why don't you go ask him?" demanded Mama.

"Because he doesn't know. You sent my daughter away before he knew she was going to have his child. I should have told him then. He would have done the right thing. But instead, I foolishly listened to that priest of yours when he said my daughter had sinned, and ruining the good Delgado name would just add sin on top of sin. I was a fool. I once feared God. But God allowed my daughter to sell herself on Mabini Street to feed that child, his child. And Mabini killed her. Well I don't fear God anymore. José Delgado must know the truth. And he must do the right thing."

"You'll not shame my husband or this family," ordered Mama. "That bastard grandson of yours is the one who stirred up all this riffraff to cause trouble. He's the reason my husband's dying and my son is dead."

"Johnny tried to stop them. It's your son that helped them," argued Yaya. "Now it's time José Delgado learned he still has a son."

I jumped at the sound of Wing's voice crying out from the other room.

"Somebody help. I think Papa's dying."

I had to go to her. I had to be with Wing and Papa. I knew Mama and Yaya heard Wing's call, because, as I turned away and headed down the hall, I heard Yaya say, "I'd love to stay and continue our little chat, but your husband's dying. That may not concern you, but I'm going to him. And he will know the truth before it's too late."

"I'm afraid I cannot allow that," stated Mama.

"Well, you'll just have to kill me to stop me," replied Yaya as I heard her turn her back on Mama and head toward the door.

* * * *

When I returned to the others, I saw that the fire'd been put out, resolving one threat, yet Casablanca wasn't safe yet. The storm seemed to have grown in intensity if that was even possible. The walls of the house seemed to flex under the stress of the pounding wind. And when I looked up at the sound of the creaking roof, I saw gaping cracks in the plaster ceiling that weren't there before.

I looked over at Johnny kneeling next to Papa with an arm around Wing and saw him looking at the same thing. Our eyes met, and I could see I wasn't the only one concerned that the house might be about to crash down on all of us.

"Wing, you're not to concern yourself about Boy," Papa was saying in a voice so weak I almost didn't recognize it. "You had no choice. That thing you killed was not the brother you grew up with, nor the son I raised. That boy we knew's been gone for years."

"I'm sorry, Papa," sobbed Wing between her tears as she lay her head on his chest.

"Shush," said Papa, still trying to comfort his little girl through his own pain. "Besides, you're not alone. You have your cousin, Lisa." Then shouting with a strength I thought he no longer possessed. "Where is she? Where's my other girl?"

I leaped to his side. "I'm here, Papa. What is it?" I asked, taking his hand.

"There you are," he said with a smile and an ever so weak squeeze of his hand. "It seems you're always here at the farm. Even when you're not. You've a farmer's soul, Lisa. And a farmer's soul is one with the land. You'll always be here. And I need you to always be there for Wing." He squeezed both our hands as Wing and I tried to see each other through our tears. "My two peas in a pod." He went into a coughing spell where I wasn't sure he'd ever catch his breath again.

But he did. And getting right back to business, "Enough of crying women. Johnny! Where's Johnny?"

"I'm right here, sir," answered Johnny, leaning into Papa's range of vision.

"Johnny, I'm depending on you to run this place."

"Me, sir?" asked a surprised Johnny.

"Who else? If you've learned half of what your uncle, the Captain, has taught you, you'll do just fine. The rest you'll just have to figure out on your own. I'm not worried. Like Lisa here, farming's in your blood. I knew that the first time I saw you ride that son of a bitch, Thunder."

Johnny smiled as Papa choked on his own laughter.

"But sir, this whole mess, stirring up the rebels. I feel responsible. I never meant anything like this to happen."

"I know that," said Papa. "You're young. You're supposed to be naive and idealistic when you're young. That's called spirit. It's when we grow up that we learn there are consequences to our actions. We grown-ups just pray that the young can learn that before they do too much damage." Papa looked Johnny in the eye. "You'll do just fine. I know it." His voice dwindled to barely a whisper. "I realize you saved my daughter's life. And now you've saved this farm. I die in your debt. My son, or whatever Boy had become, is gone. But you're still here. And you've acted as a true son should. I wish with all my heart that you were mine. It should have been you. You should have been the one."

I looked about for Yaya. Where was she? This was her chance. But she was nowhere to be found. Nor was Mama. Her husband lay dying, and she couldn't even be at his side. Well Wing and Johnny were. And so was I. I couldn't let him die without knowing the truth. It was all up to me. I had to tell him. I took a deep breath.

"Papa," I began. "Papa?" But I was too late. He wasn't there. His body was. But not Papa. Papa was gone. I remember thinking how odd it was that I'd never noticed his eyes were blue before, not until that very moment as I closed them with my hand.

Papa's death so affected me that I didn't even flinch when part of the ceiling caved in just feet from us. Sitting by Papa's side, still holding his hand, I looked up to see sky through a six-foot hole in the roof, and wondered why God was so impatient to have Papa's soul up in heaven that he needed to poke a hole in our roof. Then I felt someone pulling me up by the shoulders.

"Lisa! Lisa!" he shouted over the roar of the typhoon coming through the roof. "We've got to get out of here! The whole roof might collapse!"

It was Johnny, already organizing an evacuation. "We've got to get everyone to the church. It's made of stone. It may be the only place left standing by the time this damn storm passes." He already had the workers gathering up Papa's and Boy's bodies to carry them with us to the church.

"Lisa, you and Wing make sure all the women get out."

Hortensia and Lou were right there with the men. They wouldn't let Johnny out of their sight.

"Where's Mama?" shouted Wing.

As if in answer, Mama seemed to appear out of nowhere. "Wait for me. Don't leave without me," she called. "Make sure they bring Boy."

"Mama, are you OK?" asked Wing.

"What do you mean? Why?" she replied.

"You're bleeding."

"What?" asked Mama in surprise, looking at her blood-stained blouse. "Oh that. No, uh, that must be from your brother. Come. Let's go with the men. I guess that's everyone." She grabbed Wing by the arm and latched onto the others as they headed out the door and into the jaws of the storm.

I was about to follow them when something made me stop. Yaya. Where was Yaya? Knowing her, she probably went back for Papa's cigars. That darn woman's going to get me killed, I thought, as I turned to go find her.

But then I remembered I hadn't seen her around when Papa died. She'd been coming out of the den right behind me after Wing's call. Mama came out. But where was Yaya? On my way to the den, I saw Speed's body still on the floor by the dining table and thought how no one saw fit to bring it with us to the church. Then, for some reason I noticed the knife he'd used on Papa was gone. It was still in Speed's hand the last time I saw it.

Suddenly, my vision was filled by the look on Mama's face when Wing pointed out the blood on her blouse. I looked back down the hall toward the den and felt the vomit rising in my throat.

Chapter 22

I don't know how long I sat on the floor of the den staring at the body before Johnny came back to find me. I remember screaming at him when he told me we'd have to leave her behind. We couldn't leave Yaya behind. But my knees could barely carry my own weight, so Johnny would have to help me through the storm to the church. He couldn't support me and carry Yaya's body at the same time through 200 kilometers per hour winds. We'd have to come back for her after the storm, he insisted.

It was only the explosion from the dining room ceiling caving in that distracted me from fighting Johnny long enough for him to drag me from the house.

Once outside, I couldn't see. Blinded by the rain, deafened by wind that sounded like a freight train, my legs gave out after my first few steps. Johnny threw me over his shoulder with one arm and clawed his way toward the church with the other, dropping to his knees more than once. I thought for sure he'd give up on the church and duck for cover into the barn or the office. But Johnny already knew, from his first trip to the church, what I couldn't see through the storm. The barn and the office were already gone. They hadn't just fallen. They were gone.

* * * *

"Aye, thank the Lord!" cried Hortensia as Johnny threw me through the entrance to the church and collapsed against the door behind me. "But where's Yaya?"

I couldn't come right out and say it. "She's not coming," I offered, out of breath.

"What?" asked Lou. "Don't tell me that old battle ax insisted on riding out the storm back at Casablanca. She'll be impossible to deal with tomorrow, all hung over from Papa's good scotch."

Knowing I'd normally enjoy a good laugh at Yaya's expense, their smiling faces changed when they saw the look on mine.

"What is it?" asked Hortensia.

"Is she hurt?" added Lou.

I could only summon the strength for one word. "Gone."

"Yes, we know Papa's gone. Rest his soul," hushed Hortensia, afraid to say the words aloud. "But Yaya, what of Yaya?"

"She's gone too," stated Johnny, bringing an end to our little dance, leaving the two maids staring at each other as he helped me over to a pew to rest.

I sat at the pew, feeling so tired, I thought maybe I'd died myself. I looked about the candle lit church as if my spirit had left my body and was floating from person to person, curious to see what the living were still up to.

Johnny was flitting about with his crew of workers shoring up doors and windows against the relentless pounding of the storm. Assorted families from town, taking refuge in the church, were scattered about, dividing their time between minding unruly children and praying for their lives.

Mama was there, occupying her personal pew like royalty sitting upon her throne. I knew what she did. I never doubted that she was the one. It was Speed's knife I found in Yaya's back. But it was Mama who put it there. I wasn't stupid. No one could have taken Yaya fairly, face to face. Mama must have taken advantage of her one chance as Yaya turned to leave the den to attend to Papa.

And now she had the nerve to sit there in church as if she had that right, as if she hadn't just committed cold-blooded murder. I'm sure she thought she'd gotten away with it. And maybe she had. After all, I was the only one who knew her dirty little secret. Even Johnny hadn't had the leisure time to put two and two together. Who would believe me? My word against the venerable Mrs. Delgado. Who would ever believe she was capable of such a thing. And what was her motive? To cover up the fact that Johnny was the son of José Delgado? My story just grew crazier and crazier. I had no proof of anything. Besides, the whole sordid tale would only tarnish Papa's reputation.

As I sat there wondering what the right thing to do was, it occurred to me that I wasn't the only one who knew after all. God knew. I had hoped that that revelation would somehow make me feel better. Yet it didn't.

That's when I saw Father Rivera and tried to remember when I'd last given confession. Not that I'd done anything wrong. Well, I had killed at least one person recently, what with slitting Skinny's throat in the course of helping Johnny save Wing from the kidnappers. And then, who knows? I'd been shooting at rebels on and off all day. I just might have actually shot one or two without knowing. But I didn't know if those counted. Besides, it wasn't the killing that bothered me. It was the secrets that I couldn't live with. Yaya's murder and Johnny's parentage. I thought if I could just unload them onto someone else, a heavy weight would be lifted from my back and I'd be able to breath again. I would confess everything to Father Rivera. Let him keep Mama's secrets. And I was sure he would, what with the feud between him and Yaya. When she was alive, he and Yaya barely spoke since her daughter was sent away. She never forgave him for the part he took in that. And he was always kissing up to Mama, since his own livelihood, as well as the church's, depended heavily on her charity. He would keep Mama's dirty secrets all right. No matter. I didn't care anymore. I couldn't do it myself. Papa and Yaya were dead, not to mention the others. I'd never felt so tired in my life. I just wanted it all to go away. It was time someone else shared the burden. Father Rivera, every saint I could think of, Jesus, and God.

I struggled to rise from my pew as if the weight of the world lay upon my shoulders, and managed to make it over to where Father Rivera stood at the pulpit. I indicated why I'd come to him. His eyebrows rose at the timing of my request.

"Lisa, my child, does this storm frighten you so, that you aim to be sure you meet your maker with a clean conscience?"

"No, Father," I answered. And too tired to come up with a better reason, "I just figured we've got some time to kill here."

He frowned at my choice of words as he turned and led me toward the confessional.

* * * *

And that was that. I told Father Rivera about Mama and why she'd killed Yaya, how Johnny was really the son of Papa and Yaya's daughter. I told him everything. Oh, I know, it took some explaining, and I don't know if Father Rivera believed any of it, but it no longer mattered to me. It was out of my hands. I'd given myself, all of us, over to the Lord. Let His will be done.

I walked out of the confessional reborn. The weight was gone. My conscience was clear. I felt a sense of peace flood over me. I'd have sworn it was a beautiful summer day and the birds were singing. Well, that's how I felt. Of course, that couldn't be anything further from the truth. That damn typhoon still hadn't passed. In fact, it apparently had stalled right over us, neither coming nor going, just sitting right on top of us, pounding. And pounding. I don't know if the winds were actually continuing to grow stronger, or if it was just a matter of their continual pounding beginning to have an effect. The church was made of stone, all right, but even stone has its limits. The wind seemed to be patiently picking at the very mortar that held the stone together. We could hear slate tiles peeling off the roof like little flakes of dandruff, crashing down like missiles. Cracks were beginning to show through the church walls. It seemed as though God was really pissed about something, or someone. And that someone was inside the church.

I thought maybe Father Rivera was thinking the same thing because when we first came out of the confessional, he looked rather pale, and maybe a little frightened. But now, as he looked about his church, taking a beating at the hand of the Lord, his eyes came to rest on Mama. And they weren't forgiving eyes. There was fury in them. And those eyes never left Mama, as he returned to the pulpit and called for the attention of his frightened parishioners.

No, he wasn't going to reveal my secrets. I was right about that much. It wasn't for him to do. And it wasn't to the rest of us that Mama needed to make amends. It was bigger than that. It was with God. And God was right to lay his hand upon our church and give it a little squeeze. He was right to come for her. And now it was up to Father Rivera to save the church and the rest of us. But to do so, he had to bring Mama to God.

Father Rivera stood at the pulpit like a stone statue, his icy stare bringing even boisterous children into silence. Then, as if his stare wasn't bad enough, he began to speak. And it wasn't pretty. Have you ever heard the preachers in those old westerns shouting about eternal damnation? Well, Father Rivera made them sound like choirboys.

"How many here wish to die this day?" he shouted.

If there were any remaining parishioners still brave and confident in the face of the storm, the Father's words changed all that.

"I said, how many here wish to die this day?" he repeated, louder than the first time.

People looked about at each other wondering what to say, a few brave enough to reply, "No one. No one wants to die."

"Liars!" shouted the Father. "Liars and blasphemers!"

As if on cue, lightening must have struck the church steeple because the crash was deafening as the top of the steeple crashed into the roof, opening a hole the size of a water buffalo. As the rain poured in, the church bell, no longer securely tied to the steeple, began chiming erratically with the wind.

"Down here!" shouted Father Rivera, as faces looked up, distracted by black sky. "Don't look up to Him for your salvation! Your salvation lies here, among you!"

Some of the old ladies from town knew what he meant, and could be seen, heads bowed, praying fervently. Hortensia didn't need Father Rivera to take the lead. She hadn't gotten off her knees since she'd learned of Yaya's death.

I wasn't scared. Since my confession, I felt only a calm glow about me. I was already saved. So I sat there, in my pew, the rain slapping me in the face, serenely watching, just watching, as the world fell apart all about me. People panicking, children screaming, the roof caving in under the pounding of the wind. And through it all, Father Rivera chanting about eternal damnation as the church bell cried out, mourning the end of the world.

Johnny and the workers had given up trying to shore up the church against the storm. It was out of their hands at this point. If there were anyone in the church that hadn't found God at that point in their lives, they'd found Him now. They didn't have to look very far. That's because God had found them. He'd come from above, ripped a hole in the roof of the church, and rained right down upon their heads.

Even Mama couldn't run from Him. Her face expressed sheer terror as Father Rivera continued to chastise his flock, to blame them and their sins for the Lord's anger. Yet it was to one particular parishioner he seemed to direct the brunt of his attack. Flashes of lightening that should have been coming from above, through the hole in the roof, instead seemed to be shooting from his eyes directly at Mama.

"Repent! Cast off the devil that devours your soul! For until you do, the Lord will not rest. Not until every brick of his temple has settled upon your head! Save yourself! Save us all!"

People began jumping from their pews, rushing toward the confessional. Others couldn't wait, and began shouting right from the pews, admitting to every indiscretion they could think of, in hopes of staving off the Lord's judgment. Even Hortensia could be heard admitting to some childhood crush on a priest long since passed away.

But Father Rivera didn't waiver. Not one step did he take toward the confessional. He continued to stare directly at Mama, threatening an afterlife worse than death. And Mama's whole body was trembling as she sat in her pew, eyes squeezed shut, praying only that it would all go away. It wasn't until the storm threw aside the plywood protecting the big stained glass image of the Last Supper, and sent a shower of colored glass raining over her head, that she managed to rise on shaking knees and make her way toward the confessional.

Only then did Father Rivera calmly make his way over to the crowd pushing and shoving to be first. The panicked jostling ceased abruptly when the Father pointed at Mama and beckoned her to the front of the line. The crowd parted in deference, as it was nothing unusual for them to see Mama get preferential treatment.

At first Mama looked as if she might turn and run, flashes of lightening juxtaposing her white-faced panic against the Father's red-faced fury. The church bell pealed louder and louder in Mama's hesitation. And then it stopped. The bell, not the storm. The storm raged stronger than ever as the walls trembled with wind and thunder. But not the bell. The bell stopped. It just stopped. I didn't know at that point if a bell that size could just blow away. But I think Mama had a different idea. I think she stood there wavering at the threshold of the confessional imagining the hand of God taking the church bell in his firm grasp and silencing it, silencing it so he could better hear all Mama had to say. He was ready, ready to hear Mama's confession. Father Rivera took a deep breath, closed Mama's door, and took his place in the booth adjacent to hers. His eyes locked on mine as he slowly closed the door.

As frightened as the people were of the Father's fire and brimstone, they seemed at wits' end without him. They huddled about the confessional praying they'd have their turn before the church buried them alive in rubble, as if the only path to salvation lay through the door to that confessional. And as new holes opened up in the church roof, windows shattering as protective plywood peeled away, I began to wonder if they might be right. No matter for me. I'd already made my peace with the Lord.

Johnny'd made his way over to where I sat and held me tight, protecting me from falling debris. He soon yanked me from my seat, pulling me to the floor and dragging me with him as he crawled under the pews for shelter. We lay there in each other's arms as the world came down around us, clinging to one another lest the storm pull us apart. For as long as Johnny held me in his arms, I knew that wherever God decided to send us, we'd be going together.

Chapter 23

All their fretting turned out to be for nothing. Father Rivera needed take no more confessions that day. I woke up in Johnny's arms and we were both alive. Apparently so was everyone else, as they came crawling out from under the rubble that used to be the church, to a bright sunny morning. The confessional was just about the only thing left standing. We all found Mama still praying on her knees when we finally thought to remove enough debris to open the confessional door.

Judging by the beautiful blue sky and return of the birds, I guess God got what he came for. I just wish he hadn't taken his sweet time about it. Everything was gone. Well, not quite everything. *We* were still here, all of us. Me, Johnny, Wing, Hortensia, Lou, the workers and their families. Even Thunder came trotting in from the fields where he'd taken refuge. Oh, and the land. Don't forget the land. The land was still here too.

Father Rivera came through for Yaya in the end, after all those years of feuding. I like to think it was out of his own guilt, payback for supporting Mama all those years ago when Johnny's Mom was banished and sent to die on Mabini Street. At least that's what I like to believe, anyway.

He never had to tell Mama a word of what I'd said to him to get her to confess. That was God's doing. Or Mama's fear of Him, to be exact. And mine wasn't the only confession that never saw the light of day. Being a priest, after all, the Father never revealed Mama's either. No one ever found out that Papa was Johnny's real father. That's right. Johnny never became a Delgado. And I never told a soul. Well, except Johnny and Wing, of course. I never could keep a juicy secret from Wing. And I thought this was pretty juicy. Anyway, she had to know she still had a brother, only the good kind this time. Besides, this way I could forever tease her about the days when she had a crush on her brother. Eeyuck! That's pretty gross, isn't it?

But the public would never know the truth about Papa and Johnny. They would continue to suspect, but they would never know. That subject would remain forever a matter of tsismus.

So we buried our dead and soon got back to living. There was so much to be done, and we had little time for grieving. All the neighboring hacienderos just showed up one day, and, with all our combined workers, began rebuilding the Delgado farm. Everyone refused payment, insisting they'd expect the same from us if their farms had been hit as badly.

We were all sitting under a makeshift tent the maids had erected under which they could serve lunch. Lou made use of the only thing left of Casablanca, her huge stove standing like a monument at the base of its stone chimney. Maids from the other farms would not have insulted the legendary Lou by bringing in their own cooking. But they did supply provisions with which Lou could work her magic. And so we sat in the shade of the tent stuffing ourselves on chicken adobo and pancit, washing it all down with fresh-squeezed calamansi juice made from those tiny sour oranges we Filipinos love so much. Hortensia was losing weight, running food over to the workers resting under the huge mango trees that survived the storm over by the courtyard.

From their chairs under the tent, Ron Fanlo, Scooby Montero, and Chica-ting Arroyo had nothing but compliments for Johnny as they looked over at him sitting under the trees with the workers.

"You know," began Scooby, "he runs this place like he's been doing it his whole life."

"Captain would have been proud," agreed Chica-ting.

"And José," added Ron, watching Johnny move about among the different groups of workers with thanks for their efforts and compliments for their work. "Look at the way they stand with respect as he approaches. Take away some hair and put a gut on him and you'd think it was José Delgado himself."

"To José Delgado," toasted Scooby and Chica-ting, refilling their shot glasses with Tanduay rum.

"Yes, to José, my old friend," added Ron quietly, wiping a tear from the corner of his eye. Then, after downing his shot, "Hey, Johnny!" he shouted over to where the workers all sat. "Johnny! Come join us for a drink!"

I looked over to Johnny, who jumped up at the sound of Ron's order, but wavered among the workers, uncertain of what to do, always mindful of that fine line of distinction between worker and haciendero.

Johnny looked back at me, imploringly, letting me know he felt torn between loyalty to the crew of workers and respect for the haciendros. He didn't want to insult anyone.

I smiled back and waved for him to stay where he was, and he sat down again, relieved, knowing I'd take care of everything.

"Wing," I called, as I poured a shot of rum for Johnny. "Tell the maids to pass out a bottle of San Miguel beer to each worker. I know we were saving it for later, but one beer with lunch wouldn't hurt."

Ron and the others saw me putting on my sun hat to bring Johnny his rum, and protested. "No, I want him to come here," insisted Ron.

I smiled at him and wagged my finger. "Just because you want something, doesn't make it so. He doesn't work for you."

Ron feigned indignance. "Then who does he work for? This is totally unacceptable behavior. I demand to speak with the haciendero."

I laughed as I took Johnny's rum and followed Wing and the maids with their beer. "Then you'll have to come with me and speak to the haciendero yourself. He's sitting with the workers. Or are you old men too delicate to come out from under the shade of your tent."

No, they didn't come out from under the tent, perhaps too set in their ways to change at this stage of their lives. But they laughed just the same, and raised their glasses to Johnny, toasting both to old times with Papa, and to new times with Johnny and the next generation of young hacienderos.

You see, despite everyone's distinct recollection of Papa refusing to write a will, claiming it unwise to plan one's own death, who were we to question Father Rivera when he came forward with Mama jointly to present one?

Well, in it, Papa left half the farm to Wing, and the other half to Yaya and Captain. Though the will provided for Mama's support, there was no mention of Boy, and Mama immediately moved back to Manila. I, on the other hand, had no intention of ever leaving the farm. The farm would need me. And so would Johnny. You see Yaya's and Captain's half of the farm passed directly to Johnny. And a handsome young haciendero like Johnny would need a pretty young bride to help manage things, after all.

So, in the end, I got everything I wanted all along. The farm, Johnny, and to be a Delgado. Well, maybe not a Delgado, but a Dillinger anyway, because just as soon as the church is rebuilt, Johnny and I plan to be married and make lots of little Dillingers.

You see I never really had much Delgado blood in me. I mean, not so much that our kids would have two heads or anything creepy like that. But the sugar, now that's another story. 'Cause just like Papa's, the sugar coursing through *my* veins is pure cane.

ALSO BY DAVID ABIS

LAST GIRL STANDING

In this bittersweet ill-fated teenage romance, Audrey Spencer thought the world a safe place, until she's forced to move to a sketchy trailer park at the outskirts of a West Virginia coal town. There she befriends Zachary Ledbetter, simultaneously fascinating, dangerous, and anything but normal, that missing link between impetuous young boy and psychopath. Coming of age together while confronting obsession, rage, and survival, soon even the line between love and stalking becomes blurred, until things literally blow up at prom when shots are fired.

VOICES IN MY HEAD

Wouldn't it be fantastic if everyone could simply access social media directly with their minds? It's the year 2050, and sixteen-year-old Grace Malone is finally old enough for Voices, a tiny computer chip painlessly implanted directly into the brain to replace all those old-fashioned cellphones and computers. But when her head is suddenly inundated by a world full of political unrest and social justice warriors, Grace is having second thoughts. That's when she meets a boy named Max, a techie geek from the other side of the tracks who refuses to be chipped, and she begins to question all the social media groupthink, cancel culture, and internet bullying bouncing around her brain. Inevitably, when packs of marauding violent mobs take things too far, infiltrating the government and law enforcement, even threatening her family, Grace and Max are ultimately drawn into the battle between right, left, anarchists, police, and the military. But will they be able to stop a world gone mad with just an antique Android phone, a glitchy portable Nintendo game console, and the best of intentions? Oh, and did I mention the ballistic missile?

CALAMITY IN SWEET SPOT: A POLITICALLY UNCORRECT WHIRLWIND REDNECK ROMANCE

All they needed was a natural disaster and they'd all be living on easy street. As mayor of Sweet Spot, Mississippi, a pathetic collection of dilapidated shacks and underachievers situated smack-dab on the very buckle of the tornado belt, Buck Jones believes it's his civic duty on behalf of his little town of antigovernment moonshiners, gun-toting preppers, and born-again meth addicts, to score some of that sweet federal aid being thrown around so freely. Well, Buck Jones may be a man of vision, but the last thing he envisions is falling madly in lust with Jennifer Steele, that spitfire journalist from CNN who arrives when Buck's prayers are answered by a crew of naive Yankee reporters assigned to cover tornado victims in the rural South. Fireworks abound between the redneck flimflam man and the bleeding-heart city girl as the scheme to defraud the government threatens to blow up in their faces and the town's very existence is imperiled by a thoroughly peeved Mother Nature who finally sends Sweet Spot's chickens home to roost. In the end, it may be up to small town U.S.A. to save the day, but it's up to Buck to get the girl.

THOUGH I WALK THROUGH THE VALLEY

Her daddy was just a small-town preacher. But that was before. He ain't nothin' now… except dead. What truly happened between 19-year-old Jaime Jo Tremper, Tommy Harris, and her daddy would be the subject of conjecture for years to come. Yet secrets always trump gossip in a small town, and only those involved, and their maker, can ever really know the truth. Jaime Jo and Tommy have a history together, and the scars to bear for it, both mental and physical. No one ever expected to hear from Tommy again after being packed off to war. Yet two years later, resilient as a cockroach, the Special Forces psychopath comes home to the mountains of North Carolina to claim his girl. The overwhelmed local sheriff does his best to separate the two, but love can be a powerful thing, not everything is as it seems, and only Jaime Jo and Tommy know the truth. As a desperate young woman places her fate in the hands of her Lord, a vengeful Vietnam vet takes matters into his own, coming home to save his girl and finally end the nightmare that began the day Tommy Harris met Jaime Jo Tremper.

VILLAGE IDIOTS

Just a naive young medical student from Manhattan's Upper East Side, Benjamin Walker's cloistered world is thoroughly rocked by his very first patient on the psych ward. Angel McGovern, exotic dancer by trade, is a nymphomaniac genius with two and a half PhD's. An overwhelmed Ben is kidnapped by Angel and taken on a wild and crazy road trip to the tropics, accompanied by two other zany escaped inmates from the asylum. Makesh Guptah is a rocket scientist who believes aliens plan to destroy the Earth. Juan Martinez is a slow-witted giant who wouldn't hurt a fly, but is headed for the electric chair if found mentally competent. Will Juan beat the rap? Will Makesh save the planet? Will Angel ever scratch that itch? Will Ben make it home alive? VILLAGE IDIOTS, a sexy farce with heart, is kinky, crazy, and ultimately out of this world.

www.ingramcontent.com/pod-product-compliance
Lightning Source LLC
Chambersburg PA
CBHW070837250626
47159CB00003B/814